OXYGEN

A mission gone desperately wrong—

OXYGEN

and no way out short of blind faith....

RANDALL INGERMANSON
| AND |
JOHN OLSON

BETHANYHOUSE
MINNEAPOLIS, MINNESOTA

Published by Bethany House Publishers
A Ministry of Bethany Fellowship International
11400 Hampshire Avenue South
Bloomington, Minnesota 55438
www.bethanyhouse.com

Printed in the United States of America by
Bethany Press International, Bloomington, Minnesota 55438

Library of Congress Cataloging-in-Publication Data

Olson, John B.
    Oxygen / by John B. Olson & Randall Ingermanson.
      p. cm.
    ISBN 0-7642-2442-5
    1. Women astronauts—Fiction. 2. Twenty-first century—Fiction. 3. Mars (Planet)—Fiction. 4. Space flight—Fiction. 5. Sabotage—Fiction.
I. Ingermanson, Randall Scott. II. Title.
    PS3615.L75 O95   2001   2001001374

To Amy and Eunice—

our truest counselors,
closest friends,
and cherished wives.

JOHN B. OLSON received his Ph.D. in biochemistry at the University of Wisconsin, Madison, in 1995, and did postdoctoral work in computational biochemistry at the University of California, San Francisco. He lives with his wife and two children in the San Francisco Bay Area, where he works for a biotechnology company and heads the writing group SCUM (Super Cool Underwriting Maniacs).

RANDALL INGERMANSON earned his Ph.D. in theoretical physics at the University of California at Berkeley in 1986, and did postdoctoral research in superstring theory at The Ohio State University. He lives in San Diego with his wife and three daughters and works as a computational physicist. He is the author of a time-travel novel, *Transgression*, as well as a nonfiction book, *Who Wrote the Bible Code?*

If you'd like to know more about John and Randy and the calculations they did for this book, you're probably a bit unbalanced. Nevertheless, they invite you to visit their Web sites:

www.litany.com (John's site)
www.rsingermanson.com (Randy's site)

ACKNOWLEDGMENTS

JBO THANKS

All the SCUM who helped make this book happen: Jan Collins, Donna Fujimoto, Ellen Graebe, Heath Havlick, Nancy Hird, Kelly Kim, Kelsey Mitchell, Patty Mitchell, Carl Olsen, Amy Olson, Jennifer Rempel, and John Renning.

Roger Chylla, Josh Colbourne, Kathleen Dlugosh, Carola and Krist Gudnason, Kathy and Steve Marbert, Bill and Vickie Olson, Michael Platt, Susan Robinette, John Sullivan, and Adrian Tsingaris: for friendship, encouragement, love, hospitality, free editing, and sound advice.

Lindsey Clarke, Julian Farnam, Imre Friedmann, Ralph Gustafson, Scott Rowland, Rick Searfoss, Jim Sleeper, and Bob Spears: for answers to technical questions.

Mom and Dad, Peter and Arianna: for doing all the hardest work so I could play.

Amy, for all of the above, plus a whole lot more. How can I thank you enough?

RSI THANKS

Don Williams, Jamie Wilson, David and Becca and Sarah Poage, Mark and Gail Lundgren, Jeff Hilton, Gary and Sandy Becker, John Sabin, and Steve Wearp: for constant encouragement while I worked on this project.

Sherwood Wirt, Dave and Heather Kopp, Sol Stein, Jack Cavanaugh,

Chip MacGregor, Erin Healy, Thomas Womack, Betty Fletcher, Barb Sherrill, Steve Moore, Donna Axelrod, and Bonnie Line: some of the writers and editors in my life who've helped me along the way.

Mom and Dad and my daughters, Carolyn, Gracie, and Amy.

Eunice: who has put up with Mars much longer than anyone should.

BOTH OF US THANK

Karen Ball, Lisa Bergren, Elaine Wright Colvin, Rene Gutteridge, Lee Roddy, and Lauraine Snelling: for friendship, advice, encouragement, and much more.

Jan Collins, Brandilyn Collins, Ellen Graebe, Pete and Sherah Sleeper: our final line of critiquers.

Michael Carroll: the world's best space artist, a true inspiration and faithful guide in our quest to know Mars.

Kathy Tyers: our model for what a science-fiction writer should be.

Steve Laube: our friend and our editor.

The engineers at NASA who took the time to answer our questions: Tim Briscoe, Fred Smith, John Connolly, Jim Rainwater, Chris Hanson, Chuck Verostko, Jason Raboin, Kriss Kennedy, and Don Pearson.

Shannon Lucid and John Connolly, for technical reviews of the manuscript. All remaining errors are no doubt our responsibility, but we'll blame our editor anyway.

Holly Briscoe and her husband, Tim, for taking such an interest in this book, and for giving us an insider's look at Houston and the Johnson Space Center. Holly, we award you the Silver Snoopy Award for your efforts to make this book succeed!

PART I

Human Factors

"Man is the best computer we can put aboard a spacecraft . . . and the only one that can be mass produced with unskilled labor."

WERNHER VON BRAUN

"For long-duration manned spaceflight, the most important consideration is not the technology of the spacecraft but the composition of the crew."

SHANNON LUCID, ASTRONAUT

"To summarize in *Star Trek* terminology, what a piloted Mars mission needs are two 'Scottys' and two 'Spocks.' No 'Kirks,' 'Sulus,' or 'McCoys' are needed, and more importantly, neither are the berths and rations to accommodate them. We can do the mission with a crew of four."

ROBERT ZUBRIN

CHAPTER 1

Tuesday, August 14, 2012, midnight
VALKERIE

Valkerie woke up screaming. A viper bat clung to her face with fish-hook claws, smothering her with its thin, leathery body. She tore at her face, but the creature had dug in too deep. She could already feel its venom burning into her lungs, constricting her chest in a long, convulsive cough. Struggling for control, she traced the contours of her face with tingling fingertips. Slowly, the clinging creature melted into her skin, fading back into the world of dreams.

The nightmare gradually faded, giving way to a new, more gripping terror. Valkerie was wide awake now. There was no such thing as a viper bat. But she still couldn't breathe.

Valkerie flung herself from the camping cot and thudded to the floor. She lay on her back, gasping for breath. She was hyperventilating, but the burning in her lungs grew worse. An acrid stench filled the cabin—the smell of sulfur dioxide—SO_2.

"Oh no." The volcano was venting. "Oh God, please . . ." Valkerie rolled over and fought her way up onto her hands and knees. Dim red light filtered in through the cabin window, illuminating a large duffel bag in the middle of the room. She crawled slowly toward the bag, struggling through the coughs that wracked her body.

"Please, God." Squeezing her eyes shut against the pain in her cramping muscles, Valkerie inched forward until she felt the heavy canvas. She dug underneath a metallic thermal suit and pressed her breather to her face. Her lungs choked shut at the rush of acidic gas. *Idiot!* She flung the mask across the room. Gina-Marie had warned her

13

about the filter, but Valkerie had insisted it would be good for one more trip.

Her mind raced. If Mount Trident was venting, the whole valley could be filled with sulfur dioxide. She had to get out of there. Fast.

Valkerie tried to stand, but the room spun out of control. She crashed onto the floor, hitting her head hard on the edge of the cot. A cloud of ringing light sparkled in her mind. Her muscles relaxed, and she gave herself to the tide of darkness that washed gently across her senses. *Sleep. No more experiments. Sleep.*

An image crept into her mind. A large plastic bag filled with new sample tubes. Was it still sealed? She couldn't remember.

Groping her way forward, Valkerie swept her hands across the floor. A smooth surface crinkled at her touch. She lunged at the bag, poked a trembling finger through the heavy plastic, and pressed her lips to the hole. The air tingled in her lungs with burning sweetness.

She curled around the bag, hugging it to her body, breathing life through the ragged wound. Gradually, the needles that prickled at her consciousness started to recede, but she knew it wouldn't last. The air in the bag was getting stale—fast.

Valkerie took one last breath and staggered to her feet. Her jeep! It was just outside. She lurched to the cabin door and pushed her way out into the night. The air hit her in the face like a blast of hot tear gas. Gagging on the foul gases, she stumbled blindly forward, clinging to consciousness.

Heaving herself into the seat of the jeep, she turned the key. The starter whirred and the engine coughed to life, but then died immediately. *Idiot!* Valkerie smashed her fist against the dash. The jeep couldn't run without oxygen any more than she could.

A wave of nausea wracked Valkerie's body. Her muscles were cramping again. She fell across the seat and reached into the glove box for her knife. *Pliers.* They would have to do.

Valkerie crawled out of the jeep and threw herself on the ground by the jeep's front tire. Taking off the cap of the air valve, she crushed its metal tip with the pliers. After a few seconds of twisting and squeezing, she heard a faint hiss.

Valkerie chomped down on the rubber valve and sucked in a desperate breath. The air was black with the taste of rubber, but anything was better than SO_2. When her lungs were full, she clamped down on the valve with the pliers. Breathe, clamp, breathe, clamp. She held each breath as long as she could before letting it out.

The tire went flat way too soon. Valkerie crawled to the next tire and repeated the process. Then the next tire and the next. After she had sucked the last ounce of air from the spare, she took off running across the clearing. The valley was rugged and wide. She knew she couldn't make it out on foot, but if she could just get above the blanket of heavy gases she might have a chance.

Halfway across the clearing, Valkerie fell reeling to the ground. Red thunderbolts stabbed at her brain. A sparkling haze shrouded her vision as she fought her way to her feet. The heavy gases were thicker close to the ground. She had to stay upright. Walking on tiptoe, she made her way to the edge of the clearing, looking up at the night sky to keep her nostrils elevated.

Valkerie stumbled into a limbless old pine and crashed to the ground. Too dizzy to stand, she crawled on her hands and knees to a younger pine with limbs low enough to climb.

The rough branches cut her face and tore at her nightgown as she climbed. Valkerie lost her grip and fell, crashing into the branches below. She pulled herself up and kept climbing. Higher and higher through the darkness, until slowly, her head began to clear.

"Thank you. Thank you." Valkerie breathed in and out to the cadence of the simple litany that filled her mind. The sparkles in her eyes were fading. Below her feet, tendrils of mist danced in the moonlight, flowing along the envelope of the deadly gas cloud.

The valley reflected an angry red glow. Valkerie looked up at the peak that loomed above her. If the venting continued long enough, the gases might rise higher than she could climb. But that was the least of her worries.

She closed her eyes and wrapped her arms around the tree, hoping Professor Henderson was wrong. His solemn voice echoed in her mind: *"If it starts venting, get out. Fumarolic venting almost always presages a major eruption."*

Wednesday, August 15, 2012, 9:30 A.M.

BOB

Bob Kaganovski had shampoo in his eyes when the decompression alarm went off.

He grabbed the suction hose and ran it frantically over his face and eyes. Footsteps pounded outside the shower.

"Decompression!" shouted Josh Bennett, mission commander of the Ares 10. "Get to the EVA* suits now! We've got about fifteen minutes."

Bob popped open the Velcroed shower door and grabbed a towel. Fear knotted his gut. Only fifteen minutes! He stepped out of the shower and swiped a towel across the soles of his feet, drying them just enough so he wouldn't kill himself on the stairs.

He ran through a corridor to the steep circular stairway that led down to Level 1 of the Habitation Module. The decompression alarm beeped once every two seconds. The interval was keyed to cabin pressure. When it got down to vacuum, the beeps would merge into one steady drone. If he wasn't in his suit by then, he wouldn't hear it. For one thing, sound wouldn't travel in a vacuum. For another, he'd be dead.

Bob slipped and slithered down the metal staircase. Josh lay on the floor, with both his legs already stuffed into the lower half of his EVA suit. Bob yanked open the door of his locker and pulled out the heavy upper half of his suit.

It fell on the floor in a heap.

"Easy!" Josh said. "Don't panic. I'll give you a hand—"

"I've got it." Bob grabbed it and heaved. *Who designed this beast?* Fifty years of research, and the thing still weighed over eighty pounds. Normally, somebody was supposed to help you into an Extra-Vehicular Activity suit. But in an emergency, you could do it yourself. In theory.

Bob latched the upper half of the suit to a stability rack and laid out the lower half on the floor. He grabbed a MAG—NASA-speak for a diaper—and taped it on.

The beeping of the alarm increased in tempo.

Now for the hard part, the LCG—Liquid-Cooled Garment—a Spandex pair of long johns with feet, encased in a clunky water-cooled nightmare of tubes and gizmos. Bob struggled furiously to pull it over his damp skin. Minutes passed.

Josh was almost all of the way into his suit by the time Bob got his LCG on. "How you doing with that thing?" Josh asked.

"I'm getting there." Bob wiped the sweat out of his eyes.

"We're down to eight minutes." Josh fastened the inner connectors

---

*A glossary of NASA terms is on page 367.

at his waist, then the outer ones. "Need some help before I put on my gloves?"

Bob stuck both feet into the legs of the EVA suit and pushed in. His feet slid home into the boots and he pulled the pant legs up to his waist. "Okay, give me a hand up."

"Better hurry." Josh put on his Snoopy cap and adjusted his comm mikes. "The air's getting thinner." He pulled Bob to his feet. "Just climb up into your top. Nothing to it."

Right. Bob clumped over to his top, turned, and tried to squat. Which was almost impossible wearing the pants.

"Drop the pants," Josh said. "I need to pressurize, okay?" He pulled his helmet and gloves out of his locker.

I'm on my own now. Bob let go of the circular metal ring that ran around the belt of the pants. He squatted and tried to back in underneath the suit. Which was practically impossible for a guy almost six feet tall. Josh had it easy—he was five inches shorter and a lot more limber. Bob pushed up into the suit. The thing was the mother of all turtleneck sweaters, fifteen layers of everything from Teflon to Nomex to who-knows-what. Halfway up, his head got stuck.

His heart was hammering now, three beats for every beep of that blasted alarm. He backed down and tried again.

And got stuck again. *Force it.* He pushed harder. Harder.

The suit popped loose from the stability rack. He staggered forward, but the heavy pack pulled him back. He teetered, lost his balance, and fell on the suit's backpack with his legs pinned beneath him.

Stuck! Bob tried to roll onto his side, but he couldn't move. His head and arms were tangled inside the suit. His legs began cramping. He was trapped like a turtle on its back. Except a turtle would at least have its head out of the shell. The alarm beeped fainter, faster. Sweat poured down his face. *So this is what the Apollo 13 boys felt like. Dogmeat.*

Minutes passed. The beeps merged into a single tone. Quieter. Quieter. Off.

Hysterical laughter echoed in the small room. Bob felt strong hands grab the upper half of his suit and begin tugging.

"Congratulations. You're dead!" Josh slowly manhandled Bob out of his turtle-shell prison.

Bob opened his eyes and saw Josh with his helmet and gloves off, grinning like a maniac.

The airlock door opened and two med techs walked in. "The exercise is over," said the first one, a cute redhead with dangly earrings. "That's six times in a row you've killed yourself, Bob. You've got the record." She and Josh helped him to his feet.

The other tech grinned. "Don't sweat it, bro. You're supposed to break records, right? That's what they pay you for—to go where no man has gone before." He and Josh helped Bob step out of the lower half of his suit.

The redhead shook her head, making her earrings dance like wild men. "Okay, now let's check you over. Any parts broken?"

"I'm fine," Bob said.

It took the techs ten minutes to peel off his Spandex underwear and MAG diaper and check him over for damage. Bob stood there, buck naked, barely noticing them. He'd been in this program too long to bat an eye at the indignity of the medigeeks' inspections. But if he couldn't pass the EVA drill . . .

"You're fine, Dr. Kaganovski," said the redhead. "Next time take it slower and dry off a little better." She turned to Josh. "How's the splint on your wrist holding up?"

He shrugged. "Hey, it's just a hairline. No sweat."

"Yeah, well, take my advice and don't buy another motorcycle." She walked out of the room with the other tech.

"Yes, Motherrrr." Josh flexed his wrists and revved an imaginary bike. "Hey, Kaggo, you want to run another exercise before lunch?"

Bob looked at his watch. "We don't have time. The psych test is coming up."

"Psych test?" Josh raised an eyebrow.

"At eleven," Bob said. "Didn't you read your e-mail?"

Josh just looked at him.

"Don't tell me you weaseled out of it." They walked out of the Hab and into the locker room. Bob went to the sink and began rinsing the last of the shampoo from his hair. "Lex and Kennedy are gonna spit bile if you're the only one who doesn't have to take it."

"Nobody told me anything about a psych test." Josh stepped into his street pants. "Lex is doing T–38 proficiency training this morning. And Kennedy's running docking sims over in SES."

Bob's heart double-thumped. He went to his street-clothes locker and began dressing. "Let me see if I've got this straight. The klutz of the crew has to go have a happy chat with the shrinks, while the rest of you get to play?"

"You're not a klutz," Josh said. "You just need a little more time—"

"What do you call a guy who can't even get dressed without hurting himself?" Bob yanked on his pants and plopped down on the bench. "Seventeen months till lift-off, and they're getting nervous, that's what I think. They've still got time to unload me, bring in someone else who knows his head from a hole in the ozone."

"Just can it, will you?" Josh sounded angry. "Listen up. You know who's the most important guy on the crew? Read the mission architecture document. The flight engineer, that's who. The ace mechanic. Scotty. That would be you, in case you've forgotten."

"Mechanics are a dime a dozen."

"Yeah, right, and monkeys can do brain surgery." Josh finished tying his shoes. "You're the best mechanic in the Ares program. Anything goes wrong out there, it's you who's going to fix it, and everybody knows it. So what are you worried about?"

"Flight surgeons, that's what. They want a change. I can smell it."

"Then blow your nose. I don't care who wants a change. My main priority is getting to Mars and back with my crew alive. As long as I'm commander on this mission, you're my number-one mechanic. Got it?"

"So what's the deal with the psych test, then?" Bob jammed his feet into his shoes. "What do I tell these guys?"

"Shrinks are all alike," Josh said. "They're afraid of a repeat of the Mir fiasco. Just figure out what they want to hear and tell it to 'em."

"Oh, right," Bob said. *And what do they want to hear?*

"You'll do fine." Josh whacked Bob on the shoulder. "Believe me, you haven't got a thing to worry about."

CHAPTER 2

OXYGEN

OXYGEN

Wednesday, August 15, 2012, 6:00 A.M.
VALKERIE

A deep rumble, steady and insistent, droned in Valkerie's mind. The sound meant something. Something important. She covered her ears, but the roar hammered into her skull, setting off echoes of throbbing pain.

The volcano! Valkerie opened her eyes, blinking against a thick film of goo. The valley swayed and tilted around her as she searched the summit of Mount Trident in the gray light of early morning.

A thin column of steam rose above Trident's fourth cone. But the roar didn't seem to be coming from the volcano. She turned and blinked into the rising sun. A large military helicopter approached low over the Valley of Ten Thousand Smokes. A rescue party?

Valkerie tried to wave, but the motion set off a fit of coughing. Her lungs felt like they had been dissolved in acid, and after the coughing, her head felt even worse. She watched helplessly as the helicopter descended into the clearing by the cabin.

"Don't land! SO_2!" Valkerie's tattered voice was washed away in the rush of wind.

The pitch of the helicopter's roar dropped as the blades spun down. *Great!* The idiots either cut power or their engines were choking on the oxygen-depleted atmosphere.

Two men in business suits stepped out of the helicopter and pointed in her direction. Her rescuers? They didn't even have breathers. Half dazed, she watched them approach, waiting for them to start coughing.

Valkerie shook her head to clear her mind. The men seemed to be okay. She leaned back and uncurled her legs from around the branch she had been sitting on. Her body tingled with prickling pain. Her vision blurred with each pulse of her quickening heart.

A branch slipped from her cold-numbed fingers, and she fell, crashing down through the jagged limbs. She slammed into the ground and rolled on the gravelly cinders, struggling for breath in an ocean of dizziness and pain. Running footsteps. Shouted questions. "Are you okay?" "Can you breathe?"

Valkerie struggled to her feet, ignoring the bright lights that flashed in her brain. Her samples. She couldn't go without her bacteria. "Get back to the chopper! I've got to get my samples."

The men stared. Mouths open, eyes wide, they stood watching her— like imbeciles.

Good grief, she didn't have time for this. The volcano could erupt any minute. "Get to the helicopter. Now!" She turned and ran for the cabin.

"Valerie Jansen?"

Valkerie glanced back. The taller one was jogging after her.

"They're in the cabin. It'll only take a minute." Valkerie flung open the sheet of plywood that served as a door and stepped inside. The interior still reeked of SO_2. She fell to her knees in front of the portable sample heater and checked the dial.

"Are you Valerie Jansen?"

Valkerie picked up the oven and turned slowly. "Yeah, I'm the only one here. Gina-Marie left two days ago." She stepped toward the man, but he made no move to let her pass. "I'm sorry, but I couldn't leave without my samples. It took me five days to collect them. I . . ."

Valkerie bit her lower lip. Something was wrong. The man was in his late forties. Tall. Well-groomed. Good-looking. What was he doing on a rescue helicopter? And why was his face so familiar?

The short man appeared behind his companion, peering at her through thick, eye-shrinking lenses. "May I ask what you were doing up in that tree?" His voice was an annoying whine.

"Don't we need to get out of here? Aren't you here to rescue me?"

"Rescue you?" The tall man took a step backward.

"Trident's about to erupt. Right?"

The tall man shrugged. "We just came from your central research station. They didn't say anything about an eruption. I assume they've been monitoring."

"But it was venting all night. The whole valley was filled with SO_2. If

I hadn't found a sealed plastic bag to breathe from, I wouldn't have survived to reach the tree."

"Venting?" The tall man stepped away from the cabin and cast a worried glance up at the overshadowing peak.

"Trident isn't known for venting. It could signal a major eruption."

"Why didn't you evacuate? You've got a jeep." The small man's voice carried an accusing tone.

"In an SO_2 blanket? Who are you guys? You're not from the research station."

"I'm sorry," said the tall man. "I'm Steven Perez and this is Roger Abrams. We're from NASA. We've reviewed your Astronaut Candidate Application and were hoping for an informal interview. We've been trying to get in touch with you for weeks."

Valkerie dropped the sample heater. Blood surged into her face and throbbed with a pressure that made her nauseous. Her ASCAN application? Steven Perez? The director of the Johnson Space Center, Steven Perez? An interview? She looked down at herself. Dirty and bleeding. Barefoot and wearing a flimsy nightgown—for an interview. Not just any interview—the most important interview of her life.

Wednesday, August 15, 2012, 10:55 A.M.
BOB

Bob checked his watch again. 10:55. Almost showtime. He walked out of the elevator onto the fourth floor of Building 1 and headed for the drinking fountain, mentally cursing every flight surgeon who'd ever lived.

Flight surgeons had trashed the lives of more astronauts than he cared to remember. Jim Lovell's bilirubin. Deke Slayton's heart arrhythmia. Al Shepard's inner ear. Now they were coming for him.

Tell 'em what they want to hear.

Right. But what did they want to hear?

It was easy to guess what they didn't want to hear. Bob had spent the last six months going over the Ares 10 flight hardware with a microscope. That was his job. If anything went wrong on the mission, it'd be his neck in the noose. But some of the contractors had complained that he was too picky about safety.

Bob snorted. *Too picky about safety?* An oxymoron. Or it would have

22

been in the old days. But modern NASA had a new mantra. "Faster, cheaper, better." What about "safer"? If you forgot that, you got an Apollo 1 fire. A Challenger explosion. A Mir collision. The smart guy didn't trust his safety to anyone. *Anyone.* Trust yourself first, last, and only.

Bob swigged some water at the drinking fountain and wiped his mouth on his sleeve. *Now go. Relax. Be cool. Amble in. Act nonchalant. Don't give them anything to grab hold of.*

And tell 'em what they want to hear.

He ambled down the hall, his gut knotting up. How would Josh handle this? *With cool.*

Bob pushed open the door and smiled. "Hey, docs! Ready to shrink some heads?" It sounded stupid the instant he said it.

A severe-looking fiftyish blond woman stood up and extended a hand. "I'm Dr. Hartmann." She introduced her two colleagues. Dr. Avery, an African-American guy in his forties, very no-nonsense. And a pink-faced kid who looked fresh out of psycho school, clutching a fat notebook. Bob didn't catch his name.

"Sign this consent form." Dr. Hartmann held out a three-page document.

Bob studied it. "You're going to *videotape* this?" So that's why the side wall had a big mirror.

"Standard practice. Dr. Perez wants an objective record."

Right. Bob hadn't heard much that he liked about Perez, but he was The Man now, so you had to live with it. Bob read the entire release form slowly, including the fine print on the last page. He didn't like it, but this seemed a bad time to argue. He signed.

"Have a seat, Mr. Kaganovski."

"Thanks, Ms. Hartmann."

"That's *Dr.* Hartmann."

"Oops ... sorry." Bob felt his ears turning hot. *Great start, Kaggo. Just put that other foot on the banana peel and try for a split.* He slumped into the chair. *Be cool. There's still time to recover.*

"Dr. Perez has asked us to evaluate various relationships among the team members of the Ares 10 prime crew. Please relax and answer the questions as quickly as you can. We're interested in your *first* reactions to these questions. Is that clear?"

A smoke screen. Shrinks never, ever told you what it was really about. Bob tried to relax. "Sure thing. No problemo."

"Please tell us about Dr. Alexis Ohta. Does it bother you that a woman is on the team?"

For crying out loud, did anyone still think that mattered? "Hey, she's just one of the guys, you know?" *One of the most gorgeous guys you've ever seen in your life.* "I think she's the best man on the team."

Dr. Hartmann gave him an incredulous stare. "Best *man*?"

"Um, you know what I mean." *Great, Bob. Kick your tonsils while you're at it.* "Lex is just a . . . regular person. We kind of forget she's a girl."

"Girl." Dr. Hartmann scribbled in her notebook.

"Lady. Woman. Y-chromosome-challenged person." Bob rolled his eyes. *Oh, give it up.* "Girl." *Good grief! Lex called herself a grrrl. Wasn't that the same thing?*

Hartmann kept writing. Dr. Avery just looked at Bob. The kid studied his notebook intently, his tongue poking a knob out of his cheek.

"Fine, Mr. Kaganovski. Could you tell us about Mr. Kennedy Hampton? How do you feel about his privileged background?"

"We kind of kid him about his name." Bob leaned back in his chair. "You know, about how the only good Kennedy is—" *Oops, bad idea.* Bob cleared his throat. "Actually, Josh and I like to call him Hampster. He thinks that's funny, you know?"

"I'm sure it is." Dr. Hartmann pursed her lips and wrote for half a minute, scratching her pen noisily on the brittle paper. Dr. Avery studied Bob, his smile chilly. The kid licked his lips and kept his eyes fixed on his notebook.

"Excellent, Mr. Kaganovski." Dr. Hartmann looked at her clipboard. "I'm sorry, it's Dr. Kaganovski, isn't it?"

"It's Bob."

"Fine. Dr. Bob, could you tell us about Mr. Joshua Bennett? Do you have any question about following his orders, considering that he doesn't have a Ph.D.?"

Bob shrugged. "Josh is a terrific pilot and the best leader I've ever known. He's good at making decisions and it's his job to give the orders. If you can do that, you don't need a fancy-shmancy degree."

Dr. Hartmann nodded and scrawled something. "But you have quite a fancy degree—a Ph.D. in physics from Berkeley."

"Um, yeah, well, it's not like I'm using it or anything. I do engineering physics, not the real stuff like cosmology or quantum field theory. I'm basically a glorified mechanic."

"But suppose Mr. Bennett gave you an order about something where he lacked expertise? Suppose you considered it wrong, even dangerous?"

Bingo. It was safety after all. Here's where they'd try to nail him. *Tell 'em what they want to hear.* Bob cleared his throat and sat up straight in his chair. "That's a very good question, but the fact is . . ." He scratched his nose and then gave her his best smile. "The fact is that Josh is a pretty smart guy, and he's just not going to ask me to do something dangerous. I trust the guy." Which was mostly true.

"You'd obey his orders, then? You seem a bit hesitant."

"It's my job to obey the commander. He's not going to send me into harm's way, I'll tell you that. He's John Glenn, Jack Ryan, and Captain Picard, all in one." Bob tugged at his chin. "So, yeah, I'd obey his orders." *Unless he was wrong.*

"Thank you." Dr. Hartmann wrote something and circled it several times. Dr. Avery leaned back in his chair and shut his eyes. And the kid closed his notebook.

Closed his notebook. Bob went tense in every muscle.

Dr. Hartmann stood up. "Have a pleasant day, Dr. Kaganovski. I'm sure the mission will be very successful." She gave him a stiff smile and walked out. Dr. Avery followed her, his expression blank. The kid nodded to Bob on the way out. "Good luck, guy."

Bob's mouth hung open for a long moment. That was it? The whole interview? He'd come prepared for a one-hour dog-and-pony show, and they walk out after ten minutes? Yow!

Then he remembered that some technician on the other side of the mirror was probably still running the videotape. He stood up, trying to look unconcerned, and ambled out the door.

The shrinks had already disappeared. Bob suddenly needed fresh air. He headed down the hall toward the elevator.

One thing was for sure. They had come looking for dirt on him. And they'd found it, big time.

But how? What had he said?

Wednesday, August 15, 2012, 6:20 A.M.
VALKERIE

"Interview? Me? Now?" Valkerie backed away from the NASA director, looking wildly around the cabin for something big enough to hide behind. "I'm not dressed, I just—" She ran her fingers through her hair, trying to press down the tangled mass of frizz and twigs. "You've got to leave. I mean—the volcano. It could go anytime."

"Are you sure?"

Valkerie hugged her arms to her chest and nodded. "It was belching SO_2—" Her lungs tightened, and she doubled over, coughing. Her throat was raw and her chest was full of fluid. Dark spots moved across her eyes.

"Roger, run back and tell the pilot we're leaving right away. I'll help Dr. Jansen with her equipment."

Valkerie listened to the short man's retreating steps with a growing sense of panic. The director wasn't moving. He wanted her to go with them.

She dropped to her knees and pulled the bulky thermal suit toward her, holding it against her body as she went through the motion of folding it. Her head surged with pain. He was still looking at her. Why didn't he leave?

Perez stepped toward her and stooped to pick up the sample oven. "What else do you need? One of those backpacks?"

Valkerie followed his gaze and blushed. Her bra hung from a loop on the pack frame, and a pile of dirty underwear and socks lay in front of it on the floor. "No. Please. Just the oven. I need to change, and I . . . I won't take long." She rose unsteadily to her feet and moved to block Perez's view of her underwear. "Tell the pilot I'll be ready in a few minutes." Valkerie held her breath and waited, forcing herself to look him in the eyes.

"Of course." Perez pointed toward the door. "Pile anything you need out there." He stepped outside and struggled to shut the plywood door behind him.

"Just leave it. It doesn't close all the way." Valkerie shoved the pile of underwear into her pack and crept to the doorway to peer through the gap. Good! Perez was on his way back to the helicopter.

Breathing a sigh of relief, Valkerie hurried to a small pile of dirty clothes at the foot of the cot. Great. They reeked. She had stretched the three-day field trip to five, and all her clothes were covered with sulfur-saturated mud. It wasn't fair. Why did this have to happen now?

She stepped into a pair of stiff jeans, bracing herself against the wall. The jeans felt rough and cold, like dirty clay pots. Valkerie chose a gray sweatshirt that camouflaged the mud and changed quickly with her back to the door.

Ridiculous to interview looking like this. They'd have to go back without her. Maybe she could tell them she had to drive the jeep out.

The helicopter roared to life. Seconds later she heard a loud knock.

Valkerie stumbled to the door and poked her head through the gap. "Go ahead and fly out. I've got to drive the jeep." Her shout ground gravel into her raw throat.

Perez shook his head. "What happened to the tires?"

"Oh yeah." Valkerie looked down at her feet. "I needed the air—to breathe."

"To breathe? How did. . . ? Oh, I see. Very clever." Perez squinted up at Mount Trident and frowned. Valkerie dragged her two packs outside, and Perez followed her with the thermal suit and air tanks. She could feel the weight of his eyes on her back. Great first impression she was making. First a nightgown and now clothes that weren't fit for a mud wrestler.

They stepped across the bodies of two dead birds. "See? Ravens!" she shouted over the helicopter's engines. "Killed by the SO_2."

Perez nodded and kept on walking past her. Valkerie stumbled behind him, feeling like an idiot. She pushed her way through the helicopter-generated storm, shielding her face with her free arm. Someone took her packs and disappeared. She waited, staring at a chip of olive drab paint on the helicopter door. What if Trident didn't erupt? Some volcanoes vented for decades without erupting.

Perez appeared at the door and shouted, but she couldn't make out his words. Grabbing the doorframe, she tried to pull herself up into the bay, but her head exploded in nauseating pain. The world went black, and she felt herself falling. Unseen hands grabbed her. Lifting. Pulling. Setting her on her feet. She tried to pull away, but her legs buckled, and she collapsed into an expensive silk tie and the smell of men's cologne. Stetson. Just like her father wore. Tears welled in her eyes. Her father loved NASA. NASA and football. She had to get the job.

Valkerie opened her eyes and found herself sitting on a bench with Perez crouched before her, looking up into her face. She braced herself with her arms and forced herself to sit up straight. Feet apart, lean slightly forward, make eye contact. It wasn't too late. She could still salvage the interview.

"Is she all right?" The short man shouted above the roar. Was his name Roger? Panic surged through her. This was an interview. She was supposed to remember. Sit up straight. Eye contact. Lots of eye contact.

"Dr. Jansen? Are you okay? Can you hear me?" Perez held her by the arms, searching her face.

"What, me?" The force of her words throbbed in her head. "I'm fine. I love flying. I'm just tired. I've been collecting samples around the clock. I think I found a new bacteria that can survive one hundred eighteen degrees. It could be a really important discovery, if—"

"The bump on your head—did you fall?"

Valkerie reached to her forehead. A huge welt felt hot beneath her hand. Her face was crusty and tight. Blood? "I guess I must have scratched it."

Perez tilted her head back. "I don't like the looks of this. We'll get you to a doctor soon. Think you can make it?"

Valkerie nodded. "I'm really sorry. I know I must look a mess. If I'd known I had an interview I would at least have worn a blazer to match the mud." She forced a smile and brushed at the crust that covered her jeans.

Perez frowned. "Try not to move."

Valkerie sat rigid, afraid to relax under the scrutiny of the two men. "This was a long way to fly—just for an interview. You must have some pretty important questions to ask."

"Actually we just wanted to meet the woman Dr. Romanov keeps talking about."

"I didn't know you knew Leonid."

"Everybody knows Leonid." Perez searched Valkerie's face with a worried expression.

Why wasn't he questioning her? Had he already made up his mind? "Um, did Leonid tell you I build my own equipment? I don't have an E.E. degree, but I grew up building robotic sensors. My father—"

"Dr. Jansen. Are you sure you feel up to talking?"

"I'm fine. Go ahead. Ask your questions." Eye contact. Lean forward. Valkerie's chest constricted, doubling her over in a fit of coughing.

Perez was in her face in an instant. "Dr. Jansen, look at me. Are you okay?" Perez held her head, forcing her to look into his eyes. "Is there something we should give you? Water? Medication? Do you have any respiratory problems?"

Valkerie tried to pull away. Her brother's asthma. That's why they had come. She should have known they would do a background check.

"No, you've got to believe me. After my brother died, my parents took me in for checkups every year." Perez's face twisted in on itself, throbbing to the beat of her pulse. She squeezed her eyes shut. "It's just the gases. My lungs feel like they're filled with battery acid."

A warm coat spread itself around Valkerie's shoulders. The smell of Stetson.

"Dr. Jansen, I think you should lie down. You may be going into shock."

"I'm fine, really. I can do this."

"Dr. Jansen, please. You're going into shock. Do you know what that means?"

"Of course I do. I know I quit the surgery fellowship, but I finished the M.D. I had to quit. My father needed me."

"Dr. Jansen, please."

"And when I got accepted at Florida, there wasn't much point in going back to finish the fellowship. It—"

"Dr. Jansen—"

"When does Astronaut Candidate school start? I could finish the fellowship as soon as it's over."

"It's okay. Your medical record is fine, but ASCAN training has already started this year. That's why we're here. If you had gotten your application in four months earlier, we wouldn't have a problem, but the next session isn't for another two years, and we really needed someone now."

A black haze closed in around Perez's face. "Two years? But I've got student loans. Postdocs don't count as . . . education." Valkerie felt herself falling. The beat of the helicopter blended into a smooth and creamy roar. She knew she should say something, but what? She had already blown the interview. Two years wasn't soon enough—she needed a job now.

The helicopter lurched and the pitch of the engines fell to a low whine. Smooth fingers pried at her eyelids and a flashlight shined in her eyes. Voices surrounded her.

"How's she doing?" It sounded like Dr. Wiseman, the head of the research center.

"I'm fine." Valkerie tried to sit up, but a half dozen hands held her down. "What do Trident's seismograms look like? Has she erupted?"

Dr. Wiseman shook his head. "A little activity, but no eruption yet."

"But it was venting all night. Sulfur dioxide filled the whole valley."

Two strange men lifted Valkerie onto a stretcher and started to carry her out of the bay. Valkerie fought to sit up. "Hold up a second, I'm fine. I've got an interview to finish!"

"No interview necessary," Perez moved toward the stretcher and took Valkerie's hand. "It was good meeting you, Dr. Jansen. We can talk some other time. Believe me, you've given us more than enough to think about."

CHAPTER 3

Monday, August 20, 2012, 3:15 P.M.
NATE

Nate Harrington stalked out of the elevator. That should have been a routine press conference. Except that some pea-brained journalist had somehow found out about Josh Bennett's motorcycle accident. Whoever leaked that was going to be force-fed his own liver.

An African-American woman stood outside Nate's office alongside a small boy in a too-large wheelchair. Behind them, a video crew. And Steven Perez, smiling broadly. Anytime the cameras rolled, you could count on Perez showing his pearly whites. Even today, with the Johnson Space Center turning into an insane asylum.

Who were these people, anyway? The red light on the videocam turned on. Great. Whatever happened next would be on tape.

Steven Perez stepped forward. "Nate, you had an appointment at three with this young man, Darnell Simmons. Remember? Make-A-Wish?"

Nate clapped his hand to his forehead. His secretary, Carol, had reminded him at noon. But that was before the press conference, which should have been a walk in the park. Instead, it would be six-o'clock news, with *COVER-UP?* splashed across a picture of his sweating face.

Okay, give the kid his photo-op and get rid of him. He was dying of something horrible. And he was a space junkie. Wouldn't be alive two years from now when Ares 10 set down on Mars. Tough case. Smart kid too.

Nate hunched down in front of the boy. "Son, I'm sorry for being late. My fault. Got mauled by some pit-bull reporters who don't know

31

squat about space. Come on into my office and you can sit in the chair of the Mars Mission Director. How's that sound?"

The kid's eyes lit up.

Nate opened the door of his office and led the way past Carol into his inner sanctum.

————

Fifteen minutes later the game was over. The kid left happy, clutching a genuine hundred-percent-pure moon rock. Okay, a moon pebble—1.27 grams of lunar silicate from Fra Mauro, circa 1970. Technically, it was on loan to the kid, since the law didn't allow an individual to own lunar material. A six-month loan, if the kid's doctors were right.

Nate slumped back in his leather executive chair, massaging his temples.

Perez walked in and sat down. "I hear the press conference was some kind of fun."

"Sure, if you're the kind who likes crawling over broken glass with the Dallas Cowboys on your back. It was quicker in the good old days when they only burned you at the stake."

"Why didn't we release the accident report three weeks ago?"

"What's next? Do we report every hangnail? Does the public really need to know every little thing?"

Perez stood up. "Free and open flow of information, remember? That has been the policy of the National Aeronautics and Space Administration since Apollo 1, and—"

Nate slammed his open palm on his desk. "I don't need a history lesson, okay? I've got thirty years of service here, and I know the rule book." *And you've been here how many months?*

Perez leaned over the desk and glowered at him. "Then follow the rules." He spun around and strode out the door. A second later he poked his head in again. "You've read the transcript of the Kaganovski interview?"

"Yeah, I can read too. I'm multitalented."

"I want to discuss it tomorrow at four."

"A.M. or P.M.?"

Perez didn't crack a smile. "A.M. will be fine. Thanks for asking." He disappeared, closing the door softly behind him.

Nate shut his eyes and cursed his smart-alecky sense of humor. But come to think of it, 4:00 A.M. was as good a time as any for a lynching.

Perez would come looking for blood, but he wasn't going to get it. No way was some newbie Johnson Space Center director going to foul up a mission this soon before launch.

Carol's line buzzed. Nate grabbed the phone. "I'm not in."

"I have an Agent Yamaguchi here to see you."

"Don't know him. I'm not in."

"That's right, sir. From the FBI."

"I don't care if he's from the pope, I'm not in."

"Very good. I'll show—"

Nate slammed the phone down. Some days it rained. Some days it poured. Some days you got the whole Niagara Falls.

Carol's stiletto heels *clack-clacked* outside his door. It opened and she stepped in. "Mr. Harrington, Agent Yamaguchi."

Agent Yamaguchi turned out to be a woman, about forty-five, made up to look quite a bit whiter than she probably was. Bright red lipstick. Matching nails. What were the Fibbies coming to?

Nate shook her hand and motioned her toward a chair. "Yeah?"

Ms. Yamaguchi pulled a blueprint out of her briefcase and spread it flat on Nate's desk. "Mr. Harrington, do you recognize this?"

Nate stared at it. The Hab for Ares 10. It wasn't labeled, but it was obviously version 3.4.1B, the one with the revised shower unit. Better privacy. Perez had pushed that idea through all of about three weeks ago. Nate hadn't even seen hardcopy on it yet. "Where'd you get this?"

"So you recognize it?"

"Maybe I do and maybe I don't. Where'd you get it?"

"Mr. Harrington, obstructing an investigation is a federal crime. When I ask a yes-or-no question, there are two possible answers, and *maybe* is not one of them."

"So shoot me. Put me out of my misery."

Yamaguchi leaned back and studied him through narrowed eyes. "Mr. Harrington, let me make it clear that I am on your side."

"Before I answer any questions about this blueprint, I need to know if I'm going to have another PR atom bomb going off in my face."

"I'm afraid I don't understand."

"Long story. Watch the six o'clock news."

"All right, then. I'll cut you some slack. For the moment, you never saw these prints, and I never talked to you. Off the record, just so I can do my job, how old are these plans?"

Nate shook his head. "Maybe three weeks."

"And what are they, exactly?"

"The Hab."

"Hab?"

"Habitation Module. For Ares 10. This is the tuna can our boys and girl are going to ride to Mars in. Where'd you get it?"

"Overnight delivery. It came in this morning from Tokyo."

"Where'd they get it?"

"An autonomous radical cell. We're trying to trace connections now, but it's difficult. One reason I'm here is to ask your advice. Why would terrorists be interested in your program?"

Nate leaned back in his chair. "For publicity, I guess. Isn't that the usual motivation?"

"They typically have a political agenda. But why would Japanese terrorists care about an American space program?"

"It's probably a nationalism thing. The Ares Program is a hundred percent American. Right from the start, we cut out the Russians, the Europeans, and the Japanese."

"Why? Aren't we working with them on that other thing?"

"The International Space Station?" Nate scowled. "That boondoggle! Do you know how many years late and how much over budget that thing ran? International cooperation is great PR for the politicians, but if you actually want to get something done, forget it. No way you could get to Mars that way—not in my lifetime or on my budget. Even NASA by itself was too big and bureaucratic to go to Mars. We had to create a NASA-within-NASA to make it feasible."

"But why would terrorists care about your program?"

Nate leaned forward. "Certain countries—and I won't name any names, but their initials are France, Russia, and Japan—are mad as hornets that we're doing this on our own. It's called nationalism. They want one of their people putting footprints on Mars. And our answer is *no*. On top of that, they're really hurling a hissy fit that we're landing on July fourth."

"Why are we doing that?"

"Because we can—if we go in the next launch opportunity. July fourth happens to work, and we're not going to miss it."

"What if somebody . . . makes you miss it?"

"Then Congress zeroes our funding and we miss Mars. You've heard of Senator Axton?"

Ms. Yamaguchi nodded. "He's the guy saving us money with all the big budget cuts."

Nate clenched his fists. "He cut 40 percent of my program. If we hadn't sold the coverage rights to NBC—and we'll get the biggest payoff if we land on July fourth—we'd have missed this coming launch opportunity. We lose Mars and we'll spend another forty years picking our nose in low-Earth orbit."

"What are the antiterrorist arrangements for your Mars flight?"

Nate shrugged. "Not bad. Terrorism has always been NASA's biggest security concern. We've got the normal precautions in place. But truth to tell, on this mission we've been more worried about fundies than terrorists."

"Fundies?"

"Religious fundamentalists. They're afraid we're going to prove evolution. They stage a protest every week or so over at the Rocket Park entrance, jam up the traffic, yell their slogans. Nothing too exciting, except when one of 'em gets heatstroke."

"Mr. Harrington, I think you may need to increase your level of security against terrorist attacks. The cell we penetrated is very determined. If there are others . . ."

That's all we need. Nate picked up the phone and punched a button. "Consider it done."

Carol answered on the first ring. "Yes, sir?"

"I need to talk to whichever sorry excuse for a brain-dead moron runs Security these days."

"Right away." Carol put him on hold. Nate got an earful of some oldies station. "Stairway to Heaven." Led Zep.

Agent Yamaguchi stood to leave. "I'll get back to you when we know more."

Nate reached up and shook her hand. "Thanks for the tip. Can I keep the blueprint?"

"Do you have a safe?"

The music switched off. "Security. Daniel Collins here."

Nate nodded to Yamaguchi and made an "Okay" signal with his hand. She headed for the door. He slumped back in his chair.

"Collins, we have a problem. . . ."

VALKERIE

Valkerie stared out the oval window, watching the blur of browns and greens that rushed up to meet her plane. She shut her eyes and took a deep breath. If a plane was going to crash, it would crash on landing.

Valkerie lifted a hand to her bandaged forehead. The swelling had gone down days ago, but it still looked awful. The doctor said she'd been lucky—as if suffocation, concussion, and humiliation were things everybody aspired to. It was hard to be thankful. It had almost ruined her chance of getting into the ASCAN program.

Almost. But by some miracle the interview had been good enough to get her into the air. Dr. Abrams had called from Houston two days after meeting her. They wanted her to fly out for some tests. Abrams had warned her not to get her hopes up. He was letting her take off, but it was clear that he expected her to crash on the landing. Obviously, he had been checking up on her.

Valkerie sighed. It seemed that no matter how well she performed, she was never going to be able to escape the mistakes of her past. They already knew about her quitting the surgery fellowship. Did they know about her freshman year at Yale? She had signed the release form. Surely, they had already checked her transcripts, but maybe they didn't care about her grades. Right. More likely they hadn't gotten around to checking. When they finally did, those two D's and an F would spell "Doomed, in Debt, and a postdoc Forever."

She had been such a fool. Skipping classes. Partying every night. Going out with every guy who asked . . . After enduring four years in high school as Valbot the Metal-Mouthed Brain, she had gone absolutely crazy. If her dad hadn't flown to New Haven to talk to the vice-provost, they would have kicked her out of school. As it was, she had to endure the shame of academic probation—not to mention the look of disappointment on her dad's face. How many years had he spent working his way through college? How many hours of overtime had he put in so she wouldn't have to work at all?

After that she had knuckled down and worked her tail off. Med school. Grad school. A postdoc . . . But that one year of foolishness would haunt her for the rest of her life. No matter how hard she tried, she would never be able to shake it. Even now, it still tugged at her heart. She had felt so free. Had so much fun. Made so many . . . friends.

But where were those friends now? The fun hadn't lasted. It couldn't last. You either worked hard and got ahead, or you had fun and got left behind. In academia there was no in between. If only she could get into NASA, things would be different.

God, please let me get into NASA. Just this once, let them pass the transcripts by.

The plane taxied to a stop. Valkerie extracted her carryon from the overhead bin and shuffled forward through the crowded plane.

A wall of heat hit her the second she stepped into the jetway. She wheeled the case quickly up the long ramp, racing the dampness that prickled at her arms and legs. Once in the air-conditioned terminal, she moved self-consciously through a gauntlet of expectant faces, searching for somebody with a sign. A cold, impersonal somebody who would greet her respectfully and drive her in awkward silence to the Johnson Space Center.

"Dr. Jansen?" The voice came from behind and to her right.

Valkerie turned. "Dr. Perez?" She gaped at the director. "I . . . I'm sorry. I wasn't expecting to see *you* here."

"I wasn't sure I could get away." Perez's face lit up with a warm smile. "Welcome to Houston. Did you have a nice flight?"

"Uh, yes. Thank you. Much better than the last one."

Perez grinned and directed her down the concourse. "So has Trident erupted yet?"

Valkerie shot him a wary look, but he was still grinning. "Volcanoes are very unpredictable," she said. "It really could have erupted."

"I never doubted, but Roger checked up on you after we got back. Burst into my office raving about how you had followed protocol. He was impressed. Roger's very big on protocol."

"Well, I still feel bad about our so-called interview. I wasn't myself at all. I appreciate your giving me another chance."

"Dr. Jansen." Perez stopped at an elevator.

"Please, call me Valkerie."

Perez raised an eyebrow.

"I know it's different, but they've been calling me Valkerie since the eighth grade. It's kind of a nickname. It was the name of my first robot."

Perez pressed the button marked "Parking Garage." "Okay—*Valkerie*, I don't think Roger made our position clear. We didn't ask you here to give you 'another chance.' We're very interested in your knowledge of microbial ecology, your medical training, your equipment designs. And

the way you handled yourself out there in the Katmai Preserve....
Breathing from your jeep tires? Very impressive. That kind of resource-
fulness is exactly what we need. If you pass the physicals and psych
tests, I'll push as hard as I can to get you into the current ASCAN class."

"The *current* class. You mean I won't have to wait until the next
one?" Valkerie felt her face starting to glow. "What can I say? Thank
you!" She followed Perez from the elevator out into a dimly lit parking
garage. "But aren't you the director? Why would you have to push?"

"The *new* director. NASA is a huge bureaucracy, and bureaucracies
are very resistant to change." Perez put Valkerie's bag in the trunk of a
white Ford with government plates and opened the passenger door for
her.

She could feel the old excitement coming back—the same excitement
she felt before going off to grad school. But this time she was going to
be part of a team. She could settle down and make friends—friends who
wouldn't graduate and leave every year.

Perez slid behind the wheel and started the car.

"Are you allowed to tell me anything about the tests?"

"Pretty standard physical and psych tests. We mainly want to make
sure that you are a healthy, stable, sociable individual. With Mars loom-
ing large on the horizon, we can't afford to have our astronauts going
postal on us."

"Mars? Is there really a chance I could go to Mars one day?"

"Anything's possible. Does that worry you?"

"No—just the opposite."

"Good. The *life question* is one of the main driving forces behind the
Ares program. It has all kinds of scientific and philosophical implications. Microbial ecologists will always be a crucial part of our Mars
teams."

Valkerie nodded weakly, feeling overwhelmed. Perez drove down an
isolated freeway, surrounded by stunted hardwoods and scrubby pines.
Not nearly as bad as she had imagined. At least Houston had trees. Perez
rambled on about NASA and the unmanned missions to Mars. Valkerie
interjected a question here and there, but it was all she could do to pay
attention. If she could go to Mars ... The thought was staggering.

The trees gradually gave way to a vast wasteland of concrete, metal,
and dust. Tangled oil refineries and filthy smokestacks stretched to the
horizon as far as the eye could see. Flaming chimneys painted black
streaks across a sooty sky. Perez droned on about government bureaucracy

and budget cuts, but all she could think about was Mars. What could she accomplish if she were free from the money and time pressures of academia? What would it mean if she discovered a totally new life form on Mars? What would her father think?

By the time they left the freeway, she had already won two Nobel Prizes and was working on a third. They drove slowly through a small town dominated by parking lots and strip malls. It was a little seedy but better than the refineries. The air looked almost breathable.

"We're putting you up at the Holiday Inn." Perez pointed across the car at a large building on the right. "But if you don't mind, I'd like to get you started right away on some of the tests. We're under a huge deadline crunch."

He turned at the next intersection. A white concrete sign read "National Aeronautics & Space Administration." Valkerie watched as an outdoor exhibit of enormous rockets loomed larger. The car slowed and Perez emitted a throaty sigh of disgust. "Freaks."

Valkerie followed his gaze from the security gate to a ring of protesters, circling beneath a cluster of pines. Clumsy handwritten signs drooped across their shoulders. "Say No to Mars." "Evolution Is Dead and Mars Won't Help."

Oh no! Please. Not protesting NASA. Of all the humiliating . . .

Perez rolled his eyes. "Welcome to the Bible Belt, Valkerie. Home of fundies, freaks, and fruitcakes."

Great. Valkerie forced a smile. If Perez's hostility spilled over to all Christians, then she was dead on arrival.

Wednesday, August 22, 2012, 11:00 A.M.

BOB

Bob's personal purgatory this week was a treadmill in the Environment Simulation Lab. For two hours a day, he had to walk on the thing, the lower half of his body encased in a near-vacuum gizmo. The flight docs' idea.

Bob thought it was bogus, but no astronaut ever won an argument with Flight Med. *Flight Med.* He cringed at the name. What had he said wrong in that interview with the flight surgeons last week? He'd asked Nate about it, but Nate just skittered around the question like a puppy on ice. What had they found?

It couldn't be the safety thing. He'd promised to follow Josh's orders. But maybe they thought he wasn't careful enough? No way. Not with his record. They had to know he was fibbing. Maybe they didn't care what he said at all. Maybe they'd just been watching his body language. Maybe they'd finally caught on to him.

Astronauts were supposed to be macho, high-flying daredevils. Stunt pilots. Skirt chasers. Afraid of nothing.

Bob wasn't any of that stuff. He hadn't even planned to be an astronaut. Six years ago, when he'd been doing robotics for NASA, one of the supervisors put Bob's name on an application for the Ares program and arm-twisted him into signing it. And somehow, *somehow* he'd wound up on the crew. Because he was good at fixing things.

Nobody knew how scared he was. He wasn't a pilot. Got vertigo on anything higher than a kitchen counter. Didn't want to be a hero.

But he *did* want to go to Mars. Mars was a new world, waiting to be discovered. What would they learn about how planets worked? What amazing new materials might they bring home? Had Mars ever harbored life? Could the Red Planet provide a second home for future generations of humans? The crew's geologists and biologists would answer those questions—maybe.

But somebody had to ride along to keep the ship running.

And if that *somebody* was a fraidy-cat flight mechanic named Bob, well . . . he'd just have to swallow his fears and go. It was just something he had to do, like Sam going to Mordor. If they meant to pry him off the mission, they would have to use a crowbar.

Bob wiped his face with a towel and took another swig of the oversweet sports drink that NASA forced him to drink.

"Wow, that was fun!"

Bob turned to look.

"Sarah?" Bob stumbled forward, catching the treadmill controls hard in the chest before he could pull himself back up. *Sarah McLean?* Bob looked again. A woman at the far end of the lab staggered along beside Steven Perez. Dark blond curls. A face right off a natural soap commercial. No way. It couldn't be.

"You did great, Valkerie." Perez led her by the arm.

Valkerie? What kind of name was that? She was probably a reporter. Perez was always bringing in media people, letting them try out the equipment, staging impromptu interviews. It was nuts, trying to train with somebody always sticking a camera in your face, but after a while you got used to working in a fishbowl.

The woman scanned the lab, registering amazement at the equipment. When she saw Bob, her eyes lit up with recognition.

A chill ran through Bob's gut. Oh no! Not another interview. He always came off looking like an idiot.

Perez's cell phone chirped. He yanked it out. "Steven Perez here." A funny look spread across his face. "White House calling? I'll need to take this on a secure line." He covered the phone. "Valkerie, would you excuse me? I've been trying all week to get the president, and she's finally got a few minutes to talk. Look around, and I'll come get you as soon as I can."

Bob smiled with grim satisfaction. Perez was mucking up NASA but good. About time somebody started putting *his* feet to the fire.

Perez trotted off. The reporter turned in Bob's direction and strode toward him with purpose. She didn't seem as aggressive as most media types. She looked . . . nice.

"Hi!" she said. "Aren't you Bob Kaganovski?"

"I'm afraid so." He still didn't know what to say when strangers approached him. Not that people cared much about him. It was Josh Bennett everybody wanted to know about—especially the women.

"I read about you in the *Scientific American* article. And your paper in *Nature*. What's that contraption you're on?"

"A treadmill." Bob waited. The polite question was out of the way. Now she'd ask about Josh.

"I can see that. I'm guessing that shroud over your hips is a low-pressure unit."

Bob raised his eyebrows. *Pretty smart for a reporter.* "You know about that?"

"Does it work? Do you really get a redistribution of body fluids?"

He shrugged. "Haven't the foggiest. Far as I can tell, it's flight-doc mumbo-jumbo. They make me do it because I'm the tallest."

She looked skeptical. "You're only five inches taller than Josh Bennett. That's an 8 percent effect. What's the big deal?"

"It's supposed to be nonlinear. And I'm about twice as clumsy as Josh, which is 100 percent effect." He narrowed his eyes. "You're not a reporter, are you?"

"Excuse me?"

Bob pointed in the direction she'd come. "I saw you with Dr. Perez and figured you had to be a reporter. But you're not dumb enough."

She laughed. "Thank you ... I think."

Bob felt like a moron. "Sorry. That came out wrong. Blame it on oxygen deprivation."

Her eyes smiled at him. "No big deal."

He looked at the timer. Ten more minutes. *Close enough.* He hit the Stop switch and let the treadmill coast to a standstill. "So, um, what was your name again? Valerie?"

"Valkerie." She stepped forward and shook his hand.

Her grip felt firm and sure. Very nice. "Right. So what brings you to NASA today, Valkerie?"

"Dr. Perez asked me to come take some tests. I may be joining the astronaut corps."

"The astronaut corps?" Bob stared at her. "But the new class began training in July. You must have one hot resume. Are you a pilot?"

"A microbial ecologist." Valkerie looked down at the treadmill. Was she blushing? He tried to swallow, but suddenly his throat felt tight and constricted.

"Actually, I'm kind of dizzy about it all," Valkerie said. "Last week, I was collecting thermophilic bacteria in Alaska. Today I'm in Houston trying to figure out where to find an apartment."

"I ... uh ... I could help you with that." Bob swallowed again. This was where he always blew it, but he might as well try anyway. "Tell you what. To make up for calling you a reporter, I could buy you dinner tonight."

Her eyes glowed. "I'd like that, but Dr. Perez has me booked solid for tests through Friday. I just got here yesterday, and I've already taken three physicals."

"Well, how about Friday night? I could clue you in on where to look for apartments, and maybe we could ... you know, talk about biochemistry."

"Biochemistry?"

Oh great, that sounded pretty stupid. "I'm cross-training," he said hastily. "My main job is to be the Ares 10 flight mechanic, but I'm supposed to play backup to Josh on the biochem stuff. Frankly, I'm kind of behind. I don't think it matters, because Josh has it down cold, but you know how NASA is."

"Actually, I don't."

"I could fill you in on that, too," he said. "Anyway, I'd like to hear about your work. Microbial ecology—is that what you said?"

"That's what my degree says." Valkerie shrugged. "But I've always liked electronics and robotics. I spend most of my time building equipment. Basically, I'm just a glorified mechanic."

"Uh-huh." Bob licked his lips and reached for his sports drink. He missed the bottle and the drink toppled over the edge of the treadmill.

Valkerie caught it in midair.

Great. On top of everything else, she was coordinated.

She handed him the bottle.

Bob managed a half smile. "Thanks. And, um... welcome to the ASCAN program."

CHAPTER 4

Friday, August 24, 2012, 4:35 P.M.
VALKERIE

Valkerie perched on the edge of a sixties-era gray metal chair, glancing nervously up at the clock whenever the psychologist looked away. It was 4:35. If the test wasn't over soon, she wasn't going to have time to change clothes for her date. Bob Kaganovski. Unbelievable. She hadn't been in Houston a week and she had a date with Bob Kaganovski.

"Seven, six, four, nine, five, five, seven, five, eight, one, four." Dr. Hartmann paced back and forth in the small room. "Repeat back the list. Now!"

"Seven, six, four, nine, five . . ." Valkerie repeated back the list calmly.

"Faster!"

" . . . five, seven, five, eight—"

"Start all over. From the beginning." Hartmann tapped on a table with her pen.

"Seven, six, four, nine, five, five, eight—"

"Wrong! The next number is a seven." Hartmann scribbled in her notebook furiously. "A mistake like that could cost someone's life. Pay attention!"

Valkerie bit her lip to suppress a smile. Her interview with Dr. Abrams had been a piece of cake. They were obviously playing good shrink, bad shrink.

"Now repeat the numbers after me, and this time get it right! Eight, four, nine—"

The door to the room burst open, and a tall, distinguished-looking

44

man strode into the room. "Dr. Hartmann, we need to talk right now. This Kaganovski interview has gotten way out of hand."

Kaganovski? Valkerie jerked to the alert. Dr. Hartmann turned on the man. "*Missssster* Harrington, I'm in the middle of an important interview. If you'll just make an appointment—"

The man turned to Valkerie. "Sorry about the interruption, but I have to talk with Dr. Hartmann for five minutes. It's important."

Valkerie nodded. Did they know about her date with Bob Kaganovski? The good shrink, bad shrink routine was developing an ominous new wrinkle.

Hartmann pulled her cell phone out and punched in a number. "Hello, Dr. Perez? I'm in the middle of interviewing Dr. Jansen, and Mr. Harrington is trying to make a scene." She paused. "Would you? Thanks so very much."

"Let me talk to him." Harrington reached for the phone.

She snapped it shut and flashed him a polyester smile. "He'll be down in a moment to speak with you personally. Sir."

"Good!" Harrington crossed his arms across his chest and glared at Dr. Hartmann.

Dr. Hartmann stepped toward him. "If you'll excuse me, *Mister* Harrington, I've got thirty more minutes to put Dr. Jansen through the Richardson battery."

"The Richardson battery?" Harrington searched Valkerie's face with a disgusted look. "She's not an ASCAN. What's she doing taking the Richardson battery?"

Dr. Hartmann smoothed her yellow legal pad. "She's already passed physicals one, two, and three. Dr. Perez says she's been doing extremely—"

"What do you mean, *Perez* says? Am I missing something here? Did somebody forget to hand me my pink slip? Since when does Perez do an end run on standard procedures?"

The door flew open and Perez breezed in. "Nate! Good to see you, and I guess you've already met Dr. Jansen."

Nate. Nate Harrington? Where had she heard that name? Valkerie looked to Perez for an explanation.

"But we're interrupting an interview, aren't we?" Perez took hold of Harrington's arm. "If you'll just step outside with me, we have a few things to discuss."

Harrington yanked his arm away. "What is going on here? Did I hear right? You've hired yourself an astronaut and you've got *my* flight surgeons checking under her hood?"

"Nate—"

"And have you seen the latest recommendation of the medical board? This is no way to run a mission."

"Nate, calm down. I want you to meet Dr. Jansen. Leonid says she's the best postdoc he's ever had."

Valkerie stood up to shake Harrington's hand. He stared back at her with smoldering fury. Valkerie felt sick to her stomach. He was really angry. This wasn't part of the act.

"Nate, she builds her own equipment, *and* she's an experienced surgeon. I'm bringing her into the ASCAN class. She'll be able to—"

"Impossible. She's already missed four weeks. You can't do this."

"I can, and I will. This isn't a discussion."

"So does she have to pass the tests?"

"What tests?"

"You've already agreed. After this class, there'll be no more free rides for ASCANs. No more missed drills. No more sleeping during class."

"Nate, that's for the next class."

"As far as I'm concerned, she *is* the next class. If you want me to sign off on her after she's missed four weeks, then she's going to pass my tests—everything I throw at her."

"I'd hardly call that fair."

"Fair has nothing to do with it. Just tell me one thing, all right? Do you even care about this program? Because if you don't, if this is just some game you're playing to move your career along, then count me out. I'll retire and go fly my ultralights, if you're going to do an end run—"

"Nate—"

Harrington rounded on him. "If you want me to quit, just say so, and I'm out of here."

"I don't want you to quit."

"Then give me back my mission. According to the org charts, I'm in charge on this flight."

Perez sighed. "Okay, she'll pass your tests."

Harrington nodded and turned on Valkerie with a look of triumph. "Nice meeting you, Dr. Jansen."

Valkerie stepped toward him. "It was good—"

Harrington turned and left the room, slamming the door behind him.

Friday, August 24, 2012, 6:00 P.M.
BOB

Bob stepped into the elevator on the ground floor of Building 4S. Where was Valkerie? He hadn't seen her since Wednesday. Had she been avoiding him? There would be no reason to avoid him, unless . . . No, he couldn't go there. Innocent until proven guilty. Besides, it had been over a week since his interview with the shrinks and nothing had come of it. He wasn't going to let his paranoia drive in another wedge. Not this time.

If only he'd told her where to meet him. Had he even given her a time? He punched the button for the sixth floor and leaned back against the fabric walls of the elevator. What if she had changed her mind? He would check his voice mail one last time, but this was looking like a disaster.

The elevator *chinged* and the chrome doors slid open. Bob stepped out, punched in the combination, and opened the door of the Astronaut Offices.

Whoa! Valkerie paced back and forth in front of the Ares 10 crew office. Nice dress. Medium heels. Earrings. She had done up her hair in some kind of a . . . whatever.

Maybe he should have dressed a little spiffier. Dockers and a NASA-logo knit shirt—in Houston that was practically formal wear. He walked down the hallway on silent Nike feet. "Hi, Valkerie."

She whirled. Her face broke into a smile. "Hi, Bob! I'm sorry, but I couldn't remember where we were going to meet and—"

"My fault," he said. "I've been looking all over for you and . . . oh, never mind." He paused, wondering what to say next. "You look great."

"Thanks." Her eyes beamed. "Where are we going?"

"A little Italian place just up NASA Road One. It's called Enzo's." He told her all about it on the way out to the parking lot. "Do you like antiques?"

"Um, what kind?"

"This kind." Bob stopped at his car and swept off its reflective shade cloth with a flourish. "A 1965 Mustang with original everything."

"How nice."

Bob had known she'd like it. He unlocked the passenger door and helped her in. When he climbed in on the driver's side, she asked, "No fuzzy dice?"

He shook his head. "I'm not much of a decorator, I guess. Sorry." He turned the key and the engine throbbed to life. "I rebored the cylinders myself and did some tweaking on the carburetor." He drove toward Saturn Lane, telling her the details. When they reached Gate 1, Bob stopped and honked at a half dozen protesters standing in the right lane waving picket signs.

"Sorry," he said to Valkerie. "The rules are that you give pedestrians a full one-lane buffer. I can't go by until they move." He waved at them to step back, but they didn't budge. The security guard at the gate walked toward them. The protesters backed away.

Bob eased the clutch out and glided forward. "It's pretty ridiculous, huh? They're afraid if we find life on Mars, we'll prove evolution. So they don't want us going to Mars. Here in Houston, people take their religion *seriously*."

"Is that a . . . problem?" Valkerie asked. "I mean . . . most people have some kind of religious background, right?"

"Oh yeah, sure."

A brief pause. "Do you?"

Bob felt his shoulders tense. "I went to private Catholic schools growing up." He wanted to look over at Valkerie, try to read her face, but he didn't dare. If she was one of those anti-Catholic—

"I hear they have a pretty good educational system," Valkerie said.

"They have a *great* system. Best in Chicago. I'm glad I went to their schools."

"*Their* schools? So you're not . . . Catholic?"

Bob didn't know what to say to that. He went to Mass once in a while—enough for Kennedy to call him a choirboy. Had read the Bible all the way through. But . . . did he *really* believe in God?

Yeah, sure, in some sense. Look at the deep symmetry of the universe. The beauty of a birthing star. The stark elegance of string theory. And if a guy didn't feel some kind of numinous awe when he peered up at the velvet black sky stippled with a gazillion galaxies . . . well, he probably wasn't being honest with himself.

Was he religious? That one made him squirm. Religious people could be pretty weird. Anti-science protesters. Hare Krishnas chanting on the street. Hindus washing in the Ganges. Suicide-bomber Muslims. Bob didn't identify with anybody like that. He wasn't religious. No way. But spiritual—yeah.

"I'm sorry," Valkerie said. "I didn't mean to interrogate you about your beliefs."

"Oh no, that's fine," he said quickly. "I believe in God—just maybe not in the conventional sense. I was raised Catholic, and I admire a lot of things they do, but . . . I guess I don't quite fit in that box. I mean, there's a lot of things I don't agree with them about."

Bob gripped the steering wheel hard. Was he coming off as too judgmental? "Don't get me wrong," he said. "Everyone's got a right to believe what they want—even those folks back there with the signs. They mean well, but they're just so . . . sure of themselves. They've got the inside scoop on the Bible, and you're not allowed to ask questions."

"Questions?"

Bob turned right on NASA Road One. "Yeah, like if God created the stars six thousand years ago, how come we can see galaxies twelve billion light-years away? Sure, He could have created the starlight en route, but that's kind of deceptive, isn't it? Is God trying to fool us into thinking the universe is older than it really is? If so, why would He do that? And if so, is it wrong for us to go along with His little hoax?"

"That's . . . something to think about."

Bob sighed with relief. If she liked that question, he had a lot more. "And about that Noah's flood thing, I wonder if they ever did the biomass calculation. How many species could you fit in an ark?"

By the time they reached Enzo's, Bob had pretty well knocked the creationists out for the count. He and Valkerie took a table for two back in the corner farthest away from the smoking section.

"I heard somewhere that most astronauts believe in God," Valkerie said.

"They do and they don't. If you mean Einstein's God—some kind of deep Cosmic Purpose, yeah, a lot of us believe in that. The Force or whatever."

"What about a . . . personal God?"

Bob thought for a minute. He wrestled with that one a lot. On the one hand, the God of the Bible was a personal God. But on the other hand, He didn't seem to hang out with the boys all that much these days, did He?

Bob shook his head. "Mostly no. Of course, there've been a few deeply religious astronauts. Some of them were real heavy hitters. John Glenn. Frank Borman. Jim Irwin. Shannon Lucid. Great people, all of them. But they're the exceptions. I haven't been in space yet, but if you talk to people who have, they'll tell you that God is no closer up there than He is down here."

Valkerie took a sip of water and studied him with her large, soft eyes. "Meaning. . . ?"

This was amazing. Bob usually found it hard to talk to women. But with Valkerie, he was really opening up. And she was drinking it all in. Wow!

"Meaning this. God supposedly wants this deep personal relationship, right? I mean, He's *dying* to have a relationship with us. And yet most of us aren't exactly swamped with messages. Okay, yeah, I've met a few nutcakes who thought they were hearing from God every five minutes. God tells 'em which lipstick to use, which car to buy, which . . . person to marry. I mean, they're getting messages from God left and right. Whereas the rest of us don't hear diddly. Isn't that strange? One burning bush would go a long way, know what I mean? What's with God? Couldn't He at least send an e-mail?"

Valkerie nodded pensively. "I see your point."

Bob felt vaguely disappointed. It would have been nice if she had a spiritual side to her. Hadn't she ever noticed the grandeur of the universe? The deep symmetry and numinous awe and all that? But no, she was a scientist. She'd probably think that was nuts.

"Tell me about the Mars mission."

That was safe ground. Bob talked for two hours straight on the Ares 10 program. Training. Safety issues. Internal politics. The funding crisis. The protesters. The hope that the mission would find evidence of life on Mars. The history of manned exploration of space. Bob could not believe how well this was going.

As they were finishing off their banana cheesecakes, Bob had a brilliant idea. "Hey, if you're interested in NASA history, there's a great little outfit just up the road where the astronauts hang out. It's a little shabby, but if you'd like to see it . . ."

"What's the name of the place?"

Bob couldn't wait for Kennedy and Josh to see her with him there. "It's called the Outpost," he said. "You'll love it."

Friday, August 24, 2012, 9:00 P.M.

VALKERIE

Bob opened the door and Valkerie dropped into the worn leather seat of his antique Mustang. What a day. First a confrontation with Harrington and now this. Bob Kaganovski—the man she'd been reading about for two years—was a Christian-basher. He hadn't stopped talking about Christians since he'd picked her up. Why did her faith have to be so alienating? Why did Christians have to make such a big deal about science and evolution? Didn't they see what it was doing to people?

Bob slid behind the wheel, and the car started with a low rumble. "You'll really like the Outpost. It's the quintessential astronaut hangout. If I know Kennedy Hampton and Josh Bennett, they're probably already there."

Valkerie nodded, and Bob's face lit up with a goofy grin. He was so cute, like an overgrown puppy. If only he weren't . . . such a jerk. She'd bitten her tongue all evening, but if he made one more crack about her faith, she was going to scream.

The worst part was that he made a lot of sense. What could she say? She didn't know the answers herself. Why didn't God communicate more directly? If God really led Christians, why did He always seem to lead them to the wrong people? For example . . . why had *she* always been attracted to Bob Kaganovski?

Valkerie had been following Bob's career for years. While everyone else was oohing and aahing over Josh Bennett, hadn't it been the tall, shy engineer in the background who caught her eye? She had even read some of his papers. Maybe she couldn't always follow the physics, but his writing glowed with unpretentious brilliance. And now she was out on a date with him. In a redneck Mustang no less. Getting her faith bashed in.

Bob turned right onto a dark side street and pulled off the road. Valkerie looked around the overgrown lot. The only building in sight was a dark wooden shack with no signs or windows.

"Here we are." Bob's enthusiasm seemed a little forced.

Valkerie looked up at him nervously.

"I know. It doesn't look like much on the outside, but believe me, it doesn't look like much on the inside either."

Valkerie got out of the car and followed Bob to a small porch at the back of the building. The weathered wood panel door was closed, but the hasp didn't seem to be padlocked. A thin band of light shone past the ill-fitting door.

Valkerie stopped and listened. "It's late. I don't think they're open."

"Of course they are. It's only nine-fifteen." Bob stepped forward and pulled on the door.

Valkerie stepped timidly inside and waited for her eyes to adjust to the dim light beyond. The smell of stale cigarette smoke greeted her with the clash of billiard balls. Saloon doors separated the narrow foyer from a dirty, run-down bar. She reached forward to push open the small wooden portals but drew her hand back with a start. The doors were cut in the shapes of two curvy women wearing padded Naugahyde bikinis. Valkerie hesitated, not knowing where to put her hand.

Bob reached around her and pushed open one of the women. "Like I said. The quintessential astronaut hangout. Seems almost like that place in *The Right Stuff*, doesn't it?"

Valkerie nodded and hung back to let Bob step first into the rustic bar.

"Hey, Bob! What are you doing here?" A man with a pool cue stepped away from a shabby billiards table. Valkerie gasped when she recognized him. Josh Bennett, the commander of the Ares 10 mission. A striking young Asian woman leaned over to make a shot. Medium height, athletic, lustrous black hair. She looked even better than her pictures—Alexis Ohta, the crew's geophysicist.

"Josh! I want you and Lex to meet someone." Bob motioned Valkerie forward.

Josh flashed a smile at Valkerie and extended his hand. He was a little shorter than he looked on television, but the TV cameras hadn't exaggerated his rugged good looks one lepton.

"This is Valkerie Jansen—like Valerie, but with a 'k.' Perez is recruiting her for the corps."

"*Perez?* Recruiting?" Josh gripped her hand and gave her an appraising look. "Well this *is* an honor."

"Valkerie, this is Josh Bennett and Lex Ohta from the Ares 10 prime crew. We're teammates."

"Hi, Valkerie." Lex kept her distance. She didn't seem that excited to meet her. Valkerie wondered if she and Josh were an item.

"Valkerie, you'll be interested in this." Bob led her to the far wall near the bar.

Valkerie gaped at an entire wall filled with mission photographs and astronaut memorabilia. Most of them were signed—some by an entire shuttle crew. Valkerie studied the photographs, looking for Apollo-era pictures.

"I'll be right back." Bob walked toward the bar.

Valkerie studied the pictures. STS 90, STS 110, STS 68—they all seemed to be from the shuttle era. She scanned the rest of the room. It was covered from floor to ceiling with license plates, business cards, pinned-up dollar bills . . . but no Apollo shots.

Bob returned carrying two plastic cups full of beer. He offered her one.

"No, thank you. I don't drink."

Bob looked stung. "It's just a beer. How'd you get through university without beer?"

"Some of us found that studying worked." Valkerie knew she was being snippy, but she was too exhausted to care.

"Hey, what did I say?"

"I'm sorry. I'm just tired. I don't want to get into another argument. Really."

"Argument? Who's been arguing?"

"Nobody. It's just that . . . well, I guess that's how the last few hours felt to me. I'm sorry, I—"

"Why didn't you say something?"

"What could I say? You're entitled to your opinions. I know you didn't mean to be offensive, it's just that—"

"Offensive? What do you mean—offensive?"

"You've been bashing Christians all evening."

"But . . . you're a biochemist. I just assumed that—"

"—that I couldn't be a scientist and a Christian? Because Christians are too irrational, right? Because we're all a bunch of cross-toting, un-educated kooks."

"I didn't say that."

"No, but you implied it. Do you have any idea how hard it is to listen to someone trash your faith all night? You people love to point out how intolerant the church is, but did you ever consider how intolerant you are?"

"What do you mean, 'you people'? I told you I believe in God."

"How convenient. That's why you spent the whole night trying to prove God doesn't exist. I suppose that makes you a very spiritual athe-ist."

"I never said God didn't exist; I just said you couldn't prove—"

"Bob, I really don't want to get into an argument. If you're offended by a scientist who actually believes—" Valkerie turned and headed for the door.

"Valkerie, wait, I'll take you home."

"I'd rather walk. The hotel's just down the street, and I need the exercise."

"Walk? In Clear Lake? You can't. Let me give you a ride. I won't say another word about—"

"Bob, please . . . don't tell me what I can and can't do." Valkerie pushed through the saloon doors and stepped out into the night. It was late, but the air still felt like a sauna. She clomped to the side street and made her way toward NASA Road One. A car roared to life behind her, but she didn't look back. She'd really gone off the deep end back there, but Bob was so . . . infuriating. If she hadn't bailed when she did, she would have said something she'd regret even more.

Valkerie turned at the intersection. Where were the sidewalks? She searched the shoulder across the street. Nothing on either side but gravel and Saint Augustine grass. Apparently nobody knew how to walk in Houston.

A group of rough-looking kids riding in an open jeep slowed down to pace her. "Yo, sugar. Lookin' for your sugar daddy?"

Valkerie reached into her purse and clenched a tube of lipstick like it was a canister of pepper spray.

"Can I have your phone number? I lost mine."

A horn honked behind them, and they sped off with a roar. Valkerie doubled her pace. Her shoes were going to be ruined, but she didn't care. She just wanted to get to her room.

A car horn blared, but Valkerie ignored it. She stumbled forward, wishing she hadn't been so rash. Another honk. A beep.

Valkerie looked over her shoulder. A car was following slowly behind her, blocking traffic in the right lane. Valkerie pushed forward, not knowing whether to be mad or relieved. It was a redneck antique Mustang.

Bob shifted his weight, flexing his calves to keep from passing out on the hot stage. Nate's welcome speech was taking forever. A huge crowd had assembled on the rec field to watch the Ares 10 crew demo the Martian Rover. Bob scanned the glistening faces. Of course she wouldn't be here. He hadn't even mentioned the demo. And after his spectacular foul-up last night, he'd be lucky if Valkerie ever spoke to him again. She certainly wouldn't have braved the 103-degree heat to watch him ride around in an air-conditioned Mars buggy.

Nate finally got around to introducing the crew. Bob waved to the crowd and did his best imitation of a sincere smile. Where could she be? He'd called her hotel room, the astronaut offices, the gym. . . . Nobody even knew her schedule. They were all too busy with the Johnson Space Center Open House. The campus was boiling with tourists. It was insane. He'd been forced to park on the street and run half a mile to make it to the demo on time.

Kennedy Hampton leaned over and whispered in Bob's ear. "You look like you could use a stiff dose of antifreeze. Wanna help me warm up the Rover's air conditioning?"

Bob shrugged. Anything to get off the stage. Kennedy stepped forward and waved to the cheering crowd, then leaped off the stage, setting off a chorus of excited squeals. Bob walked over to the side and took the stairs.

Fighter pilots. Everything was a competition. Kennedy seemed to take Josh's popularity as a personal challenge. Like a down-in-the-polls politician, he never passed up an opportunity to grandstand.

Bob waited inside the roped-off area for Kennedy. A peleton of women clung to him as he pushed his way through the milling crowd. Finally Kennedy arrived. Bob followed him to the Rover. *Women.* Kennedy threw himself into the chase as if it were an Olympic event. Fine, let him. If that was the game, Kennedy could have the gold, silver, and bronze.

Kennedy opened the airlock door in the side of the mammoth six-ton, eight-wheeled Rover. Bob leaped up the steps into the cool interior.

Kennedy followed him in and shut the door. "Okay, what gives, Kaggo?"

Bob plopped down into one of the rear seats and peered through the darkened glass at the crowd outside. "They're expecting us to show off the Rover."

"Not until you spill. Josh said your date last night was hot." Kennedy sat down on the bench across from Bob.

"It wasn't even a date. She's new in town, and I was just showing her around."

"And I'm sure she begged you to take her to the Outpost, seeing that it's such a well-known landmark."

Bob shrugged. "She's interested in NASA, and I thought she might appreciate the history."

Kennedy grinned. "Yeah, right. The Outpost is very historical. Come on, admit it. You were bringing her home to meet the family. You wanted to get Papa Kennedy's approval."

"*Your* approval? I've known her for all of about three days. We didn't even hit it off."

The airlock door opened, and Lex and Josh climbed into the Rover.

"Okay, Hampster. You're the pilot." Josh slid along the bench to sit beside Bob. "Pilot away."

"We're talking. Bob's worried I'm not going to approve of his new girlfriend."

Lex plopped down next to Kennedy. "Okay, Bob, spill!" She fixed him with an expectant look.

Oh, for crying out loud, not Lex too. "Come on, guys, the people are going to think something's wrong with the Rover. Let's get this show off the road."

"Hampster?" Josh motioned forward to the driver's seat.

Kennedy growled. "Come on. Y'all at least got to meet her. I'm in the cold here."

Josh turned to Lex. "You're the backup pilot."

Lex shook her head adamantly.

"Okay, *I'll* drive." Bob stood up. Josh and Kennedy pushed him back down.

Kennedy shot a pleading look at Lex.

"Okay, okay. I'll be the martyr." Lex went forward and climbed into the driver's seat with a grin. "But if you guys don't talk so I can hear, I'll crawl back there and throttle you." She started the Rover and drove it toward the field of rocks the grounds crew had brought in for the show. Kennedy and Josh looked at Bob.

"Come on, guys. Lighten up. It was no big deal. Valkerie seemed lonely, so I offered to show her the sights."

"I'll bet you did." Kennedy smirked. "What are you going to show her on your second date?"

Bob pressed his palms against his eyes. Good grief, they weren't going to quit badgering him until he'd told them the last putrid detail. "Okay, I'll admit it. I was really interested in this girl, but I blew it, okay? Another disaster for Kaggo. A foul-up of epic proportions. Satisfied?"

Josh's face softened. Kennedy reached across the aisle and whacked him on the shoulder. "As bad as last time?"

"Worse. She walked out on me. Wouldn't even let me drive her back to her hotel."

The Rover reached the field of rocks. Lex slowed down and let the beast show off its eight-wheel independent suspension.

"She must be nutso. Unbalanced." Josh stood up and grabbed an overhead bar. "Don't beat yourself up over it, okay, Kaggo? She's the one with the problem."

"No, it was my fault. I deserved it."

Kennedy snorted. "You're just out of practice. It takes a little time, that's all. You probably just started putting the move on too early."

Bob shook his head. "You wouldn't understand."

"If you guys don't talk louder, I'm going to start spinning donuts!" Lex shouted from the front. "Remember, Hampster. Nate thinks you're driving."

"So what happened?" Kennedy shouted at the driver's seat.

"We started . . ." Bob looked down at his feet. "*I* started talking about religion. I guess I was trying to impress her, but I ended up hurting her feelings—bad. I feel like scum."

Josh laughed. "What is she, a Buddhist or something?"

Bob shook his head. "Christian."

"So what's the problem?" Josh asked. "Sounds like a match made in heaven."

Kennedy grinned. "She probably doesn't like choirboys."

"Apparently, she's fresh off the fundie farm," Bob said.

Kennedy laughed out loud. "You went out with one of those picketers? What did you expect? If you ask me, I say good riddance. I know plenty of women who would love to go out with you. How about tonight? I could set something up for dinner."

"Forget it," Lex shouted. "Kaggo's too classy for your ilk. Bob, you need a lady of quality. I've got a friend who would be perfect for you."

Bob shook his head. "Thanks, guys, but—"

"I bet things aren't as bad with Valkerie as you think," Josh said. "Are you sure you aren't being too hard on yourself?"

"If anything, I'm being too easy. I was a jerk."

"Maybe if you talked to her. Apologized. You could work things out."

"Assuming I wanted to work things out."

"What?"

The Rover ran up and over a huge rock. The entire frame tilted hard to the right. "Take it easy, Lex!" Josh sat back down next to Bob.

"Talk louder, or you're gonna get more of the same."

"You heard the boss." Josh nodded at Bob.

"Valkerie and I are totally incompatible," Bob called out. "It could never work in a million years."

The Rover jerked to a stop. Lex turned in the driver's seat and looked back at Bob with fire in her eyes. "You don't know that. No matter what you said, no matter how bad she hurt you or you hurt her, if you like her, you have to try."

"No, I don't." Bob searched his friends' faces. "Guys, this is ridiculous. I know I don't get out much, but I can tell when a relationship isn't going to work. Believe me, this is one of those times."

"All right. Fair enough." Josh shrugged. "But she seemed pretty nice to me."

"I'm not saying she's not nice. It's just that . . ."

"Just that what?" Lex strode back toward them. "What are you always so afraid of?"

"Not afraid. Cautious. Trust me. I have all the reason in the world to be cautious—especially with fundamentalists."

Bob stood up. The Rover had grown uncomfortably quiet. "Come on! Let's drive over some more rocks." He turned and looked out the window at the crowd, searching through the faces for . . .

Good grief. What was it with him? He was such a moron. Hadn't he learned anything after Sarah?

Let it go, Kaggo. From now on you're thinking with your head. Your heart's never given you anything but trouble.

CHAPTER 5

Monday, August 27, 2012, 5:00 A.M.
VALKERIE

The Vomit Comet—not the world's most reassuring name for an airplane. Valkerie patted the thigh pocket of her olive green flight suit. Two genuine NASA barf bags lay inside. Of the twenty-plus pieces of equipment she carried in the thirteen pockets of her flight suit, the barf bags were the most accessible. Apparently they were the only items they expected her to use.

She turned to search the faces of the three men sitting against the wall behind her: Nate Harrington, Dr. Abrams, and a green-suited trainer. Abrams looked mad enough to spit blood. Valkerie wondered when Harrington had sprung the flight on him. He had called her at 4:00 A.M. with the "good news." The 3:00 P.M. flight with the ASCAN class was canceled, but if he was lucky, he could get the KC-135 at 5:00 A.M. What a thoughtful guy. With judges like him, who needed a jury?

Valkerie looked up at the timer at the front of the padded bay. They'd go parabolic in five minutes. She scanned the stack of cards tucked into the plastic sheath of her sleeve. Harrington wasn't giving her any slack time. She'd have thirty seconds of weightlessness to free float, somersault, and walk down a patch of Velcro on the plane's ceiling. Then after pulling some heavy gees at the bottom of the sine wave, the whole thing would start over again. She flipped through the cards. Forty cycles in all, and every one of them was a different test. Why even bother to try? Harrington had designed the whole thing to make sure she'd fail. She had talked to an ASCAN in the cafeteria, and he told her that his class didn't even have tests. To him, the Vomit Comet had been something they did for fun. Right, some fun.

Valkerie forced down the anger rising in her chest. She certainly hadn't been making many friends in Houston. Nate Harrington was willing to schedule a private flight just to get her out. And Bob Kaganovski. Who knew what he must think of her? After the way she had treated him? His uncertain smile burned in her memory, making her sick to her stomach. She had been so mean. It was worse than kicking a puppy.

A million butterflies began flapping in her stomach. What was happening? The plane wasn't supposed to dive for three more minutes. She felt a sharp rap on her shoulder. A man stood upside down on the ceiling above her. The trainer in the flight suit.

"You're upside down, astronaut. I want you on the ceiling standing in front of me—now!"

Valkerie looked up at the timer. Twenty-eight, twenty-seven, twenty-six . . . Of all the cheap tricks. She unclasped her seat belt and started to stand but thought better of it just in time. Curling her knees to her chest, she thrust her feet upward and pushed off with her hands. She hit the ceiling harder than she expected and rebounded. Arms flailing, body twisting, world spinning, she fell slowly through space, hitting her back on the padded floor of the plane.

Before she could bounce off, she thrust her feet upward again, but this time more gently. The force of her kick sent her twisting toward the ceiling. She absorbed the impact with bent knees and planted her feet firmly on the Velcro strip.

Straightening her body, she swung around to face the trainer. Her universe inverted itself, and she and the trainer were right side up in a world turned upside down.

"How do you feel? Nauseous? Light-headed? Disoriented?"

Valkerie shook her head warily.

He tossed a ball to her. She reached out a hand to catch it, making a last-second adjustment when she realized it wasn't going to arc back down. Down no longer had any meaning.

"Back somersault. Right now!"

Valkerie kicked free of the Velcro and tucked into a tight backward roll. After two rotations, she opened out her body and rebounded off the floor to spin back up onto the ceiling. "This is so cool! Can I do another one?"

A beep sounded, and Valkerie fell softly to the padded floor of the bay. The gees built up quickly as the KC-135 pulled out of its dive. She struggled into her seat and waited for the next dive. So far so good.

After another half hour of testing, using every dirty trick Valkerie could imagine, the trainer turned to the rear of the plane. Harrington scowled, shook his head, and turned his thumb down. Abrams looked as if he was about to be sick.

"The flight's over," the trainer announced.

"Why?" Valkerie turned on Harrington. "We were supposed to do another thirty runs."

"It's clear to me that you're going to pass the test. I don't want to waste your time."

"Waste my time? None of the other ASCANs even had to take tests. The Vomit Comet was supposed to be fun."

"None of the other ASCANs applied four months late. You've missed a lot of training. It's only natural that you need to work an accelerated schedule. As soon as we land I've scheduled you for two hours of physical training, followed by—"

"Physical training!" Valkerie wanted to shriek.

"Is something wrong?"

Nothing except that I'm exhausted. "Um, not really."

"If you can't hack it, just say so."

"I can hack it."

"Good. And after PT, Perez has you on console at SES."

"SES?"

"Systems Engineering Simulators. Building 16. It's all here on your revised schedule." Nate patted a manila folder on his lap. "I hope you appreciate this. Perez had to bump Bob Kaganovski to get you a slot."

"Thanks." Valkerie bit her lip to keep from screaming. All Bob needed was another reason to hate her.

Monday, August 27, 2012, 9:00 A.M.
BOB

Bob groaned as he stepped out of his Mustang. It was already 9:03 A.M. An overturned tanker had cost him the two most productive hours of his day. He hurried through the parking lot toward Building 29. A limo cruised by him and stopped outside the building. Probably a Congress-critter doing a little fact-finding mission on the taxpayers' nickel. The driver popped out, came around, and opened the door.

Kennedy Hampton stepped out. "Thanks a lot, Senator Axton!"

A jowly man in a business suit sat inside. Bob's jaw fell open. "Hack-saw" Axton himself. The guy was bad news for any kind of science program. He made Proxmire and his bozo Golden Fleece Award seem like the good old days. Why was the Hampster hobnobbing with a jerk like Axton?

Bob hurried toward Building 29. He'd almost reached it when he heard a shout.

"Hey, Kaggo, wait up!" Kennedy strode up, shaking his head. "You missed a chance to talk to Axton."

"I've got nothing to say to guys like him." Bob opened the door. *What in the world?*

"Mornin', Dr. Kaganovski, Commander Hampton," said the security guard.

"Good morning, Shane." Bob raised an eyebrow at the brand-spanking-new X-ray machine. "Planning on starting an airport?"

Shane grinned at him. "New rules. Came down from The Man. No big deal. Just put your briefcases here and walk on through the metal detector."

Bob put his briefcase on the conveyor and stepped through the white arch. No beeps. Bob grinned back at Kennedy. "Guess it didn't notice my fillings."

Kennedy followed him through. "Kaggo, listen, you need to learn to deal with these politicals, okay? They pay our salaries—"

"Yeah? Well, last time I checked, I pay their salaries too." Bob walked with Kennedy toward the Hab bay. A security guard stood outside the door. *Huh?* Did they think someone was going to walk off with the Hab?

"Can I ask you something?" Kennedy followed Bob into the bay. He didn't seem that surprised by the new guard. "How'd things go with the flight docs a couple weeks ago?"

"Lousy." Bob threw his briefcase on a desk and logged on to a workstation. "If they want my hide, I gave it to them—with a parsley garnish."

"Bob, something's coming down. Axton's not talking, and Nate is twitchier than a hound dog on a coon hunt."

"It's me," Bob said. "If you threw me overboard, the storms would magically calm down. I guarantee it."

Kennedy studied Bob with a puzzled expression. "You really are paranoid, know that?"

"Where did you hear that? From Hartmann?"

Kennedy laughed and disappeared into the Hab. "I've got news for you, bud. It ain't exactly a well-guarded secret."

Bob slumped in his chair. So Kennedy thought he was paranoid. Was that what Josh and Lex thought too? Impossible. They were counting on him to get the ship to Mars and back. Weren't they? Or did they already know what Flight Med was up to? Great. Now he was sounding paranoid again. But how could you tell whether you were paranoid or people really were out to get you?

Bob checked his schedule for the day. Great, he had a flight-sim exercise in twelve minutes. One of those totally pointless things. The other three crew were ace pilots, but if they *somehow* got incapacitated, he had to know how to fly the ship. Right. Either the thing flew itself, or he'd be dogmeat. He was lucky if he could fly an elevator. But no use pointing that out. His position was precarious enough right now.

If they replaced him, he had a pretty good idea who they'd bring in. Valkerie was too good for NASA to ignore. A medical doctor. A Ph.D. biochemist. Healthy as all get-out. Coordinated. And a crackerjack mechanic. Oh yeah, she was sociable too, unlike Kaggo over in this corner, Mr. Social Misfit.

Bob walked out of the lab, cut across the lawn past the duck ponds, and into Building 16. He didn't get over here much, but it was hard to get lost. Walk in, take a left, and follow the big pipe that ran along the ceiling—all the way back to the flight-sim lab.

Steven Perez stood on the stairs leading up to the large metal dome. "Okay, run that one again, Valkerie."

Bob stopped. *What was going on?*

Perez hurried down the stairs. "Good morning, Bob! I came by your lab half an hour ago, but you weren't in. I know we had you scheduled for some training, but I wanted to give Dr. Jansen a crack at this too." He put a hand on Bob's shoulder. "Realistically, I think you've gotten about as good as you're going to get on this machine, and it's not likely you'll ever need to use this training anyway. So if you don't mind...?"

A cold knot tightened around Bob's gut. *Smile. Act calm. Don't go postal.* "That's just fine, Dr. Perez. I'm anxious to work on the Hab some more, anyway." *Don't act so stiff. Lighten up.*

Perez nodded. "I appreciate all the work you've done to improve the human factors on the Hab. That's especially important for our female crew members."

Bob nodded and felt his insides go numb. *Female crew members.*

Plural. The last time he'd checked, Lex was the only female on the crew. Since when was "one" plural?

Perez's cell phone rang. He flipped it open. "Perez here." His face darkened. "Well, uh, *hello*, Senator Axton! What a pleasure to have you visiting today! Yes, I can meet you in about . . . five minutes. You're in my office now? How nice. I'll be right over."

Perez jammed the phone in his pocket. "Um, Bob, could you maybe give Valkerie a few pointers on the sim? The trainers aren't in yet, and I've got a little forest fire to put out."

"Sure, no problem." Bob took a deep breath. A little time alone with Valkerie. He hadn't been expecting this, but he might as well take advantage of it. He had an apology to make, and now was as good a time as any.

He poked his head inside the half-dome. Valkerie lay in the pilot's seat, totally absorbed in the sim. She looked bone tired. At nine-thirty in the morning! Poor kid. "Valkerie?"

She didn't answer.

"Valkerie, I'm really sorry. I was a . . ."

Bob stepped all the way into the sim and came around to look her in the eye. He froze.

She was asleep.

Monday, August 27, 2012, 9:45 A.M.
VALKERIE

Valkerie woke with a start. Bob Kaganovski's face filled her blurry vision. "Bob! What are you doing in my bed—" She blinked her eyes, trying to make sense of the control panels that surrounded her.

Bob stepped back and shuffled uneasily beside her. "I'm sorry. Dr. Perez asked me to help you run the sim, but I didn't have the heart to wake you."

"To wake me?" Valkerie looked around the room, trying to get her bearings.

"You look really tired."

Valkerie nodded. "Harrington's been working my tail off. I'm beginning to wonder if being an astronaut is worth it."

"Probably not. Axton's on the rampage again. Chances are you'd only get halfway through the ASCAN program before Congress cuts our funding. Who knows what's going to happen if Ares 10 doesn't get off the ground?"

"Ares 10? Why wouldn't—" Valkerie put a hand to her mouth. *Bob's here for the simulator. Idiot.* "I'm so sorry. This was supposed to be your time. I didn't . . . Perez didn't ask me before bumping you from the schedule." Valkerie slid out of the seat and tried to stand, but her legs wobbled under her like overcooked spaghetti.

"No, sit down. Please." Bob reached out for her arm but hesitated and took back his hand. "Are you okay?"

"I'll be fine. I'm just tired." Valkerie pulled herself up by a handle on the wall. Her feet felt hot and swollen, and her lower back burned with dull pain. "Harrington scheduled me for the Vomit Comet at five and then had me on a treadmill program for over two hours."

"Nate Harrington? Are you sure? That doesn't sound like Nate."

"I'm sure, all right. He's trying to break me. Trying to get me to withdraw my application."

"No way. He's on our side. Nate would never—" Bob froze. He looked as if he'd just swallowed a bumblebee.

"Nate wouldn't what?"

"Oh, nothing. I, uh . . . was just thinking that I wanted to apologize for Friday night. I was really a jerk. I—"

"You were fine. I'm the one who needs to apologize. I was tired . . . I wasn't myself at all. I totally overreacted." Valkerie paused. Bob didn't seem to be paying attention. A frown creased his forehead.

"Are you sure Nate made out your schedule? Nate Harrington?" he asked.

"I'm positive. He called me up at four and told me himself."

"Four A.M.?"

"I know it sounds ridiculous, but I promise it was him. I just saw him . . ." Valkerie looked at her watch. "Oh no! I've got to get to Building 8. I've got a 'Bruce protocol' test in ten minutes."

"Hold on a second! Let me get this straight. Nate scheduled you for the Vomit Comet at five, then two hours of PT, and now you have a Bruce protocol test at ten?"

"Look, Bob, I'm really sorry. My behavior Friday night was inexcusable, and I don't blame you a bit for being mad, but I've got an appointment in nine minutes, and I really can't afford to be late." Valkerie ducked past Bob and hurried through the door of the dome.

"Valkerie! Wait!"

Following the pipe at a quick jog, she mentally kicked herself every step of the way to the main entrance. Had she said something wrong? She pushed through the doors and ran across the campus lawn toward Building 8. And why did Bob have to be so . . . irritating? She entered the building at a quick walk. Two minutes later, she was standing out of breath in the exercise room.

"Valerie Jansen?" A man in a white lab coat walked into the room from an adjacent office.

"Sorry I'm late. I just came from Building 16."

"Well, I hope you didn't run. This is a maximal-effort stress test, you know. I'll need to get your BP and heart rate during exercise and at rest."

"*Maximal* effort?"

"Yes. Basically, we'll run you to exhaustion."

Valkerie felt the blood drain from her face. She was so tired she could hardly stand. She wouldn't have a chance. Harrington was going to win after all.

CHAPTER 6

Bob stormed past Carol's desk and into Nate's inner office. Nate stood staring vacantly out the window.

"Excuse me!" Carol called. "I don't think—"

Bob slammed the door. "I want an explanation for this."

Nate turned and slumped heavily into his chair. He looked as if his pet dragon had just died. "How'd you find out so fast?"

Bob sat down on the edge of a chair. "She told me."

"Who told you? Carol?" Nate pressed his hands to his temples. "She doesn't know a thing about it. I just finished talking to Axton five minutes ago."

"I don't care about Axton. I want to know why you're treating Valkerie Jansen like road kill."

"Oh. Um, right. Valkerie." Nate's face darkened. "She came late, and she's way behind the other ASCANs."

"And that's her fault?"

"Bob, there's a lot going on that you don't know—"

"Nate, I do know this. Valkerie is going to make a fabulous astronaut someday. She'll be a star on the Space Station. Or the Ares 14 mission, if there is one. But she's not going to make it if you keep pounding her into the dirt. Vomit Comet runs at 5:00 A.M., followed by two hours of PT. That's outrageous! And then you have the gall to schedule her for a Bruce protocol stress test. What kind of a sadist—"

"If she's not tough enough, it's better to find out early."

"Tough enough for what? Fifteen rounds with the Olympic heavyweight champion? *I'm* not tough enough for the kind of stuff you're dumping on her. Neither is Josh. Or Kennedy. I don't think even Lex could handle it. What gives you the right to—"

"Listen, Bob, if you knew what was coming down the pike, you'd thank me."

"What's that supposed to mean?"

Nate swiveled his chair and stared out the window.

Oh no, they really are thinking of replacing me. "No, don't tell me. I don't want to know. But you lighten up on Valkerie, okay? Does Perez know what kind of schedule you've got her on?"

"Perez went around me to bring her in. If he doesn't like her schedule, he can dump her on somebody else." Nate opened an aspirin bottle, shook two tablets into his hand, and washed them down with coffee. "Any other Excedrin questions?"

"Yeah. Want me to tell Perez you said that?"

"Go ahead, make my—"

"Mr. Harrington, am I late?" A woman's voice at the door.

Bob spun around. A middle-aged Asian woman stood framed in the doorway.

"Ah, Ms. Yamaguchi, come in, please." Nate turned to Bob. "Thanks for dropping by, Bob."

Bob stood up. *Now get lost.* "Nate, I want you to lighten up on Valkerie. I don't care what's coming down the pike, what you're doing to her is wrong." He stalked past the woman and out the door. Perez was going to hear about this.

Behind him, Carol called out, "Oh, Agent Yamaguchi? Your office called and left a message for you."

Bob's pulse picked up a notch. *Agent* Yamaguchi? As in FBI? Why were they bringing in the FBI? And what had Perez done to get Nate so riled? Nate was almost autonomous. Perez didn't carry much clout over him, except in building allocations and . . . personnel.

Personnel. Perez controlled astronaut assignments. And the only astronauts Nate had were on the Ares 10 prime and backup crews.

Kaggo, we have a problem.

Tuesday, August 28, 2012, 11:30 A.M.
VALKERIE

Valkerie leaned back in the flight chair and watched the universal docking port rotate on the monitor in front of her. She took a deep breath and let it out slowly, willing her sore muscles and aching neck to relax. "Come on. Just a little more . . ." She tapped the joystick a hair to the right, and the docking port stopped rotating. She brushed the thruster control, and the port began to grow larger. "Adjusting attitude. Once more, and . . . there!"

"Maneuver Successful"—the message flashed green on her computer screen. She looked around the dome. Good. Still alone.

Valkerie searched the menu for another maneuver to practice. So far it was working. Perez had her down for SES training all morning. Did he know how badly she needed it? She must have done horribly on the Bruce protocol test yesterday. The doctor didn't say anything, but her resting pulse and blood pressure had to be off the chart. And she reached exhaustion embarrassingly soon. She tried to explain her schedule to the doc, but he didn't seem to care. Apparently Harrington had already gotten to him. The race was fixed. Why even bother to run?

Valkerie chose another docking maneuver and scanned the instrument panels. Oh great. The space station was coming in way too fast. She fired the forward thrusters, but the ship didn't respond. What was going on? She pitched the ship around 180 degrees and fired the aft thrusters long and hard. Nothing.

Great. Must be a glitch in the program. Oh well, crash and burn time—unless . . . She pitched the ship another ninety degrees and rolled so that it was coming in broadside. Overriding the lockouts, she fired the RCS side thrusters simultaneously. The ship shimmied and started rotating, forcing her to switch from one set of side thrusters to the other and to keep a constant hand on the joystick to counter rotation. Good . . . she was slowing. One hundred meters, eighty, seventy. She fought to position the ship. Thirty meters. Just about there . . . She yawed the ship around in an ultraslow cartwheel to the docking port. "Attitude. Rotate, rotate . . . yes!"

The green "Maneuver Successful" message flashed once on the monitor and then the screen went blank. A message appeared one letter at a time on the monitor. "Beautiful work. Couldn't have done better myself."

Valkerie rotated in the flight seat and looked back through the dome window. Josh Bennett waved at her with a grin. He motioned down at her vid screen.

A message appeared. "Want to do another one?"

Valkerie turned around and shook her head. She had gotten lucky. The odds were one in a million that she could pull off a repeat performance.

Josh ducked away from the window and appeared at the simulator door. "That was terrific! They told me you weren't a pilot."

"I'm not, but Dr. Perez is letting me play on the equipment anyway. I think he knows how much I need a break."

"Well, I've been flying since I was thirteen, and it took me two tries to get the Wilcutt maneuver right. Most people don't even think of it. You're a natural."

Valkerie smiled. Josh's eyes sparkled with excitement. Most guys she knew would be threatened, but he seemed truly pleased—as if he had made an important new discovery.

"I guess I should tell you my secret. I thought the computer had glitched. I was just goofing off and happened to get lucky. Too bad the trainers weren't here to see it, huh?"

"Oh, they'll see it all right. Everything you do on this machine is recorded."

"Everything? But ..." Valkerie tried to remember—how much time had she spent playing around? "It's not fair. If I'd known I was being monitored, I'd have taken it more seriously."

"I'm sure you did fine."

"That's not the point! This place is—it's worse than Big Brother. Last night one of the security guards insisted on searching my pack before he would let me leave. Why do you put up with it?"

"I don't know why the security's so tight right now, but I'm sure there's a good reason for it. They're doing it for our protection. Everything. The tests, the training, the monitoring. If you were fifty million miles away from the nearest human being and you had to execute a perfect Wilcutt maneuver to save your life, would you be happy knowing that NASA had left that part of your training up to chance?"

"Yeah, right. Like I'll ever have a chance at a space flight."

"What makes you say that?"

"Nate Harrington. He's made it very clear he wants me out of the program."

"I wouldn't be so sure. The way they're pushing your training, I'd say they've got you slated for Ares 10 backup. For . . . Susan's position." Josh's face darkened and he looked down at Valkerie's console.

Valkerie waited for Josh to look up. "Who's Susan?"

"Susan Dillard. She was a friend of mine."

"Was?"

"We were out in the desert on my bike. I guess I was going too fast. I didn't see a section of barbed wire until it was too late."

"Did she. . . ?"

Josh shook his head. "Broken hip. Not bad. It'll heal in time, but she's out of the corps." Josh looked off into space. "And she blames me."

"I'm really sorry. Were you . . . dating?"

"No. We were just friends, but I . . ."

Valkerie watched the emotions racing across Josh's face. He was silent for a long time, but it was a comfortable silence. She felt at ease with him.

"I know that NASA has taken a lot of hits in the last ten years, but it's still a great organization. It's so important. So vital . . . I was an idiot. In one burst of blazing stupidity, I could have ruined the mission. I could have killed NASA."

"Don't you think you're being just a little overdramatic?"

Josh shook his head. "Some senators would like nothing better than to dismantle the entire space program. If a rocket doesn't carry a warhead, they don't want to have anything to do with it."

"That's what Bob said. He thinks Congress may cut NASA's budget again."

"They may have already done it. Senator Axton visited yesterday, and I've been getting weird vibes from Nate and Perez. Nate just set up a meeting with me at one. He sounded like a funeral director."

"But you're so close to launch. Surely they wouldn't cancel the mission now. The country would be furious."

"They might not cancel this one, but I'm worried about the big picture. Going to Mars once doesn't mean we'll get to go back. If the Ares 10 mission isn't a smashing success, if we don't bring back more than just a few dry, red-tinted moon rocks, then there won't be an Ares 14. NASA as we know it may cease to exist."

Tuesday, August 28, 2012, 1:30 P.M.
BOB

Bob walked into Building 1 and punched the elevator button. This had to be some kind of a record, going to see Nate twice in two days. After the run-in yesterday morning, Nate wasn't going to be thrilled to see him today. But the morons over at AresCorp had been giving him the runaround all day. The Inertial Measurement Unit was glitching on the test stand, and nobody wanted to take responsibility. AresCorp wasn't even admitting there was a problem. Time to bring in the sledge-hammer. Nate was good at dealing with contractors who tried to weasel out of their obligations.

Carol looked up when Bob came steaming in. "Dr. Kaganovski! Mr. Harrington's busy at the moment, but—"

"I'll wait." Bob sat down.

Carol leaned forward. "Did you see that FBI woman who came by yesterday morning? Wasn't she a *trip*? Don't tell anyone, but I think she and Mr. Harrington are an *item*. She comes to see him every *day*."

Bob stood up and began pacing.

"If you want, I can call you when Mr. Harrington is available."

"Who's talking to Nate?"

"*Officially*, nobody's in there."

Bob stopped. "What do you mean, nobody's in there?"

"That's what Mr. Harrington *said*. Officially, nobody's seeing him, and he's not here *either*."

"What's that supposed to mean?"

The door to Nate's office opened. Josh Bennett lurched out.

Bob straightened up. "Josh! You won't believe what AresCorp is trying to pull on us this time."

Josh nodded to him stiffly. "Later, okay?" He staggered out into the hallway.

Bob stared after him. "Josh. . . ?"

"Dr. Kaganovski? Mr. Harrington's free now, if you want to see him."

Bob reluctantly turned and went into Nate's office.

"Um . . . hello, Bob." Nate sat hunched over his desk, his chin cupped in both hands, elbows on his desk. He looked as deflated as one of those helium balloons, the day after the party.

Bob sat down. "Everything all right? I just saw Josh on the way out and—"

"You wanted to see me?"

Bob took ten minutes to explain the AresCorp problem. Nate listened but said little.

"I'm fed up with AresCorp," Bob finished. "They need to get their act together now, or this flight is not going to happen."

Nate nodded vacantly. "I'll take care of it."

Bob felt his jaw drop. *That was it?* Just one little monotone sentence? No flying tirade, no blazing bazookas, no thunder and lightning?

Nate flipped open his PDA and checked something. He swore. "Lex is in California again."

Bob shrugged. "She's been doing a lot of proficiency training lately." Pilots never thought they had enough training.

"She won't be back till tonight." Nate turned to his computer and banged away at the keyboard for thirty seconds. "I'm sending out an e-mail now to notify you and the rest of the crew that we'll have an All-Hands Meeting tomorrow at 9:00 A.M."

An All-Hands Meeting? That usually meant something major. Bob shifted in his chair. "Um . . . what's on the agenda?"

Nate stood up. "You'll find out at the meeting. See you then."

Bob stood too. A queasy feeling shimmied inside his gut. Something was wrong in NASAville. Really, really, really wrong. So wrong, it made the problems with AresCorp look like kitty litter.

And it didn't look like something a flight engineer could fix.

CHAPTER 7

Valkerie took two more steps and leaned on her arm pole to rest. The EVA suit weighed a ton. She scanned the boulder-strewn horizon. The gold-coated visor of her helmet painted the rocky landscape with an amber tint, giving it an artificial feel. Still, it was good to be outside and away from her phone. She was sick to death of Harrington calling her with a new schedule.

He seemed to be getting better, though—ever since the Bruce protocol test. Valkerie had been able to spend the whole morning on the sims at SES. This afternoon, she was getting to help test the new EVA suits— with three of the current ASCANs. Maybe he was going to relent and let her join the class after all. Maybe she'd done better on the endurance test than she thought.

Well, might as well bang on some more rocks. Valkerie collapsed onto her knees, and swung the small pick at a stony outcropping. The handle turned clumsily in her hand. So much for NASA's new and improved gloves. It was an effort to close her hands against the air pressure that filled them. Her fingers were already sore. She tried to imagine Bob and Josh working on Mars in these suits for one and a half years. They were crazy.

Valkerie tried to stand up, but the PLSS pack on her back threw her off balance. She fell forward onto her hands and knees, then collapsed with a grunt. Might as well rest for a minute. That was an important activity too. Even with one-third the gravity of Earth, Bob would have to rest on Mars. Probably a lot more than he'd use a pickax.

Something tapped on her shoulder. Valkerie fought her way up to her knees. Cowboy boots, blue jeans, a white shirt. Josh Bennett knelt next to her. His eyes squinted against the afternoon sun, giving him a wild, desperate appearance.

He reached out and flipped the clasps that secured her helmet. The helmet lifted off with a swoosh. The coastal humidity crashed in on her face and filled her lungs.

"What are you doing out here?" Valkerie asked.

"I heard you were on the suit test, so I came out looking for you." Josh seemed agitated. Nervous.

"For me? Why? Is something wrong?"

"No. Everything's fine. I just . . ." Josh's eyes swept the desert terrain. "The other ASCANs are already done. Could I, uh, give you a ride home?"

"Sure, I guess." Valkerie answered tentatively. She didn't know Josh that well, but she could see that something was bothering him.

He helped Valkerie to her feet, and the two of them walked slowly back to the truck. Josh seemed preoccupied. He had said "other ASCANs." Did he know something she didn't?

The suit technicians helped her out of her suit, and she ducked into the trailer to change out of her Liquid-Cooled Garment. When she stepped back into the sunlight, Josh was kicking impatiently at a pile of rocks and sand. The three ASCANs were already in the van.

Josh directed Valkerie to a silver pickup truck. "I already talked to the trainers. They said it's fine for me to take you home."

Valkerie climbed into the truck. "Is everything okay?"

"Sure." Josh started the engine and sped across the gravelly desert road. He started to speak three times, but each time he shook his head and lapsed back into uneasy silence.

"I don't envy you having to spend so much time in those suits. They're incredibly heavy."

"They'll feel a lot lighter on Mars. They . . ."

Valkerie waited.

"You're a biochemist. Do you think we'll find life on Mars?" Josh stared across the seat, his eyes intense.

"I doubt it. If there's liquid water on Mars, it's got to be deep underground."

"But what about ALH-84001? Have you read much about that—the

Mars meteorite they found in Antarctica? The one with the micro-fossils?"

"A little. The PAHs, carbonate globules, and magnetite crystals are intriguing, but I'm a bit skeptical about the so-called microfossils. Twenty nanometers is just too narrow. They couldn't possibly have been living cells."

Josh nodded thoughtfully. "But what do you *hope* is true? Do you hope we find evidence of life on Mars?"

"Hope? Well, it would be exciting to be sure, but I'm a scientist. I try really hard to be objective. I hope you guys find the truth—whatever it turns out to be."

Josh drove in heavy silence. Valkerie watched him from across the seat. Conflicting emotions rippled across his face. She could see a question forming but had no idea what it could be. After what seemed forever, they pulled into the NASA entrance. He pulled the truck to a stop in the parking lot and jogged around to open her door.

Valkerie waited uneasily. "Thanks for the ride. It was really nice of you to pick me up."

Josh shrugged. "I uh . . . I was wondering. Would you like to go out to dinner with me—tonight?"

Valkerie almost fell over. *This was the big question?* "Sure, that would be great." She couldn't believe it. Josh didn't seem the type to agonize over a date. He was so . . .

Josh flashed her a big smile and walked around the car to the driver's door. "Is seven okay?"

"Seven is . . . oh no! I forgot. I'm doing three hours of observation at Mission Control tonight. Can we make it tomorrow?"

"Tomorrow night? Um, sure. How about seven-thirty?"

"Seven-thirty sounds fine." Valkerie paused. Bob Kaganovski was walking toward the parking lot. His face wore a terrible scowl.

"Okay, see you at seven-thirty." Josh climbed into the truck and raced off.

Valkerie stood fidgeting in the parking lot, waiting for Bob. A guilty pang stabbed through her conscience. "Hi, Bob."

Bob didn't even look at her. "He's dating someone, you know."

"What?" Valkerie stepped backward.

"Just thought you might like to know." Bob kept walking. "She's a bacteriologist too—on a research trip in Antarctica. They've been going together for over a year."

Wednesday, August 29, 2012, 7:00 A.M.

BOB

"Morning, Shane." Bob tossed his briefcase onto the X-ray scanner belt and walked through the metal detector. A young blond woman rifled through his briefcase. "Dr. Kaganovski, please look into this eyepiece with your right eye." She pointed to a device on the table.

Bob peered in. "I don't see anything."

She keyed in something on a computer. "Okay, you're in the system now."

"They've finally decided I really work here?"

"It's a new biometrics security system, sir. You'll find a retinal scanner like this one at all entry points."

Great. A new way to prevent actual work from getting done. Bob headed for the Hab bay. He peered into the new retinal scanner at the door. The lock clicked. He pushed open the door.

Now what?

A dozen security dweebs holding clipboards milled around the Hab. None of them were smiling. Bob strode up to the group. "What's going on?"

One of them turned around. Daniel Collins. Head of Security at JSC. "Mornin', Dr. Kaganovski. We're just adding a few extra security cameras. Nothing special."

Nothing special? Bob counted five new videocams ringing the exterior of the Hab. A workman walked in through the open airlock with another. Lex came out, looking a little dazed. What was she doing in at work at 7:00 A.M.? Normally, it took two miracles and an earthquake to get her in before ten.

She caught his eye. "Hey, Kaggo, what's going on here? I'm gone for two days and the KGB takes over. And what are you doing in so early?"

"Hate to break it to you, Miss Night Owl, but this is when I always get in."

"They've got ten cameras in the interior," Lex said. "There's even one in the head. Can you believe that?"

"When the paranoids take over, they don't mess around," Bob said. "So what brings you in so early? This is 5:00 A.M., California time."

"Just felt like it." Lex scratched her nose.

Since when did Lex just *feel* like getting up early? Something strange was going on. "Where's Josh?"

"How should I know?" Hostility slashed across Lex's face.

Bob didn't know what he'd said wrong, but it wasn't worth pursuing. He might as well try to get some work done before the All-Hands Meeting. He had a six-point universal docking port prototype on the test stand, and it was fritzing again. He'd pretty much decided yesterday that the cables were shot.

He went out of the lab and down the hall to the supply room. A couple of workmen were installing something when he arrived. Bob spotted the supply room manager. "Morning, Hank. I need about six feet of coaxial cable."

"I'll get it." Hank disappeared into the guts of the room.

Bob turned to watch the workmen. Whoa! They were installing a retinal scanner here too.

Hank returned with the cable. Bob filled out a standard requisition form and signed it. "So what's with all the eyeball scanners? This is really going to mess up JSC."

Hank shrugged. "As far as I know, it's only our building."

One of the workmen looked up. "Nope. ESTL too."

Bob raised his eyebrows. Energy Systems Test Lab? It made sense to tighten security over there, with all the explosives. But why the Ares program?

Two hours later, he had the docking port put back together with a fresh set of cables. Good. Now he could play some. He heard a step behind him. Smelled a woman's perfume. Bob reached for his wrench. "Yeah, Lex?"

"Come on, Kaggo, we've got that All-Hands Meeting over in Building 4."

Bob straightened his back. "Any idea what's going to hit the fan this time?"

"I'm guessing Senator Axton is trying to cut the Ares project off at the knees." Lex sounded worried.

Bob followed her. "Congress can't do that. We've already bought the hardware. Quitting now would throw all that away—for nothing. It's crazy."

"Politics isn't about logic."

Bob felt his heart shudder. *Great. Just great.* He'd been doing eighty-hour weeks for six years now—for what? So some lame-brained politico could blow it all sky-high? He trudged beside Lex, wondering how things could get any worse.

Five minutes later, they walked into a small room. Josh sat at the head of the table. Kennedy sat beside him, looking glum. And Nate . . .

Wait a second, where's Nate?

Nate was the Mission Director. If there was bad news, he ought to be here to deliver it himself. Unless . . .

Bob sagged into a chair. A scene from the movie *Apollo 13* flashed into his mind. Three astronauts, sitting together in a room. *Just the crew.* Ken Mattingly was getting axed from the flight. And Commander Jim Lovell had that sick look on his face that Josh wore right now.

Lex shut the door and dropped into the fourth chair.

A pregnant pause followed.

Josh cleared his throat. "Bad news, people. There's going to be a small change in personnel for Ares—"

"They can't do this, Josh!" Kennedy slammed his fist on the table and shot a look of sympathy down toward Bob. "We're a team. We're going to stand together and tell them all to jump off a—"

"That's right!" Lex jumped out of her chair and began pacing. "Suck it up, Josh! Go in there and tell them we're not going to fly without our crew. Our whole crew."

Bob leaned back in his chair and shut his eyes. He'd seen it coming, and still it hit him like a cannonball in the gut. Six years of training, down the tubes. Just like that. *Wham, bam, sorry, Sam, you're out of the plan.*

"Listen up, people," Josh said in his Air Force voice, the one he used when Congress-critters and NASA mucky-mucks came around. "The decision is made, and it's my decision. It's final."

Bob tasted bile in the back of his throat.

"You don't have the right!" Lex jabbed her finger at Josh. "In seventeen months, we're taking a three-hundred-million-mile cruise, and we want the best on our team. And we *are* the best. Hampster's the best pilot in the navy. I'm the best geoscientist on the planet. And Kaggo's the best mechanic in the known universe. It's our lives on the line. Don't give us that rot about you-have-the-right-to-decide."

Bob massaged his aching temples. *Denial.* Wasn't that the first stage of grief? They could scream all they wanted. They'd get through that pretty soon. Then they'd start bargaining. Then they'd . . . whatever the other stages were. Finally, acceptance. *Face it, pals. You're going to Mars without me. Deal with it. Josh already has. No wonder he looked so sick yesterday afternoon in Nate's office.*

"People, you can make this easy, or you can make it hard, but—"

"No buts!" Lex walked around behind Bob and put her hands on his shoulders. "You bump one of us, and we all drop! Have you got that?"

"That's right," Kennedy said, but his heart didn't sound in it. "Right, Bob?"

"Um, you guys . . ." Bob shook his head. "I appreciate the gesture, but the mission is more important than any one of us." He opened his eyes and stood up. "Josh, if it's better for the mission that I not go, then I'll step down. Just say the word."

Josh's eyes widened in surprise. "Kaggo, have a seat. Lex. Hampster." Josh leaned forward, squared his shoulders, and looked them each in the eye. "It is my duty to inform you that I am resigning as Mission Commander of the Ares 10. I'll be working this mission as prime Capcom here on the ground."

Lex slumped forward onto the table.

Kennedy's shoulders sagged.

Bob felt his whole universe lurch, sway, and break free from its foundations. Josh? Off the mission? Absurd! He was the glue that held this team together.

Without Josh Bennett, how on earth was this mission going to fly?

CHAPTER 8

Wednesday, August 29, 2012, 3:00 P.M.
NATE

Nate crushed a sheet of paper into a ball and threw it in the waste-basket. He'd lost. Perez had won. Time to try to salvage this mission.

A soft knock at the door interrupted. "Come on in!" Nate shouted.

The door opened and Steven Perez walked in. Valkerie Jansen followed him. Perez looked neither triumphant nor apologetic. Exhaustion lay like a mask over Valkerie's face. Both sat down.

Perez cleared his throat. "Valkerie, we have some good news for you. We've decided to invite you to join our current class of astronaut candidates. Congratulations. You blew our ASCAN tests into orbit."

She didn't show much emotion. "That's . . . great. Sorry if I don't jump up and down, but I'm a little tired right now."

Perez raised an eyebrow toward Nate. *Your turn.*

Nate fidgeted in his chair. "There's been a reason for all this, Dr. Jansen." *Actually, a lot of reasons, but you don't need to know all of them.* "We're also going to offer you an unusual opportunity, and we needed to make sure you were up to the challenge."

Valkerie sat up straighter. "Opportunity?"

Nate handed her an official letter, signed by himself and Perez. "In January of 2014, the Ares 10 will be lifting off for Mars. We'd like you aboard as Mission Specialist."

Valkerie dropped the letter and gaped at Nate.

Perez rescued the letter and handed it back to her. "Valkerie, it's only fair to tell you that a mission to Mars will be somewhat risky—on a par with the Apollo missions, or possibly even more dangerous. The crew will be on its own for two and a half years, with no outside help available in an emergency. Your personality traits are exceptional for dealing with what we call five-sigma days."

Nate felt his jaw tightening. The odds of a five-sigma day were one in three million. He and Perez had gone round and round on this thing and—

"But I don't get it," Valkerie said. "A fifth crew member—plus food, oxygen, water, and all that—adds a lot of weight, doesn't it? You can't redesign a mission this late in the game."

Nate drummed his fingers on the desk. "We've made a slight reconfiguration in the crew." *Right. We threw the best man off the team. We are such geniuses.*

"Reconfiguration?"

"Let me explain," Perez said. "A team is more than the sum of its parts. Before I joined NASA, I did a lot of work in human factors studies for the Navy. Submarines, in particular. What we've found in restricted environments is that the ability of a crew to deal with a crisis depends on the particular personality mix of crew and commander."

Nate gritted his teeth while Perez went on and on about his psychometric analyses, his crisis-adaptability predictors, his psycho-whatsamahoodle teamwork index. You handed out the tests, took the numbers, crunched them through your computer, and out came the index of the team. The computer didn't care how good each crew member was individually. It wanted to know how good the *team* was—as a team. The computer gave the current team an index of 3.2 out of a possible 4.0. Good, but not outstanding. *Unless the whole thing is a crock.*

Then Perez's computer had run the same predictor with every possible combination of pilot, mission specialist, ASCAN, and starry-eyed nutcake who'd ever applied to NASA.

"And with you on the team, Valkerie, we came up with an index of 3.98," Perez said. "That's the best we've seen by a very significant margin. The team will be about seven standard deviations above the mean."

"But . . . if I join, who's *not* going to be on the team?" Valkerie asked.

Nate picked up a ball-point pen and began clicking it. In and out. In and out. "We showed the data to Josh Bennett, along with the transcripts of some interviews by our psychologists. In the end, we let Josh make the decision. We feel it was the right one."

Valkerie sat forward on her chair. "So . . . who's not going? Bob? Did you kick Bob off the team? I don't think I could accept that. He's not the easiest person to get along with, but he's vital to the success of—"

"Kaggo's in," Nate said. "He's the most important man on the team. If anything breaks on the Starship Enterprise, Scotty has to fix it. Kaggo is our Scotty. That, in fact, was critical to our thinking." *Our shrinks' thinking, anyway.* "We found that one team member dramatically reduced Kaggo's critical thinking skills."

"Alexis Ohta?" Valkerie said. "She doesn't get along with Bob?"

"Lex is in." Nate put the pen back on the desk. "She's an expert geophysicist and an ace pilot. She's a little aloof and was the least affected by any of the others from a personality perspective." *Wonderful. I'm starting to sound like Perez.*

Valkerie leaned back in her chair. "Kennedy Hampton?"

Nate scratched his neck. *I wish.* Of the four, the shrinks liked the Hampster most. Which was probably why Nate liked him least. He was too much the rich frat boy who had everything handed to him on a silver starship. Perfectly balanced? Nobody was perfectly balanced. It wasn't normal. "Kennedy's the best seat-of-the pants pilot we've got, and a pretty good mechanic," Nate said. *I hate to admit it, but he is.* "Kennedy will be the new commander."

"You mean. . . ?" Valkerie's eyes filled with horror.

Nate looked at his watch. "As of this morning, Josh Bennett has resigned as Mission Commander of the Ares 10." *Josh Bennett—the best astronaut, leader, and all-around good guy you ever met—that Josh Bennett is off the team. Because of a teamwork index in a lame-brained computer program.*

Perez sighed. "Josh is a terrific individual, but we found that his strong leadership personality tended to subsume the critical thinking skills of the rest of the crew. They'd follow him into a fire-ant-infested black hole if he led them. That's not what you want your crew doing in blind faith. I'm sorry, but we had to take Captain Kirk off the team. Josh made this decision himself."

"Congratulations, Valkerie." Nate stood and extended his hand. "We were looking for someone who could think outside the box, but we also needed someone who was physically and mentally tough. You've proven yourself on all counts. Welcome to the Ares 10 team."

Valkerie shook her head. "I'm sorry to disappoint you, but I'm not at all sure I can accept."

Nate felt a shot of liquid oxygen shiver through his veins. She had to join the team.

"Not sure you can. . . ?" Perez looked as if he were about to have an aneurysm.

"I don't want to be the reason Josh gets bumped off the team."

"Josh's resignation doesn't have anything to do with you." Perez pulled his chair closer to Valkerie. "Josh is off the team no matter what you decide."

"Uh huh . . ." Valkerie nodded somberly.

"We very much want you on the team," Perez said. "We believe you'll be critical to its success."

She fidgeted in her seat. "When do I need to let you know my decision?"

Nate leaned forward. "As soon as possible, of course. We'd like to schedule a press conference for tomorrow to announce your acceptance. Or Friday at the latest."

"And you're just assuming I'll accept it?" She looked incredulous. "After the way you've treated me these past two weeks?"

Perez stood and put a hand on Valkerie's shoulder. "Let me point out one thing that might sway you, Valkerie."

She folded her arms across her chest. "I'm listening."

"We don't have any other candidates we consider suitable," Perez said. "And without Susan Dillard the Ares 10 backup team can't even be considered. If you don't join the team, we're going to miss this launch opportunity."

Valkerie's face stiffened. "But you could . . . try again in two years. Couldn't you?"

Perez shook his head. "We talked to Senator Axton on Monday. If we don't make it to Mars on this launch opportunity, we won't get a second chance. He's got the votes to shut us down."

Nate turned to look out the window. *And if we get shut down now, we're never going to Mars. Not in my lifetime. Maybe not in yours either, Cupcake.*

Wednesday, August 29, 2012, 3:30 P.M.

VALKERIE

Valkerie wandered out of Harrington's office in a daze. Mars! What could she say to them? Of course she couldn't go. It was too sudden.

Too cruel. She couldn't take Josh's place. The press would eat her alive. Josh would hate her.

His mood yesterday suddenly made sense. He already knew. That's why he was acting so strange. And all that time she thought he was agonizing over asking her out. He must have been dying inside. But why ask her out? Was he really interested in her? Or was he hoping to talk her into stepping down?

Valkerie hurried out of the elevator and past the security guard to the glass sliding doors. Her leather flats clacked across the old brick floors, echoing sharply off the marble walls. She ran across the mall toward Building 29. Maybe she could catch Josh before he went home. She couldn't make any decisions without talking to him first.

Valkerie waited impatiently at the security check and hurried down the hall to Josh's lab. She was probably the last person on earth that he'd want to see, but he *had* asked her out. At least she could try to explain. It wasn't her fault.

Valkerie listened at his door. Nothing. Maybe he had left the Center. Who would blame him if he left and never came back?

She fidgeted in her pack for her keys. Maybe she should call it a day. The last thing Josh needed was—

The door opened and Josh appeared, leaning against the doorjamb. "Hi, Valkerie."

"Um, I could come back if this is a bad time. . . ."

"No. Please . . . come in." Josh's arms hung heavily at his sides, but his eyes were soft . . . almost inviting.

"Really, I know this is a bad time. I'm sure I'm the last person you want to see right now. I can come back later."

"No! I mean, you're not . . . the last person I wanted to see." Josh stood back and motioned her inside.

Valkerie followed him into the tiny lab. Amazing. The room was chock full of equipment. All the latest. Some of it still in the packaging. "Wow. This is all yours? How many research assistants do you have?"

Josh shook his head. "Just a dishwasher."

Valkerie circled the room. "Quite a setup. I don't even know what some of this stuff is."

"That makes two of us." A smile lit his face. "Nate thought all he had to do was throw equipment at me and I'd magically become a research scientist."

"That's an engineer for you."

Josh laughed. "It's the NASA way—at least it was until Perez got here."

Valkerie turned to search his face. He didn't seem bitter—he was even smiling.

"Josh, I came here to tell you ... I didn't know anything about—what happened today. If I'd known, I'd..." Valkerie set her purse on the bench and slid onto one of the lab stools. "Look, I'm not going to accept the position. I think what they've done to you is wrong. It's not fair and I'm—"

"Steven Perez is right, you know." Josh's voice was surprisingly soft.

Valkerie studied his expression. He looked light-years away.

"You are a much better fit for this mission than I am."

"But I don't know the first thing about flying—"

"This mission doesn't need another pilot. The ship's got four redundant flight computers that can each steer the ship better than the best flyboy ever born. What the mission needs is someone who can find something spectacular out there. Something worth going back for."

"But what if I can't find anything? What if there's nothing to find?"

"You've found life before—in some pretty harsh environments. *Thermospira aquaticus, Thermophilus sulfataria, Thermis rhodacans, Thermophilus edwardi...* If you can't find life on Mars, I doubt anybody else could find it either."

Valkerie slid off the stool and moved toward a bench at the far end of the room. "You've read my papers?"

"I've read your test results too. Psych, med, flight, stress, training. Very impressive."

Valkerie could feel the heat creeping into her face. She turned away from Josh and started flipping some of the parafilmed Petri dishes that littered a bench.

Footsteps tapped behind her. She caught her breath.

"Steven told me about your adventure in Alaska. Did you really breathe the air in your jeep tires?" Josh's voice was low. She could almost feel his breath on her neck.

Valkerie's heart pounded at her throat. What was wrong with her? What was she thinking? She flipped over a Petri dish and started counting the plaques. Sixteen colonies of bacteria, dark against the amber medium. "The volcano erupted a cloud of SO_2 gas. I couldn't breathe."

"We're lucky you made it out alive."

We? Valkerie reached for a freshly tooled stainless steel cylinder. She could feel her pulse throb against its comforting weight as she hefted it in her hand.

"You're an amazing woman." Josh reached around her and gently took the cylinder from her hand, letting his fingers linger several seconds around hers. "You'll make an amazing astronaut."

Valkerie turned slowly, backing away from his penetrating gaze. He reached a hand around her shoulder and walked her away from the bench.

"So are you ready to go out? We could break early today. There's something I want to show you. It will take a little while to get there, but I think you'll find it worth the trip."

Valkerie looked into his eyes. The eyes of the man whose career she had just ruined. Seas of crystal blue. Not even a speck of reproach. She smiled and nodded her head ever so slightly as he guided her through the door.

Wednesday, August 29, 2012, 8:00 P.M.

BOB

Bob watched his computer monitor as the test of the Inertial Measurement Unit continued. The IMU combined gyro measurements and accelerometer data to estimate attitude and velocity. And it was glitching again.

He slammed his open palm on the table. That guy from AresCorp had lied to him. Either that, or he was grossly incompetent. Which was odd, because Lex said he was some kind of a hotshot engineer. She'd known the guy since grad school.

Bob checked his watch and decided to take a hike over to Josh's lab. Only 8:00 P.M. Maybe Josh would still be in there, playing with his chemistry set. Bob needed to vent a little. And Josh had an awful lot of explaining to do. This late at night, they could talk freely without worrying about the walls having ears.

It didn't make sense. Josh Bennett was Chuck Yeager, John Glenn, and Neil Armstrong. Nate and Perez were throwing that away? Why? Over some stupid teamwork index?

Buzz Aldrin missed being the first man to walk on the moon just because the door opened the wrong way. Jim Lovell missed out on the moon altogether because of one fried switch. Now Josh Bennett was going to lose Mars because of a teamwork index—a figment of some academic's imagination.

Who was going to replace Josh?

Nobody knew, but Bob's money was on Valkerie. She was perfect for the mission. A medical doctor. A Ph.D. biochemist. Cool under pressure. Fit. Intelligent. Attractive. She was so . . . perfect. Except for one thing.

Bias. What if she found life on Mars? Would she try to cover it up? Wasn't there a point where your philosophy was more important than your raw qualifications? Probably. But Perez would have caught it if she were that bad. More likely Bob had misjudged her. After all, he was basing his assumptions on only one data point. Maybe he should give her another chance.

When Bob got to Josh's lab, he found it locked. He pounded on the door. "Hey, Josh! Open up! I need to talk to you."

No answer. Maybe he had gone to the bathroom, or whatever. Bob punched in Josh's security password on the keypad and opened the door. "Josh!"

Still nothing. He left the door ajar and walked in farther, scanning for signs of intelligent life. There was plenty of the other kind, sitting in those Petri dishes.

A purse? On Josh's workbench?

Bob opened it up, found a wallet, and flicked it open. Valkerie's photo stared up at him. Unbelievable. She even looked good on her driver's license. Fresh. Clean. Talk about your girl next door.

Bob snapped it shut, reached for the purse and . . . it fell, spilling its contents all over the floor. Clumsy fool! He knelt down and began scooping stuff into it.

"And just what do you think you're doing in here?"

Bob dropped the purse and spun around. A night watchman shined a fat flashlight in his eyes. He wore a security badge, a gun, and a radio, and looked like the type who enjoyed pushing his authority around. Bob had never seen the guy before.

"I work here. I'm Bob Kaganovski, one of the astronauts."

"You're not Josh Bennett."

"True and tautological. If I'm Bob, I can't be Josh."

The guard didn't crack a smile. He whipped out a cell phone and punched in a number.

"Is there some problem?"

"Nobody belongs in here when Josh Bennett ain't here. That's my orders."

"Where is he, anyway? I came looking for him."

The guard pressed the phone to his ear and waited. Finally, he gave up and thumped in another number. Another long wait. "Yeah, hello, Mr. Harrington? This is Officer Sheldon on the night watch in Building 29. We got a situation here I thought you should know about. I'm in Mr. Bennett's lab, and my orders are that nobody is in here when he isn't, not even the janitor. He told me I should call him first, and you second, in case of any trouble. There's a guy in here, claims to be an astronaut. Bob Something."

"Kaganovski," Bob said.

"Yeah, Kanga-whatever-it-is. That's what he *says*, anyway." Another pause. "Yeah, he's got his picture ID, and it looks kinda like him." More waiting. "Okay, I'll do that."

The guard flipped his phone shut. "I'm supposed to verify your identity on one of those eyeball things, and then you have to call Harrington."

Bob walked out of the lab. The guard locked up behind him. Two minutes later, Bob had passed his retinal scan check. The guard left him with a warning.

Bob dialed Nate's cell number.

It rang once. "Harrington."

"Nate, this is Bob. Thanks for calling off the wolves."

"Bob, just exactly what were you doing in Josh's lab? It's almost eight-thirty."

"I was waiting for him. He's usually in at this hour, and I had a question. Thought he'd gone to the john or something, so I just went in."

"His door was *unlocked*?"

Bob hesitated. Thin ice here. "I know the combination." That was true, as far as it went. Except that Josh hadn't given Bob the combination. Bob had cracked it.

"I'll bring that up with Josh. It's against regulations. What did you want to talk to Josh about?"

"Oh, the usual. Sports. Women. And how funny it is that one day you can be going to Mars and the next you just up and resign for no good reason. Chitchat like that."

"Bob, you know there were some very good reasons."

"I haven't heard one yet."

A long silence. Nate sighed. "Maybe I shouldn't tell you this, but you're part of the reason."

"*I* am? Do I need a stronger deodorant?"

"You remember that interview you had with the shrinks a couple weeks ago?"

Bob scratched his head. "The one where I pretty much shot myself in the head? Yeah, I thought for sure they'd put me on the chopping block after that. They didn't like me."

"You're essential, Bob. Without you, we don't have a mission."

"I'm touched. What's this have to do with Josh?"

"You said you'd follow Josh's orders. No matter what, you'd obey."

So I fibbed. Josh told me to tell 'em what they wanted to hear. "And?"

"And they went nonlinear over that. Started quacking about loss of critical thinking due to overly strong leadership. Alpha-male psycho-babble."

Bob closed his eyes and leaned against the wall.

"Still there, Kaggo?"

"I'm here. Just thinking." *Like what an idiot I am.* Bob felt his heart racing. He'd messed up. Big time.

"Can you hold? I've got a call on another line." The line went dead, then immediately came alive again. "Hello, Crystal?"

"Sorry, my hormones must be acting up again. I'm still Bob."

"Oops, hold one minute." The line went dead again.

Bob waited. Who was Crystal? Not Nate's secretary, nor his ex-wife. Maybe a daughter? Or maybe . . . hmmm. This might be a good time to put two and two together and try to get seven. *What was that FBI woman's name?*

"Hey, Bob, I'm back."

"How's Ms. Yamaguchi doing this evening?"

"She's . . . fine." Nate sounded nervous. "How'd you know that was her?"

You just told me. "I have ways of finding things out." Bob decided to take another flier while he was hot. Yamaguchi was Japanese, wasn't she? And FBI. And there had to be some reason for the sudden ramp in security. "So what's the deal on those Japanese terrorists?"

Shocked silence. "Kaggo, have you been bugging my office?"

"No, I'm psychic. All physicists are. We're in league with Satan."

"You're getting weird, Kaggo."

"That often happens when I lose a mission commander for no reason."

"It wasn't my idea." Nate coughed. "Blame Perez if you have to."

Keep rolling. "When are they going to announce Valkerie's joining the mission?"

"When she accepts the offer. If she accepts it."

If? Bob blinked. Was there a human being on the planet who would think twice about going to Mars?

"Hello?" Nate said. "Are you there?"

"Yeah, I'm here. One more question. What was stolen from Energy Systems?"

"What are you talking about?"

Bob tried to sound surprised. "Oh! So you're not in the loop on that one?"

"I'm in the loop, but you're not supposed—"

"I'm psychic, remember? Now, if you'll excuse me, I need to go perform some unspeakably evil rituals with the head of a goat." Bob hung up and wiped the sweat from his forehead.

He'd caught Nate off-balance and guessed well. Now he had to figure out what it meant. Bad things were happening. Security didn't have a handle on it. And Valkerie was going to be on the mission.

If she said yes. But who, in their right mind, would turn down Mars?

On the other hand, with all the security lapses, safety issues, and political machinations, who in their right mind would want to go?

Bob shook his head, wondering what was wrong with him. Maybe he was crazy, but he still wanted to go. He still wanted Mars. Wanted it bad.

Valkerie could have Venus.

CHAPTER 9

OXYGEN

Wednesday, August 29, 2012, 9:00 P.M.
VALKERIE

Valkerie walked with Josh down a dark corridor. Her body still tingled from their flight. A T-38 Supersonic Trainer. It was amazing. She'd never dreamed anything could move so fast. It was like being shot out of a gun—a gun with a barrel that twisted and turned like a roller coaster. Josh was right. The baby could really "yank and bank."

Valkerie walked in silence, listening to the echo of their footsteps against the concrete walls. The Vehicle Assembly Building. She still couldn't believe they were in Florida. They'd made the trip in less than 100 minutes. And Josh said he could check out a T-38 anytime he wanted. He could fly anywhere in the country with about as much effort as most people exerted driving across Houston.

"And you really think Lex has a boyfriend in California?"

"Why else would she log five trips to Moffett Field in one month?"

"Maybe she likes the weather."

Josh snorted. "What? Better than Houston? What could be better than heat and humidity?"

Valkerie giggled and leaned closer into Josh. She felt happy. Alive—almost light-headed. If it was endorphins from flying, then she had to fly more often.

"Okay, shut your eyes." Josh stepped up to a steel door and peered into a retinal scanner. Valkerie stopped and shut her eyes. She heard a faint ping and the hum of a powerful motor. Josh put his hands reassuringly on her shoulders and started to guide her forward. She suppressed the urge to feel her way with her hands. Josh wouldn't do anything to hurt her.

"Just a second. Don't peek." Josh's hands slipped off her shoulders and she heard a click followed by a distant buzzing sound. His hands were back in an instant, and he guided her forward again. The sound of their footsteps was swallowed up in a great void. Like the cavern in Mammoth Cave—her last vacation with both of her parents. She squeezed her eyes shut to keep from peeking.

"Just a little bit more. We're almost there." Josh guided her to the right and then pulled her a few steps back. His hands closed gently around her head, stroking her hair back from her eyes. He tilted her head back. "Okay," he breathed. "Open your eyes."

An outline slowly took shape before her, drawing her eyes upward. Higher and higher still, it towered above her, crushing her with its immensity. She felt light-headed, dizzy, as if she were standing at the brink of a great chasm. A cavernous chamber stretched out above her like the night sky. And filling the cavern, a colossal pillar to hold up the heavens, stood an enormous rocket.

"It's huge." Valkerie whispered. "Huge." Nothing else could be said. Words weren't adequate.

Josh leaned into her. "Makes you feel insignificant, doesn't it?" His voice was hushed. Almost reverent. "And this is only a tiny fraction of the effort we're expending to send our crew to Mars."

Valkerie nodded slowly, still awed by the spectacle that towered above her. "Is this the Ares 10?"

Josh shook his head. "Ares 9. It's the launch vehicle for the ERV—Earth Return Vehicle. They'll launch it a month before the Ares 10. It will take the slow, fuel-efficient trajectory to Mars and orbit there for four years, waiting to take the crew of Ares 14 back to Earth. There's another one just like it already waiting for you at Mars."

"It's . . . it's mind-boggling."

"That's not all. There's already a base camp on the surface of Mars. It's manufacturing fuel and oxygen to use on the return trip. It was launched on yet another ship just like this."

"All that for four people."

"Valkerie, this is so much bigger than any four men or women. Our hopes, dreams, comforts, fears—they're all irrelevant. This is the hope of all mankind. The sum of all our dreams. Our future. This determines whether we as a race will stagnate and die or rise up to face the challenge of our potential. To be born anew as a civilization. You and I stand at the crux of all history. The critical pivot point. The future of mankind is ours to decide."

Valkerie stared up at the rocket. All this—for four tiny people. And they wanted her to be one of them. Even Josh wanted her to go. It was staggering.

"Valkerie, you have the chance to change the course of civilization. As much as I'd like to go, I can't. But you *can*. You can make the mission work. You can find a reason for us to keep going back. Please tell me you'll go. Tell me that this—all we've worked on for so long—isn't going to be for nothing."

"Okay." Valkerie's whisper sounded small and weak in the dwarfing chamber.

Josh spun her around and held her in front of him, staring at her with penetrating eyes. "I'll help you, I promise. I'll train you myself. I'll be with you every step of the way. Promise me you'll tell them tomorrow. Promise me."

Valkerie nodded, taken aback by his intensity. "I'll tell Mr. Harrington first thing in the morning. I promise."

Wednesday, August 29, 2012, midnight
BOB

Bob shut the door of his office and locked it. Time to play Sherlock, and he didn't want anyone thinking he was Professor Moriarty. Technically, this would be illegal. Technically.

Nate had let the cat out of the bag. Somebody had raided the cookie jar last night. For what? And how'd they get past security? An inside job? Bob shivered. The best security in the world failed when you had insiders.

He checked his watch. Midnight, Houston time. He needed a drone account someplace where the sun was shining. Maybe Japan?

He pulled out his PDA, punched in his password, and went to his little black book.

Very good. His password cracker digital agent had seven different accounts on university computers in Japan. The University of Tokyo would do nicely.

Bob logged in to the machine in Tokyo. It belonged to somebody he didn't know, a female art student. Tomorrow, she'd lose her account and get grilled by the authorities. They'd quickly discover she had no clue about a hacker break-in at the Johnson Space Center in the United States, and she'd be off the hook.

Meanwhile, Bob would have the information he needed. Untraceably. It was a shame he had to work this way—especially when the computer he was breaking into couldn't be more than a few hundred yards away.

From the Tokyo machine, he telneted into the JSC through a hole in the firewall. Not the official one, but another one Bob had created that nobody knew existed. From here on, everything would be illegal. He sighed. Life wasn't always simple, even when it was easy.

In a few seconds, he had linked in to the supply-room database of the Johnson Space Center. He had a theory. If there had been a break-in, Security would have run an audit to figure out what was missing. What had they learned in that audit?

When he brought up the database, he held his breath and tried the Administrator functions. He had the password, but there might be a digital tripwire, or a keystroke metric. If so, he was playing with fire. He punched in the password slowly with one knuckle to disguise his characteristic typing pattern.

The Administrator screen came up. He scanned the available functions. Add Users. Delete Users. Change Passwords. Audit Inventory.

Yes! That one. Bob typed in the Audit command, brought up another screen, and studied it. First do a quick date check and . . .

And the last audit for the ESTL supply room was this morning—the same morning the retinal scanners were added to all the doors. Just as he'd expected.

Somebody named P.T. Henderson had signed off on the audit.

Bob typed in the command to show discrepancies and sort the results by date. Obviously, whatever was missing would be at the top of the list. He drummed his fingers on the table while he waited for the results to display. He was walking in a minefield. For all he knew, somebody could be watching activity in the Administrator account right now. They could be running a traceback to Tokyo. And from there, Houston was just one link. Maybe he should have used a second cutout account. Too late for that now.

The search results began filling up the display window. Bob scrolled down the list, looking for discrepancies. He scanned all the way down. As he approached the bottom, his gut tightened. What was he looking for, anyway? Fishing expeditions could go on forever. Meanwhile, the sharks could be closing in on him.

Nothing interesting.

Bob ran a search to see what other activity P.T. Henderson had logged. Strange. There were only three entries. Had he fouled up? No, the search date went all the way back to 1973. Whoever Henderson was, he had made only three transactions. All today.

The last record was the audit. Bob checked the first and second records.

Very early this morning, P.T. Henderson had checked out a couple of NASA Standard Initiators. NSIs for short. Two hours later, he checked them back in again. Minutes later, Henderson had signed off on the audit.

Quarks and bosons! NSIs were space-rated explosives. You could use them in a vacuum, underwater, anywhere. With those, a battery, and a Radio Shack timer, you had a bomb.

Bob shut down the telnet session, logged off the Tokyo machine, and scrubbed the password entry from his PDA. No fingerprints.

Who was this Henderson guy, anyway?

Bob turned to his computer and pulled up the personnel list for the entire Johnson Space Center. He found several Hendersons. None of them had the initials P.T.

Bob leaned back in his chair and shut his eyes. This couldn't happen. A nonperson named P.T. Henderson had faked a check-out entry to cover the theft, then restored the missing NSIs, run an audit, and found nothing amiss. A cover-up? Why? Why not raise a fuss and alert the site that there'd been a theft? Notify the press. . . .

Right. The one thing NASA didn't need right now was bad press. Let there be a hint of this in the press, and poof! People like Senator Axton would be baying for an investigation. Not to get the facts. Axton didn't give a rip about facts. He'd be looking for an excuse to shut down NASA. Or at least the Ares program.

To prevent that, this person Henderson was violating regulations. Bob had no choice but to blow the whistle.

Except for one thing. He didn't have any evidence. None that he could have obtained legally, anyway. He had no way to blow the whistle. It would blow up in his face.

Catch–22, Kaggo. You're hanged if you do. Hanged if you don't. Have a nice day.

Thursday, August 30, 2012, 10:00 A.M.
VALKERIE

"Valkerie Jansen?" Harrington's secretary looked up from her monitor. "Mr. Harrington got called away. He should be right back. Would you like to wait for him in his office?"

"Oh, um . . . sure." Valkerie stepped into Nate's office. Both visitor chairs were six inches deep in papers. Valkerie perched on the arm of the chair closest to the door and glanced nervously about the room. What was she going to tell Harrington? She shouldn't have promised Josh. And she should have asked for more time. They couldn't possibly expect an answer so soon.

Valkerie stood up and walked across the office to look at the mission photos that lined the wall. It would have been so much easier if her father had said no, but he was surprisingly supportive on the phone— once he was able to say something besides "I can't believe it." He'd said he was proud of her, but how proud would he be if she quit halfway though the training? How proud would he be if the media found out about her freshman year? Life was so unfair. . . .

"Valkerie?"

Valkerie spun around. A tall man in a gray suit stood framed in the door. "Bob? Oh, my goodness. I almost didn't recognize you."

"Yeah, I've been meaning to get a haircut for a long time."

"And that suit. You look fan—um, nice."

Bob grinned and stepped uneasily into the office.

"Nate's not here yet. He's supposed to be back soon though, if you want to wait."

"Actually, I was hoping to see you . . . to welcome you to the team. I think you're . . . I mean, I just talked to Josh, and he and I both think that they couldn't have picked a better person to take his place. I really mean that."

"Thank you. But what if . . ." Valkerie bit her lip. What was she going to do? She couldn't take Josh's place. The media would tear her apart.

"Valkerie, are you okay?" Bob crossed the room and stood looking down at her with concerned eyes.

"I don't know." Valkerie's vision went suddenly blurry. "I don't know if I can go through with it." She looked down at the floor.

"It's okay, you'll be fine. If I can do it, anybody can."

"It's not that. It's just . . ." Valkerie felt a light touch on her shoulder.

"It's just what?"

Valkerie blinked back her tears and looked up into Bob's eyes. "The newspapers. All the reporters. You've been in the limelight. How . . . personal do they get? Do they . . . dig into your past?"

Bob looked surprised. "Not really. A little, maybe, but certainly nothing that *you'd* need to worry about. But I'm sure you're Mother Teresa compared to Kennedy."

Valkerie shook her head. "Bob, I've made a lot of mistakes. I've done so many stupid things. I'd just die if—"

"It's okay. We all have. Hey, I wet my pants in seventh-grade gym class. What could be worse than that? But nobody cares. What they care about is what kind of person you are now. That's what matters. On that score, believe me, you've got nothing to worry about. The press will love you."

Valkerie closed her eyes, and hot tears streamed down her cheeks. She looked at the floor. "You don't know that. You don't know me. Bob, I can't do it. I just can't."

"Valkerie, it's okay. You don't have to go. They can get someone else."

"But Perez said they'd cancel the mission. All the work. Billions and billions of dollars. I don't have a choice. I've—" A tide of emotion welled up inside her, shaking her body in its irresistible wake.

"It's okay. Don't worry about Perez. It's your decision."

Valkerie buried her face in her hands.

"Would it help to talk about it?" Bob's voice was timid. Gentle.

Valkerie took a deep breath and held it for several seconds. "When I was a freshman . . ." She dabbed at her eyes. "Bob, I was such a geek in high school. When I went off to college, I was so desperate to fit in, to make friends. I . . ." Valkerie looked up at Bob. His eyes were intense. "Bob, I've never told this to anyone. Promise me you won't tell anyone. Please, promise me."

Bob nodded soberly. "All right." His voice was a whisper. "I promise."

"You see I met this guy. Sidney Nichols. He and I—"

"Sorry, I'm late, but—" Nate Harrington burst into the room.

Valkerie jumped away from Bob and ran a hand across her eyes.

"Bob . . ." Nate stopped. "I . . . wasn't expecting to see you here."

"I just came by to congratulate Valkerie." Bob moved uneasily toward the door. "But, I, uh, Valkerie and I can finish our conversation later. Okay, Valkerie?" Bob looked her in the eye. "Okay?"

Panic rose inside her. Should she ask him to stay? Could she go with him?

Bob nodded slowly and walked out the door.

"Well." Harrington cleared off one of the office chairs and motioned for her to sit down. "What's your decision?"

"I was just telling Bob that I was worried . . . about . . ."

Nate sat down on the edge of his desk and waited. "Maybe I exaggerated the risk yesterday. In a lot of ways, it's safer than the Apollo missions. Just a lot longer, that's all. But every piece of technology on this mission is space tested. We've put gigabucks of research into this baby. You'll be fine."

Valkerie took a deep breath. All that money. All that work, and she was worried about a tiny blow to her ego. *God, forgive me. Please let this be the right decision.* "Mr. Harrington, my worries aren't that important—not compared to the mission. I've decided to join the Ares 10 team—if you'll still have me."

Thursday, August 30, 2012, 8:00 P.M.
BOB

Bob paced his living room floor. Valkerie had decided to join the mission. She was on the team.

Bob grabbed up the phone. Nine-nine-two . . . He slammed the phone back down. What was he thinking? They were co-workers now. Good grief, they'd practically be living together—for two and a half years.

He stormed back across the floor. They'd have to be just friends. Like he and Lex were friends. Oh, brother, what was he going to do?

Bob flung himself onto the sofa and grabbed his laptop. "Valkerie Jansen." He pounded the name into the search engine and scanned the list of sites. Journals, symposiums, proceedings . . . Not exactly what he was looking for. *Drop the "k." Valerie Jansen.* The third entry jumped off the screen at him: www.EdwardJansen.com. Wasn't her father's name Edward? Where had he heard that? He followed the link. Robots, Eurobotica.com, Family . . . "Family." The link brought him to a page covered with photographs. Valkerie as a baby, Valkerie as a child . . . A mischievous grin was painted across almost every picture. She had been so incredibly cute. He followed the links slowly, soaking in each stage, each nuance. Valkerie in elementary school. Valkerie winning the RobotWars championship. Valkerie in high school. Going off to college . . . Wow. He hit the Print button as if in a trance.

Bob hurried over to his printer. Valkerie smiled back at him under the mortarboard cap of her graduation picture. She was . . . stunning. He carried the photo back to the sofa. So she had gone to Yale. . . . He never knew that.

I met this guy. Sidney Nichols. Bob did a search for "Sidney Nichols" and "Yale." Sixty-nine entries. Mostly zines and news archives. He looked up one of the news articles. June 21, 2000. The end of Valkerie's freshman year.

A photo of a young man carrying a sign materialized. Dark hair. Piercing black eyes. Way too good-looking. Bob read the headline. "Yale Students Barricaded in Fetal Tissue Cloning Lab." *Quarks and bosons!* Bob's heart pounded in his throat as he scanned the article. They had gotten caught trashing a research lab. They were barricaded inside the lab. Threats of a bomb . . .

Bob clicked on the next article. "Yale Student Killed in Standoff With Police." *Sidney Nichols, a third-year political science major, was killed in an explosion. . . .*

Bob picked up Valkerie's graduation photo. She was . . . she could be just like . . . Sarah. What had he been thinking? He *didn't* know a thing about her. The picture quivered in his hands. Taking a deep breath, he tore the photo slowly in half.

The two halves blurred into one as the room dissolved into splotches of yellow and gray.

Friday, August 31, 2012, 10:00 A.M.
VALKERIE

Valkerie squinted into the lights. Teague Auditorium was filling fast with reporters. Videocam operators pressed their way to the foot of the stage, jockeying for position.

Valkerie swallowed against the lump in her throat. Bob sat rigidly next to her at the long table on the stage. She leaned forward and smiled at him, clearing her throat to get his attention. He stared determinedly ahead. Probably nervous. He didn't seem to like the limelight any more than she did.

Josh sat on her right. He nodded and flashed her a big smile. He was completely in his element. The whole world was coming out to see him, and he was the master of the occasion.

Kennedy Hampton and Alexis Ohta walked in, followed by Steven Perez. The roar of the crowd instantly dropped to a low murmur. All eyes focused on Perez as he took his place behind the podium.

"Ladies and gentlemen, I'm sure you have lots of questions, so I'm going to make this brief. As you all know by now, Mission Commander Josh Bennett will be stepping off the Ares 10 flight crew in order to direct the mission from the ground as prime Capcom. Pilot Kennedy Hampton will move up to Commander. Mission Specialist Alexis Ohta will become Pilot. Dr. Valkerie Jansen will join the crew as Mission Specialist. Valkerie earned an M.D. from Johns Hopkins University and a Ph.D. in microbial ecology from the University of Florida. She . . ."

Valkerie cringed. Why was Perez talking so much about her? Everybody loved Josh Bennett. They were going to despise her. She sank lower in her chair as Perez rambled on and on. Her face burned as he told about her "interview" in Alaska. Murmurs. Silence. Laughter.

"At this time I'd like to open up the floor for questions."

The room exploded in a cacophony of shouted questions and raised hands.

Valkerie looked to Josh, relieved that he would finally take control. He was a master of the media. His confident smile and witty Bennett-isms had been filling the airwaves for years.

Perez pointed to a reporter in the back of the room.

"Dr. Jansen, Dr. Lyons at Johns Hopkins is quoted as saying that you're one of the most brilliant med students he ever graduated, yet you quit medicine to take care of your father after your mother died. Could you comment on that?"

Valkerie turned to Bob in confusion. They knew about her father. They knew about Dr. Lyons. They probably knew about Yale too. Valkerie swept the room with wide eyes. Every eye was fixed on her. They all knew, every one of them. The room sparkled in a blinding eruption of electronic flash pyrotechnics.

"Thank you for your concern. My father is much better now. He's the dearest man in the world. He loved my mother so deeply, so completely. I've never seen a purer or more passionate love. 2006 was hard for all of us, but especially for him. The time I got to spend with him in his grief was a great privilege. A whole universe opened up to me that I didn't even know existed. If I'm ever loved half so much as my mother was, I will count myself the second most blessed woman that ever lived."

Silence hung over the auditorium. Reporters stared up at Valkerie with frozen, astonished faces.

A pair of hands clapped slowly in the back of the room. More hands. More, until the whole auditorium shook with applause. Valkerie looked down at the table and sighed with relief. They could have made her the villain, but they had chosen to make her the hero instead. For now. How many mistakes would they allow her before they changed their minds?

PART II

The Point of No Return

"Launch is a high-risk enterprise no matter what safety features the engineers design into the launch system and precautions management has taken, no matter how thoroughly and meticulously the rocket has been prepared, and no matter how well-trained and competent the crew. Sitting on top of a bomb is and will always be a dangerous venture."

JERRY LINENGER, U.S. ASTRONAUT, MIR COSMONAUT

"NASA exaggerates the reliability of its product to the point of fantasy. . . . For a successful technology, reality must take precedence over public relations, for Nature cannot be fooled."

RICHARD FEYNMAN,
NOBEL LAUREATE PHYSICIST, ON THE CHALLENGER DISASTER

"Space is a completely unforgiving environment. If you screw up the engineering, somebody dies (and there's no partial credit because *most* of the analysis was right . . .)."

DAVE AKIN

CHAPTER 10

Monday, December 9, 2013, 11:00 A.M.
BOB

A monstrous forklift lumbered across the runway and up the ramp into the belly of the Super Guppy. Kennedy was helping direct it. Not necessary, but never mind. It gave the photographers a focal point. Behind Kennedy sat the Hab on a titanium pallet, encased in a triple layer of plastic to maintain its clean-room integrity. A perfect shot of the Ares 10 and its commander. Just perfect.

Forty-seven days until launch, and Bob felt ready. The last year had been murder. Final checkouts on the Hab. Flight sims. Machine-shop training for the entire crew. Underwater work in the Neutral Buoyancy Lab to simulate weightlessness. Splashdown training. A solid week with the crew locked alone in the Hab, simulating light-time delays in communications with Josh and the other Capcoms. Desert training. The Mars Arctic Research Station on Devon Island.

They were ready to rocket—Bob knew that. Believed it. But late at night, when the rational side of him was sleeping, the irrational side lay wide awake, staring at the ceiling with pounding heart and screaming imagination. This wasn't a moon mission—three days out, three days back, with a day or two of flags-and-footprints photo-ops against a silver-cratered backdrop. This was Mars—five months out, five months back, with a year and a half to survive in a hostile alien land. Earth would be ten long minutes away by radio.

NASA had never tried anything like this before. And if anything went wrong, nobody would try it again for a long, long time.

But they were ready. Josh was the perfect Capcom. Kennedy would be a good commander—not the Picard Josh would have been, but a decent Riker. Lex, still the best man on the crew, was running a 10-K every morning just to warm up. Valkerie had zipped through training in record time. And when Lex dislocated her shoulder the previous summer, two days into isolation training in the Hab, Valkerie relocated it in all of about five seconds. Kennedy hadn't complained about having an M.D. on the crew since. She was an awfully good microbial ecologist too, judging by her *Science* article on thermophilic bacteria from that volcano in Alaska.

They were a smooth, sharp, professional team. *Professional.* Bob meant to keep it that way. It was embarrassing, the way some of the media people leered at you in an interview. *Two men, two women? Wink, wink. Off the record, Dr. Kaganovski, what are the prospects for a relationship on this mission?*

If they only knew. Lex had always been aloof—ever since Bob had known her. But in the last year, she'd grown even more distant. You had to wonder sometimes if she was in the same time zone. Sometimes she'd disappear for days on end and come back vacant and moody. Despite a horrible article about her in one of those junk men's magazines, despite her stunning good looks, she was anything but the goddess of love. Which was fine with Bob. He was on this mission to do a job. Period.

And Valkerie? Sure, she was pretty—some would say gorgeous—but Bob wasn't susceptible to that kind of thing. Not that she had time for any kind of social life, anyway. She had spent the last fifteen months training hard. Hard, even by NASA standards. So the media had her pegged as an upright, clean-living John Glenn type. As far as Bob could tell, they were right. She was a good, hard worker. And smart. A great pick for the mission. Very professional.

Kennedy, however, was a different story. He was a navy pilot, and it was no secret that he had been living the high life straight out of *The Right Stuff.* Flying and drinking, drinking and driving, drinking and groupies. The NASA brass overlooked all that. Let him get it out of his system now. There wouldn't be any groupies in space.

Except that . . .

Six or eight months ago, Bob and Kennedy had been playing pool at the Outpost. They were both about six brews into the evening, and Kennedy had a local honey hanging all over him. After missing a shot, he turned to Bob with a sloppy grin and said, "Dibs on Valkerie."

That's all. Just that one comment. *Very* unprofessional. Bob hoped that Kennedy had been kidding, that it had been the alcohol talking, but deep down inside he knew better than that. Maybe the Hampster was an officer, but he sure wasn't a gentleman. There would be only two women on that ship. One was sweet, young, attractive. The other was Fort Knox. A guy like Kennedy wouldn't have a lot of choices.

Bob wouldn't stand for any messing around in space. There were not going to be any *relationships—wink, wink—*on board the Ares 10.

————

They waited at the Vehicle Assembly Building for over two hours before they were allowed to enter the clean room. Security goons hovered everywhere, and they had *guns*. Bob submitted to a retinal scan twice within fifty yards. They X-rayed his briefcase and walked him through a metal detector.

When the team finally reached the Hab inside the mammoth clean room, they found it surrounded by security geeks. The wrapping was off it, and everyone wore bunny suits. Normally, the KSC techs would be doing the visual check of the exterior. But this was not normal. Only the crew, with Nate and Josh, were allowed near the Hab.

Bob wasn't about to gripe about that. The fewer people who touched it at this stage, the better he liked it.

The entire crew did a once-around of the exterior of the Hab at ground level. Everything looked spotless. They wheeled in several sections of catwalk and repeated the inspection at the midpoint of the Hab. Perfect.

They walked inside the Hab. Kennedy led, with Bob right behind. Valkerie and Lex were tasked to record the inspection with videocams. Which was absurd, but some NASA mucky-muck had ordered it. The complete visual inspection took over an hour.

"All right y'all, let's call it a day." Kennedy clomped down the stairs. "Tomorrow we've got the electrical systems checkout. We've got a ton of work to do. Everyone needs to get here at 7:00 A.M. sharp."

"That's 6:00 A.M. in Houston," Lex said. "How about cutting us some slack?"

"We've got five months to cut ourselves some slack on the way to Mars," Kennedy said. "Our schedule is right to the wire, people. We need to get that electrical checkout done by close-of-business tomorrow."

Bob shook his head. "Nate, how are we supposed to get anything done with this security dog-and-pony act every time we turn around?"

"It's ridiculous," Lex said. "You'd think we were terrorists."

"What about it, Nate?" Kennedy said. "We're not exactly federal prisoners."

"I requested the tightest possible security," Nate said. "We have excellent reason to—"

"Nate?" Josh motioned Nate off to one side and talked to him quietly for a few minutes.

When they came back, Nate was sweating. He cleared his throat and looked around the circle. "Okay, team, I see your point. There *is* a need for tight security, and we're going to meet that need, but I'll see to it that it doesn't impact your ability to do your job."

For Nate, that was practically a groveling apology. As they headed for the exit, Bob whacked Josh on the shoulders. "Thanks, buddy. What kind of dirt have you got on Nate to make him back down like that?"

Josh gave him a mysterious smile. "You'll never know."

Friday, January 24, 2014, 8:00 P.M.
VALKERIE

Valkerie looked across a concrete drainage channel at the small clusters of friends and family gathered to send off the Ares 10 astronauts. She snuggled down into her coat, shielding her ears beneath her flapping collar. The night was chilly and clear. The launch tower loomed above her like a colossal offering to the gods. Bright spotlights polished the powerful heavy-lift launch vehicle to a gleaming white, filling the night sky with a dull orange glow. The tower of Babel. She swallowed back the disturbing thought. It settled into the pit of her stomach like a bitter pill.

Valkerie turned to watch her fellow crew members laughing and talking with their family and friends across the dividing moat. She had worked with them for over a year now. Practicing, drilling, training. The four of them functioned together like a space-age pit crew, but when it came to real life, they might as well have been speaking different languages. At the end of the day, while the others were lingering over dinner or hanging out at their favorite bars, she was memorizing manuals and practicing on simulators. Trying to cram into a year and a half what they had learned in six.

She had excelled to be sure. Mastered the material in record time.

Valkerie was the toast of the trainers. But she knew deep in her heart that she was a failure. Somehow, during all those joint exercises, she had failed to connect. A year and a half of her life was gone, and what did she have to show for it? Memorized flight procedures to back up Kennedy? Wiring diagrams to back up Bob? Zero-g surgery in case somebody got sick? She had spent a year and a half training to be an emergency backup system. A piece of baggage that nobody expected to use until they got to Mars.

A burst of laughter rang out from the small crowd gathered across from Kennedy. Overdressed and overloud, they reminded her of a group of politicians at a campaign rally. Kennedy was their candidate. Their hero. He strutted and preened in front of them—the host at his own late-night talk show. Valkerie searched the group, wondering if he had the gall to invite any of his groupies. The thought left her feeling uneasy. Flight Med had put her on birth-control pills—ostensibly to lessen the severity of her periods during the mission. But she couldn't escape the fear that she was looking at the real reason.

Valkerie pushed the thought from her mind and turned her attention to the quiet Asian women that clustered in front of Lex. Her sister and mother? Her mother and grandmother? It was hard to tell. Of her three crewmates, Valkerie knew Lex the least. Josh said Lex had been aloof from everybody lately, but she couldn't help wondering if he was just saying that to spare her feelings. Lex seemed to get along with Bob just fine.

Valkerie sneaked a glance at Bob. Three guys stood across from him— off to the side and away from the rest of the crowd. Hands in their pockets, hunched shoulders, shuffling feet, they seemed almost as uncomfortable as Bob. Were they brothers? She didn't see any family resemblance. More likely friends. Drinking buddies.

Bob nodded back at her, and she looked quickly down at the ground. How did he do it? He always seemed to know when she was looking at him. It wasn't like she looked at him that often. Ever since her first day on the team, Bob seemed to grow more and more distant. It wasn't their fight at the Outpost—they'd both apologized a dozen times for that. Something else was bothering him. Something deeper. More systemic. Josh had noticed it too, but Bob wouldn't talk about it with him. Maybe Josh was right, maybe Bob was getting a severe case of cold feet. Maybe that was what was wrong with Lex too, but Valkerie doubted it. She couldn't help wondering if Bob would have been a lot happier with Josh on the team.

"You're awfully quiet tonight."

"Dad!" Valkerie spun in the direction of the moat. Her father stood across from her, blowing a cloud of steam through his hands. "What took you so long? I was starting to worry you wouldn't make it." Valkerie looked at her watch. They had taken him to the Houston airport over six hours ago.

"My flight was delayed. I had to tip the taxi driver a hundred bucks to get me here this soon. No way was I going to miss the traditional send-off—not after my baby worked so hard to get me VIP tickets." A swell of emotion rolled across his face like a sheet billowing in a summer breeze. Suddenly she felt miserable and all alone. Two and a half years was an eternity. She didn't know if she could do it.

"Nervous?"

Valkerie nodded. "Scared, I guess. I'm going to miss you. I'm going to miss—everything."

"I'm going to miss you too." Her dad's voice quivered.

Valkerie took a step toward the moat but stopped short at its painted edge. Why couldn't she go to him? Her father needed her. She needed him. Just one more hug. What would it hurt?

"Yes sir, I'm going to miss all those lemon meringue pies you have to make me when Michigan humiliates Wisconsin." Her father grinned at her from across the moat.

"Michigan humiliates Wisconsin? Dream on. You haven't eaten lemon meringue in four years."

"Oh, I get it now. Just as soon as we finish rebuilding, you decide to run off to Mars. Well, it's not going to work. I'll expect two pies the minute you get home."

Valkerie smiled but didn't rise to the taunt. Her dad stood straight and tall on the other side of the moat, watching her with a contented, satisfied expression. He would always be there for her. That was enough. No matter what happened in between, things with him would be the same when she got back.

A black car pulled close to the moat and a tall air force officer stepped out. Valkerie frowned and glanced at her watch. Only ten more minutes. She forced a smile and turned back to her father. He nodded and smiled but remained silent. It was a comfortable silence. He had visited her all week while she was quarantined at crew quarters in Houston. Reminiscing. Smuggling in pizzas. It was nice. Like their time together after her mother died. But this time they could talk about the past. It was the future that they studiously avoided. And this time it was her father who played the role of nurse—a role he performed with comical ineptitude.

"Expecting someone in particular?"

Valkerie nodded. Josh Bennett had said that he would stop by to see her off. She'd talked to him on the phone, but she hadn't seen him for two weeks. This was her last day. You'd think he would at least stop by to say good-bye.

Her eyes drifted back to the parking lot. The air force officer stood outside his car, clutching his hat in both hands. Who was he there to see? Lex? Someone in Kennedy's party?

Another car swept into the parking lot and pulled to a stop behind the roped-off visitor section. Josh sprang from the car and headed straight for Valkerie. He seemed to be out of breath.

Valkerie's dad turned expectantly.

"Mr. Jansen." Josh shook her father's hand. "It's a pleasure to finally get to meet you. Valkerie's told me all about you."

"The pleasure is all mine. I've heard nothing but good reports about you—for years."

Josh shrugged. "Well, you know how biased the media can be." He nodded at Valkerie and flashed her a big smile.

Valkerie looked down at her feet, suddenly uncertain how to respond. She cocked her head to the side. Bob was talking with one of his friends. The other two must have already left.

Bob turned slowly and stared back at her with big, questioning eyes. Valkerie looked back down at the ground. Somehow he always knew.

CHAPTER 11

Bob poured himself another bowl of Cheerios.

"Hey, Bo, you better get you some bacon and grits," Kennedy said. "That kiddie food won't last you long."

Bob wanted to say something about not wanting to heave up a big breakfast, but he didn't dare. Not with the NBC cameras right in his face.

Today was the day. Launch Day. It had to be today, and everyone knew it. The Saturday before the Super Bowl. The timing was perfect. NBC's ratings were gonna hit the stratosphere. And NASA would get another billion dollars to pay off some of its bills. Then *if* they reached Mars exactly on July fourth, there'd be a multibillion dollar payday from NBC, and the mission's debts would be covered.

What a way to design a mission—with NBC picking the dates.

At the other end of the table, half a dozen cameras clustered around Valkerie. Which was fine with Bob. She was articulate and photogenic. That's what brought in the network money. Great. Now he was starting to sound like Perez.

"Dr. Jansen, what's the first thing you plan to do when you get into space?" A reporter wearing a surgeon's mask shoved a microphone in Valkerie's face.

"I suppose I'll have to deal with crew-acclimatization issues first."

"What exactly are those?"

"Dizziness, hand-eye coordination, possible vomiting. The usual problems. It's called Space Adaptation Sickness."

"Are you concerned about your safety?" asked an earnest young man with slick black hair and a bow tie.

Valkerie gave a half shrug. "It's like any kind of flying—the most dangerous parts are takeoffs and landings, right?"

"Aren't you afraid?"

"I'm confident that we've done everything we can to make this voyage as safe as possible." Valkerie pointed toward Bob. "Thanks to people like Dr. Kaganovski, the Ares 10 is probably the safest space vehicle ever built."

Bob set down his spoon in his unfinished bowl of Cheerios and managed some sort of a smile as the cameras zoomed in on him.

Good answer, Valkerie. Right out of The Right Stuff. *And I bet you're scared spitless. Just like I am.*

Because when you got right down to it, sitting in a chair with ten million pounds of rocket fuel strapped to your tail could be bad for your health.

Unlike Lex and Kennedy, Bob had never flown a shuttle mission. This would be his first launch. This morning he'd woken up with his heart pounding, knowing that this could be the day. Would be the day, if the weather was anything near okay.

When he'd heard the forecast, he'd almost lost his cool. Winds above 20 mph, with possible slacking in the late morning. Possible.

You couldn't launch in winds above fifteen miles per hour. The rocket could get blown into the tower. Launch time was set for 1:47 P.M., with an eight-minute launch window. If they missed that, they'd have to launch tomorrow, right during the Super Bowl pregame show.

And Nate would blow a brain gasket. Perez too. They could not afford to lose a gigabuck. Which was why Bob was scared out of his gourd. Would they launch, or wouldn't they?

"What about you, Dr. Kaganovski?" It was the bow-tied reporter. "Aren't you just a teensy bit worried?"

Like every astronaut who ever lived, Bob lied through his teeth whenever he got that question. He took a swig of orange juice, wiped his mouth, and gave a careless shrug, letting the tension build. "Not at all," he said. "Compared to driving the Houston freeways at rush hour, a launch into space is like a walk in the park."

Saturday, January 25, 2014, 8:00 A.M. EST
VALKERIE

After breakfast, Valkerie retreated to her room in crew quarters, locking the door behind her. The reporters were in a feeding frenzy. She needed time to think. They were leaving the earth in less than six hours, and she had this terrible feeling that she was forgetting something important. But what was there to forget? NASA had done all the packing. Ten thousand people were working full-time to make sure nothing was forgotten.

Valkerie undressed and pulled on her diaper. No, not diaper—MAG. Astronauts were too macho to wear diapers. Maybe that's what MAG stood for. Macho Astronaut Garment. She climbed into her cooling garment, tugging hard to get the stubborn meshwork of plastic tubing over her shoulders. She zipped it up and cracked open her door. Good. No reporters. The last thing she wanted was to have her picture taken in ridiculous-looking long johns.

Valkerie stepped out into the hall. A sober-faced technician met her. Kennedy and Lex were already dressed and stood waiting outside Bob's room.

"Need any help in there?" Kennedy called through the door. "The long set of sleeves are for your legs. The short ones are for your arms."

Bob stepped out of the room with a goofy smile. "I was wondering why the rear was so drafty."

The technician escorted the four astronauts to the suit-up room. Two female suit technicians greeted Valkerie and led her to a white table.

All of her personal gear was arranged neatly on the table, waiting for her inspection. A lanyard knife, survival radio, vomit bag, signal mirror, whistle, sunglasses . . . The suit technicians triple-checked all her gear before stuffing it into the pockets of her orange Partial Pressure Launch and Entry Garment. What a clunky name. Why didn't they . . . Valkerie laughed out loud. She finally realized why NASA didn't use an acronym for the suits.

The techies pressurized her suit to test for leaks. "Looks good, Dr. Jansen," one of them said. The other made the sign of the cross, her eyes glistening. "God go with you, Dr. Jansen."

Valkerie stopped, unsure what to say. The tech watched her with an expression bordering on awe. Valkerie felt suddenly alone, as if she were already a million miles away. She wanted to reach out to the woman, to tell her that she was just like her. To ask her about her family, take her by the hand . . . but the others were already leaving.

Valkerie turned away slowly and followed her crewmates down the ramp to the Astrovan. Their faces were somber. Professional. Determined. They seemed so different in their suits, as if they had left their humanity behind with their street clothes. One at a time, a technician helped them into the van, and the doors locked shut behind them. Locked away from a world she would soon be leaving. Trapped in a cell with three familiar strangers. The urge to escape was almost overpowering. She wanted to run back to the suit tech and give her a hug. For all she knew it might be her last chance for a hug for two and a half years.

Saturday, January 25, 2014, 9:00 A.M. EST

BOB

By the time they were halfway up the elevator, Bob was regretting that he'd drunk so much orange juice at breakfast. His kidneys had gone into overdrive. When they reached the top, Bob was the first one out of the elevator, looking for the bathroom. He was not going to go in his Maximum Absorbing Garment if he could help it.

The plumbing was primitive, but it worked. When he came out, the others were standing in the White Room, preparing for ingress to the launch vehicle.

"You're first," Kennedy said. "Wave to the cameras and take one last look at the good green earth, because the next time you go outside, there isn't going to be any lawn within a hundred million miles."

Bob gulped. *I can't believe it. We're really leaving. If the winds drop a little.*

Saturday, January 25, 2014, 11:30 A.M. EST

VALKERIE

Valkerie lay on her back with her feet locked into place overhead—waiting. They had been strapped in their seats for over two hours. If Launch Control knew they weren't going to launch today, why didn't they just let them go home? The winds were too high.

115

Valkerie closed her eyes and tried to relax. The ship vibrated beneath her like a finely tuned automobile. A strange noise made her jump. Kennedy whistling softly under his breath. Bob and Lex began to snicker.

What was so funny? Kennedy's whistling? Or was it another private joke? Valkerie was sick to death of being left out. Just once she'd like to know what was going on.

"Time for the astro comm checks." Josh's voice came in through her earphones. He sounded tired, but at least he could get up and walk around. "MCC to Ares 10, how do you read?"

"CDR, loud and clear," said Kennedy.

"PLT," said Lex.

Valkerie hesitated. "MS1."

"MS2." Bob sounded calm, confident. That helped Valkerie a little. If he wasn't afraid, why should she be?

"Ares 10, this is Launch Control," said the Launch Director. "Ready for hatch closure. The winds are at one-five-decimal-two and steady. We are at T-minus one hour and forty minutes."

More than an hour and a half! Valkerie tried to cross her legs, but the molded seat and harness held her legs in place. She had to go bad—and having her feet above her head wasn't helping matters. If they didn't scrub the launch soon, she was going to have to . . . Oh, so maybe that's why Kennedy was whistling.

The Launch Director came on again. "Hatch is closed and latched for launch?"

"That's affirm." Another voice, probably one of the closeout crew.

Lex started whistling. This time Valkerie joined in the laughter.

Saturday, January 25, 2014, 12:41 P.M. CST
NATE

Nate wiped his forehead and tried to will the wind-speed indicator to drop. The rolling average over the past five minutes was 15.1 mph. One tenth of a lousy mile per hour too high. The instantaneous wind speed was 14.8. If it stayed down for another minute—

"Mr. Harrington, are you going to launch, or aren't you?" The network rep stood with his hands behind his back, feet spread apart, looking for all the world like a gunslinger.

Nate pointed at the clock. "Let me spell it out for you. Our launch window closes in fourteen minutes. We are at a built-in hold at T-minus seven minutes. If the average wind speed dips below fifteen, then we proceed. Otherwise, no. Any other brilliant questions?"

"Dr. Perez, can't you talk sense into him?" The network rep jerked his thumb toward Nate. "You have to launch today. We've got a lot of money riding on this."

Perez walked up to the rep and stared at him coldly. "I've got four lives riding on this, and that is my only consideration right now. If that's a problem to you, then walk. We've got a mission to run. Or we will as soon as they clear the tower. Until then, Launch Control in Florida runs this launch."

The average wind speed dropped to 15.0.

Nate switched to the Launch Director's circuit and keyed his mike. "LD, this is Mission Director Nate Harrington. We are go for launch at MCC-Houston."

"Roger that," said the Launch Director. "All technical issues on site are now closed. White Room is deconfigured. We are clear to fly."

The Launch Director went down the checklist of engineering teams, getting a *Go* from each. The last was the crew itself.

"CDR?"

"Go!" said Kennedy.

"Count will resume on my mark," said the Launch Director. "Three . . . two . . . one . . . mark!"

The clock began ticking down from seven minutes. The average wind speed dropped to 14.9.

The network rep put a hand on Nate's shoulder. "Mr. Harrington, does this mean we're definitely going to launch today?"

Nate yanked off his headset and spun around to glare at him. "Listen, you imbecile, and listen good. Nothing is definite until the solid boosters ignite at T-minus 1.8 seconds. After that, God himself can't call back the launch. Now get out of here."

"I want a definite guarantee that—"

Steven Perez stepped in. "Thank you for stopping by. We have work to do. You will leave now." He pushed the rep bodily out of the room.

Nate wiped his face again, his eyes riveted to the wind-speed indicator. *Don't you dare change. We cannot afford to miss this launch. We can't. We just can't. Stay at 14.9.*

Please.

Saturday, January 25, 2014, 1:44 P.M. EST
BOB

"Ares 10, this is Houston," Josh said. "The clock is ticking again. Good luck, and godspeed!"

The clock resumed its countdown. Bob tightened his grip on the arm of his chair. *In fifteen minutes, we'll be in space.*

Or dead.

Saturday, January 25, 2014, 12:49 P.M. CST
NATE

The clock passed T-minus two minutes without incident. Nate's heart hammered in his rib cage. The instantaneous winds had been fluctuating between fourteen and sixteen for the last five minutes, but the average was below threshold. *Two more minutes and we're home free, baby, and we can start paying our bills again, and—*

15.0

Nate stared at the indicator. Just a gust. It had to be.

"Flight, this is LD," the Launch Director's voice came through Nate's headset. "We are at threshold. Recommendations?"

The Flight Director down in Mission Control took only an instant to pass that buck on up the ladder. "Nate, this is Flight. What's your opinion on this?"

Perez was at Nate's side in an instant. "Is fifteen safe?"

"Technically, yes. It's marginal."

"Is it safe?"

"It's—" Nate tugged at his hair. "Flight, hold the countdown."

"LD, hold the count," said Flight.

The clock stopped. Two seconds later the phone rang.

Nate picked it up and slammed it down.

Sixty seconds ticked by. No change in the rolling average. The instantaneous speed bobbed around between fourteen and sixteen.

Perez put a hand on Nate's shoulder. "It's not moving up."

Nate was hyperventilating now. "I see it. Shall we go?"

"If we can do so safely. Your call, Nate."

Which was a lie, and Nate knew it. They had too much invested in this thing to back down. If it was marginal, they had to go. They had to.

"Flight, this is Harrington," Nate said. "Recommend we proceed with launch."

Saturday, January 25, 2014, 1:51 P.M. EST

VALKERIE

"Ares 10, this is Josh. Resuming the count."

Valkerie watched the clock start ticking down again. A minute fifty. A minute forty. This was it. It was really going to happen. *God, please keep us safe. Please don't let this be another Challenger.*

She exhaled slowly. Had Christa McAuliffe been praying the same thing? If so, what good had it done her?

Saturday, January 25, 2014, 1:52 P.M. EST

BOB

Bob watched the seconds tick off. Average wind speed was holding at 15.0 exactly. T-minus fifty-eight seconds. The launch window would close in three minutes. One more delay, and the launch would be off for today.

This is no way to run a mission.

The Ares 10 had almost ten million parts, each of which had to work for this mission to succeed. Had they checked them all? They must have, a thousand times. There were procedures for everything.

Written by humans. What if there'd been a glitch they hadn't caught? What if they hadn't thought of every contingency? What if some terrorist somewhere had a SAM ready to blow them out of the sky? What if?

The instantaneous wind speed dropped to 14.5, then to 14.2.

Bob felt his pulse slowing. *Okay, this is it. No more what-ifs. We're going to Mars, no matter what.*

Saturday, January 25, 2014, 12:53 P.M. CST
NATE

Nate was breathing again. Average wind was down to 14.9 and holding steady. T-minus twenty seconds. *Come on, baby!*

Fifteen point zero. Nate sucked in his breath and held it. T-minus fifteen seconds, and the announcer began the traditional countdown.

"Fifteen . . . fourteen . . . thirteen. . . ."

The instantaneous wind gusted to 15.3.

Nate toggled his headset mike. "Flight, recommend you maintain countdown."

"Roger that, over. LC, recommend you continue the count."

"Ten . . . nine . . . eight . . ."

The wind speed jumped to 15.5, then to 15.9.

Nate jumped out of his chair. "Flight, that's just a gust. Rolling average is fine. We are still go for launch. Go, go, go!"

Wind speed 16.4.

"Five . . . four . . . main engine ignite . . . three . . . two."

Nate's eyes were riveted on the screen. The six solid boosters lit off. No turning back now.

Wind speed 16.9. *God have mercy.*

Saturday, January 25, 2014, 1:53 P.M. EST
BOB

T-minus zero. Somewhere down below, eight explosive charges severed the ten-inch restraining bolts. The rocket leapt off the pad, pushing Bob deep into his seat. The entire ship lurched and shimmied. He checked the instantaneous wind speed. 17.2. 17.5. *Just let us clear the tower.*

The rocket shuddered with a deafening metallic groan. Bob checked the altimeter. They had cleared. They were at 100 mph, with a lateral wind speed of 18.2. He could feel the buffeting as the dynamic air pressure climbed rapidly.

"Hang on, people," Bob yelled into his mike. "We are in for a *ride.*"

Saturday, January 25, 2014, 12:53 P.M. CST
NATE

A collective gasp hissed around the consoles in Mission Control. Had a stabilizer fin nicked the edge of the tower? Nate couldn't be sure. A blast of static filled the room. What was causing all that noise?

It was now seven seconds into launch. Deep in the guts of some computer, somewhere, control of the rocket passed from the Launch Center at Cape Canaveral to Mission Control Center in Houston.

Tag, you're it.

Saturday, January 25, 2014, 12:54 P.M. CST
VALKERIE

Valkerie's monitor rattled and pitched, a cold blue blur that flickered at the edges of her terror. A deafening roar filled her brain, punctuated by pings and ear-piercing groans. Voices shouted in her ear. Something was wrong. She couldn't hear above the roar. What were they trying to tell her? What was she supposed to do? Something flashed red on her monitor. A purple haze on a field of fuzzy blue.

"I can't hear you!" Valkerie shouted into her microphones, but she couldn't hear her own voice. Her arms were made of lead and her tongue was dull as stone.

"I can't hear you! What do you want us to do?"

Saturday, January 25, 2014, 12:54 P.M. CST
BOB

Something snapped way down in the guts of the ship. Bob twisted his head frantically. Had something broken? They couldn't bail out now. They were sixty seconds into the launch—about the point that the Challenger had exploded—and traveling 3000 mph. Way too fast for an emergency egress.

The ship vibrated like a paint shaker. And the worst was coming any second now. Max Q, the point of maximum dynamic pressure. If anything was going to blow, it would be here. The ship was shaking so bad,

Bob couldn't see a thing. He narrowed his eyes to slits and tried to watch the clock. The roar of the ship filled his ears.

Valkerie was screaming something. Bob couldn't understand her. The noise battered his senses. They would hit Max Q at T-plus sixty-four seconds. He watched the clock. *Sixty-two. Sixty-three. Sixty-four.*

Sixty-five. And they were still alive.

For the time being.

Saturday, January 25, 2014, 12:54 P.M. CST
NATE

The camera inside the ship was shaking like an epileptic. Something had gone terribly wrong. They were in some kind of resonance mode, and the nozzle gimbals couldn't keep up—they were probably out of phase and causing positive feedback. The screen filled with static.

"Flight, we've lost telemetry!" That was TELMU, and he sounded frantic.

"Flight, I've lost track of the ship!" GNC jumped out of his chair and hammered on his console.

A babble of voices filled the Flight Director's channel. Nate switched to the Capcom link. This was reserved for Josh and the crew.

"Ares 10, do you read me? Come in. You have passed through Max Q," Josh shouted into the microphone.

Nate tightened his grip on the edge of the table. The monitor now showed only the view of Ares 10 from the ground telephoto lens.

"Ares 10, we've lost telemetry. Can you hear me?" Josh's voice had a frantic edge to it.

No response.

"Ares 10, this is Josh. Do you copy?"

Nothing followed but static for a long minute. And then . . . Lex's voice. "Houston, this is PLT. We are . . . a little shaken up, but it's getting better."

Mission Control erupted in cheers.

"How about the rest of you? Kennedy, you okay?"

No answer.

"Valkerie, are you there?"

"This is Valkerie. What happened? That wasn't in the sims."

"We're checking into that right now, but we've lost telemetry. Bob, what can you tell us? We're going to depend on you until telemetry comes back online."

Saturday, January 25, 2014, 12:55 P.M. CST
BOB

Bob couldn't focus on his monitor. This was insanity.

"Bob, this is Josh. Can you hear me?"

No telemetry. A possible hull breach. They were trapped like worms on a hook. They were dead. There was nothing they could do.

"Bob!" Lex's shout cut through the roar. "Do you have comm?"

"I can hear you. Comm's okay."

"Well, check off with Houston."

"Sorry, Josh." Bob fought to keep his voice level. "I'm hanging in there."

"Roger that, Bob. How about you, Kennedy? Are you all right?"

"Kennedy?" Bob could hear Lex's shout through his helmet.

"Pipe down. I've got a ship to fly." Kennedy's reply was faint and uneven.

"Just hang on a little longer," Josh said. "We are at T-plus two minutes even. Solid rockets separating in five seconds . . . three . . . two . . . one . . . now! Should be smooth sailing from here on."

Saturday, January 25, 2014, 1:01 P.M. CST
NATE

Nate watched the clock as it ticked through the eight-minute mark. The crew was alive and the ship was still in one piece. That was the main thing. Something had gone wrong, but it hadn't been a catastrophe. No ignition failure, no terrorist missiles, no busted O-rings. Another half minute and they'd make it to Main Engine Cutoff. Then in another thirty minutes, they'd do a short burn to circularize into a parking orbit for a full systems checkout. As long as the boys and girls on console could communicate with the crew, they still had a chance. Hopefully, nothing was damaged. If not . . . well, Bob was a cowboy. He could fix it. Or bust an aorta trying.

123

Eight and a half minutes into launch. Twelve seconds to Main Engine Cutoff.

"Stand by for MECO," Josh said.

"Standing by." Lex's voice crackled through the static.

Nate watched the seconds flash by. 8:40. 8:41. 8:42. The engines shut down. A spontaneous cheer swept through Mission Control. Ares 10 was in orbit.

Nate wiped his face. That had been the worst fifteen minutes of his life, but they'd made it. The scary part of the mission was done. Now let them sit in a parking orbit for a few hours while they got used to micro-gravity, checked out all systems, and fixed anything that was broken.

After that, on to Mars.

CHAPTER 12

OXYGEN

Saturday, January 25, 2014, 1:01 P.M.
VALKERIE

The roar faded to silence, and Valkerie felt herself lift off her seat. Weightless. They were in orbit.

She hung limply in her harness, waiting for the cheering to start.

Lex moaned. Someone was throwing up. Was it Bob?

"Is everyone okay?" Valkerie unbuckled her harness and floated free of her seat. Voices buzzed in her earphones, but she ignored them. She pulled the antinausea medication from the mesh bag at her command station. This was where she finally got to be useful. This was where they'd start appreciating her.

Lex sat in the pilot seat massaging her temples. She seemed to be okay. Valkerie turned to Bob, who was wiping his mouth on the towel attached to his vomit bag. He was a little green, but nothing serious. Kennedy lay still in his harness, arms floating motionless in front of him.

"Kennedy?" Voices were yelling in Valkerie's earphones. She pulled her Snoopy cap off and moved in to examine him. "Kennedy?"

Kennedy rocked back and forth in his seat, teeth bared, eyes clamped shut, forehead furrowed in pain.

"Kennedy, are you okay?" Valkerie pushed her way to Kennedy's side.

Unshed tears bulged at the corners of his eyes.

"Kennedy, what's wrong? Can you hear me?" Valkerie shouted.

Kennedy brushed at his face with his sleeve. "Quiet! I'm trying to listen."

"I'm sorry, I thought you—"

"Shhhh!" He repositioned his microphones and turned away. "That's a negative, Houston, but there was a bit of turbulence. We are commencing to check for damage." He popped his seat restraints and pushed off for the central stairwell. "I'm checkin' Level One!"

Valkerie stared after him in surprise and turned to see if the others had noticed his strange behavior. Lex had already released from her seat and was starting to type at the NavConsole.

Bob floated above Lex like a phantom. "Keep your eye on the cabin pressure. If it so much as hiccups I want to know about it." He moved deliberately, clutching his vomit bag tight. His eyes jittered like his world was moving faster than his equilibrium could keep up.

"Bob, let me give you something for the nausea." Valkerie held up a syringe. "I think Kennedy needs something too."

He waved her away without even looking at her. "Get below deck and help Kennedy. I want every ORU pulled. Every system double-checked."

"Is something wrong? I heard a crash, but I thought it might be—"

"Now!" Bob snapped. A second later he looked suddenly apologetic. "Please, Valkerie. Telemetry is out. I really need you downstairs."

Valkerie pushed off for the stairwell. At the hatch, she turned to look back. Bob was typing furiously at the master console. A fresh vomit bag was floating in the air next to him. His face was pale and glistened with a sheet of sweat.

"This really will help." She flicked the syringe packet in Bob's direction and pulled herself into the central stairway. If he was afraid of a little needle, that was his problem. Her job was to offer it.

Valkerie pulled herself through the stairwell tube using the steps that were folded back against the walls of the metal cylinder. The lower deck was lit by a dull orange glow. Something was wrong. The main lights were out. She hurried through the circular corridor. Kennedy was in the equipment bay shining a flashlight across the back wall panel.

"Is everything all right?"

"Huh?" Kennedy swung around and caught her in the beam of his flashlight.

"Bob's worried about the ship. He wants me to help you with checkout."

Valkerie squinted into the light. Kennedy's head was cocked at a funny angle. He didn't look good at all. "Are you feeling okay?"

Valkerie pushed herself closer. "Need an antinausea shot?"

Kennedy shook his head and turned to face the wall. "I'm fine. No problems at all. But I could use some help checking the ship." He swept the wall haphazardly with his flashlight. "I've already checked this area. You check the decontamination bay." He floated past her with his head still cocked to the side.

"Are you sure? What about the lights?"

"I'm about to check them right now. You make sure none of the hoses vibrated loose." He pulled himself through the door and disappeared from sight.

Valkerie pulled a flashlight from one of the charging stations and flicked it on. An odd flash caught her eye. She played her light along the walls of the room. A shiny spot on the back wall reflected the light back at her. The same part of the wall that Kennedy had been examining.

Valkerie pushed herself over for a closer look. A large patch of the lower section of the wall glistened with some kind of a residue. She ran a finger across the patch. It was wet, oily. An organic solvent? She examined the patch closer. It was streaked with a strange pattern. Like somebody had wiped it with a cloth.

"Juice."

Valkerie jumped at Kennedy's voice. She spun around to face him. "What?"

"My drink bag sprang a leak." Kennedy brought out a clean towel and wiped at the spill.

"But—"

"This isn't exactly a spectator sport. Didn't I ask you to check the decontamination bay?"

Valkerie held her ground. "That wasn't juice. I checked—"

"The decontamination bay," Kennedy growled.

"But that wasn't—"

Kennedy pushed his way past her with a look of irritation. Valkerie watched him leave, too surprised to say another word. Kennedy was hurting bad—he had to be. Either that or . . . Valkerie pushed off the wall and headed for the decontamination room. The faster they checked the ship, the better.

BOB

Bob moved a shaky finger down the column of data on his computer screen. Life support—stable. Cabin pressure—stable. Over two hundred indicators of structural integrity—all of them read stable. He couldn't believe it. A stabilizer fin had winged the tower—a video analysis on the ground had confirmed it. They could have been killed so easily. The vibrations alone could have torn them apart. One loose hose. One weak O-ring. There were millions of failure modes, any one of which could have killed them. And that was just in eight minutes. How many billions of failure modes would there be if they went all the way to Mars?

What had he been thinking? Up till now, he'd been brushing aside his fears as trivial things, as phantoms to be mastered by his mind. But what if the phantoms were real and his logic a slave to an illusion? That had never occurred to him. He had been a fool. If the Hab had broken up during launch, if it had exploded in a bright orange fireball that repeated itself over and over on his parents' big-screen television—how would that have been substantially different from committing suicide? Sure there was a chance that he'd make it back from Mars. But there was a chance he'd survive a jump off the Golden Gate Bridge too. Failure to think through consequences wasn't a valid excuse. How many times had the Sisters taught him that lesson? How many times did the ruler have to smack his knuckles before the message finally lodged in his bony little head?

He turned slowly to face Lex, careful to avoid the kinds of sudden motion that had been making his inner ear send out general distress signals to his stomach.

"How are you doing with the Guidance and Nav checkout?" His voice pounded in his head. His face felt bloated, as if he were hanging upside down. No gravity to pull the fluids down. They had warned him about that too, but of course he hadn't paid attention. He hadn't considered the possibility of death, much less issues of general discomfort.

Lex looked up from her console and shook her head. "The primary IMU is glitching. I'm resyncing it with the secondary."

"Great." Bob closed his eyes and sighed. The Inertial Measurement Unit had glitched on Earth under a lot less severe shaking. Of course it wasn't working. And the IMU was mission critical. If they didn't have both secondary and primary working, they'd have to scrap the mission.

Yesterday the thought would have ticked him off but good, would have pumped him full of determination to *make* this mission succeed. But now . . . now he felt almost relieved.

Because after the beating they'd just taken, there was no way this ship was going anywhere but to a docking port with the International Space Station. He'd just looked the Reaper in the eye and walked away in one piece. A normal, everyday life on Earth was suddenly looking like a pretty good deal. A wife. Kids. Minivan. House in the 'burbs. If they twisted his arm, he'd even take the white picket fence.

"Hey, Bob, this is Houston." Josh's voice sounded tinny and thin. "EECOM and TELMU want to know when they're going to have telemetry back on line. We're feeling kind of lonely down here with all our consoles flatlined."

"Roger that, Houston," Bob said. "The answer to that is not very soon. The telemetry data bus is fritzed, and our Ku-band antenna seems to be locked up pretty good. It may take a spacewalk to fix the antenna, and that is not going to happen today."

"That's another thing," Josh said. "Flight is asking if maybe we shouldn't push back the trans-Mars injection burn a little bit. We'll miss prime time, but I don't think we have any other choice."

Trans-Mars injection? Josh was still thinking there was a chance to do TMI? The Hampster would set him straight on that real fast. "Um, Josh, hasn't Kennedy sent you his report yet?"

"That's affirmative, we have Kennedy's preliminary report. All life-critical systems are online and in order, but we've got no data down here. Zero. Zippo. So you need to be our eyes and ears. We need an exact accounting of what's broken and what isn't."

"Roger that." Bob checked his console. "Looks like the Hampster and Valkerie have already fixed the problem with the lower level lights. They're downstairs right now kicking the tires on the fuel cells, but I can see from our power usage that those are in good shape."

"EECOM is concerned about the integrity of the solar panels," Josh said. "They weren't designed to take that kind of stress. Recommend you deploy them and check for damage. That's a mission critical function and it's gonna take a few hours to deploy those, so you need to get started right away."

"That's affirm. Beginning deployment of solar panels." *Like there's any chance of saving this mission.* Bob flipped open the procedures book, read through the first section, and began toggling switches. They hadn't planned to deploy the solar panels while in orbit. It would take a couple hours to reel them out, another couple to bring them back in. And who knew how long in between to check them out. Busy work. The boys on the ground were obviously stalling. Giving themselves time to work out an emergency rendezvous with the International Space Station. The Hab was designed to land on Mars, not Earth, so they'd have to rendezvous with the ISS and wait for the next shuttle. A day catching down to the ISS, a few weeks on the station, and they'd be back on *terra firma*. They wouldn't be heroes, but they'd be alive.

Which sure beat the alternative.

Saturday, January 25, 2014, 4:00 P.M.
NATE

Nate scanned the faces of Gold Team. They had just finished their shift, but every one of them had volunteered to hang around and back up Maroon Team. "All right, kids, that was a tough launch. What's our status?" He jabbed a finger at EECOM. "You first."

EECOM was a short, thin woman with bright red hair and hunched shoulders. She licked her lips nervously. "I do not have data at this time. Bob is investigating the situation. We seem to have multiple failures in telemetry. The data bus has failed, and the Ku-band antenna has a malfunction. That is all he knows at present."

"Telemetry is mission critical," Nate said. "Is it fixable?"

TELMU shrugged. "Too early to say. The Ku antenna should be easy. Don't know about the data bus. But let's assume so for now."

Nate scratched his neck furiously. "What a royal mess. So what have we got? Does anybody have any hard data?"

GNC cleared his throat. "Josh talked to Lex about the Guidance and Nav. They had a glitch in the IMU, but she resynced it with the secondary. Other than that, she's happy."

Josh nodded. "Lex is ready to rocket. I also talked to Kennedy, and he's done a pretty thorough checkout downstairs. All life-critical systems are fine, and he's pretty gung-ho to move on to the next phase. Bob is being . . . Bob. We had a question on the mechanical integrity of the solar panels, so I asked him to deploy those and test them thoroughly. That'll take a few hours."

"What about Valkerie? Have you talked to her?"

"She's worried about neck injuries and wants to examine the crew right away. Flight Med concurs and has put it on the schedule."

Nate leaned back in his chair. "Okay, obviously we're not gonna make the burn for Mars tonight. My question for you all is real simple. How long before they're ready to break orbit?"

"The bottleneck is currently in the solar panel checkout," EECOM said. "Once Dr. Kaganovski completes that procedure, we can pronounce the ship good to go."

"Assuming we get telemetry fixed," said TELMU.

Nate turned to the Flight Dynamics Officer. "What's our deadline?"

"We need to do the burn as soon as possible," FDO said. "Every day we wait is gonna cost us about eighty meters per second of delta-V, and we're marginal now. We should have launched a week ago."

"Tell that to NBC," Nate said. "Any other issues? Everybody comfortable with where we're at?"

Heads nodded around the room.

"Okay, people, go keep an eye on Maroon Team." Nate stood up. "As soon as we're ready to do that burn, I want to know about it."

Saturday, January 25, 2014, 8:00 P.M.
BOB

Bob studied the powerflow diagnostics. "Um, Houston, good news/bad news on the solar panels."

"Yeah, Bob, go ahead." Josh's voice cut through the static. "EECOM is begging me to give her some numbers."

"Okay, Panel B is good. It's operating at something like 99.8 percent of nominal." Bob took a sip of juice. "The real problem is with Panel A. I'm seeing just about 48 percent of nominal power. I deployed the CamBot out there to do a visual, and we have some serious damage near the middle of the array. I'm talking busted semiconductor, dangling wire, and structural damage."

The signal cut out. When it came back on, Josh was still swearing.

"I'm gonna estimate we're operating at a combined level of about 74 percent of rated power," Bob said.

"I think that's below our safety margin," Josh said.

Which means we don't fly. "That's affirm."

"I'll pass that information along, and we'll see if there's any way out

131

of that," Josh said. "Any other damage reports? We need to know everything, Bob. If you've got a broken toilet paper dispenser, we need to know, okay?"

"Roger that," Bob said. "Lex is monitoring the primary IMU to make sure it doesn't go hinky on us again. The Hampster should be sending his next report in a few minutes. Stand by."

Bob pushed off toward the stairwell. The mission might be dead, but nobody was going to say that he didn't give it his best effort. Bob floated down the stairwell and entered the brightly lit lower level. "Hampster! Shake a leg!"

Kennedy came around the corner, looking like he had a migraine. "Hey, Bo, sound don't travel in a vacuum. No matter how loud you yell, they aren't gonna hear you back in Houston."

"Sorry." Bob looked around. "Where's Valkerie?"

"She's working on the bioreactor. One of the hoses pulled loose, and we lost a little water."

"Like how much?" Bob pulled out his PDA to make a note.

"Not even enough to report," Kennedy said.

"Houston wants everything reported."

A pained expression crossed Kennedy's face. "Hold on." He floated back into the service bay, where a panel had been yanked out of the wall. "Valkerie, is the bioreactor fixed yet?"

"Just about."

Kennedy turned back to Bob. His face had taken on a slight greenish cast. "It's online again. There's nothing to report."

"Are you feeling okay?" Bob asked.

"I'm fine, and you're not my mother, so back off, all right?" Kennedy's eyes narrowed to slits. "Did you hear me? We're not going to report that bioreactor."

"Um . . ." Bob didn't want to make a scene, but he didn't feel comfortable, either.

"Look, they wanted a list of what's broken, right? As in present tense? So if it's fixed by the time you check in with Houston, you are not going to mention it. They've got enough to think about down there. How do the solar panels look?"

"Panel A is busted up pretty bad," Bob said. "Definitely not fixable. We'll be below margin on energy production when we hit Mars."

"We can turn off some of the flight computers," Kennedy said. "That's not going to be an issue."

How do you know? You haven't even seen the data. Face it, Hamp-ster. The mission is over. Bob scanned the checklist on his PDA. "Okay, what else do we have glitching?"

"Everything else is fine."

"What about the Reaction Control System? Have you checked it yet?"

"RCS is fine. There's a busted valve in one of the hypergolic fuel lines, but we've got enough redundancy that it's not an issue. We can easily keep station with fifty jets."

Bob narrowed his eyes. "Just one valve? We've got fifty-two jets."

"Okay, it's two valves, but we aren't going to bother reporting them to Houston. You know how Perez is—he'll freak out over any little thing. The solar panel is the main thing." Kennedy looked at his watch. "Time for my report." Kennedy pushed past Bob and ducked through the hatch of the stairwell.

Bob let him go. Denial. And after denial came resignation. Or was it acceptance? The Hampster would be all right. He just needed a little more time. They'd all work as hard as they could to salvage the mission, but in the end it wouldn't happen. It wasn't in the stars. Still, acceptance would be a whale of a lot easier knowing they'd given it everything they had.

Bob floated toward the lab. "Valkerie, I'm sorry about yelling . . ." He stopped outside the door. Soft tones drifted from the open chamber. Humming. No. Not humming. She was singing to herself. A heavy lump formed in his throat. He stopped himself at the door. She was busy. He could come back later. The apology would keep.

Bob hurried up the stairwell and floated back to the CommConsole. Kennedy was talking into the headset. "That's affirm, Houston. Holding steady at 80 percent nominal power."

Bob pulled himself over to look at the powerflow readings. Had something fixed itself?

"Roger that, Hampster. We're going to push back TMI until tomorrow morning. Noon at the latest." Josh's voice crackled over the comm speakers. "Valkerie's report has Flight Med in a tizzy. We've added med exams and a final systems check to the schedule. Oops, we're hitting Loss of Signal. Acquisition of Signal in six minutes—pick you up on TDRSS-east." Static filled the speaker.

"Hampster, that's 74 percent nominal power," Bob said.

Kennedy looked at the numbers again and let out a low whistle.

"You're right, Kaggo. I must have messed up the calculation. That was stupid. Is Valkerie done downstairs?"

"I didn't . . . um, she was still working when I left." Bob switched screens to check the ship's vitals. "Did you report the bioreactor and the RCS jets?"

Kennedy pulled out an aspirin packet and ripped it open. "I reported everything."

Bob turned his head sharply to look at Kennedy. *Did that mean yes or no?*

"You wouldn't believe the headache I've got." Kennedy swallowed the aspirin dry. "I need to take a few minutes' break, crew. Lex, you're in charge of the ship." He disappeared into his cabin.

CHAPTER 13

Saturday, January 25, 2014, 10:00 P.M.
VALKERIE

Valkerie shook a tiny drop of water loose from the tip of her pipette and let it hang shimmering in the air. She touched it with a glass slide, and it stuck to the charged surface of the glass. Clipping the slide under the microscope, she examined the free-floating microorganisms. Everything looked fine. Their water-recycling bioreactor was good to go. She looked up from the scope and checked it off her list.

Kennedy poked his head into the lab. "Computer systems are all 100 percent."

"What?"

"I've checked the hull, the scrubbers, the fuel cells, RCS, navigation.... Everything's fine. Nothing to worry about."

"Then why are you telling—"

Kennedy disappeared. She listened as he bumped and thumped his way down the circular corridor. Something was definitely wrong. In the year and a half that she'd trained with him, never once had his actions been so erratic—even when he was drunk. He was really starting to scare her.

And why was he reporting every little thing to *her*? She wasn't the flight engineer. She had a feeling that it had to do with the spill. But if he didn't want her to know what was on the wall, wasn't that his business?

Maybe he just had a headache. Something two aspirin and a . . . Valkerie looked at her watch. Oh no! She didn't have her gear together, and she was supposed to start Bob's physical in three minutes.

135

Valkerie dabbed the slide dry with her sleeve and ricocheted her way down the hall and up the stairwell. Lex was hovering over the Nav-Console, typing away.

"Where's Bob?"

Lex didn't look up. "In his cabin."

"So how are you doing? Are you feeling okay?" Valkerie pulled out the med supply bin and started stuffing supplies in the med kit.

"I'm fine."

"It was a pretty rough launch." Valkerie tested a stethoscope and clamped it around her neck. "Any headaches? Dizziness?"

"Listen, Valkerie." Lex pushed herself back from the console. "I've got a tight schedule to keep to—and that schedule doesn't have me down for a med exam until 2300 hours."

"I'm sorry. I just thought I'd—"

"If this ship isn't in tip-top shape soon, Houston is going to start having second thoughts. We've got a ton of work to do, and we're running out of time. And your little med exams aren't helping."

Valkerie felt like she had been slapped. "I'm sorry. I'm just trying to do my job." She retreated around the stairwell to the crew's quarters.

She pushed herself through the corridor and grabbed a ceiling strap outside Bob's door. First Kennedy and now Lex. Was it her or just them?

"Come in." Bob's voice sounded loud and clear through the thin plastic door.

Valkerie sucked in her breath. Had she made that much noise? Did he know how long she had been there?

"Hey, Bob. Ready for your med exam?"

"Sure. Come on in."

Valkerie hesitated. It had been a long time since her intern days. It was going to be hard to get back that sense of professional detachment. And it didn't help that she was starting out with a house call.

She opened the door and floated awkwardly into the tiny cabin. Bob was leaning over his computer station. His legs were hooked around two pull-down bars that served as a zero-g chair.

"How are we doing?" Valkerie asked.

Bob pressed his hands to his eyes. He looked exhausted. "I hope I'm missing something simple, but the data bus diagnostics are not looking good. I was just checking the manuals and . . ." He shook his head.

Valkerie nodded. "Um, do you mind if I ask you a question while you work?"

"You just did."

"I'm sorry. If you're busy, I can come back later." Valkerie turned toward the door.

"No, I'm fine. Really. I'm sick of this manual. You may doctor at will." Bob turned to face her. He didn't seem angry.

"What's wrong? You look like you're expecting me to sprout fangs," he said with a grin.

"To be honest, after dealing with Kennedy and Lex, fangs wouldn't be that bad."

"I've noticed. That's why I'm hiding in here. If Lex was wound any tighter, we could use her as a NavGyro."

Valkerie nodded and pulled down the stethoscope that floated out from her neck. "So . . . how are you feeling?"

"A little tired of having to go to the bathroom every fifteen minutes, but fine other than that."

"It'll taper off soon. All that fluid has to go somewhere. You don't have gravity pulling it down into your legs anymore."

Bob's face clouded.

Valkerie regretted her words immediately. He knew that. Of course he knew that. Why did she have to be so patronizing? Why did . . .

"Valkerie. I've been wanting to . . . I really need to apologize for barking at you this afternoon after MECO. I was way out of line."

"Um, sure . . ." Valkerie didn't know what to say.

Bob stared up at her. Waiting. She dropped her eyes, fidgeting with her stethoscope.

"So! How's your neck? Any headaches?"

Bob shook his head.

"Let me just check." She anchored her feet to a Velcro strip and reached a hand to Bob's shoulder. His muscles tensed at her touch.

"The launch really did a number on your back. Your shoulders are as tight as steel-belted radials." Valkerie started kneading his shoulders. "Are you sure you haven't been bothered by headaches?"

"Maybe a little." Bob rolled his shoulders and rotated his head in a slow circle. "This feels . . . nice."

Good, his voice was mellowing. He was beginning to relax. "Bob, I need your advice."

"Shoot."

"How long have you known Kennedy?"

"About eight years. Why?" His voice was cautious.

"Oh, no reason. Just wanted to know more about him." Valkerie worked at a knot in his back. "So I take it you know him pretty well?"

Bob nodded.

"What's he like? You know, his character ... I mean is he the kind of guy you can depend on? Is he a good friend?"

"From what I hear, he's pretty typical for a navy pilot. They kind of live by their own code. You could trust him with your life—just don't ask him to watch your beer."

Valkerie chuckled. "Okay, I need to get your blood pressure and listen to your lungs." She pulled a sphygmomanometer out of her bag. "Then I'll check your eyes and ears and get out of your way."

Bob watched her intently as she wrapped the cuff around his arm and pumped it up. A barely perceptible smile danced at the corners of his mouth—as if he knew something she didn't. Something important.

"What's Kennedy's family like? Has he ever been married?"

Bob's smile wilted into a frown. "Why are you so interested in Kennedy all of a sudden?"

"One-forty over sixty. Normal for this soon after launch." Valkerie put the cuff away and pulled out her ophthalmoscope. "I've just been thinking about him lately. He really ... wants to make this mission work."

"What about me? I want to make it work too."

Valkerie checked Bob's eyes. "Sure, but you're not—you know—as much of a gunner."

"A gunner isn't going to get us to Mars. If there's a problem, we've got to know about it. It's my job—"

"I agree. Being cautious is very important. It's just that Kennedy—"

"Kennedy is cautious too, you know. He doesn't always play the foolhardy commander. He can be downright obnoxious in his attention to detail."

"So you'd say he's cautious?"

"Sure, he just does a better job hiding it."

"That makes me feel a lot better."

"What?" Bob turned to stare at her.

Valkerie examined Bob's ears. They seemed fine

"So how does he feel about women?"

"Kennedy? Are you kidding?" Bob gave a short laugh. "He's a total—well, let's just say that he sees a lot of women."

"He's not threatened by them? Do you think he looks down on women?"

"Valkerie, trust me. Forget about Kennedy. He's not worth worrying about."

"Are you sure?"

"Trust me."

Valkerie nodded. Maybe Bob was right. Maybe she was just being paranoid. Maybe Kennedy's behavior was normal for a commander on a mission. Speaking of which. She looked at her watch.

"I've got to go. I'm five minutes late for Kennedy's exam."

"What's the rush? You were late for my exam too. I thought you wanted to ask my advice."

"Never mind. It's probably all in my head." She packed up her bag and propelled herself to the door with a push from her fingertips. "Okay, I'll be back later with something to loosen up those trapeziuses. In the meantime, get some rest."

Bob shook his head. "I've got a schedule to meet."

"Take an hour off," Valkerie said. "Doctor's orders. You're going to lose efficiency unless you get some rest." She pushed out into the hallway before he could argue.

Saturday, January 25, 2014, 10:00 P.M.

NATE

Nate strode into Mission Control. "Okay, Gold Team! I need another powwow!"

The team left their stations behind Maroon Team and headed for the door. Incredible! They were six hours into the Maroon Team shift, and not one of them had gone home. Which was why they were Gold Team.

The team settled into chairs in the conference room with little chit-chat. EECOM handed Nate a report. "I just received this from my support team. It's an analysis of the energy budget we are going to use on the mission."

"If we continue the mission," Nate said.

"What do you mean, *if?*" Josh jumped up and began pacing. "We have to continue."

"I know that, and you know that, but somebody forgot to explain it to Mother Nature." Nate opened the report and stared at it blankly.

"Okay, I need your frank opinions, people. Are we good to go? Blunt opinions—don't sugarcoat this for me. Josh, if you were on that ship, knowing what you know, would you abort the mission?"

"No way."

"Why?"

"It's real simple," Josh said. "Every life-critical system is known to be good, with a working backup and a working fail-operational option. So our team can safely go."

"What about mission-critical systems?" Nate asked. "Any word on the telemetry?"

TELMU shook his head. "Bob's been working on the data bus, but no joy yet."

"The primary IMU was glitching, right? Without that, our kids don't know where they are."

"It glitched *once*," GNC said. "Josh verified that with Lex. It glitched once, and she synced it with the secondary."

"Any other problems? Reaction Control? Fuel cells?"

"Both fine," Josh said. "I talked to the Hampster in person, and he verified that."

Nate narrowed his eyes. "Where was Bob?"

"Reading manuals in his cabin. Lex said he's still a bit queasy."

"Any medical problems besides space sickness?"

"Valkerie's not done with the exams. We won't get her report until midnight."

Nate stared at the energy budget report. *I don't have time to read this thing.* "Okay, EECOM, give me the rundown on this. In plain English. I need to fill in Perez and the president in an hour."

EECOM folded her hands on the table in front of her. "The solar panels are designed to produce 125 percent of the nominal energy requirements at the worst-case distance from the sun, which is Mars at a distance of 1.67 astronomical units from the sun. We've lost a fraction of our power. According to Commander Hampton, we've lost 20 percent. Dr. Kaganovski said it was 26 percent, but I believe he gave a pessimistic number."

"Sounds like Kaggo. So we've got 80 percent of 125 percent. You're telling me we have no margin?"

"Incorrect," EECOM said. "Mars moves in an elliptical orbit with moderate eccentricity. The greatest distance the Hab will reach from the sun during this mission is only 1.52 AUs. Since the solar power function is an inverse-square function of radial distance, the solar arrays will produce a decreasing amount of power until they reach Mars, at which point they will *still* be producing 11 percent more power than required, even with Dr. Kaganovski's pessimistic numbers. So we have a margin all the way. We are good to go."

Nate wondered how he was going to translate that geek-speak to the president. "Any reason *not* to continue the mission?"

"None that I am aware of." EECOM looked to Josh and the others.

Heads shook all around the table. "Ditto." "My systems are good." "Let's boogie."

Nate shook out an antacid tablet and chugged it down with the last tepid dregs of his coffee. "When are we going to get back telemetry? I don't like having the console boys and girls flying blind."

"Once they solve the data bus problems, we can patch together a data channel through the S-band," TELMU said.

"So our data rate is gonna be, what, one percent of normal?"

"In *principle*, we could do the whole mission at low bandwidth if we have to," TELMU said. "It worked with the Galileo probe. It was way hard, but they ran the mission."

"When are we gonna fix the Ku-band antenna?"

TELMU leaned forward. "Not before the TMI burn, that's for sure. It's a simple fix, but we haven't got time to do a spacewalk before tomorrow noon, and that's when we need to do the burn. Right, FDO?"

The Flight Dynamics Officer nodded. "If we want to land on July fourth."

"We have to land on July fourth," Nate said.

EECOM's eyes narrowed. "With respect, sir, nobody is holding a gun to our heads."

"We're still in the hole," Nate said. "We're sitting on a pile of debts with more zeros than you want to think about."

"We made a pile on the launch," Josh said.

"We made diddly. Launches are a dime a dozen. This country wants to see flags and footprints in red dirt." Nate leaned back in his chair and fiddled with his empty coffee cup. "We knocked a G-bill off our debt. We've got 3.8 left to pay down. If we hit a home run on July fourth, we might break even."

"Sir, what happens if we scrub the mission?" EECOM asked.

"Then we scrub the Ares program, because we're out of business for good," Nate said. "Lock, stock, and Ku antenna."

VALKERIE

Valkerie pushed over to the command center. Lex was stationed behind one of the computers going through a system check with Houston.

"Where's Kennedy?" Valkerie asked.

Lex motioned to the stairway.

Valkerie looked at her watch. Eight minutes behind schedule. The controllers weren't going to be happy. She hurried down the stair tube and emerged into the lower level. A hissing noise directed her around the stair column to the locker cabin. Kennedy was floating sideways beside an open panel in the back of the room. He was welding a valve on a pipe with a small oxyacetylene torch.

Valkerie waited for Kennedy to finish the weld. "Nobody said anything about a damaged pipe."

Kennedy started—like a child caught with his hand in the cookie jar. "It's just a precaution. It looked a little loose, so I decided to reinforce it."

"Right." *That's why it was leaking all over the wall.* What was it with this guy? He was almost suicidal in his zeal to save the mission.

Valkerie averted her eyes as Kennedy started a new weld. "As soon as you're done, I need you to stop by the Med Center for your physical."

"Impossible. My schedule for the next three and a half hours is mapped out to the last minute."

"So repairing that pipe was on your schedule?"

"No. I was scheduled for a medical exam, but the *doctor* didn't bother to show up."

"Well the *doctor* is here now, and I have orders to check you out."

"You *had* orders. Right now your orders are to help Bob reel the solar panels in." Kennedy turned off the torch and threw back his mask.

"I've ordered Bob to get some rest. He's been going hard almost ten hours straight."

"You what? Where do you come off giving orders?" Kennedy snapped on the torch. "Get this straight. We've got one goal and one goal only: to get this ship to Mars and back. Am I making myself clear?" Kennedy dipped the torch so that it pointed toward Valkerie. She could feel the heat of the flame on her face.

"My first duty . . ." Valkerie fought to control her voice. ". . . is to the safety of the crew." She turned and pushed off for the stairwell.

"And repairing the ship quickly is the best way to ensure our safety." Kennedy's voice rang out behind her.

Valkerie jumped up the stairwell and swung through the door. Ignoring Lex's questioning look, she headed for her cabin and closed the door behind her.

She floated in the darkness, waiting for the fit of trembling to subside. *He threatened me. He actually threatened me.* She still couldn't believe it. What had happened to the easygoing guy she had trained with? Something was wrong. Bad wrong.

She pulled her headset off the Velcro strip on the wall. Josh was going to hear about this. No way was she flying to Mars until Kennedy had a complete checkup—medical and psychological.

CHAPTER 14

Bob was dreaming about a little house with a white picket fence when Lex woke him up. "Hey, Kaggo? Josh wants to talk to you."

Bob rubbed his eyes. "Can't it wait? Valkerie told me to get a little shut-eye."

Lex shook her head. "Josh says it's important. He wants you to take it on the encrypted comm link here in your quarters." She disappeared without waiting for a reply.

What was this all about? It had to be bad news. Bob closed the door and put on his comm headset. "Josh, this is Bob."

"Kaggo, this is Josh. How you doing up there? Keeping busy?"

Bob relaxed a little. Just hearing Josh's voice made him feel that somewhere down there was a human being who actually cared about him more than the mission. "It's been a little busy, but we're getting things under control. Wish you were up here, buddy."

"Me too, Kaggo, but somebody has to look after you guys down here, right?"

Bob began fidgeting. "So . . . um, what's up? Why the private comm link?"

"First off, this is just between me and you, all right?" Josh's voice sounded tight. "Completely off the record, and nobody else will ever know anything about this. Okay?"

Bob felt his pulse speed up a notch. *Why the cloak-and-dagger?* "Sure, Josh."

"I need you to do something tough, Kaggo, so if this gets a little uncomfortable, I'm sorry, but I really need to know."

"This is a little late for me to get counseling for my unhappy child-hood."

Josh didn't laugh. "What's your read on Kennedy? Is he . . . doing okay? What's his mental state?"

What the devil? Bob tried to think. Did somebody seriously think Kennedy might be off-balance? "The Hampster's doing pretty good, ac-tually. He had a little space-sickness early on, but not as bad as Lex and me. And he's way less uptight than I am about the ship. Not that there's any serious problems with the ship, but you know, I'm always way cau-tious." *Good grief, I'm babbling.*

Silence.

"I'm listening," Josh said.

Bob's heart was pounding now. What did Josh want to hear? "You know, we're all pretty tired up here. Stressed. That was a horrible launch, you want my opinion. Next time, I say we scuttle the launch if it's that windy, okay?"

"Sure, Bob." A slight pause. "How's Valkerie doing?"

"She's . . . okay. She kind of freaked during the launch—and I don't blame her."

"So I heard."

"Did Lex tell you that?"

"Sorry, I can't say."

"But she's calmed way down since then. Even Kennedy's been kind of jumpy, and he's done a bazillion shuttle missions. Josh, what's the big deal here? You worried about Kennedy? Or Valkerie?"

"I'm just concerned. About all of you."

Bob closed his eyes. Josh had to be fibbing. Obviously, he was more than a little concerned. Otherwise, why the encrypted comm link?

"So . . . how *is* Kennedy holding up?"

"Listen, I think the Hampster's doing as good as any of us, maybe better. We're all a little tired and cranky, that's all. Valkerie even ordered me to take twenty winks."

"That's it? You kids just need naps and you'll be fine?"

"Yeah, that's it."

"Gotcha. Okay, that's all I wanted to know." Short pause. Then, in a casual voice, "How's Valkerie doing?"

You asked that already. Bob cleared his throat. "She looks pretty frazzled, if you ask me."

"Frazzled? Give me some examples." Josh sounded worried again.

"Well, you know, she's tired. And she's been after Kennedy. Keeps checking on him, and he's busy, and—"

"What kind of checking? Does she seem suspicious? Paranoid?"

What in blazes was this all about? Had Kennedy told them Valkerie was weirding out? Or vice versa? Bob cleared his throat. "No, I wouldn't call her paranoid. Tired, yes, like the rest of us. We got up at 5:00 A.M. Houston time, and it's almost midnight now."

"Uh-huh."

"Listen, Josh, I need to know what's going on here. Isn't this a little late to be doing the flight-surgeon head games? We're already launched, for crying out loud. We're all okay. Tired, yeah. A little queasy from Space Adaptation Sickness. But we'll be fine once we get a little rest."

Silence.

"Okay, Josh? Are you listening?"

"Let me make sure of two things," Josh said. "And I'm going to be very blunt here, so I want you to forget I asked, five seconds after you answer. First, are you certain Kennedy is fit for command?"

Bob swallowed. So that was the crux of all this. "Sure, Josh. Kennedy is good to go." *I hope. Because whether we dock with ISS or do that burn for Mars, Kennedy's going to be driving the bus.*

"Second, is Valkerie showing any signs of paranoia?"

"Valkerie is fine," Bob said.

"Great." Josh sounded relieved. "How's the ship? Any problems besides that solar panel and telemetry?"

"Nothing important. A few glitches. I've got 'em mostly resolved." Bob closed his eyes. There he went with the can-do NASA-speak again. Any more of that and Nate might send them all to Mars despite the condition of the ship.

Bob smiled. Not likely. Not with Kennedy and Valkerie already under the scrutiny of Flight Med. He might as well give the flight docs his name and Lex's too. At this point none of them were feeling too chipper.

Saturday, January 25, 2014, 11:45 A.M.

NATE

Nate took off his headset and nodded to Josh. "Good job. What's your assessment?"

"I trust Bob's judgment," Josh said. "Kennedy and Valkerie just had a little tiff. That's all."

"And her concerns about Kennedy? What do we do with that?"

Josh shook his head. "She's tired. Listen, Nate, we've driven these people for eighteen months, and this was supposed to be their big day in the sun, and then we went and gave them a lousy launch. Frankly, I'm not surprised they're having a little friction."

Nate's gut was burning from twenty hours of coffee and donuts. "We've got the go/no-go meeting in eight hours. You know the team better than anyone else. Is there any psychological reason we might want to bail out of the mission?"

Josh thought for a minute. "None. As long as the ship's fine, the crew is good to go."

"You'd better be right," Nate said. "Because once we do that burn, we're committed. There's no off-ramp for the next three hundred million miles."

Sunday, January 26, 2014, 1:30 A.M.

BOB

Bob's brain was buzzing with fatigue, and he could not run another data-bus diagnostic, even if they held a gun to his head. He floated up to the NavConsole and hooked his legs on the bar to anchor himself.

It was now 1:30 A.M., and Valkerie and Kennedy had been assigned to catch a few Zs. Bob checked that the doors to their sleeping quarters were shut. "Lex, what's up with those two?"

Lex gave him a knowing look. "I had an . . . interesting conversation with Josh."

"So did I." Bob studied her closely. "Any idea what started that?"

Lex shrugged. "Who knows? The flight doc probably had too much time on his hands and started reading things in that weren't there. I think Kennedy's fighting a migraine or something. Maybe that launch shook a few screws loose. He's tired, I can see that."

"What about you?" Bob asked. "You tired?"

"Let me tell you about tired," Lex said. "Tired is when you're nine hours into the Ironman, you've still got twelve miles of a marathon left to run, you've got a blister the size of a quarter on your right heel, and your calves are cramping. No, I'm not tired."

"I'm tired," Bob said.

Lex nodded pensively. "How's the ship doing? Any show-stoppers?"

"Yeah, our telemetry is gonna be out for who knows how long. Nate won't let us fly like that."

"We could go a few days without telemetry," Lex said. "After all, we're designed to be autonomous. By the time we hit Mars, the round-trip radio time will be about twenty minutes, so telemetry isn't exactly mission critical. I want the bottom line. Ignoring telemetry, are we good to go? You're the only one who really knows this ship, Kaggo."

"If you'd asked me five hours ago, I'd have said no way. Now?" Bob shrugged. "What if I were to tell you I just plain don't know? What if—"

"Don't give me what-ifs," Lex said. "Just tell me your opinion. Because whatever you say, I'm with you." She closed her eyes, then brushed at them with the palms of her hands. "But I'll tell you something. There are only two things I've ever really wanted to do in my life. Go to the Olympics. And go to Mars."

"The Olympics?"

She nodded, swallowed hard. "Volleyball. I don't usually tell people this, but I could have been on the team for the 2000 games in Sydney. Broke an ankle three weeks before tryouts and had to miss out. I was going to try again in 2004."

"And. . . ?"

"And when 2004 came around, I was two years into my Ph.D. at Stanford and racing the clock to finish so I could apply for ASCAN training. There was no way I was going to miss Mars, not even for the Olympics."

"You knew you wanted to go to Mars way back then?"

"Ever since I was eight years old." Lex opened her eyes. They were wet and bright and full of fire. "Take me to Mars, Bob."

Sunday, January 26, 2014, 8:00 A.M.

NATE

It was 8:00 A.M., and the mood in the conference room was tense. "Okay, Gold Team, I need your verdicts." Nate rapped on the conference room table. "EECOM?"

"EECOM is go."

GNC nodded. "No problems on Guidance and Nav."

"Flight Dynamics works," said FDO.

Perez stepped forward "What's our basis for all this? We don't have telemetry, right? So how do we know what's good and what's not?"

"Our basis is the say-so of Kennedy Hampton and Bob Kaganovski," Nate said. "TELMU, when is telemetry coming back online?"

"Good news on that," TELMU said. "It's mostly fixed. They are not gonna be done before the TMI burn, but they're talking just a few more hours of work. Based on that, I'm go."

"Fine," said Perez. "Is everyone comfortable with this flight?"

Heads nodded around the table.

"Okay, here's what we'll do, then," Perez said. "We'll talk to the crew and get their opinions. But it has to be unanimous to go. The world does not end if we scrub the mission."

"Of course." Nate kept his face perfectly straight, but his heart was hammering out a different message in Morse code on his rib cage.

Dead wrong, Dr. Perez. Dead wrong.

Sunday, January 26, 2014, 10:00 A.M.

BOB

Bob was sweating. The four of them huddled around the radio mike, about to decide the fate of the mission.

"Ares 10, this is Houston." Josh's voice crackled with tension. "I have Dr. Perez and Mr. Harrington here with me. Do you copy?"

"Copy, Houston, this is CDR," said Kennedy. "What's your verdict?"

"Our understanding is that you've got failures on two systems—the solar panels and the telemetry. Is that correct?"

"That is correct," Kennedy said. "The solar panels are operating at approximately 80 percent."

Bob leaned closer to the mike. "That's 74 percent."

"Bob's right," Kennedy said. "But EECOM tells me we had a lot of margin because of the mission geometry, so that's not an issue. As noted, we have a problem with the telemetry system, but we believe it can be fixed with a spacewalk."

"Dr. Kaganovski, we need your assessment." Perez's voice.

"Actually we have two problems with the telemetry system. The data bus is—"

"I've got it mostly fixed already," Kennedy interjected.

Bob raised his eyebrows and stared at Kennedy.

"While you were sleeping." Kennedy grinned. "The problem wasn't as bad as it looked at first. I'll need your help to wrap it up, but it's a couple hours' more work."

"Anything else, Kaggo?" Josh sounded tense.

Bob hesitated. He'd really have liked to have looked at the data bus himself. "Okay, other than the solar panels and the telemetry, I don't see that there are any significant issues with critical systems that can't be worked around."

"Bob, what about noncritical systems?" Josh asked. "Do you have anything else to report?"

A tremor ran around the four astronauts. Kennedy handed the mike to Bob, his face tight. Lex's bright eyes stayed glued on Bob. Fear flickered across Valkerie's face. And something else. Bob tried to place it.

Trust. That was it. Valkerie trusted him. The thought terrified him. All of them were looking to him for reassurance.

And he didn't know. He had the diagnostics on every system on the ship. They all looked good, but . . . how could he be sure?

Bob scratched his nose. "Houston, the ship is clearly not at a hundred percent. We have two known problems, and it's possible that there are others."

"Ares 10, we need to make a go/no-go decision soon," Josh said. "We can't afford to let you take days in orbit to check everything out. The longer we wait, the faster you'll have to go to make Mars on our target date. FDO says the orbital mechanics are getting worse by the hour. Are there *any* known issues at all in life-critical systems?"

Bob didn't need to think to answer that. "Negative."

"Are there any other known problems in mission-critical systems?"

"Negative."

"Ares 10, we are giving a provisional go to the mission. But we need a go/no-go decision from each of you. It must be unanimous to go. If not, we can dock you with the ISS and bring you home on a shuttle. We do not have to run this mission. Is that clear?"

The four astronauts looked at one another. "Clear." "Affirmative." "Yes." "Very clear."

"Dr. Ohta, go or no-go?"

"Go!"

"Dr. Kaganovski, go or no-go?"

Kennedy reached for the mike, muttering, "Go, go, go!"

Bob yanked it away. As CDR, Kennedy would give his vote last.

Kennedy grumbled something and let go of the mike.

Bob wiped the sweat from his forehead. Why was he so afraid? Other than the close call at the launch, there was no rational reason for it. With telemetry all but fixed, the only real problem was one bad solar panel. They could live with that—even if the whole panel died, they could make Mars by cutting back to emergency power levels. There was some risk. But he had accepted a certain amount of risk when he signed up for ASCAN training, hadn't he? This wasn't exactly a job in accounting. He couldn't very well back out now just because there was a risk of something unknown going wrong. It wouldn't be right. Could he really waste billions of taxpayer dollars just because he was afraid? What would people think?

Bob glanced at Valkerie. She frowned down at the table, avoiding everyone else's eyes. He realized she wasn't going to vote go. She had radioed Houston with some kind of concern about Kennedy. It had to be her. So it didn't matter what he voted. They weren't going to Mars. It was as simple as that.

"Go," Bob said.

"Dr. Jansen, go or no-go?"

Valkerie looked paralyzed with fright.

Lex put a hand on Valkerie's shoulder. Kennedy gave her an encouraging smile. Bob kept his face expressionless, calm. But inside, his guts were churning.

"Dr. Jansen, go or no-go?"

Valkerie was trembling all over.

"Dr. Jansen, go or no-go?"

Valkerie cleared her throat again. "Before I decide, could I ask a few questions?"

Lex's face tightened. She wasn't known for being a good loser. Bob wondered what she'd do when Valkerie voted no-go.

"Go ahead, Valkerie," Kennedy said. "Take your time. Ask as many questions as you like."

Valkerie stared at him. She looked surprised. Confused.

"My first question is for Josh. Josh, what do you think about the concerns I expressed earlier? What's your honest opinion—as a friend?"

"Valkerie, I want you to know that I took your concerns very seriously," Josh said. "I investigated them myself, and although I can't be certain, I'm convinced that what you observed was due to the extreme stress of the moment. I don't think the problem will be repeated."

Valkerie nodded thoughtfully and turned to Bob. "My second question is for Bob. Bob, are you absolutely sure that this ship is sound?"

Great. Dump it all back in my lap. Of course I'm not sure. Who's sure about anything in life? "All I can do is repeat what you already heard. We have some problems, but I voted go. The riskiest parts of a mission are the launch and reentry. We survived a tough launch without busting up. I believe the worst is behind us." Bob shrugged. What more could he say?

Valkerie sighed and turned to Kennedy. "My last question is for Kennedy. What happens when I vote no-go?"

Lex sucked in her breath and her face went rigid. Kennedy put a hand on her arm. She shut her mouth and stared at Valkerie with fiery eyes.

Kennedy shook his head and looked steadily at Valkerie. "I wouldn't like that decision, but I can't ask you to risk your life against your will. So if you vote no-go, we'll abort the mission. Possibly, some of us might fly to Mars on a later mission, but you are aware of the budgetary constraints. There probably won't be a next mission."

Valkerie nodded pensively and looked around the circle at their faces. Silence hung heavy on the group. Bob held his breath.

"In that case I vote . . . go."

Sunday, January 26, 2014, Noon
VALKERIE

"Stand by for trans-Mars injection in one minute, thirty-five seconds." Kennedy's voice boomed through the flight deck of the Hab.

Valkerie leaned back in her flight chair. This was it. The flight computers were set. All they had to do was initiate a command sequence, and they'd be on Mars on July fourth. *If* the ship didn't fall apart, and *if* the guidance systems didn't miss the planet, and *if* they didn't kill each other first.

She pulled her harness tighter to force herself down into the seat. It was hard to sit in zero-g. Without gravity the body didn't want to bend.

The others talked among themselves in hushed voices. They had pretty much left her alone since the meeting. As if they were afraid she would change her mind if they disturbed her. Hopefully they'd loosen up after the burn—after they were committed.

But what if they didn't? Could she stand two and a half years with Kennedy? Had she made the right decision? Valkerie didn't know anymore. She had been so sure that Kennedy was going to be a problem, but he seemed fine now. Mostly . . .

"TMI in thirty seconds."

Dear God, please keep us safe. Please don't let anything happen. A pang of guilt stabbed her conscience. With all the agonizing she had done, had she even prayed once for guidance? It had all happened so fast, she couldn't remember. But wasn't God in control whether she prayed or not? Surely He wouldn't bring her this far just to have her quit and let everybody down. They had spent billions of dollars to get to this point in the mission. To quit would have meant her career.

"TMI in fifteen seconds."

God, please help this to be the right decision. Please keep us safe.

"Five, four, three, two, one. Firing main engine."

Valkerie was pushed back into her seat. Not the gorilla-on-your-chest pressure of launch, but after a day of weightlessness, it felt just as intense.

Her senses reeled as what had been forward suddenly became up, and what had been behind suddenly became down.

Kennedy's voice filled her mind as he counted off the seconds. "TMI plus ten . . . TMI plus twenty."

Please God, help us. Please don't let this be too late. Please . . .

"TMI plus one eighty. TMI plus one ninety." Kennedy paused. Valkerie's heart fluttered.

"I hope nobody wants to go back, ladies and gentleman, because we are past the point of no return."

PART III

The Belly of the Beast

"As aviators and test pilots had discovered since the days of cloth and wood biplanes, cataclysmic accidents in any kind of craft are almost never caused by one catastrophic equipment failure; rather, they are inevitably the result of a series of separate, far smaller failures, none of which could do any real harm by themselves, but all of which, taken together, can be more than enough to slap even the most experienced pilot out of the sky."

JIM LOVELL, COMMANDER OF APOLLO 13 MISSION

"Psychiatrists and psychologists agree that piloted missions to Mars may well give rise to behavioral aberrations among the crew as have been seen on Earth in conditions of stress and isolation over long periods of time. . . . At the present time, little effort has been spent developing techniques for crew selection that will adequately guarantee psychological stability on a voyage to Mars and back."

NASA's MARS REFERENCE MISSION DOCUMENT

CHAPTER 15

Thursday, April 3, 2014, 5:00 P.M.
VALKERIE

Valkerie smiled into the handheld camera, squinting against its light. Bob hadn't taken the camera off her for more than a minute during the entire press conference. What was wrong with him? Did he like watching her squirm? He'd better be planning to edit the tape before sending it back to Earth. They were now more than two months into the mission, and the radio delay had grown to almost four minutes—too long to hold a press conference in real time, even if their Ku-band antenna had been working.

Bob pressed the Play button, and they listened to the next pre-recorded question from the NASA moderator down on Earth. "Another question for Dr. Jansen," the moderator's voice filled the main cabin. "Jon Simon, a sixth grader from Placentia, California, would like to know: How are you going to get back home?"

Lex twisted in her seat. Kennedy cleared his throat impatiently. Valkerie turned toward them and gave an apologetic shrug. This was the third question in a row directed at her. The others were starting to get irritated, but what could she do?

Valkerie forced a smile for the camera. "As you know, Jon, we don't have the rocket fuel to turn around. The only way we can get home now is to go on to Mars first. We have a nice comfy module waiting for us there on the surface of the planet. That'll be our home for about a year and a half. Then we'll fly a small rocket up to join the Earth Return Vehicle that's already waiting in orbit around Mars. We'll come home in that. I know it all sounds very complicated, but Commander Hampton is a very experienced pilot. He'll get us home safe and sound. Don't you worry."

Bob pressed the button for the next question. "A question for Dr. Ohta, from fourth grader April Townes, in Atlanta, Georgia. She would like to know: Are you ever afraid?"

Valkerie sighed with relief as Bob turned the camera to Lex.

"No way!" Lex leaned forward, her back straight as an arrow. "I love it up here. I've been waiting all my life to go to Mars. We're going to learn how Mars was formed and whether there's ever been any life there. And most importantly, we're going to find out whether humans can turn Mars into a New World where you, April, might come to live someday."

Bob pressed the button again. "The next question is for Commander Hampton, from eighth grader Jason McCready in Denver, Colorado: Are you going to be weightless for the entire journey to Mars, and if so, will that cause you any problems when you get there?"

Kennedy flashed a big smile at the camera. "When we left Earth orbit two months ago, we had intended to reel out our last rocket stage on a long tether and set the ship spinning around it. The centrifugal force would feel just about like gravity to us. We haven't been able to do that yet because of all the plumbing problems. Having gravity would just make things worse. But we're almost done fixing those problems, and Dr. Kaganovski has finally patched up our data bus. Tomorrow we're planning a spacewalk to fix our broken antenna. After the spacewalk we'll do our centrifugal force trick and then we'll have gravity for the rest of the trip. So we don't expect any problems, um, Jay, when we reach Mars. We should be in great condition."

Bob pressed the button again. "The next question is from Shannon Winslet, a third grader from Rock Hill, South Carolina. Dr. Jansen, what's it like going to the bathroom in space?"

Valkerie felt the heat rise to her face. "As you can imagine, going to the bathroom in space can be a challenge at times. Zero gravity makes a lot of things more difficult. Exercise, for example . . ."

Kennedy leaned in front of Valkerie. "Shannon, our toilet here on Ares 10 is specially designed with foot stirrups and clamps to hold you down. The Ares 10 isn't the only thing that gets launched by jet propulsion. Want to see our toilet? If Dr. Kaganovski will just follow me with the camera, I'll be happy to show you our bathroom. It's only the size of a small closet, but it gets the job done."

Valkerie shut her eyes and let herself go limp the second Bob took the camera off her. She hung motionless in the air, every bone in her body tingling with fatigue. The last two months had been a nightmare— a mad scramble to fix one piece of broken equipment after another. The cooling system had started leaking right after trans-Mars injection— right behind the panel that Kennedy had supposedly spilled his juice on. And working on cooling systems was no picnic. She'd ingested enough antifreeze to keep her warm on Pluto.

Then there was the data bus. Kennedy had said it would be an easy fix. What a joke. Bob didn't finish it until this morning—after eight weeks of painstaking work. Which meant it *finally* made sense to repair the Ku antenna. For the moment they could only transmit data over the S-band, and that would take forever—especially for compressed video. Americans wouldn't get their first glimpse of their tax dollars at work until tomorrow night. Valkerie wondered if anyone would think the video was worth the cost.

Kennedy's voice got louder. They were coming back. Valkerie wind-milled her arms and kicked her legs, but she was too far away from the floor to push off. She couldn't reach the ceiling either.

"Hey, Bob, get in here, quick!" Kennedy's shout shot up her spine like an electric shock.

Valkerie stopped her flailing and hung motionless in the air. She wasn't going to struggle. Wouldn't give him the satisfaction.

"Hi, Valkerie," Kennedy beamed and stepped in closer. "Mind telling our audience why you're lying sideways?"

"I'm not sideways, you are." Valkerie smiled at the camera.

"Are you stuck? Would you like a hand?" Kennedy extended his hand with exaggerated formality.

"No, thank you. I'll drift to the ceiling eventually. Are there any more questions?"

Bob clicked the button. "Dr. Jansen." The moderator's voice. "Fifth grader Liz Smith from Ogden, Kansas, wants to know if it's possible that the first man on Mars might be a woman? If so, would you like to be first? And the same question goes for Dr. Ohta."

Valkerie looked to Kennedy and Lex. She felt her cheeks flushing again. What could she say? Of course she wanted to be first. "Honestly, I haven't thought that much about it. I would certainly be honored if I were chosen to take that first step. But I'm . . . uh . . . not really sure how that gets decided." *Oh great. I just went on record as being the most ambitious person on the crew.*

Bob turned the camera to Lex.

She didn't hesitate. "Absolutely, it would be wonderful if a woman were the first to step out on a whole new planet. Just like Dr. Jansen, I would love to have that honor, but unfortunately I don't get to decide. By tradition, the commander of the crew makes decisions like that." Lex looked to Kennedy. "Commander Hampton? America wants to know whether you're going to choose the first man on Mars to be a woman?"

Kennedy hesitated.

"I don't think Commander Kennedy could possibly be expected to make such an important decision right now," Valkerie said. Bob switched the camera back to her. She could see Kennedy scowling at her out of the corner of her eye. "Um, Mars is still three months away. A lot could happen during that time."

And in the meantime, a little kid from Kansas has just thrown another monkey wrench into life on board the Ares 10.

Thursday, April 3, 2014, 8:00 P.M.

BOB

Bob closed the video-editing software and compressed the final version of the press conference. He started up the transmission process. The video upload would tie up the S-band channel for the rest of the night. Editing it had taken forever, and they didn't have much time. He had a lot of repairs to make before the spacewalk. Since trans-Mars injection, he had discovered four separate problems. Problems that should have been reported. And three of them were on systems that Valkerie and Kennedy had checked. There was absolutely no excuse for such negligence. Valkerie was new. He could understand that she might miss something. But Kennedy? He was the second engineer. Kennedy should have checked her work personally.

Bob rummaged in a drawer for some work clothes. A disturbing thought burned in his gut. What if Kennedy had been checking something else out instead? It was hard to imagine him being so irresponsible, but it certainly would explain some things. Like Josh's mysterious concerns about Kennedy's mental state—and the bad vibes that had sprung up between Kennedy and Valkerie almost immediately after launch. Bad vibes? What if their bickering was just a cover? They seemed to get along well enough now. Too well.

Bob pulled some coveralls out of a stowage bin and tried to think about something else. Kennedy and Valkerie could work things out for themselves. He had a job to do. The Hab was heating up again. Right before the press conference, he had studied the computer 3-D image of the temperature sensors aboard the ship. No doubt about it, there was a heat source down in the service bay. Which meant yet another problem in the cooling system.

He changed clothes slowly, careful not to make any noise. Blue Team—Lex and Kennedy—were on sleep shift, and he didn't want to disturb them. Kennedy in particular seemed exhausted. Eight hours would do him a world of good.

Bob slid his door silently aside and peered out. Valkerie was scheduled for an exercise session on the treadmill in the main cabin. If he was really quiet maybe he could sneak past her and duck downstairs without a confrontation.

Things would have been a lot easier if Kennedy hadn't switched Valkerie to Red Team. The last thing Bob needed right now was to have to spend social time alone with her. It was hard enough working with her. He still couldn't figure out why Kennedy had made the change. Maybe Kennedy made another pass at her, and she shot him down. Yeah, that was probably it. It was inevitable. Kennedy was the type to make passes, and Valkerie was the type to shoot guys down. Besides, she was a professional. She could never be interested in a guy like Kennedy. *Kaggo, you've been imagining things.*

Bob floated quietly through the corridor. Voices! He froze. Whispered voices. Coming from the main cabin. Why would Valkerie be whispering?

He pushed himself forward into the cabin and froze. Kennedy was huddled close to Valkerie at the conference table. Valkerie looked up at Bob with wide eyes. Consternation puckered her features.

"Bob, I was starting to worry you wouldn't come." Valkerie's voice seemed strained. "Please, join us. We were just talking about you."

I'll bet you were. Bob leveled his gaze at Kennedy. "What are you doing still up?"

"Valkerie and I started chatting, and I lost track of time." Kennedy didn't look Bob in the eye.

"He was telling me about your first trip on the Comet. Did you really give the instructor a black eye?" Valkerie's laugh sounded forced. She fixed Bob with pleading eyes and motioned with her head toward Kennedy.

Bob felt suddenly uneasy. What did she want from him? If she wanted him to leave, she could just say so. He didn't have time for childish mind games. "The trainer was anchored too close to me, that's all." Bob glared down at Kennedy. "Right now, I've got work to do. There's another coolant leak on the lower deck, and *somebody* has to fix it."

"It looks like a big job," Kennedy said. "I noticed it right before my shift ended, but Valkerie *needed* me to help her with the bioreactor filters . . ."

Bob felt his ears getting hot. What was that look from Kennedy supposed to mean? What was he insinuating?

"Bob, please. Sit down and talk." Valkerie twisted out of her seat and started toward him. "You have to take a break sometime."

Bob swallowed hard and yanked himself toward the stairwell with a ceiling strap. "I need to get to work. The coolant leak won't wait." He turned as he ducked through the hatch and caught Kennedy looking at Valkerie with a self-satisfied smirk. "If I were you, Hampster, I'd get some sleep. Tomorrow's the big spacewalk."

Bob pulled himself down the stairwell, not waiting for Kennedy's reply. He let out a deep sigh when he reached the lower level. Something was definitely going on between those two, but what? Was Valkerie trying to butter up the Hampster so she could be the "first man on Mars"? Kennedy wasn't going to give that one away. Not cheap, anyway. Valkerie was playing with fire if she wanted to go kissing up to Kennedy. She didn't know what kind of guy he was.

What was with her, anyway? Didn't she know better than to look at guys like that? One wide-eyed, innocent look from her could seduce a monk at thirty paces. Valkerie had to know what it did to guys, but still she kept it up. It was driving Bob nuts.

Was she just toying with him? Trying to make him suffer? He had known girls like that in high school. Rough girls from the public schools. Shouting lewd comments. Flirting with every uniformed boy they saw. He had known they were just teasing him, but secretly he liked it anyway. Before he'd met Sarah, those suggestive jokes and shouted taunts were as close to a social life as he had ever come.

But now . . . he wasn't a schoolboy now. He could keep pushing her away until she got the message. But Kennedy was another matter. If she kept it up with the Hampster . . . well, she was flirting with trouble.

Big time.

CHAPTER 16

Valkerie's feet pounded silently against the treadmill. Her hips chafed under the tug of the four large elastic bands that pulled her down against the belt. She let go of the handrails and swiped a towel across her face. The Hab was stifling—seven degrees above normal. Only fifty-five minutes and already her legs felt like kinked garden hoses. She dialed in a higher speed and pushed through the pain to keep up. Heat or no heat, she wasn't going to lose bone mass without a fight.

Valkerie swung her left arm in a sweeping arc, pulling against the bungee cords built into her penguin suit. She punched with her right—a jab for Bob with his haunting eyes and silent disdain. A left, a right. Kennedy with his sugary politeness and wandering eyes. Why did he have to be the only one who ever talked to her? An uppercut—maybe that would get Lex talking. A right, a left, a right. Perez, Harrington—Josh. Another right. Josh had said he would be there for her. A left. She heard his voice, but it was all NASA-speak. Words beamed twenty million miles through dark, cold space—to say nothing.

The timer buzzed and Valkerie jogged the machine to a standstill. She unbuckled the strap that held the elastic bands to her waist and pushed off for her room, careful not to dislodge the sheet of sweat that clung to her back. She was too tired. The last thing she wanted was to chase blobs of sweat around the cabin with a towel.

Grabbing clean clothes from her room, Valkerie circled around the central stairway to the thirty-by-thirty-inch shower compartment built into the wall next to the toilet ORU. The unit was barely big enough for her to maneuver in. How did Bob manage? Probably didn't even notice. Valkerie slammed the shower door shut. These days all Bob seemed to think about was repairing the ship. She couldn't believe he'd just walked away and left her to fend off Kennedy by herself.

Valkerie squirmed out of her sweaty clothes and pulled the handheld shower nozzle out from the wall. She wet her clothes with a tiny blob of water and rubbed soap into them until they were a ball of floating suds. Then she sprayed herself gently, letting the water encase her body in a thin, shimmering sheet. The water was much warmer than usual. It felt nice, but the warmth wouldn't last. She lathered herself quickly, using her soapy clothes as a washcloth. When she was done, she used the vacuum hose to suck off all the soapy water. After vacuuming the last film of water from the sides of the shower, she rinsed herself with a clean spray of water and vacuumed herself and the shower walls dry. Ah . . . it wasn't exactly relaxing, but at least she was clean.

Valkerie dried off quickly and got dressed. She and Bob were scheduled for a break, but what could she do? Kennedy and Lex were both asleep, and Bob had made it abundantly clear that he didn't want to have anything to do with her. Sixty-eight days into the mission, and already she was sick to death of life on the Ares 10. How could she hold out for two and a half years? What had she been thinking? She'd be thirty-five before the mission ended. Thirty-six or thirty-seven before life was back to normal—assuming it ever went back to normal. Her dad's last message said he'd received over two hundred e-mails from men wanting to communicate with her. One even asked him for her hand in marriage. What kind of man would do that? Had she thrown away her only chance at a normal life? What about friends, marriage— a family?

Valkerie pushed off for the stairs. Maybe if she just talked to Bob . . . if she could find out what was bugging him, maybe they could patch things up. It was worth a try. Things couldn't continue as they were. Not with Kennedy getting more familiar by the day. Something about him made her uneasy—not to mention all those stories she'd heard in Houston. She pulled herself down the stairwell and wriggled through the door.

Bob lay stretched out against the back wall of the lower deck, examining the pipes behind the wall panel that Kennedy had spilled his "juice" on.

"Bob? Could we talk?"

"Sure. Go ahead." Bob didn't turn around.

"Um . . ." Valkerie moved across the room and anchored herself to the floor stay next to Bob. "Have I done something to offend you?"

"Of course not. Why do you ask?"

"A couple of hours ago with Kennedy. You didn't seem that eager to . . . talk."

"As I said, I had work to do." Bob grabbed a flashlight from his belt and thrust it deep inside the wall.

Valkerie's stomach churned. "You don't care about anything but work, do you?"

Bob pulled his head out of the wall. "What's that supposed to mean? Of course I care—"

"Then why didn't you help me with Kennedy?" Valkerie demanded. "Is it some kind of a guy thing? A noninterference pact?"

"What are you talking about?" Bob stuck a long vacuum hose into the wall and turned on the motor. A high-pitched whine filled the chamber.

"I was practically begging you to stay, but no, you ran back to your tools where it's warm and safe. Where you wouldn't have to deal with anyone else's pain."

"Pain? Did Kennedy hurt you?" Bob pushed himself upright and grabbed a ceiling strap with a white-knuckled hand. His eyes smoldered with fury.

Valkerie backed away. "No, but being around him is so . . . awkward. . . ."

"Awkward? Is that what this is all about?" Bob shook his head incredulously. "You're bent out of shape because your social life isn't working out the way you planned?"

"Bob, Kennedy's been acting weird—ever since we left Earth. He hasn't done anything yet, but—"

"Awkwardness isn't pain." Bob pushed himself back down and reached inside the wall panel.

"You've been hurt, haven't you?"

Bob grabbed a wrench and started tinkering with a pipe inside the wall.

Valkerie waited for several minutes and turned toward the door. "I'll pray for you."

"Don't talk to me about prayer." Bob's voice echoed inside the wall.

"As far as God and I are concerned, the problem of pain is still an open question."

"*The Problem of Pain?* Have you read C.S. Lewis?"

"C.S. Lewis wrote that book before he even knew what pain was." Bob grabbed his wrench and leaned farther inside the wall. "He wrote it before he met Joy Davidman, you know that? I think a guy who's going to write about pain ought to first meet the woman of his dreams, and ask her to marry him, and then have her yanked away for no good reason at all. Why would God allow that to happen?"

Valkerie hesitated. It was a good question. A hard question. You got into all kinds of issues like free will, God's sovereignty. . . .

"Don't have an answer, do you? Well, before you answer that one, you have to answer another, more basic question." Bob backed out of the wall again and mopped his hands and wrench with a DriWipe.

"I'm listening."

Bob studied her, his haunted eyes suddenly very intense. "Has God ever spoken to you?"

"Well . . . yes. Lots of times."

"Out loud so you could hear?"

"What do you want, a megaphone?"

"I'd settle for an honest answer."

"Okay. It's . . . kind of a gentle leading."

Bob hung his head. He looked almost . . . disappointed. "Of course it is. So gentle you have a hard time knowing if it's Him or your own imagination. So answer this. Why doesn't God speak out loud—in a voice I can understand—if He wants so much to have a relationship with me?"

"He wants us to have—"

"Hold on." Bob held up his hands, palms outward. "Don't answer now. Just think about it. You're a scientist. Think like a scientist."

CHAPTER 17

Friday, April 4, 2014, 4:00 P.M.
BOB

Bob pulled on his gloves and locked the wrist connectors onto the sleeves of his EVA suit.

"Hampster, are you sure you didn't do anything to spook Valkerie? A crude remark? A joke she might have taken the wrong way?" Bob took another breath of pure oxygen and looked at his watch. They still had another five minutes of prebreathing to go.

"No way! She came to me—not the other way around. I didn't do a thing."

"I really don't get her. Sometimes she can be so . . . normal. Intelligent. Hardworking. Interesting. But other times . . ." Bob took a deep breath and shook his head to clear his mind. He was exhausted. After working all night on the cooling system, he'd barely had time for a shower and a few hours' sleep.

"Listen, Kaggo, just humor her, okay? We're going to have her as our crewmate for the next thirty months, so let's try to bond with her a little better." Kennedy kept his eyes on the stairwell. "She looks like she'd be a nice bond, if you take my meaning."

Bob didn't want to take his meaning. "Do you think she's unstable? Because she's on point while we're doing the walk. If she goes hinky on us—"

"Hey, Valkerie!" Kennedy said in a jovial voice, his eyes looking past Bob. "Are you ready to ride herd on us?"

Bob turned to look at Valkerie emerge from the stairwell, moving slowly because of her EVA suit. Had she heard their conversation?

She looked a little apologetic. "Sorry for the wait, guys. I was just upstairs helping Lex on the console. Ready to turn on comm?"

Bob set the frequency on his comm link and flicked it on. "Bob, comm check, over."

Lex's voice floated in through his headset. "Bob, this is Lex. I read you loud and clear. Hampster?"

"CDR, comm check."

"Loud and clear," said Lex. "Houston, this is Lex. We are go for the spacewalk. I'm at the console, Valkerie is suited and manning the CamBot, Kennedy and Bob are wrapping up their prebreathing."

Bob felt a little nervous about this EVA. Nobody had ever done one like this in interplanetary space, millions of miles from Earth. If anything went wrong, they'd be a long way from the nearest gas station.

"Okay, crew, let's do it." Kennedy gave Valkerie a thumbs-up and pointed to the CamBot she'd be operating remotely. "Take some great shots for the kids back home, okay, Big V?"

She looked mildly irritated at this new nickname. Bob felt his hackles rising. *Great. Out we go, and you've just annoyed the person who has to let us back in. Nice move, Hampster.*

Kennedy unlocked the hatch to the airlock and stepped inside. Bob followed him in. They sealed the hatch and pressed the button to pump air back into the Hab.

When the pressure got down to a few millibars, Bob flicked another switch, and they evacuated the remaining air into space. Amazingly, the airlock didn't have a safety mechanism. He turned the handle and the outer hatch popped ajar.

"This is CDR," Kennedy said. "We are egressing the Hab now." He pulled himself out.

"MS2 following," Bob said on his way out.

Quarks and bosons! Nothing in the world prepared you for a spacewalk. It was just plain weird to be out in space, with nothing holding you to civilization but a thin little tether. The EVA suit's bulk made your legs pretty much useless. You moved by grabbing and pulling. And you tried not to look down—whatever "down" meant. And don't even think about the fact that a good shove and a broken tether would send you tumbling away from the ship on a nice elliptical orbit around the sun. And you'd just keep going for a billion years or whatever, until the sun swelled up and fried you.

Bob was hyperventilating. *Stop it! Don't think about it.*

It was a head thing—a lot like walking on one of those four-by-four beams in a kiddie playground. If the thing was six inches off the ground, you could walk it with no sweat. But raise the bar a hundred feet up and try walking that same beam. Most adults couldn't do it. Wouldn't do it.

Now raise the bar twenty-five million miles, put on a hundred-pound EVA suit, and bring along some tools so you can do repairs.

And make it look easy for the kids back home. Bob's heart was hammering in his chest. He could do this. Had to do this. Was going to do this.

Kennedy looked back. "How you doing, Kaggo? Need a hand?"

"Just getting my bearings."

They had egressed near the aft section of the Hab, at the opposite end from the antenna. Bob pulled himself awkwardly along. He noticed the CamBot tracking him, its red LED lit. He stopped and waved to the camera.

"Looking good, Bob," said Valkerie. "Hey, Kennedy, what's that?"

Bob turned to look. Kennedy hovered inches from the Hab, peering intently at something.

Bob pulled himself over to have a look. "What's up, Hampster?"

"Nothing major," Kennedy said. "Looks like we've already absorbed a kinetic energy event."

Bob examined the hole. It was small and jagged and showed a carbon streak on the white exterior of the Hab. The Hab was covered with a synthetic, multilayered foam construction, designed to absorb the impacts of space debris in low-earth orbit and micrometeorites in deep space. A pebble moving at ten kilometers per second had more energy than a rifle bullet. "Looks pretty energetic," he said. "Probably went in several centimeters."

Kennedy pushed his index finger into the ragged wound. "Three or four inches, at least."

Valkerie's voice broke in. "Kennedy, remember to decontaminate that glove after ingress. Just in case of organics."

Bob smiled. Like there was any chance of catching a virus hitchhiking on a micrometeorite. But procedures were procedures.

Kennedy pulled his finger out. "Roger that, Valkerie. We are now continuing on to the antenna."

They traveled the length of the ship, moving slowly and carefully. When they reached the antenna, Kennedy took his position on the far side. Bob moved in on the near side. Both of them attached short secondary tethers to the ship.

Bob studied the antenna. The servo motor was shot, just like the CamBot had shown. He reached into the web bag strapped to his side, pulled out the spare, and handed it to Kennedy. A couple of minutes' work with the wrench and the bad servo came out.

He guided the new one into position, tightened it down with a wrench, and connected the power cable. No big deal.

"Smile for the cameras, Kaggo," said Kennedy.

Bob looked up in time to see the CamBot propelling itself carefully into place. "Show them the old piece, Hampster."

"Good work on the repair, Kaggo," said Lex. "Step back, boys. I'm going to test the motor."

Bob and Kennedy unlatched their secondary tethers and eased backward.

"Testing on my mark," said Lex. "Three, two, one, mark!"

The servo began turning and the antenna tilted.

"Way to go, guys!" Valkerie said.

"I'm all set to activate the antenna and try a transmission," Lex said.

"Don't turn on the juice until we get away from this antenna," Kennedy said. "I don't want to get my brains fried. By the way, I think we should do a quick visual inspection of the solar panels. What do you think, Kaggo? Maybe we can fix the panels?"

Right. Fat chance of that.

"Bob, this is Lex. Do you concur?"

Bob hesitated. He was feeling queasy, but he couldn't say no. This would probably be Kennedy's last spacewalk ever. "Affirm on that, Lex," Bob said. "Let's do a quick visual on both panels."

Solar Panel A was a paper-thin collapsible structure about two meters wide and extending fifty meters straight out from the ship.

"Lex, this is Bob. Solar Panel A has good structural integrity for about the first twenty-five meters. Beyond that, there's a complete disconnect."

"Roger, Bob," said Lex. "Does it appear to be repairable?"

"Negative."

"I concur on that," said Kennedy. "Proceeding to Solar Panel B."

When he reached the other panel, Bob was beginning to feel fatigued. The pressure inside the EVA suit made it hard to bend his arms and legs.

NASA had never yet solved the flexibility problem. EVAs were exhausting.

Panel B looked a little dinged up near the base. Bob inspected it all the way around, then clipped his secondary tether to the side of the Hab. "Valkerie, bring the CamBot around and photograph this. It appears that we had some mechanical torsion on the panel during deployment, with associated scraping on one side. I am observing several exposed wires with heavily abraded insulation. Kennedy, what do you make of these?"

Kennedy was breathing hard in his helmet mike. The sound made Bob nervous. "Lex, I concur with Bob's assessment. There appears to be some mechanical deformation at the base of Panel B, with collateral electrical damage."

The CamBot arrived. Valkerie quickly targeted the bot's powerful light on the wires.

"Okay, guys, good news," Lex said. "I activated the Ku antenna and have been transmitting the CamBot feed to Earth. They've acquired signal and the engineers are looking at the video now. We've got a long radio delay, but maybe they can give us some advice."

Bob reached in alongside the CamBot and pointed to the wires. "These red wires are for carrying current from the solar panel. What's this green one? It appears to have come disconnected from something. The end is free and exposed. Is that for control? Or sensors? I don't recognize that." Which made Bob nervous. There shouldn't be a single piece of this craft that he didn't know inside out. He ought to know what that wire did, but it was . . . totally new to him.

Lex's voice came in over the headset. "Guys, I am examining the online schematics for the Solar Power Electrical System. It appears there are no green wires in that system."

"What about blue wires? Our visors are plated gold." Kennedy's breathing was coming faster, rasping in Bob's ears.

"Negative, there are no blue or green wires." Lex's reply seemed fainter. Bob's stomach churned. Cold sweat prickled at his skin.

"Bob, this is Lex. There should be some plastic shielding covering those red wires."

"It's partly gone," Bob squinted at the wires, trying to bring them into focus. "I would guess it broke off during deployment of the panels. Some of the wires are heavily abraded."

A new voice cut in. "Bob, this is Houston, Jake Hunter here. Great job you did on the Ku repair. Our engineers have been looking at that video feed, and we are recommending that you not touch that green wire."

"Okay, um . . . roger that," Bob said. "Do not touch the green wire."

The Capcom continued. "Bob, our engineers are a little concerned about the integrity of the insulation on those abraded red wires. Those are supplying most of the juice for the ship. Recommend you test those to see if they're hot. Over."

"Affirmative on that," Bob said. Kennedy handed him a multimeter.

Bob clipped the ground lead to the frame of the solar panel. Was the meter set to Current? He squinted and thumbed it to Voltage.

The CamBot edged in closer, coming between Bob and the Hab. "I'm going to move around on the other side so I can see better," Kennedy said. He disappeared beneath the solar panel. A moment later, he said, "Okay, Bob, coming up behind you."

Bob reached in with the probe. A bead of sweat rolled down into his left eye. He blinked several times.

"Kaggo, watch out for that green—"

A flash of light exploded out from the solar panel deployment bay.

CHAPTER 18

Friday, April 4, 2014, 5:00 P.M.
VALKERIE

Valkerie spun through the air, pressing her hands to her ringing ears. What happened? She ricocheted off a wall, kicking and twisting to get her bearings. A high-pitched beep assaulted her senses. A woman's voice yelling. Screaming.

Valkerie grabbed a ceiling strap and the world slowly righted itself. The yelling stopped, but the alarm continued. The beeps were getting closer together—less intense.

The decompression alarm. What had happened? An explosion? And why were the lights so dim? She could hardly see.

Valkerie flung herself toward the EVA lockers. With her breath coming in shallow gulps, she flung open her locker and pulled the bubble helmet down over her head. She snapped down the clamps and reached for her gloves. First one glove and then the other. Her lungs were on fire, but she fought the urge to start the oxygen flow. Not until the last glove was . . . clamped.

Valkerie flipped a switch on her chest pack, and the roar of rushing air filled her suit. Cold air blasted into her chest, burning her lungs like a wildfire. Desiccated in the vacuum of space.

"Lex, do you hear me?" Valkerie adjusted the comm link on her helmet. "Bob?"

Silence.

"Kennedy?" Heavy breathing echoed in her helmet—a man's breathing. She turned the volume down. "Bob? Are you all right?"

No answer. Just a low, throaty rasp.

"Lex?" Valkerie screamed into the comm link. She knew Lex had been on console and hadn't been wearing a suit. Grabbing a rescue bubble from the EVA station, she pushed her way up through the stairwell, still hearing the labored breathing in her helmet. Then a metallic clank—the sound of the hatch to the airlock?

"Bob? Kennedy? Get in here quick! Hurry. Lex wasn't wearing a suit." Valkerie pushed across the deck to the command station. It was vacant.

"Lex?" She followed the curve around the stairwell and almost bumped into her crewmate—floating in the corridor, her body limp.

"Lex!" Valkerie unfolded the rescue bubble while quickly assessing her crewmate's condition. Lex's skin was red and blotchy, her mouth open. Valkerie could see the saliva boiling off her tongue. She seemed to be conscious . . . barely.

Valkerie shoved Lex into the bubble and zipped it shut. She pulled out the release pin, and the bag slowly inflated. Lex floated inside the plastic bubble, still not moving. She had oxygen, but Valkerie didn't remember how long it was supposed to last. The rescue bubbles were a holdover from the early shuttle days. They were designed for emergencies—not long-term survival. Nowadays NASA mainly used them to test ASCANs for symptoms of claustrophobia.

Valkerie let go of the bubble and pulled herself to the main cabin.

"Bob? Kennedy? Are you there?" she shouted into her comm link. "If you can hear me, Lex is still alive. I put her in a rescue bubble. We don't have much time."

Valkerie turned up the volume on her helmet again. The breathing hadn't quit. If anything, it was even heavier. Whoever it was could be going into shock. Tetany? No matter how serious it was, she couldn't do a thing to help until she got the cabin repressurized.

"Guys? I'm guessing that the explosion occurred near Solar Panel B, so I'm checking there first for the hull breach." Valkerie paused and visualized the layout of the Hab. If she was right, then the explosion occurred somewhere at the base of the main cabin wall. Great. The whole wall was lined with racks of white stowage bins. Spotting the leak wasn't going to be easy.

Valkerie yanked on the stowage bins, sending them and their contents flying into the cabin. Soon the whole room was a swirling mass of food packets, empty bins, and equipment.

"I sure could use some help in here!" Valkerie swiped at the volume dial and got an earful of breathing. It sounded bad, but at least . . . somebody . . . was still alive. Why wasn't the other one answering? She pushed the thought aside. One thing at a time.

Valkerie tore at another set of bins and shined her flashlight back through the metal scaffolding. There were so many floaties in the room that she almost didn't see it. A long half-inch-wide gap in a welded seam.

"Found it!" She shouted so loud, it hurt her own ears.

Valkerie dove through the swirling stew, pushing the bins aside with the sweeping strokes of a swimmer. She was in the lower deck shop in an instant, digging franticly through the supplies. *Surely they thought to pack a metal plate!*

Forget it. There isn't time! Valkerie grabbed the oxyacetylene torch and pushed away from the shop, pounding on the walls as she floated by. Plastic. Plastic. Curse NASA! Everything was made of plastic. Plastic or Nomex.

Valkerie paused at the hatch to the stairwell. This was going to have to do. She lit the torch and adjusted it so that its flame was an almost invisible cone of blue. Shielding her eyes with her arm, she cut through the metal of the heavy hatch door, guiding the torch slowly in the shape of a warped rectangular plate.

"Got it!" She jumped back to keep the hot metal plate from floating into her. It was hot enough to melt right through an EVA suit.

Picking the plate out of the air with a pair of pliers, Valkerie leaped up the stairwell and pushed her way through the cluttered main cabin to the empty racks that lined the wall. She wedged the hot metal plate between a rack and the floor to hold it and tried to pry the rack from the wall. No use. It was bolted solid. But somehow she had to get back there to fix the breach.

Valkerie flipped on the torch and started cutting her way through the scaffolding, one bar at a time. "Guys? Are you still there?" She jammed a hot bar into an empty bin and started on another one. One more and she'd be able to get to the wall.

Valkerie turned up the volume another notch as she worked, listening for the breathing. Still there. A pang stabbed through her. What if Lex died? What if she were left alone with Kennedy?

The last bar came free, and she pushed aside the thought. She couldn't allow herself to panic. One thing at a time, and her first job was to repair the breach in the hull. Valkerie retrieved the metal plate and pushed herself through the opening in the rack. The gash in the hull was longer than she had first thought. It ran almost eight inches along a welded metal seam. The plate she had cut was barely long enough.

She placed the metal plate over the seam and laid down four beads with an aluminum feeder rod, then checked her watch. They were running out of time. It would take a while for the cabin to repressurize.

"Okay, guys. Hold tight. I'm coming to get you."

Valkerie wriggled out of what remained of the rack and pulled herself to the stairs. The pressurized suit fought her every move.

She headed straight for the oxygen tanks. "Thank you, God." The tanks that fed the fuel cells were almost full. They had better be enough. It was a big ship.

Valkerie screwed open the valve and jumped back as a liquid oxygen geyser filled the room with a white cloud.

"Okay, guys!" She pulled herself to the hatch of the airlock. Good, the outer door was secure. Valkerie overrode the fail-safe and threw open the hatch. Her heart double-thumped. There was only one man inside.

"Bob?" Valkerie's voice was a shriek. "Kennedy?"

The man didn't move.

Valkerie grabbed a leg and hauled the suited figure into the ship.

Oof! He kicked out and caught her square in the chest. She lurched backward and slammed against the wall. He kicked his feet and thrashed his arms wildly to right himself.

"Hey. Calm down!" Valkerie worked herself above the man and shined her flashlight into his faceplate. Wild, terror-filled eyes stared back at her. It was Kennedy.

"Kennedy! Where's Bob?" Valkerie held their faceplates together, trying to stare some sense into him.

Kennedy clamped his eyes shut, squeezing out twin pools of tears.

"What happened to Bob?" Valkerie shook Kennedy to make the words sink in.

Kennedy's eyes went wide with recognition and surprise. He opened his mouth to speak but clamped it shut again with a grimace. His eyes rolled to the side, then closed in concentration. "I don't . . ." His breathing was getting heavier.

"What happened to Bob?"

"I . . . think . . . dead," he said between hoarse pants. "Killed . . . in the explosion." He turned his head, twisting his face in an expression of agony.

"No!" Valkerie pushed Kennedy away from her and scrambled into the airlock. *No! It couldn't be. Please God. No.* She sealed the hatch and hit the evacuation pumps to evacuate the chamber. No, it couldn't be. He was lying. She'd seen it in his eyes. He had to be lying.

The pressure gauge needle moved to zero, and Valkerie threw the outer hatch open. Space opened up around her like a dizzying black pool. She attached her tether and pulled herself along the side of the ship, sweeping its length with her eyes.

"Come on, Bob. You can do it. Hold on a little while longer."

Valkerie pulled herself to the point of the explosion—a crater in a twisted mass of metal, foam, and plastic. She scanned the area with her flashlight, taking in the scene with terrifying clarity. The solar panel was gone. And so was Bob.

Valkerie gulped hard and blinked against the tears that welled in her eyes. Too late! She should have come out right away.

She closed her eyes. *Think!* Lex needed her. She had to get back into the ship.

Valkerie pulled herself back to the hatch. She knew she should maintain contact with Kennedy, but she was too sick to talk. To him anyway. Her right hand snagged on a line, and she had to pause to untangle herself.

What was Kennedy hiding? What hadn't he. . . ? Valkerie yanked on the other line. A tether! Something was attached to it—she could feel its weight moving toward her from the other side of the ship. She tugged at the line, reeling it in as fast as she could move her sore, trembling hands. A white blob moved toward her through the shadow of the ship.

"Bob?" Valkerie went rigid, stunned by the still white specter that floated ominously toward her. "Bob?" The body struck her a glancing blow, wrenching her hands free of the ship. She tumbled backward into the void, her mind frozen in a gut-wrenching scream. Grappling with the body, fighting against the waves of revulsion that pounded against her, she floated out into an inky black sea.

Valkerie clung to a lifeless leg. It was real. Solid. A stay against the overwhelming grip of oblivion. She took a deep breath and felt her reason returning. She and Bob were still attached to the ship. As long as their tethers didn't break, they would be okay.

Valkerie reached out with one hand and felt for her safety line. One gentle tug propelled them back to the ship. She clipped Bob's secondary tether to her own EVA belt and pulled herself toward the hatch, dragging Bob behind her like a giant helium balloon.

She opened the hatch and pulled Bob into the airlock with her. He was stiff, lifeless.

She sealed the hatch and flipped the pressure equalization switch. It took only five seconds for the pressure gauge needle to stop moving. Apparently the cabin didn't have much pressure.

Valkerie threw open the hatch and pushed Bob into the dim interior of the ship. She searched his suit for punctures. The arms and chest were blackened, and a few shiny specks of metal were embedded in the suit, but on the whole the damage didn't look too bad. She swallowed hard and shined her flashlight into his facemask. Bob's features were frozen in a deathlike pall.

She pulled the helmet to her, hugging the glass dome to her chest. She couldn't know for sure. Not until the cabin pressure was high enough. But if Bob wasn't dead, he was getting there. Fast.

CHAPTER 19

Friday, April 4, 2014, 6:00 P.M.
BOB

Bob drifted lazily upward in a sea of pain. He could sense the surface as he floated higher, higher, higher. Finally, his face broke the surface.

His eyes fluttered open.

"Bob! Can you hear me?" Valkerie's voice battered his ears.

He blinked, winced. His skull felt as if somebody had buried an ax in it. The whole right side of his rib cage throbbed.

"Kaggo! Are you alive?" Kennedy asked. "Talk to us, buddy!"

"Where am I?" Bob tried to raise his head.

"Relax," Valkerie ordered. "You'll find it hard to move in your EVA suit anyway."

"Help me . . . take it off." He motioned feebly with his hands.

"Not yet," Kennedy said. "We lost pressure in the Hab. We're repressurizing from the reserves, but it's not coming up very fast."

"What about Lex?" Bob asked. "She's not in a suit!"

"We put her in a rescue bubble," Valkerie said. "There was no time after the explosion to put her in a suit."

"What explosion?" Bob closed his eyes and reopened them. Nothing made sense. Why were the lights so dim? Why did his head ache? What was with his ribs?

"Bob, do you remember testing the wires on the solar panel?" Valkerie asked. "Then there was an explosion and we lost pressure in the Hab."

It was starting to come back now. The wires. The multimeter. The flash before blackness. Bob stared vacantly. "Bomb . . . that was a bomb, wasn't it?"

"We don't know that," Kennedy said. "Blast this stupid pressure indicator! What's going on? We're only up to three hundred millibars!"

"Lex doesn't have much air in that bubble," Valkerie said. "Can we pop it open and give her a breather?"

"Not yet," Kennedy insisted. "We need four-fifty, at least."

"What's taking so long?" Valkerie asked.

"I told you, I don't know," Kennedy said. "Aren't you listening? It's not coming up; that's all I know. Kaggo, can you take a look at this?"

Bob raised his hand in the air and waved it. "Help me up. I'll try."

"Stay still," Valkerie ordered. "You've got a concussion, probably some bruised ribs."

Bob waved feebly at Kennedy. "Get the pressure up. We can't leave Lex in that bubble very long."

"I'm working on it." Kennedy slammed his palm on the computer. "I don't get it. Something's wrong here. We're pumping Nitrox out, but the pressure's coming up too slow."

"We've got a leak, then," Bob said.

"We *had* a leak," Valkerie said. "I patched it."

"Try releasing some of the helium reserves," Bob suggested. "That'll speed things up."

"We're gonna be singing like sopranos." Kennedy tapped some keys and waited a minute. "Okay, we're up to four hundred. Valkerie, head upstairs and get ready to check on Lex."

Valkerie disappeared up the stairwell. "Let me know the second it's okay to open her bubble."

"Here it comes, here it comes," Kennedy said through clenched teeth. "Four-thirty. Come on baby, move!"

Bob pushed against the floor and slowly rotated up and forward.

"Four-forty, let's go, let's go," Kennedy ordered. "Four-fifty. Valkerie, you are go to open Lex's bubble, but get her on a breather quick."

"Roger that." Valkerie's voice sounded clipped and cold.

"Say, Hampster," Bob said. "Are we clear to take off these helmets?"

"You can, but I'd like to get the pressure up higher."

Bob's pulse pounded in his skull. Valkerie had said he probably had a concussion. Because of the explosion. Because of the bomb.

And a bomb implied a bomber. Which meant what? Sabotage? Bob felt sick to his marrow. The bomb had depressurized the hull. Somebody had tried to kill them. Who? Asian terrorists? European nationalists? An inside job?

Whoever did it had access to space-rated explosives. Not easy to get. But once upon a time . . . two pyros went missing from Energy Sytems. They'd never been recovered. Was it possible? Were two pyros enough?

"Five hundred millibars," Kennedy said. "Valkerie, report on Lex."

"I've put a breather on Lex. She is still unconscious. Over."

Bob grabbed a strap and steadied himself. Kennedy stood over a console, watching it intently.

"Five-fifty," Kennedy said. "Hang on team, we are almost to a decent cabin pressure. Let's get it up to six hundred and we can take off our helmets. Hang tight, we are at five-sixty. Seventy. Eighty. Ninety. Six hundred. Clear to remove helmets."

Bob unlocked the wrist couplings and pulled off his gloves, then reached up and unlocked his helmet. He took it off, breathing a sigh of relief. The air in the cabin was really thin. But he could talk now. Using real sound waves in real air with real people. He'd had enough of disembodied voices in his ear. "How you doing, Hampster?" His voice was up half an octave.

Kennedy looked grim. "We're not out of the woods yet, Kaggo."

Friday, April 4, 2014, 6:30 P.M.
NATE

Nate paced back and forth beside Capcom Jake Hunter, quietly going nuts. "Try again on vox. Do we have the Ku-band back yet?"

"Negative," Hunter replied. "Ares 10, this is Houston, do you read?"

Nate mopped his forehead. The crew had suddenly dropped comm about ninety minutes ago. The high-bandwidth telemetry was gone, and so was vox.

Static crackled from the speaker. "Houston, this is Kennedy, do you read?"

Nate spun around and stared at the speaker. Thank God! Vox! They were alive.

"We read you loud and clear, Kennedy. What's the status? We lost signal eighty-seven minutes—"

"Houston, we have a . . . problem. Bob somehow touched off an explosion in the solar panel deployment bay. We breached the hull and had complete loss of cabin pressure. Bob suffered a concussion, possibly other injuries. Valkerie and I were able to rescue him. Lex had to be put in a rescue bubble but suffered massive decompression injuries. We have repressurized the cabin from our reserves and cannibalized the fuel cells, and we are now at a breathable level and rising. But other than that . . . Houston, we are under control."

Hunter turned to Nate. "What do I say first?"

"You can start by telling them we've lost the Ku-band signal. The S-band telemetry is telling us there's a power fault in Main Power Bus B. There is zero power in Main Power Bus B. Get confirmation on that. The telemetry data may be wrong."

Hunter adjusted his headset. Nate could see him putting on his be-calm-because-I'm-in-control face. "Okay, Ares 10, we have a report that Main Power Bus B is at zero power. Please confirm, power fault on Main Power Bus B. Over."

But long before the message could have reached the ship, the radio crackled again. "Houston, this is . . . uh . . . Bob."

Nate's throat tightened. Kaggo didn't sound too good.

"We suspect . . . we have been bombed."

"What is this nonsense?" Nate shook his head. "Ask them again about the power bus."

"Ares 10, this is Capcom. EECOM is reporting a fault in Main Power Bus B. Please confirm. Over."

A buzzing sound blared from the tinny speaker. Capcom looked at Nate in shock. "Cabin depressurization again!"

"They said they fixed that," Nate said, surprised. "Ask them about the power bus. What's with these people?"

"Ares 10, please report on Power Bus B. Over."

No answer.

Capcom's face had gone completely white. "Sir, I think we may have an Apollo 13 on our hands."

Nate turned to the Flight Director. "Get all your crews in here."

Steven Perez dashed in. "What's the status, Nate?"

Nate plopped down in a chair. His guts felt hollow, his heart cold. "All I can tell you at the moment, sir, is that this is not going to be NASA's finest hour."

CHAPTER 20

Friday, April 4, 2014, 6:45 P.M.
VALKERIE

The decompression alarm stabbed through the dark cabin like a screaming dentist drill. Valkerie jumped backward, sending her unconscious patient barrel-rolling across the narrow bunk.

"Bob? Kennedy? What's happening?"

"We're decompressing!" Kennedy's shout sounded shrill on Valkerie's earphones. "Get Lex back into that rescue bubble."

Valkerie shook her head in disbelief. The collapsed plastic shell floated in the corner of Lex's cabin, curling inward around a long gash. "Impossible. I had to cut it open. She's on a breather, but we've got to put her in the hyperbaric chamber!"

Valkerie shot out of the cabin and flew down the stairwell. Kennedy was already pulling the portable hyperbaric chamber from the locker.

"Why aren't you with Lex?" Kennedy shouted.

Valkerie did an about-face and pushed off for the stairs. By the time she reached Lex's cabin, Kennedy was right behind her.

He pushed her roughly aside. "You should have put her in this right away. Don't just stand there. Deploy the chamber while I put her inside!"

Valkerie grabbed the top of the basket-weave Kevlar chamber, pushed up off the floor, and attached it to a ceiling strap. The chamber looked like a children's toy teepee. Kennedy crawled in through the slit at the bottom, hauling Lex behind him. He zipped it shut from the inside.

"I should be in there with her!" Valkerie shouted. "She needs medical attention right now."

"Go help Bob!" Kennedy ordered. "I've got EMT training. I'm pressurizing now." The chamber's walls rapidly puffed out.

Valkerie stared at the chamber in exasperation. It was too late to do anything now. Kennedy and Lex were inside at normal pressure. If she opened the chamber, they'd decompress again—and that could kill Lex.

The beeps of the alarm seemed to be getting closer together, but gradually. A slow leak.

Bob's voice cut through the alarm. "I've deployed the powder. Still no sign of the new leak."

"Powder?" Valkerie glided down the curved corridor, pushing floaties out of the way.

"Found it!" Bob's shout drowned out her words. "The powder's pointing to your patch. I'm going to need a hand. I can't get in there with the torch. Hurry!"

Valkerie grabbed a ceiling strap and jerked herself forward, smashing her shoulder against a doorway. "Ouch!" She deserved that and more. It was her fault. None of this would be necessary if she had done a better job.

Bob spotted her through all the floaties and motioned her to the rack. "See? The flux lines in the powder? The bottom seam of your patch is leaking."

The black powder in the air formed a perfect funnel pointing to the base of her patch.

"Sorry." Valkerie kept her eyes turned to the seam. She had fouled up. If only she had taken the time to test it before throwing open the reserve tanks. If only she . . .

Valkerie looked up slowly. Bob was watching her intently. Studying her every move.

"What do you want me to do?"

Bob bit his lip and frowned. She could almost hear his mind churning. What was he thinking? Was he angry? He almost looked . . . sad.

He took a slow, deep breath. "Just . . . help me fix it. I can't get through the bars."

Friday, April 4, 2014, 7:30 P.M.

NATE

Nate hovered right behind Jake Hunter, his gut twisting like barbed wire. The pressure in Ares 10 was finally back up to normal. And Kaggo had gone berserk.

"Houston, we want Josh Bennett, and nobody but Josh Bennett." Bob's voice crackled over the speakers.

Nate checked his watch. Josh had been at home today, recovering from the flu. He should be here in five minutes. If he flew that Porsche of his instead of taking the freeway.

Dr. Abrams pursed his lips. "They're displaying classic symptoms of crisis-induced paranoia," he whispered to Nate. "If you'd just let me talk to them—"

"He's here!" Perez shouted from out in the hallway.

Nate spun around. Josh ran in, wearing a pair of pants but no shirt. "I'm up to speed—Perez filled me in while I drove." He strode to the mike. Jake Hunter stepped quietly out of his way. Dr. Abrams leaned forward. "Mr. Bennett, let me give you some advice on how to handle—"

Josh keyed the mike without a glance at Abrams. "Ares 10, this is Josh. Talk to me, kiddos. Everything's going to be all right." His tone was light, but Nate could see he was devastated. Everything was not going to be all right. But thank God Josh was here.

There followed four minutes in which Bob continued repeating his demand that Josh and only Josh be put online. "Josh!" Bob shouted. "Is that you?"

"Affirmative, Kaggo." Josh sat down. "Give me an update, buddy. Be aware that the radio delay is now two minutes each way, so just calm down and try to give me information in large blocks. I need a complete status report. How are things in Aresville?"

Dr. Abrams put a hand on his shoulder. "Mr. Bennett, the first thing to remember is that—"

Nate grabbed his elbow. "Dr. Abrams."

Abrams spun on him. "This is important. Trust is a very fragile thing—"

That was more than Nate was going to take from an overpriced, underpowered shrink. "Out!" he hissed. "I have a mission to run, and you are not going to interfere."

Steven Perez stepped up. "Dr. Abrams, could I have a word with you?"

Abrams' eyes went wide, and his face tightened in fury, but he followed Perez out.

Nate turned back to see what Josh was up to.

"—sure you're right about that, Kaggo, but let's do first things first, shall we? We've got a little engineering problem. EECOM is telling me she's reading no power on Power Bus B. Can you confirm that?" Josh's tone was cool, but his face twisted in anguish.

Bob's voice crackled with tension. "We have just survived a bombing. Have you got that? This is sabotage, and I want some answers. I want to know who had access to Ares 10 after we arrived at KSC in December."

Nate leaned into Josh's ear. "You guys are getting into a time warp here. Bob said this two minutes ago and he hasn't gotten your message yet, so let's pick up this thread and run with it."

Josh nodded. "Regarding your comment about a possible bombing, Kaggo, we are initiating a complete check of all personnel who had access to Ares 10 during final assembly of the launch package. I'll tell you right now, it could be dozens of people." Josh scrawled a note and handed it to Nate. Nate read it. *Get me that list.*

That was simple enough, but Josh was wrong. Nate would have Security check the tapes, but only six people had unrestricted access to the Hab during the assembly phase—Nate, Josh, and the four crew members. He'd made sure of that. So Bob had to be wrong too. This was an accident, not a bomb. Nate wrote the six names on the note and held it up for Josh to read.

Josh's eyes went wide. He shook his head. "Okay, Kaggo, I've put through that request, and we'll get you that information just as quickly as we can. In the meantime, let's do a status check. First off, are all of you healthy?"

There followed four minutes of gut-twisting radio silence.

"Negative, Houston." Valkerie's voice. "Lex is unconscious in serious but stable condition. She is suffering from ebullism, hypoxia, DCS, and arterial gas embolism. Kennedy has her in the hyperbaric chamber under oxygen and a pressurized IV. It's too soon to know her prognosis. All we can do is pray that she comes out of it alive. Bob suffered a mild concussion and some compressive injuries to his chest, but he is mobile and alert. Kennedy experienced some disorientation after the explosion, but he's fine now. I have minor abrasions on my left hand—nothing serious."

A hush settled around the room. Nate was sweating cannonballs.

Josh pressed his hands to his eyes. After a long pause, he leaned into the mike. "Ares 10—Valkerie, Kennedy, Bob, and especially Lex—please be aware that our prayers are with you."

Nate hadn't prayed since fifth grade, and he wasn't going to start now. The only thing that could help Ares 10 was a good solid team of engineers. He handed Josh another note: *STATUS CHECK NOW!*

Josh picked it up. "Um, Ares 10, if we could run that status check on Power Bus B, I'd like to be able to tell EECOM that there's just a glitch in her telemetry data. Could you look into that for me, Kaggo?"

Another long, horrible pause. Then Bob's voice, tight. "Serious problem here, Houston. Solar Panel B is gone."

Josh stared at Nate. "Does he mean it's gone offline?"

Bob sounded close to panic. "Solar Panel B was blown away by the explosion."

"It's disappeared!" Valkerie's voice broke in. "We can't even find it on radar. Josh, what are we going to do?"

Friday, April 4, 2014, 11:00 P.M.

BOB

Bob sat slumped at the conference table while Valkerie dressed the wounds on his right arm.

"No more shrapnel." Valkerie taped on a bandage. "Just a couple of massive hickeys. You were lucky. We all were." Valkerie's voice trembled.

"Ares 10, this is Houston." Nate's voice came over the comm.

Bob lunged for the receiver and turned up the gain.

"We have no definitive word yet on whether that was a bomb or an accident. We are still reviewing the evidence. But we do have an answer to your question about access. A team of federal agents has reviewed our security records. The tapes show that only six people had unsupervised access to the Hab. The Ares 10 prime crew plus Josh Bennett and myself. Repeat, we are still reviewing the technical evidence, but the security review seems to rule out a bomb or any kind of sabotage. Please confirm. Over."

"It was a bomb, all right," Kennedy muttered. "Nate, this is CDR confirming. Only the crew, Josh, or you had unsupervised access. You haven't finished analyzing the evidence yet. Now here's my two cents. I was there. I saw the explosion. It was definitely a bomb."

Bob felt woozy, disoriented. The crew, Nate, or Josh? Impossible. It

188

had to be an outsider, somebody that could get through the security system and . . . The audit leaped into his mind. P.T. Henderson. Who would steal JSC pyros rather than bring a bomb in from the outside? Who could get past the heightened security? All the evidence pointed to an inside job.

Bob looked up from the table. Kennedy's eyes darted back and forth between him and Valkerie. Valkerie looked as if she was going to be sick.

Nate? Josh? Absolutely not, he'd known them for eight years. The crew? Ridiculous. It was suicide. What could possibly be worth . . . oh God, no . . . *Sidney Nichols.* He'd given his life for a stupid research lab. What would a guy like him have sacrificed to stop Mars?

Bob felt sick. A damp chill spread itself across his back. He couldn't breathe. He twisted free of the table bars and gathered his legs under him to push off for the bathroom.

"Where do you think you're going?" Kennedy's voice froze him like a slap in the face.

"To the bathroom." Bob's own voice sounded hollow in his ears.

"Not now, you're not," Kennedy growled. "We've got to talk. We told you not to go near that wire, and you touched it anyway. I want to know why."

"It was an accident!" Bob spluttered. "That multimeter somehow got switched to measure resistance, and when I touched the power wire—"

"What do you mean, *somehow* got switched?" Hostility tightened Kennedy's face. "How?"

"I tried to set it to Voltage, but I was having a little vertigo out there, and my vision was playing tricks on me."

"Why didn't you call off the spacewalk, then?"

"Because *you* wanted to stay out and play. I wanted to come in—"

"Then why didn't you say so?"

Bob glared at Kennedy. "What are you trying to say? You think *I'm* the bomber? That's real bright—I was the one who got hit the hardest."

"So maybe you're suicidal," Kennedy said. "Maybe you wanted to go out with a bang. The rest of us would have lingered, but you'd have had the easy way out."

"That's . . . bogus." Bob turned away from the table. "You've known me how long? Eight years? And you think I'm suicidal?"

"Guys, stop it." Valkerie put a hand on each man's arm. "Nate's got to be wrong. There have to be more suspects than just us six."

Bob shook his head. "No . . . I think he's right. When somebody breaks a really secure system, it's usually an insider."

Kennedy nodded. "It's true. And I hate to say it, Kaggo, but you make a pretty good suspect."

"What's my motive?" Bob jutted his chin at Kennedy. "Give me one good reason why I'd want to blow up this ship. Go back and read your Sherlock Holmes, Hampster. Motive is everything. Without that, you haven't got a case."

"I agree," Valkerie said. "Bob would never bomb this ship."

"Okay, fine," Kennedy growled. "If it's motive we're looking for, how about Josh? He got cheated out of this mission by a stupid teamwork index. That had to make him bitter."

Bob thought about that idea, trying it on for size. Would Josh try to kill them . . . just because Perez had derailed his career? Not in a million years. If he were going to take anyone out, it would be Perez.

"Um, guys," Valkerie said. "I went to talk to Josh right after he stepped down from the mission. I thought he was going to hate me. And . . . and he didn't. His only concern was for the mission. If it doesn't succeed, he won't get a chance at the next one. If you're looking for a motive . . . all I can say is, you're barking up the wrong tree. Josh would never do anything to hurt us."

Kennedy rubbed his eyes. "She's got a point, Kaggo."

Bob felt his heart constricting.

"I hate to say this, but what about Lex?" Kennedy asked. "What was Lex doing while we were out there? Valkerie, did you see what she was up to?"

"No way," Valkerie said. "Lex is the last person who'd want to sabotage this mission. She's been a Mars freak since she was eight years old."

"Did you know her when she was eight years old?" Kennedy asked. "What do we really know about Lex, anyway?"

Valkerie leaned forward. "Lex is the ultimate Mars fanatic. She'd never do anything to wreck the mission."

"Nice cover story, anyway," Kennedy muttered. "Maybe she's been pretending all her life. Maybe she . . ."

"Maybe she *what*?" Valkerie asked. "Be serious."

"I *am* serious," Kennedy said. "Lex is a little secretive, isn't she? Have y'all ever had any kind of deep conversation with her?"

"She doesn't talk much," Valkerie admitted.

"And what about that IMU that kept glitching on the test stand?" Kennedy asked. "Kaggo, you traced that back to that guy at AresCorp, that friend of Lex's."

"And she defended him," Bob replied.

"That's what friends do," Valkerie said. "This is ridiculous. I don't believe Lex put a bomb out there any more than you do. Do we even know for certain it *was* a bomb? What makes you so sure, Bob? I mean . . . doesn't a bomb need oxygen to explode?"

"Not if it's a NASA pyro," Bob said. *And I know where it came from.* He pulled out his PDA and opened up his personal work log.

"It wouldn't take much of a charge," Kennedy added. "That was a small explosion."

"Got it." Bob pointed to the record in his PDA. "August 29, 2012, the day Josh resigned from the mission. Lex came in real early that day. Got there before I did, and I—"

"So?" Valkerie said.

Bob closed the PDA and put it in his pocket. "That was the same day a storeroom in Energy Systems was broken into. When I got in that morning, they were installing retinal scanners on all the rooms in our building and in ESTL."

"Do you have a point here?" Kennedy asked.

"An audit showed that storeroom to be missing a couple of pyros."

"I never heard anything about this," Valkerie said.

Kennedy leaned forward. "So you're suggesting Lex moseyed in early, broke into the storeroom in ESTL, stole some pyros, made a bomb, and planted it in the deployment bay?"

"I'm not saying Lex did it, but somebody—"

"It couldn't be Lex," Valkerie insisted. "She'd rather die than miss Mars."

Bob remembered Lex practically begging him to take her to Mars. No . . . she didn't plant that bomb. He was sure of it.

"There's one thing you haven't explained yet." Kennedy's bloodshot eyes flickered in the dim light. "Who told you about the missing pyros?"

Bob felt his ears going hot. Somebody at JSC had gone to a whole lot of trouble to cover up the missing explosives. The information had never gone public.

"That's a good question," Valkerie said.

Kennedy held out his hand. "Give me your PDA."

Bob didn't move.

"That's an order."

Bob slowly pulled it out and handed it over.

Kennedy flipped it open. "It's password-protected." He held it out to Bob.

Bob felt his guts lurch. There was a lot of stuff on that PDA. His personal journal. Passwords he'd hacked. And data he'd gotten from secure NASA databases.

"Do I need to order you to do this?" Kennedy asked.

Bob took the PDA and punched in the password. "There's personal stuff on here—"

"I'm not going to steal your girlfriends' phone numbers," Kennedy said. "But right now, you're our main suspect."

"*I* am!" Bob shouted. "That's ridiculous!"

Kennedy eyed him coldly. "You know more about explosives than any of us. You'd know where to set them to do maximal damage to the Hab. You knew pyros were missing, and none of the rest of us did. And you set off the explosion."

Bob shook his head and stared down at the table.

That's real fine logic, Hampster, except for one minor problem. I didn't plant the bomb.

Which means somebody else did.

CHAPTER 21

Friday, April 4, 2014, 11:15 P.M.
VALKERIE

Valkerie listened in stunned disbelief as Bob and Kennedy argued. Ridiculous. They couldn't really believe it. One of them—a killer? It didn't make any sense. What possible reason would anyone have for not wanting the mission to succeed?

Bob yanked his PDA out of Kennedy's hand. "That isn't the issue! I did *not* plant that bomb!"

"And I want to know where you got those access codes! Why do you even have them?" Kennedy lunged for the PDA. Bob jerked it away.

"I'm ordering you. Give me that computer right now!"

Bob snapped the PDA shut and handed it to Kennedy.

"Okay, now the password. I'm ordering you to give me your password!"

"Not until we finish our discussion—then I'll come clean with everything. I have nothing to hide."

"Nothing to hide? I already have enough evidence to lock you—"

"If you want to talk about hiding, what about—"

"Would you two stop it!" Valkerie's shout echoed off the main cabin walls.

Kennedy turned on her with a scowl.

"I hope you're done bickering, because it isn't helping. Lex is in bad shape, and without that solar array we're hurting for power. If we don't grow up and start working together, we're not going to need a saboteur to kill us. We'll do it ourselves." Valkerie stared back at Kennedy through tear-saturated eyes.

Kennedy shot an accusing look at Bob. "All I'm asking is for Bob to tell me why he had a list of access codes."

Bob bristled. "I got those codes because I'm nosey, okay? I just wanted to know what was up with all the cloak-and-dagger stuff back at Houston—or didn't you notice?"

"I noticed a lot of things, but I didn't have any reason to worry. Unlike somebody—"

"Guys. Stop it!" Valkerie snapped. "Nobody here is trying to destroy the mission. Think about it. Do you seriously believe that one of us is a suicidal maniac? We know each other."

Bob sighed. "So you think it's somebody on the ground?"

"Maybe." Valkerie scratched her nose. "What if somebody got to the Hab while it was en route to the Cape?"

"Not a chance." Kennedy turned to Bob. "Bob and I were there. Nate had the Super Guppy wired tighter than Big Brother."

"So is NASA security always so tight?" Valkerie asked.

"Apparently Nate knew something that we didn't." Kennedy turned to Bob. "Did you notice that Nate ramped up the security right after *she* got to Houston?" He nodded in Valkerie's direction without looking her in the eye.

Valkerie bit her lip. She didn't need to defend herself. Let them play their little games and get it out of their system. She glanced at Bob. His face glistened with a sheet of sweat.

"What about Nate?" Bob took a deep breath. "He could have done it."

"Nate?" Kennedy said. "He was Mr. Security before the launch. Even brought in that FBI chick to work with him."

"So what if it was a cover?" Bob said. "This is a long shot, I know, but I'm just trying to think outside the box, okay?" A look of quiet desperation crossed his face.

Kennedy gave a harsh laugh. "Out of the universe, you mean."

"No, it makes sense in a weird kind of way," Bob said. "Look, if this was a John LeCarre novel, it *would* be Nate. Just because it can't be Nate. You follow?"

Kennedy snorted. "If it were Nate, he would have made sure he wasn't one of the six suspects. Either that or he would have left enough holes in the security to take the pressure off himself."

"But if he were really smart—"

"Come on, Bob, you don't believe that for an instant. We've known

Nate for years. Valkerie, on the other hand . . ."

"What about you, Hampster?" Bob looked to Valkerie for support. "How do we know it isn't him?"

"What's my motive?" Kennedy sneered.

"You're a big chum of Senator Axton," Bob said. "Maybe you want to destroy NASA like he does."

"I can think of a lot more comfortable ways to destroy NASA than bombing my own mission," Kennedy sneered. "Give me a real motive, Sherlock. Why would I do it?"

"How should I know? But you *have* been playing Grand Inquisitor tonight," Bob said. "That's exactly the role I'd expect the real bomber to play."

"If I were the bomber, why'd I suggest checking out the solar array? Wouldn't I be afraid that you'd discover the bomb?"

"Maybe you already knew the wire was broken. Maybe you were trying to—"

"Then why let *you* investigate? If I were the bomber, I'd have ordered you back and set it off myself. Just like you did."

"Me? Okay, then. What's my motive?"

"I'm still working on it. But I do know one person with a motive." Kennedy turned wolfish eyes on Valkerie. "Bob told us you were a Christian fundamentalist—just like those picketers in Houston."

Valkerie glared at Bob, who looked miserably down at the table.

"And what about that leaky patch?" Kennedy demanded. "That could have killed us all. Why didn't you check it before throwing the LOX tanks open?"

"I was trying to save your lives! Get a clue, will you, Kennedy? You were freaking out in the airlock, Bob was unconscious outside the Hab, and Lex was dying in a vacuum. If I were trying to get us killed, all I had to do was nothing! The job was done. But I didn't, did I? I saved the mission! I put Lex in a bubble, patched the leak as fast as I could, and then brought you guys back in! Why does that bother you? Because I made some mistakes along the way? Sorry! I did my best. Funny thing, I don't recall training for this particular failure mode."

Bob gulped. "*Valkerie* brought me inside? I thought . . ." He looked at Kennedy. "Didn't you bring me in?"

Kennedy shook his head. "I was groggy. I thought you were dead and on your way to Neptune. But that doesn't change the fact that Valkerie here is the only one with a motive."

"But why would she rescue me? Why bother to patch the ship at all?"

Kennedy snorted. "Why did the Crusaders slaughter the Muslims and then care for their wounded? Why do pro-lifers shoot abortion doctors? Why do they worship love but preach hate and intolerance? Maybe it's cognitive dissonance. They're full to the brim with conflicting ideas. That's got to weigh on them. Or maybe she just wanted to drag out this disaster as long as she could."

Valkerie hung her head. It was too much. She couldn't believe any of this was happening. She felt sick—like the day her mother died.

"She's the only one with motive, Bob. She had motive. She had opportunity. And none of the security weirdness happened until she got here. What do you think?"

Bob didn't say anything.

"Simple question, Bob. Needs a simple answer."

Bob turned away from Valkerie, his face an unreadable mask.

Kennedy leaned forward. "Answer me, Kaggo. At least you have to admit that she's a prime suspect. Right?"

Bob pressed his fingers to his eyes, his head moving in a barely perceptible nod.

"That's . . . ridiculous." Valkerie's voice shook with emotion. "Leave me alone, Kennedy. You know I didn't do anything."

"Leaving you alone is the one thing we're *not* going to do." Kennedy's voice filtered through the pounding in Valkerie's ears. "From now on, nobody on this ship moves a finger without someone else watching. Until we figure this out, we don't trust anybody."

Friday, April 4, 2014, 11:45 P.M.

NATE

Nate looked around the conference table. "Okay, Gold Team, give it to me straight. I don't want any sugarcoating—just the facts. Where do we stand?" He pointed at GNC first. "How do you see it?"

GNC shuffled his papers. "We're good. The Inertial Measurement Units are working fine. The StarTracker is keeping 'em in line. They can navigate all the way in."

"Fine," Nate said. "FDO?"

FDO didn't even look at his papers. "All clear. No problems."

"Good." Nate pointed to EECOM. "We'll be operating on reduced power, obviously. How we doing there?"

EECOM's face looked green. "We aren't, sir."

Nate stared at her. "I thought you had a team working on that."

She bit her lip. "My team just finished the numbers five minutes ago. And we cannot complete this mission. Solar Panel B is gone—blown away to heaven knows where. Solar Panel A is still operating at 48 percent. Their total power production is only 24 percent of nominal, about 6.7 kilowatts. That's well under the design requirements. We have reduced to emergency power usage. Even so, we only have about 260 watts of surplus power."

"So we can bring them in to Mars if we're very careful?" Nate asked.

"Incorrect. Their current distance from the sun is 1.23 astronomical units. When they reach Mars, they'll be at 1.52 AUs. The solar power decreases like one over r-squared. So they will lose 35 percent of their power, and that's a lot more than our surplus."

"Don't give me that," Nate said. "They can reduce power for comm, for the computers, for a lot of things—am I right?"

"I told you, we have done that already. We even cut power to the food freezers. We are running the ship *below* the rated emergency power usage. We've turned off every spare computer and navigation device. They are sending no telemetry and will be transmitting vox only at specified times. But the ship has to operate. And we cannot turn off life support. Oxygen production and carbon-dioxide scrubbers by themselves need a couple of kilowatts continuous power."

"You're telling me . . ." Nate couldn't say it.

"They're going to die, sir." EECOM covered her eyes. "They've got six days, and then their power production will go below their requirements. The fuel cells could have covered the deficit for some weeks longer, but those have been discharged. Mars is ninety days away. They cannot last that long. It's impossible."

"No!" Nate slammed his hand on the table. "Listen, people, failure is not an option! We're going to—"

"You are *not* listening," EECOM said. "We have *done* the numbers. Backward. Forward. Inside out. Unless you want to nicely ask all of them to stop breathing, they are not going to make it. Possibly with a crew of one. We could take Valkerie, or Lex, or Kennedy individually all the way in. Bob probably would not survive because of his higher metabolic requirements. But even a crew of two cannot possibly survive. Four is beyond impossible. I've got the numbers. And, sir, you cannot simply wave your hand and make it go away, like Gene Kranz did for Apollo 13. We need three months, not three days. The numbers are not even close."

It hit Nate all at once, like a bullet in the gut. His crew was going to die. He could save one if he sacrificed the other three—right now.

But only if he gave up. As long as he kept fighting, there was hope. Maybe.

He looked around the table. "Okay, listen up, team. I am not giving up yet. There's got to be a way. I want a team of you to look at ways we can cannibalize oxygen. Maybe the LOX in the fuel cells—"

"I told you, the fuel cells are already drained," said EECOM. "Valkerie dumped the oxygen from the fuel cells to restore pressure after the first leak. The second leak drained all their atmospheric reserves. We're running a 20–20–60 mix of oxygen-nitrogen-helium, which means they won't require prebreathing on their next EVA. But we have nothing left, sir. Nothing." Tears spilled down her face. "I'm so very sorry."

"There's got to be a way," Nate said. "And we're going to find it—hopefully before the crew figures it out themselves."

Dr. Abrams stood up. "Mr. Harrington, the crew has probably developed a full-blown case of crisis-induced paranoia by now. If you lie to them and they find out—"

"We're not going to lie. We're going to withhold information until we have a solution," Nate growled. "If you can't be constructive, then get out of here."

"What about the press?" asked EECOM. "They were expecting to see video of the spacewalk tonight on the six-o'clock news."

"Stall the press," Nate said.

"What about 'free and full flow of information'?" said GNC. "That's the rule."

"If we tell the press, they'll tell the public, and our crew is going to find out," Nate said. "We can't control their e-mail."

"Sure we can," said GNC. "It goes through our computers."

"And it's encrypted for privacy," Nate growled. "Sure we can hold it all back, but they get two hundred e-mails a day. They'd notice in two hours and start asking questions. So we cut this thing off at the source. I'm issuing a gag order on all communications with the press."

EECOM cleared her throat. "Sir, we're going to need an order from higher up on that."

"Fine," Nate said. "Dr. Perez?"

Perez nodded. "In this case, I think it's justified—"

"Sorry." GNC shook his head. "If you expect us to keep quiet on this, you've got to cover us all the way up the chain. We want the president."

"I'll call her," Perez said.

Nate cleared his throat. "Listen, team, I wouldn't ask you to do this except for one reason. Lives are at stake. If our boys and girls up there find out they've only got enough life support for one, what do you think's going to happen?"

"Murder on the Ares Express," somebody said in a horrified whisper. "Last one standing gets to breathe."

"You got that right," Nate said. "And if that happens, I'll hold each one of you *personally* responsible, is that clear?"

Heads nodded around the table.

"All right, go out there and dig me up some oxygen. And if you need a magic wand to do that—get one."

CHAPTER 22

OXYGEN

Saturday, April 5, 2014, 9:00 A.M.
VALKERIE

Valkerie wiped Lex's arm gently with an alcohol swab. It was hard to see in the dim emergency lights, but the scarlet blotches that covered Lex's skin were beginning to fade to a sickly blue. Lex was still on ventilation, but her lungs seemed to be clearing. She was still unconscious, though—not a good sign.

Valkerie opened a syringe and jabbed the needle into the septum of a sealed vial. She could barely make out the label.

"What's that?"

Valkerie jumped. "Bob, you scared me to death!"

"What is that stuff?" Bob demanded.

"It's Propentofylline—for Lex." She ignored Bob's frown and turned back to her patient.

"What does it do?"

Valkerie gave Lex the injection. "For your information, it's an NMDA antagonist. It protects the hippocampus and dorsal thalamic nucleus from hypoxia-induced calcium influx. Are you satisfied, *doctor*? Do you agree with my treatment?"

Bob shrugged. "You're not supposed to do anything that could be construed as hostile. We all agreed. If anything happens to Lex—"

"Something already happened to Lex!" Valkerie snapped. "I'm doing all I can for her, but you have to trust me. We have to trust each other."

"You're saying you trust him?" Bob nodded to the sleeping form of Kennedy. He floated vertically in a Sleep Restraint Unit attached to the wall, his arms floating out in front of him like a zombie in an old black-and-white movie.

"I have to trust him. Our survival depends on it."

Bob moved to the control center and flipped through the monitoring systems.

"Bob, all this paranoia is ridiculous. If you wanted to destroy the ship, you could do it right now. How would I be able to stop you?"

"The ship has built-in safeguards. Redundant controls. Self-monitoring subsystems to block out dangerous commands."

"And you could get through those in a second, couldn't you?"

Bob turned back to the screen and a stream of clacks erupted from the keyboard. "Whoa . . . look at this!"

"What?"

"The day before the explosion you wrote Josh four e-mails, and he only sent one reply."

Valkerie moved toward the computer station, trying to remember if she had written anything embarrassing. "Don't you dare read my mail. Those are private messages."

"I'm sure they are," Bob said grimly.

"For your information—"

"Uh-oh . . . get this."

Valkerie peered over Bob's shoulder. The screen showed a log of sent and received messages.

"Lex got six messages from an rjanderson@gimli.usaf.gov—all the day before the explosion. The server shows sixteen unopened messages since then. Did she ever mention anyone named Anderson to you?"

Valkerie shook her head. Something was familiar about that address. USAF, the air force . . . "You know. There was an air force officer that came to our prelaunch send-off. I thought it was odd at the time, because he never talked to anyone. Just stood in the back watching. I think he was watching Lex."

"Are you sure? He never said anything?"

"Nothing. He may have signaled to her, but that would have been all. He didn't stay long."

"Come on!" Bob pushed away from the command station and pulled himself across the room.

"Come on, where?" Valkerie followed him to Lex's room. "What are you doing?" She stopped outside Lex's door and watched as Bob went rifling through Lex's gear.

"Just trying to save our tails." Bob brought out Lex's computer and aimed his PDA at her IR port.

"We can't do this. Her computer's password-protected."

Bob stared at the screen of his PDA. "Come on, baby..."

"Bob. What—"

"Yes!" Bob pocketed his PDA and began hammering at Lex's keyboard.

"You have a cracker on your PDA? Those are illegal."

"Yeah, yeah. Look at this."

Valkerie craned her neck to see the text file on the screen. "It's encrypted."

"Look at the subject headers," Bob said. "Those are easy enough to read."

Valkerie squinted. "I'll miss you." "Maybe you should wait." "My last and final message."

"Makes you think, doesn't it?" Bob flipped the laptop shut.

Valkerie nodded. Lex had been so guarded during training. So quiet. Maybe—

A loud knock filled the ship. It sounded as if it came from the control room.

Bob dashed for the doorway, leaving Lex's computer spinning in midair. Valkerie pulled herself after him. Could it be Lex? Was she finally waking up? Valkerie careened off the wall of the hallway and bounced into the control room.

The room was still. Lex and Kennedy lay in their Sleep Restraint Units. Kennedy's right eye twitched. His face wore a taunting smirk, and his head bobbed up and down to the throb of his pulse. Valkerie examined the SRU that held him against the wall. Had it been unzipped before? She couldn't remember.

"Uh-oh . . . more trouble."

Valkerie followed Bob's gaze across the room to the command center. A red light flashed on the console. She couldn't tell from where she floated, but it looked like the life-support emergency alarm.

Saturday, April 5, 2014, 9:30 A.M.

BOB

Bob floated to the console. What was that flashing light? "WARNING: Current Power Usage Is Within 200 Watts of Available Power."

He checked the power usage stats.

Quarks and bosons! Life support was using an awfully high percentage of total power. He ought to have thought about that, but he'd been so tired. At midnight Lex had gone into a crisis, and it took all night to get her out of the woods, with all three of them watching each other like hawks. He desperately needed a sleep shift. But he couldn't leave Valkerie as the only person awake. If she were the bomber—*she couldn't be*—but if she were, then . . .

"What's up?" Valkerie settled in close behind Bob. Uncomfortably close.

"We got a warning from the system about power usage." Bob moved to give Valkerie more room. "I checked, and we're not using much. But about 44 percent of that is for life support."

"Um, remind me," Valkerie said. "Our solar panels won't generate as much energy when we get farther away from the sun, right?"

"Yeah, it's an inverse square law. Worst case on this mission: Mars is about 1.5 times as far from the sun as Earth is, and we're at maybe 1.2 astronomical units now, so we'll get a power reduction by a factor of . . ." *Impossible!* "When we get to Mars, we'll be getting only about 64 percent of our current power!"

He looked at Valkerie and saw in her eyes that she could subtract.

"But we're using almost all available power right now," she said. "Can we cut the power on the ship any further?"

Bob spun to the CommConsole. "Houston, this is Ares 10, come in." While he waited, he scanned the power usage stats again. The ship was down to a bare-bones budget already.

Four minutes later Josh's voice floated in over the speakers. "Ares 10, this is Houston. How are you on this fine day?"

"Josh, listen, I've got a major concern here. Valkerie and I did a hand calculation, and we see an energy crisis coming up as we get closer to Mars. Has anybody down there noticed this?"

More minutes passed. Bob was beginning to hate this two-way delay in radio-signal time. Four minutes was a long time when you just wanted to talk to a human. *We are a long, long way from Kansas, Toto.*

"Roger on that, Ares 10," Josh said. "Be assured, we are working on that now. Over."

Bob tapped his fingers on the console. *That was it? They were working on it?*

"Why haven't they bothered to inform us about this?" Valkerie asked.

"Good question." Bob keyed the mike. "Houston, we see this as a serious issue. What is wrong with you people? Why haven't you mentioned this to us yet?"

Again, the pause. This one seemed longer than usual. "Affirmative on that, Ares 10. We also are taking this very seriously. Over."

Bob turned to stare at Valkerie. "He didn't answer our question!"

"Let me talk to him." Valkerie leaned over the console. He could feel her body heat, could almost smell her anger. "Josh, this is Valkerie, and I want you to get one thing perfectly clear. We are not going to tolerate you keeping us in the dark on things that affect our safety. Over."

"You tell him, sister," Bob said.

"Don't get sarcastic with me."

He sighed. "Valkerie, I'm not being sarcastic. That was a compliment."

The next few minutes passed in frigid silence.

"Valkerie, Bob—this is Josh." He sounded contrite, humble. "I must apologize for that error in judgment. Please believe me when I say that we intended to bring up the power crisis with you after your next sleep shift. We didn't feel it was wise to discuss it when you're exhausted. We do have teams working around the clock on it right now."

Bob felt a stab in his heart. *Power crisis? Working around the clock? What was going on?* "They're scared," he muttered.

Valkerie clutched his arm. He turned to look at her.

"They're not the only ones," she said.

Then it hit him—a rush of cold fear that shot through his body, a bolt of raw adrenaline in his veins, little prickles of terror in his palms. He shivered.

"Bob?" Valkerie still clung to his arm.

He swallowed hard.

"Bob?"

He looked down at Valkerie. Her eyes were frightened. Trusting. Like a little girl's. His heart pounded in his throat. "Yeah?" He choked out the word.

"We're going to be okay, right?"

He swallowed again and swiped at his eyes with the back of his hand. Even if she were the bomber, she was still scared. She was still human. He took a deep breath and wrapped a protective arm around her.

"Yeah." His voice sounded thick and distant, and there was a ringing in his ears. "Yeah, we're going to be okay."

CHAPTER 23

OXYGEN

Saturday, April 5, 2014, 10:00 A.M.
NATE

Nate lay on a cot, staring up at the ceiling of the war room. Footsteps sounded outside.

The door flew open and Josh stormed in.

Nate leaped to his feet, heart pounding. *Had they blown the ship up completely?*

"They know." Josh wiped his eyes. "Nate, what are we going to do? They know they're going to die, and there's not a thing we can do about it."

"Josh, listen, it ain't over till the gravitationally enhanced lady sings."

"It's over!" Josh shouted. "This isn't Apollo 13. Will you get that through your head? We don't have a lifeboat on board this time."

"Josh . . ."

But Josh had already stomped out, slamming the door, swearing like a sailor. A few seconds later his bellowing cut off in midcry.

Nate rushed out. If Josh had a heart attack now, that'd just be cherries on the old cheesecake, wouldn't it? But Josh was still on his feet, staring into space.

"Josh? You okay?" Nate hurried up to check on him.

"What did I just say?" Josh spun and grabbed Nate's arm. "Nate, what'd I say?"

"They're dead."

"No, after that. We don't have a lifeboat on board. Isn't that what I said? But we do have a lifeboat!"

"What are you talking about?" Nate wondered if he ought to order Josh to take a rest. The guy was sick as a dog and had stayed on duty all night. Anybody could crack—

"The Earth Return Vehicle, Nate! It's waiting for them at Mars right now. They were going to come home in it. Why can't they use that as a lifeboat?"

"Josh, that's crazy. The energetics are all wrong. You'd have to bring it back from Mars, intercept the Hab, stop the ERV on a dime, turn it around the other way, catch up to the Hab, and then dock. You know what kind of delta-V you'd need for that? We thought about that years ago, for the Mars Sample Return mission. The *best* case we could design cost twenty-five kilometers per second of delta-V. The ERV has three."

"Okay, forget the ERV that's at Mars now. What about the one we launched in December for the next mission? It's halfway to Mars. All we have to do is bump its trajectory a little, intercept the Hab, dock it, and they're home free."

Nate shook his head. "That's like saying all you have to do is toss a Coke bottle from your T-38 into the open cockpit of a 747 and hit the pilot in the eye. You're talking about hitting a bullet with a bullet in deep space. We talked about it for Mars Sample Return and it's doable— in theory. But we don't have the operations experience. And anyway, the biggest problem—"

"So you don't even want to try?"

"Josh, my master's degree was in orbital mechanics, okay? I kind of have a clue here. The energetics for a catch-up or a catch-down with a one-month launch separation are all wrong. Not as bad as an opposite- direction rendezvous, but it's still impossible."

"Impossible—just like that? Just because it's never been done?"

"Josh . . ."

"I can't believe this. What kind of a steely-eyed missile man are you? Human lives are at stake. If there's even a chance—"

"Josh. Listen to me. This isn't helping. Go home and get some rest. We've got a team looking at reducing scrubber power requirements using the Sabatier process."

"Whatever." Josh smeared his sleeve across his eyes, turned, and walked away.

Nate watched him go, feeling . . . nothing. What was the matter with him? He brushed a hand across dry eyes. Josh had him figured wrong, he decided. It wasn't his eyes that were made of steel. It was his heart.

————

Hours later Josh broke in on a meeting Nate was holding with the life-support team. Josh looked as if he'd just survived a flogging. His eyes were bloodshot, his hair was wild, and his borrowed shirt had huge sweat stains at the armpits.

Nate stood up. "Josh, I told you to go home."

Josh beckoned to somebody out in the hallway. "I've been talking to Cathe Willison. You know her, Nate? She's got a master's degree too—in orbital mechanics. And she's got a hot little simulation program for calculating rendezvous. You want to see it? Cathe, get in here."

A slender young woman wearing a New York Marathon T-shirt walked in. She held out her laptop to Josh.

Josh flipped it open and double-clicked on an icon.

"Operation Lifeboat," said a soft, sexy voice. It was the laptop. Nate wondered if that was Cathe's voicefont, or something she'd gotten off the web.

The laptop's display flashed to a backdrop of the solar system. "December 28, 2013," said the laptop in its silky voicefont. "The Earth Return Vehicle launches from Earth on a seven-month minimum energy transfer to Mars. The intended arrival date is July 24, 2014."

On the display, a tiny ERV launched from Earth, and the whole solar system began slowly moving. A little calendar zipped up and began highlighting dates sequentially.

"One month later, on January 26, 2014, the Hab launches on a somewhat faster trajectory intended to bring it into Mars orbit on July 3, 2014." A tiny model of the Hab blipped up from Earth, circled it several times, and then did a trans-Mars injection burn.

The display cycled forward a couple of months, then froze at the current date, April fifth.

"Operation Lifeboat requires the ERV to perform one burn to intersect the Hab's trajectory, then another burn to match velocities so it can dock with the Hab. The crew will then live in the ERV temporarily, until they transplant an ERV solar panel to the Hab, restoring energy production to near-normal levels. Finally, the crew will return to the Hab and continue safely to Mars."

A couple of small ellipses projected out from the positions of the Hab and ERV, showing where they'd be at various dates and how they'd intersect with the orbit of Mars. Nate grimaced. Any fool could see how hard it would be to do the intercept in time. Right now the two ships were three million miles apart.

"The Hab has no additional fuel to burn," said the laptop. "But the ERV has sufficient fuel to perform two burns with a combined delta-V of approximately 3.1 kilometers per second. The ERV can rendezvous with the Hab at any time after May 16, 2014."

A red conic section projected out from the ERV, demonstrating a sample trajectory.

Nate slouched in his chair. "Nice job, Cathe." He put his head in his hands.

"You don't look too happy," Josh said. "This is flat-out brilliant, if you ask me. I say Cathe gets a Silver Snoopy Award for this."

"It is brilliant," Nate said. "But there's only one problem."

"What's that?" Cathe Willison sounded exactly like the voicefont on her laptop.

"The Hab runs out of oxygen April ninth or tenth," Nate said. "The rendezvous is gonna be about five weeks too late to save the crew. I've been trying to tell you that, Josh, and you wouldn't listen."

"What about that Sabatier idea you were working on?" Josh asked. "Couldn't that stretch things out?"

"We've been looking at that," Nate said. "It ain't gonna work. You need a ruthenium catalyst, and there isn't any on the Hab."

"What about if you . . ." Cathe stopped. "This is going to sound cruel, sir, but has anyone considered the possibility that one or two of the crew could survive till rendezvous, if . . ."

"If two or three of them perform a noble sacrifice?" Nate stared at her. *This was one stainless-steely-eyed missile chick.* "Um, no, we haven't considered that option."

"Hold on a second," said one of the life-support engineers, a kid named Howard. "I'm going to run four life-support simulations, each with only one of the four Ares 10 crew members, and with energy production at . . ." He looked at Nate.

"Twenty-four percent of nominal."

Howard fired up a program on his laptop, punched in some numbers, and waited. "Okay, sir, any one of the four could survive till the rendezvous."

"We know that," Nate said. "Any one of them could survive all the way to Mars."

"Fine, I'll run the same simulation with all pairs of crew members."

He fiddled with the program for a few minutes. By now the other engineers had gathered round to watch. "Gotcha!" Howard said. "Any *two* of them could make it to the rendezvous on May sixteenth."

Nate sat up. That was progress. "What about three crew members?"

"I'll try that." Howard ran the program again. When the results flashed on the screen, he slumped in his seat. "Sorry. No combination of three can survive that long."

An audible hiss ran around the table. Nate could hardly breathe. The idea was ghoulish. No. He wasn't going to order the deaths of two crew members, hoping to save the other two.

"There's a chance," Josh said. "Nate, if we can save two of them, we have to try!"

"You're telling me I have to order two of my team to commit suicide," Nate said. "Plus, I have to burn all the fuel in the ERV, just so *maybe* it will get within radar range so *maybe* we can dock those vehicles, and *maybe* cannibalize a solar panel so *maybe* they can limp in to Mars? Josh, do you see how many *maybe*s we're fighting? And that ERV costs a couple of billion dollars. If we throw that away on a fool's chance—"

Josh stood up and flung the door open. "Well, excuuuuuse me. I hadn't realized there was a dollar value on human life." He stomped out.

"Josh!" Nate started to stand.

Cathe Willison put her hand on his arm. "Mr. Harrington," she purred in that sultry voice of hers. "Sometimes the calculus of suffering gives you an answer you don't like. That's too bad, but numbers don't lie. You *can* save two of them—"

Nate yanked his arm away. *Calculus of suffering?* She was a cold one. This solution was not acceptable. He was not going to order two crew members to kill themselves. He had to save them all. To do that, he needed every engineer he could scrape up. He couldn't afford to spend any of them on half a solution, especially one with so little chance of working.

The conference room phone rang. Nate grabbed the phone. "Harrington."

"Mr. Harrington, you'll be very sorry if you hang up prematurely. This is Jane Seyler with NBC News. We're about to run a story on a certain mishap yesterday, unless you give us good and sufficient reason why we shouldn't." A brief pause. "Are you there, Mr. Harrington?"

It seemed like a good time for a heart attack, but somehow Nate's ticker held together. "Who told you about this?"

"Mr. Harrington, I've been a journalist for twenty-three years and have never divulged a source."

"Was it Josh Bennett?"

"Our story, as it stands right now, is that Ares 10 has had an Apollo 13-type accident. Is that correct, Mr. Harrington?"

Nate breathed deeply. "Ms. Seyler, I happen to be under a gag order at the moment regarding Ares 10."

"That would be an Executive Order, signed by the president herself, correct?"

"I'll neither confirm nor deny anything."

"Mr. Harrington, if I run this story, what are the potential risks to the crew of Ares 10?"

"I'm not allowed to talk to you about any of this."

"Fine. Don't talk. I'll run the story and you can obey your orders."

Nate swore at her.

"Was that on the record, Mr. Harrington?"

"What do you want from me?"

"I understand some of your engineers have developed a lifeboat-type concept not unlike that which saved Apollo 13."

"It's totally different," Nate said. Oh, great—he'd just confirmed everything. "Ms. Seyler, I hope you realize that I'm going to prosecute Josh Bennett to the fullest extent of the law."

"That wouldn't be wise, Mr. Harrington."

"Are you threatening me?"

"Are you, or are you not, going to make an attempt to save your crew? On the record."

"I don't have to talk to you."

"Look at your watch, Mr. Harrington. It's five minutes before 6:00 P.M., Eastern Time. Do I, or do I not, run my story?"

"What's it to you? You're a journalist. You have to run a story if you think it's correct."

"Are you going to launch that lifeboat, Mr. Harrington?"

"How many people in your organization know about this?"

"Only me. Are you going to launch it?"

"Just tell me one thing. If I say yes, why should you hold that story?"

"Because Alexis Ohta"—Jane Seyler breathed deeply—"Lex Ohta . . . is my niece."

Which was just crazy enough to be true. Lex's paper work didn't list a father, but Nate knew she was half Caucasian. She had been raised by a single mom, a nice Japanese girl from Santa Barbara who made a mistake with some frat boy from back East.

"Mr. Harrington? Two minutes."

"What do you want from me?"

"Launch that lifeboat."

Nate stared at the seconds ticking away on his watch. He was gonna strangle Josh for this. There was no chance this could work. None.

"Showtime, Mr. Harrington. I need an answer *right now*."

There was no way to win this. If he said yes, he'd have to launch a fool's errand. If he said no, there'd be a fire storm in the press. In three days Nate would be off the mission, and some other poor schmuck would be forced to launch the lifeboat, with that much less chance of success. "Okay, you win," Nate said. "We'll fly the lifeboat."

"You won't regret it."

Nate slammed the phone down. He already regretted the decision. But it was too late for that. He was in this up to his armpits.

Nate looked around the table at his team. Some looked mystified. Some seemed to be puzzling it out. Cathe Willison looked satisfied. "We can save two of them, Mr. Harrington. You've got several days to choose which two."

Nate stood up. "Team, I want you to go back to square one. Analyze every chemical on that ship. Cannibalize every ounce of oxygen you can find. I want a team looking for alternate catalysts for that Sabatier scrubber. We're gonna launch Operation Lifeboat. If there's any way to do it, we're going to save that crew. The *whole* crew."

The team erupted in chatter. Nate stood up and strode out.

"Sir, what's the point of raising false hopes?" Cathe pattered after him. "You can't save them all, but you *could* save—"

"The point is that I said we're gonna try it," Nate growled. "Now get busy optimizing that solution. I want you to shave it down to the wire till you have a solution where they dock with zero fuel left in the ERV. And when you've got it perfect, make it better."

"When do I stop, sir?"

"When they're dead. Now get out of my face." Nate stopped and looked for Josh. "Bennett!" he bellowed. "Get yourself over to the Capcom console. We're gonna talk to the crew about Operation Lifeboat."

Josh appeared from somebody's cube, looking thoroughly confused. "What's going on? I thought—"

"You know perfectly well what's going on. We're gonna try it and see what happens." *And when this is all over, I throw you to the wolves for breaking that gag order.*

Josh turned and trotted for the Capcom station. Nate chugged along behind him. It wasn't going to work. The numbers said it couldn't work. But he had no choice.

No choice at all but to try.

Saturday, April 5, 2014, 9:00 P.M.
VALKERIE

Valkerie went through the motions of calibrating the pH meter. She thrust the electrode into a sample from the bioreactor. Its fragile glass tip clinked against the wall of the glass vial—probably broken, but what did it matter? She flung her duty schedule across the room. What did any of it matter? It was all pointless. Busy work from Houston with one and only one purpose—to keep them from dwelling on the fact that they were all going to die.

Valkerie pushed her way through the dark lab and made for the upper deck. Kennedy was still locked in his room—sulking. He hadn't said a word since Bob ran Houston's lifeboat plan through the simulation program.

Valkerie pulled herself into the command area and hung limp in the air. Bob was still working on the computer, but she could tell by the sluggishness of his movements that he hadn't found anything new. He'd run the lifeboat simulation a hundred times and the results were always the same. Even if they could beat the one-in-a-million odds of docking a bullet with a bullet, they'd all be dead before the Earth Return Vehicle got anywhere close—unless they could hold their breath for six weeks.

Houston was lying to them. What hurt the most was that Josh had been the one to give them the news. The one man they thought they could trust was in on the lie.

A drum roll of key taps broke through Valkerie's thoughts. She rolled in the air to check on Bob. No change in his expression. Just frustration. They were all frustrated.

Valkerie pressed her hands to her eyes. Why couldn't NASA just tell the truth? It was better to know the truth—no matter how painful that truth was. She pictured Josh's animated face—so full of energy and purpose. What would she have done if she were in his place? What if he were the one forced to endure the agony of waiting for a slow and sure death? Was a false hope better than no hope at all?

Valkerie pushed the questions from her mind, suddenly uncomfortable with the direction they were leading her.

God, you have to be real. Life had to be more than a series of chemical reactions. There had to be meaning. Christianity couldn't be a false hope. It just couldn't. But what about six weeks of slow suffocation? Where was the point in that?

Valkerie drifted around and watched Bob typing at the console. A tap here. A flurry of taps there. At least he was real. Too real usually. He ran a hand through his tousled sandy hair, floating lightly in zero-gravity. He looked a lot better now that his hair was growing out. It softened him, somehow. Made him more approachable. What would he do if she slipped up behind him and gave him a hug? She smiled at the thought. No, he wasn't that approachable. He'd probably throw her across the room.

"I don't believe it!" Bob spun suddenly around.

Valkerie looked away, embarrassed to be caught staring.

"I think I know what they're planning." Shock and disbelief registered in his voice.

"What?"

"I just ran a simulation. If only two of us . . . were still alive . . ."

The implication pressed its boot into Valkerie's gut. "You think they want us to . . ." Valkerie's mind recoiled at the thought. "The simulation—it showed two of us could make it?"

Bob nodded. "With days to spare."

Valkerie hung in the air. The silence of the ship pressed in on her like a sepulcher. "No . . ." She shook her head. "There has to be another way."

"I don't like it any more than you do." Bob moved closer. Valkerie watched as a battle of emotions played across his face. "I . . ." He lifted his hand and then snapped it back down. "I've run a thousand simulations. It's the only way."

Valkerie's vision grew hazy. She turned away. Bob's presence pressed in on her from behind. She could hear his breath, hoarse and strained, could feel his warmth.

"Bob? Whatever you do . . . please, don't tell Kennedy." Valkerie glanced behind her. Bob was chewing on his lip thoughtfully.

"He may already know. . . ."

"I seriously doubt that. Promise me. Please. I don't know what he would do if he knew."

Bob nodded. "Okay, I won't tell him. Now that I think of it, I shouldn't have told you. As long as the saboteur thinks we're doomed, there's no reason for him to try anything else."

"Would you get off the saboteur thing?" Valkerie reached for a ceiling strap and pulled herself over the bunk on which Lex lay. She started checking Lex's vitals. Good. Her lungs seemed to be clearing. They would be able to take out the high-frequency ventilator tube soon. "Don't you see that suspicions and negative thinking only make our situation worse?"

Bob moved toward Lex's bunk. "Excuse me, but I haven't been trained in the fine art of ignoring reality just because I happen to prefer the way a fantasy makes me feel."

Valkerie ignored the jab and checked Lex's pulse. Still shallow and weak. What was Bob's problem? Didn't he realize that they were going to die? Why was he so bent on bringing everyone else down?

"Look, Bob, I really don't feel like arguing, okay? I'm having a very bad week."

"Fine." Bob looked down at the floor and swallowed hard. "I suppose we should all be trying to make the most of our time, but if you ask me, Lex is the lucky one. At least she doesn't have to . . . to . . . what?"

Valkerie launched herself toward the command station. "Bob! What have you been using for our metabolism rates?"

"What?"

"Our oxygen consumption. What have you been using in your calculations?"

"About a pound per day—basal consumption assuming sleep and minimal movement."

"Lex is in a coma. That probably reduces her consumption by a third—maybe even a half!"

Bob entered some numbers and launched a simulation. "Nope, not even close."

"You said two people could make it with days to spare. What if three of us were in comas?"

"Why not all four of us?" Bob started adjusting the numbers.

"Somebody has to stay awake to revive the others."

"Okay—at half consumption for three people, here goes." Bob tapped the Enter key to start the simulation. "Days to spare!" He jumped up in the air and bumped his head on the ceiling. "Do you think it could work? Can they really put us in comas?"

Valkerie nodded. Her heart was pounding a million beats per minute. "I think so. Maybe. We have a lab and a ton of starting materials."

The excitement drained from Bob's face.

"What's wrong?"

"You're forgetting one thing. One of us wants this mission to fail. How are we going to choose who gets to stay awake?"

"Bob, there is no . . ." Valkerie bit her lip. What if the explosion really was caused by a bomb? Didn't the tiny bits of bright shrapnel in Bob's suit prove it? What if Kennedy really was a killer? Valkerie shuddered. She could still see him threatening her with the torch. But was Bob any better? He hadn't exactly been friendly—and he *was* the one who caused the explosion.

"I guess we'll just have to figure out who the bomber is. We don't have much time."

CHAPTER 24

Bob took another swallow of coffee. The stuff wasn't working anymore. He'd been awake for almost two days straight. If he were going to keep this up much longer, he'd have to go to something stronger. But Kennedy was holed up in his room, and Bob wasn't about to leave Valkerie with the run of the ship.

"Ares 10, this is Houston, come in."

Bob's head jerked up. Had he been dozing? And was that Nate's voice? How could that be? Nate wasn't a Capcom. Bob keyed the mike. "Houston, this is Ares 10, Bob speaking."

Valkerie abandoned her lab work and floated over to join him. They waited in silence as four minutes ticked off.

"Ares 10, this is your Mission Director, Nate Harrington, with a special message for the full crew. Dr. Kaganovski, please summon all four crew members, if possible. I do hope Dr. Ohta is now conscious. Over."

"Check in on Lex," Bob said to Valkerie. "I'll go get Kennedy." He pushed off from the console, floated over to Kennedy's door, grabbed a ceiling strap, and pounded on the door. "Hampster! Special message from Nate! He wants to talk to all of us together."

Half a minute later, the door slid sideways and Kennedy came out looking groggy and irritated. What was with him? He'd been in there for way more than eight hours, but the beauty sleep didn't look like it was working.

When they got back to the CommConsole, Valkerie was already there. "Lex is still unconscious," she said.

Bob grabbed the mike and set it floating at the midpoint between the three of them. "Houston, this is Bob. With me are Kennedy and Valkerie. Lex is still unconscious." He nodded to Kennedy and Valkerie. "Say something to verify you're here."

"Bang, bang, we're dead," Kennedy said in a toneless voice.

"Actually, three of us are conscious and cognizant," Valkerie said. "Lex is still in a coma, but her signs are stable. I expect she'll recover—at least partially."

"Over," Bob said.

The three of them waited in awkward silence. Bob tried not to breathe too deeply. Kennedy's body odor was getting awfully ripe.

"Ares 10, this is Mission Director Nate Harrington. We've evaluated the suggestion Bob and Valkerie sent, and we think it has a chance of success."

"What suggestion?" Kennedy asked. Bob put up a hand to shush him. Nate was still talking.

"Our evaluation says that sodium pentothal together with Raplon will work best for inducing a coma and minimizing your need for oxygen. We believe you can do it safely for up to sixty days, which is more than the forty days to the rendezvous date with the ERV. There remains the question of who will stay conscious during that time. Any one of you could do it, in principle. Valkerie has the lowest oxygen needs, so if you choose her, you'll have the biggest safety margin. Kennedy is next, then Bob. You could have as many as four days to make your decision, but the error bars on that figure are pretty large. You need to decide as soon as you're finished synthesizing the drugs. I'm sending synthesis pathways and instructions in an e-mail document. Over."

Kennedy's eyes were bugging out. "What is going on here? What's Nate talking about?"

Valkerie quickly filled him in on the plan.

When she finished, Bob took the mike. "Nate, this is Bob. We still need final answers on the questions I asked after the explosion. First, do you agree that this was a bomb—not an accident? Second, is there anybody else who could have placed it there?"

Bob knew immediately that he'd hit a nerve. A frozen silence engulfed the Hab. Kennedy and Valkerie didn't like the implications of his questions. But so what? He wasn't trying to make friends at this stage. He was just trying to stay alive.

"Ares 10, this is Houston." Nate's voice sounded tense. "For your first question, Bob, I've had a team go over all the data, including the video of your spacewalk up to the final frame when the CamBot got blown up. And our answer is an unequivocal *yes*. That was definitely an explosion, and there is no possible explanation other than some sort of bomb. There should have been nothing in that bay that could explode. So I believe the only explanation is sabotage."

Bob felt his pulse pounding in his throat. *Please let it be someone down there.*

"As for the question of security," Nate said, "we have not found any additional suspects. It has to be either me or Josh or one of you four. And ..." Nate's voice cracked. "I hope you know it wasn't me. Over."

Kennedy took the mike. "Nate, this is Kennedy. We have a big decision to make. We'll think it over and get back to you ASAP. Over and out."

Bob could hardly believe the change in Kennedy. Ten minutes ago, he'd been acting like they were all on Death Row. Now, all of a sudden, he was Mr. Take Charge.

Kennedy set the mike on its Velcro patch. "Okay, we need to think about this. Bob, I have to apologize to you. It looks like your initial idea was right—we've been sabotaged. First off, we need to figure out who it could have been. Then we decide who has to baby-sit the others until the rendezvous with the ERV. So. Who do you think did it? Valkerie, any ideas?"

"Um ... this is kind of awkward," Valkerie said.

No kidding. Bob cleared his throat. "This is life and death."

Kennedy hesitated. "Okay ... How about if we each write down the name of our primary suspect on a piece of paper?"

Valkerie floated to the CommConsole and pulled off three sticky notes and a pen. She handed out stickies to each of them.

Bob sat there, frozen in horror. Who was the bomber? He knew the answer. Knew it in his head, but he still couldn't believe it. But how could you fight the logic?

Neither Nate nor Josh would kill their own crew. They just wouldn't. Kennedy? A weasel, but an ambitious one. The road to glory for him lay through Mars. Lex? She was a Mars fanatic. She was willing to die to get to Mars—not the other way around.

And Valkerie? Would she die for something—for some Cause greater than herself? Bob closed his eyes. *Sidney Nichols.* He'd used a bomb too. And he'd died for his cause. Had Valkerie been in on it?

If there were any other answer . . .

But there wasn't. And when you'd eliminated every possibility except one, then by Sherlock, you had the answer. Like it or not.

Bob opened his eyes, scrawled *Valkerie* on his sticky note, and folded it over and over. Valkerie and Kennedy had already written something on theirs.

Valkerie collected them all in a beaker, put her hand over the top, and shook it. As if that would scramble their handwriting.

Kennedy reached into the beaker and pulled out a name. "Valkerie," he read out loud, then showed it to the others. Bob recognized his own writing. Valkerie scowled at him.

Kennedy pulled out another. "Bob."

"That's ridiculous!" Bob said.

Kennedy held it up for all to see. Bob squinted at the large block letters, deliberately disguised. Was that Valkerie's or Kennedy's writing?

Kennedy pulled out the last sticky and opened it. His face flushed. "Somebody doesn't trust me." He thrust out the sticky so they could see *Kennedy* in scratchy, thin letters.

Obviously, Kennedy hadn't voted against himself or against Valkerie. So Kennedy didn't trust Bob. And therefore Valkerie didn't trust Kennedy. Bob sat there digesting this information. The others were obviously coming to the same conclusion.

"So," Kennedy said. "We've got a little round robin. What do we do?"

"If I may make a comment . . ." Valkerie seemed hesitant.

"Go ahead, Valkerie. Your comments are very important." Kennedy reached out and touched her arm. "We're all in this together."

Bob felt his blood pressure rising. Kennedy was already soliciting her vote, trying to get on her good side.

"It seems to me, we don't need a witch hunt, so much as we need an angel hunt," Valkerie said. "Sure, it would be nice to know who put that bomb there. It'd be nice to know his or her motive. It'd be nice to know a lot of things . . . for example, why God doesn't send e-mail." She threw a little glance at Bob.

Great, now she's kissing up to me.

"But the really important thing to know is who *didn't* put the bomb there. That's the person we want taking care of us and the ship until the rendezvous. If we can prove beyond all doubt that one of us is innocent, then that person should be chosen. Let's find us an angel, not a witch."

Oh, nice thinking, Miss Angel-Face. Let's see who's holier than who. And while we're doing that, let's not forget what kind of people drank poison Kool-Aid in Jonestown to make a point. Or got themselves burned to death in Waco. Or who blow up abortion clinics every other month. Nice people. Solid, everyday, ordinary people. Because the sad truth is that nice people sometimes do horrible things—when they think it's for a greater good.

"Valkerie, that's a very good idea," Kennedy said, still using his agreeabler-than-thou voice. "Maybe the first thing we could do is agree to search the private stuff we each brought along. Any objections to that? You can search my things first."

Bob shook his head. "No objections from me." He had nothing to hide. And besides, anyone who disagreed to that would be asked why. From now on, each of them had the burden of innocence. Good grief, it was going to be a righteous few days.

Valkerie nodded. "By the way, I think it's obvious that our final decision is going to have to be unanimous. As soon as any two of us can settle on the third it will be settled. So we should make it a rule that nobody is allowed to vote for himself until the other two have voted for him. That should prevent a deadlock."

"Of course," Kennedy said in his most agreeable tone.

That ticked Bob off. From now on, Kennedy would just be agreeing to anything Valkerie said—anything to get her to change her vote.

"There's just one problem," Bob said.

The other two looked at him.

Oh great, now I'm the odd man out. Bob hesitated. "Even with that rule, it's still logically possible to deadlock. What happens if we can't make a decision by the time we're finished with the synthesis? After that, we *have* to choose, and then we'll be forced to take whoever's got the best safety margin at the other end. Which would be Valkerie. So Valkerie can force herself as the choice, just by intentionally deadlocking."

Valkerie and Kennedy looked at each other. Obviously, they hadn't thought of that.

"We need to decide quickly. If we can't agree in forty-eight hours, I say we bring Josh into it," Bob said. "Let him decide, if we can't."

"What if Josh is the saboteur?" Kennedy asked.

Valkerie flushed. "Josh is not—"

"Then it won't matter who he votes for, because all of us will be innocent," Bob said.

"I want Nate in on the decision," Kennedy said. "He's the Mission Director. Let him and Josh decide together."

Valkerie frowned, but finally nodded. "Okay, we'll let them be the arbitrators if we can't decide. Good idea, Bob."

Bob felt a little surge of triumph. He knew how Valkerie felt about Nate, but she had to agree, because she was trying to curry favor with him. And Kennedy would agree with Valkerie for the same reason.

"You're absolutely right, Valkerie," Kennedy said. "I'll notify Nate of that right away." He went to the CommConsole.

Bob and Valkerie waited quietly. Bob's mind was churning. This three-way politics looked balanced, but it wasn't. He'd just discovered the first instability in it. If you made a suggestion that was remotely reasonable, the other two would agree to it. They had to, because they were each trying to win somebody's vote.

Were there other ways to tip the scales? There had to be. And Bob was going to find those ways and use them.

Because no matter what anyone said or did, he was *not* going to let Valkerie put him in a coma. That would be suicide. If it came down to that, he'd ... what?

He'd think of something.

Sunday, April 6, 2014, 11:00 A.M.

VALKERIE

"Kennedy, there's nothing there. We searched her clothes a million times." Bob sounded irritated.

Valkerie rummaged through Lex's toiletry bag for the third time. Where were her birth-control pills? It didn't make sense. *Why would they make me take them and not Lex?*

"Just trying to be thorough." Kennedy held up a pair of panty hose. "Doesn't it seem strange to you that Lex wasted her weight allotment on such impractical clothes?"

"Who cares? Let's get on with it. You still haven't searched my room." Valkerie stuck the toiletry bag to the wall and spun around for the door.

"Wait." Kennedy held up a hand. "We still need to interpret the messages on Lex's computer."

"We haven't got time," Bob said. "Let's ask Nate to track down this Anderson guy."

Valkerie followed the men to her cabin. She waited in the doorway while Bob and Kennedy went through her stuff. Kennedy was moving like a three-toed sloth on Prozac. He'd been stalling all morning. Every second he wasted was one more reason not to vote for Bob. The way things were going, they were going to deadlock. Nate and Josh would end up deciding.

If Josh couldn't vote for Bob, who would he vote for? The question had been haunting Valkerie all morning. She'd like to think that he'd vote for her—after all, she was the most qualified person to monitor the crew. But Josh had known Kennedy a lot longer, and he *was* the best choice to pilot the docking rendezvous. Plus he knew the ship better than Valkerie did. No, whatever she did, she had to keep Bob in the running. Josh would probably pick Bob over Kennedy. Bob knew the ship better than anyone, and there were still a lot of repairs that needed to be made.

Bob pulled a packet of birth-control pills out of Valkerie's toiletry bag and cast a sidelong glance at her.

Valkerie pretended not to notice, but her burning face gave her away. She looked quickly down at the floor. Where could Lex have hidden her pills—and why? It didn't make any sense. Maybe Kennedy was right about it being strange to bring fancy clothes. But at least she could wear them. That was more than could be said for Kennedy's baseball and glove. And what about Bob's "optional luggage"? The mini-oxyacetylene torch she could understand. But beer and beef jerky? He'd brought enough beef jerky to get a homesick cowboy to Mars and back.

"What are these?" Bob asked suspiciously. "Valkerie?"

"What?" Valkerie looked up. Bob was holding out her bag of oil paints. "What do they look like?"

Bob took the cap off one of the tubes and started to squeeze it into a towel.

"Bob, no!" Valkerie yelled. "They're just paints."

"What's the matter? Something in here besides paint? See?" Bob showed the tube to Kennedy. "This tube's been opened. Why would she bring paints that have already been used?"

"Because they were my mother's." Valkerie reached for the tube of paint, but Bob jerked it away.

"Please . . . don't waste them; they're all I have with me." Valkerie looked up into his eyes, forcing him to pay attention.

Bob swallowed hard. He squeezed a little paint onto his forefinger and rubbed it with his thumb, bringing it up to his nose. "You realize we'll have to analyze this?"

Valkerie nodded. "Just don't waste them. Please. I didn't make you open your beer."

"But I offered—"

"Hey! Take a look at this!" Kennedy pushed Valkerie's computer in Bob's face. "It looks like Josh and Valkerie are an item. No wonder she was willing to let him have a vote."

Bob's eyes narrowed. "That's okay. Give Nate the whole decision and keep Josh out of it."

"You can't change the rules now!" Valkerie was indignant. "We already decided."

"We brought Josh in because we thought he would be impartial," Kennedy said. "That assumption no longer seems to be valid."

Valkerie skimmed the portion of the e-mail message visible on the screen. "Is this what's bothering you?" She pointed at the last paragraph. " 'I'm counting down the seconds until your return.' Come on. We're just friends. He's just being an encouragement."

"Yeah, right," Kennedy scoffed. "If he was that encouraging to me, I'd deck him."

"And he doesn't end his e-mails to me 'Love, Josh,' " Bob added.

Kennedy held up a hand. "All in favor of making Nate the sole arbitrator say aye."

"Aye," Kennedy and Bob chorused in unison.

"I'm calling Houston." Valkerie twisted around and pulled herself through the door.

"Not so fast." Kennedy followed her out the door and grabbed her by the arm. "We're not finished searching your room, and we already agreed—we have to stick together."

"Go ahead and search. I can wait. But as soon as you're done, I'm calling Houston."

Kennedy shrugged and turned to watch Bob, who seemed to be engrossed with another message on Valkerie's computer. Kennedy searched Valkerie up and down and smiled. Valkerie backed away as he leaned in close to her ear. "I could change my vote about Josh—given the right inducement."

Valkerie went cold. "Not a chance." She pulled herself away from Kennedy and retreated back into her cabin to float near Bob.

Kennedy grinned at her triumphantly.

Valkerie shuddered. Nate was almost sure to vote for Kennedy. If she couldn't convince Bob of her innocence . . . no, it was too horrible. She had to convince Bob. No way could she let Kennedy put her into a coma.

Even if he wasn't the saboteur, Kennedy was anything but innocent.

CHAPTER 25

Nate had set up a desk out on the floor of Mission Control. He wanted anybody and everybody to have access to him.

And they were doing it. The line was finally down to three people. The first was a communications specialist named Hanson.

"Sir, we've tracked down this person R.J. Anderson that Dr. Ohta was getting so many e-mails from." Hanson held out a fact sheet. Ronald J. Anderson was an Air Force lieutenant colonel stationed near Sacramento. Born January 14, 1978. Graduated from the Air Force Academy, June 2001, second in his class. Sports—scuba diving, basketball, volleyball, you name it. Marital status—single.

Nate looked up at Hanson. "So what's the connection to Alexis Ohta?"

"We're checking that now, sir," Hanson said. "Lex graduated from the Academy in 2002, and it appears that she knew Anderson there, but they didn't run in the same circles. Other than that, we don't see a connection. For some reason, Dr. Ohta put Anderson on her list of visitors for the last meeting the night before the launch."

"What about Anderson's political ties?" Nate asked. "Any contact with terrorist organizations? Or right-wing or left-wing political organizations?"

"Sir, he has a top secret security clearance. He's clean. He's a registered Republican."

Nate leaned back in his chair. "Check their telephone records. See if they've been in voice contact. Then I want you to haul in Anderson and hit him with every fact you've got. Ask him point-blank what's his connection to Lex. This is important."

Hanson nodded and left.

Josh Bennett was next. His shirt looked rumpled, his hair hadn't been combed in days, and he had a coffee stain on his left elbow. "Nate, I've got another idea on the catch-down problem—"

A door slammed. "Mr. Harrington!" Crystal Yamaguchi's voice.

Nate looked up. Crystal looked excited. And scared. She rushed up and handed Nate a note. "Read this. I need to talk to you. Privately."

Nate opened the note and scanned it. His heart lurched. *Josh? Josh Bennett?* No. This did not compute. Somebody was letting their imagination go way overboard.

"We need to talk," Crystal said. "Right now."

"A breakthrough?" Josh said.

Crystal tensed. Her eyes clearly said, *Do not tip him off.*

Nate reached for the paper on his desk. "Josh, actually, I've got something important for you. The crew's been asking about a certain friend of Lex's, this officer Anderson. I need you to go read this info sheet to them."

"But—"

"It's important, Josh."

"Okay, fine." Josh took the sheet.

"And then you need to get some rest," Nate said. "Four hours' sleep. That's an order."

"How can I sleep when my crew's in danger?"

"Josh, I need you sharp. The next few days are going to be critical. I may need you to help me make a tough decision soon. And you can't do that if you're brain-dead tired."

Josh hesitated, then nodded and left.

Crystal pulled on Nate's sleeve. "Have you got a secure room?"

Nate nodded and led her out and down the hall to a conference room. "Guaranteed bug free, sound-proof, and all that. Now what's this dirt on Josh?"

Crystal opened her briefcase and pulled out a folder. "You remember that blueprint of the Hab that turned up in a Japanese terrorist cell a year and a half ago?"

"How could I forget?" Nate said. "That's how I met you."

"We just connected them to a group of university students in Tokyo. Japanese security raided their computers and found a copy of the blueprint as an e-mail attachment. It came in through an anonymous re-mailer in Finland."

"A what?"

"And we had Interpol get a court order to open their files. Guess where the e-mail originated?"

"You're going to tell me Josh sent it, and I'm going to tell you you're nuts."

Crystal shrugged. "Try to be objective. I can't say for sure that Josh sent it. But it did originate from his computer. That, we can prove beyond any reasonable doubt."

"So what are you trying to tell me?"

"Just this. Right now, Josh Bennett is our prime suspect."

Monday, April 7, 2014, 5:00 P.M.
VALKERIE

Valkerie loaded another tiny sample onto the high-pressure liquid chromatograph. At this rate, they'd be out of oxygen before she got the drug synthesized. The mission design team obviously hadn't expected the crew to do any organic synthesis. Whoever heard of trying to do preparative work on an analytical instrument? It was crazy.

"So what do I do if their pulse rates fall below that level?" Bob's voice sounded less than a foot behind Valkerie's head.

Valkerie stifled a growl. The Mr. Nice Guy routine was really getting old. Bob had been hovering around her all day, feeding her one question after another about the drug she was synthesizing.

"Bob, look . . . you don't have to do this. I'm already planning to vote for you. I don't trust Kennedy as far as I can throw him." Valkerie glanced over at Kennedy, who was sleeping upside down on the laboratory wall. "In Earth gravity, I mean."

"Just trying to prepare myself." Bob floated to Valkerie's side. "If I run out of the drugs, I need to be able to do the synthesis myself."

"Good luck. I used up all our starting materials. If it's not enough, we're in big trouble." Valkerie pointed to a flask of liquid rotating under vacuum. "See this flask? It's the sodium pentothal precursor. Do you know how easy it would have been for me to flush this into our water system? I could break the flask right now, and you wouldn't be able to stop me. Know why I don't?"

"Because you need it to look like an accident? Because you're too softhearted to face the people you're trying to kill? Because you'd rather do it with the poison you're—"

"Bob! Stop it! I know you don't believe that. You can't. Look me in the eye and tell me you think I'm a killer. Seriously. Look me in the eye." Valkerie stared defiantly up at Bob. He looked back at her, then diverted his gaze. He swallowed and opened his mouth but didn't say anything.

"You can't, can you? Want to know why? Because you don't think it's true."

"No." Bob scowled. "I'll admit that I don't *know* that it's true, but it *could* be. Don't you see? The whole notion that someone could have sabotaged our ship is mind-bogglingly crazy. But it's a fact—no matter how unlikely it may have seemed before it happened. Of course I can't believe you did it. I can't believe that *anybody* would do such a thing. But that doesn't change the fact that it happened."

"But what if nobody did it? What if it was just a bizarre, low-probability accident?"

"You mean like life on Earth?"

Valkerie rolled her eyes. Bob was nothing if not persistent. "An accident—like using feet instead of meters."

"Okay, an accident—that just happened to involve a bomb that just happened to be placed at just the right spot to cripple sixteen different systems—"

"Most of which weren't critical."

"—that were just critical enough to guarantee a slow prolonged death and two or three weeks of media-grabbing publicity. That's what the saboteur would want, right? To scare the public so bad, they'll never send another mission to Mars. To drag it out as long as possible—"

"If it were me, why would I suggest the coma? Why didn't I just let you freeze in space?"

"Two or three weeks of media-grabbing publicity."

"But I was the one who fixed the hull breach. I was the one who rescued Lex."

"Two or three weeks of—"

"Stop it!" Valkerie snapped. "Was I the one hogging the camera during the press conference we did last week? Was I the one giving everybody a tour of our toilet? Kennedy's the camera hog. Not me. He's the one who pushed for that press conference. Don't forget, he's the one who bullied, lied, and cheated to get us to leave Earth in a crippled ship."

Bob held up a hand. "I don't trust Kennedy either. Does that make you feel any better? I can't afford to trust him."

Valkerie considered Bob's words. He didn't know how to trust people. That was his problem. But why? "Something happened to you, didn't it? Something in your past that makes it hard for you to trust people."

Bob's neck flushed. "Right, I'm fighting for my life, and you're trying to psychoanalyze some hidden trauma. How about the fact that my life depends on it? Isn't that reason enough?"

"But you should at least be willing to consider the facts—"

"I didn't plant that bomb and that means someone else did. Until I find out who that person is, I can't afford to trust anyone."

"I didn't do it either, but I'm willing to trust you. Why can't you trust me?"

"See? Another reason not to trust you."

"What?"

"The only way you could know for sure that I'm not guilty is if you were guilty."

"Not necessarily. I'm just a good judge of character. I know you didn't do it. I can see right through that titanium-reinforced aluminum shell of yours. Underneath, I see the generous, warm, loving heart of a good man. Deny it if you want, but I know it's there."

Color rose to Bob's face. "Why would I want to deny that?"

Valkerie reached toward Bob and rested her hand softly on his forearm. "I don't know. I wish you would tell me."

Bob went rigid. His jaw muscles clenched and unclenched, and the tendons stood out on his neck. He turned suddenly and made for the door.

"Bob?"

He disappeared up the stairwell. She made a move to go after him, but then stopped. What could she say that she hadn't already?

"Don't worry, I'll get him," Kennedy said.

Valkerie jumped. How long had he been awake?

Kennedy peeled back the Velcro-fastened meshwork of the bunk. "I must say I'm surprised. Not so much at your tactics, but that Bob actually turned you down. Interesting."

Valkerie started to protest, but stopped. Why bother? He was going to vote for her anyway. Hmmm . . . if he switched his vote to Bob, then

Bob would win, and she wouldn't have to worry. What if she tried to convince Kennedy that she were the saboteur? She could force him to vote for Bob.

"Kennedy?"

He regarded her with a wary expression.

No, it was too risky. They'd all choose Kennedy, if they thought she was the saboteur. "I'll go get Bob."

"Oh no you don't. It's your turn to sleep." Kennedy moved toward Valkerie menacingly.

Valkerie shrank back from him. "But I'm not tired. I have to finish the synthesis."

"And deprive me of my chance at rebuttal? Not on your life. Come over here and lie down. And don't try anything funny while I'm gone either. I'll be listening."

"I thought you trusted me." Valkerie circled around Kennedy and started to squirm into the sack.

"What gave you that idea?" Kennedy floated above her with a sneer.

"Well, for one thing, you voted for me to stay awake."

Kennedy laughed and turned to leave the lab. "I voted for myself. You're just too dumb to realize it yet."

Monday, April 7, 2014, 5:15 P.M.
BOB

Bob felt his pulse pounding in his temples. How dare Valkerie try to tell him what was wrong with him? That was some kind of gall, trying to tell him he had a problem with trust, when she was the one with the death wish. And of course she could trust him. Why shouldn't she? He hadn't done anything except . . . blow up the ship.

He pounded the wall. That explosion wasn't his fault. It was a freak thing. Bad luck to have the multimeter on the wrong setting. Bad luck to have the detonator wires so close to the power cables. Bad luck that any of those wires had been exposed in the first place.

So if it was all bad luck, what was the original plan? That just flat out didn't make sense. When had the saboteur intended the bomb to go off? On the landing? Boy, wouldn't they have gotten some great TV coverage then?

He shook his head, trying to clear the swirl of thoughts. You'd never get anywhere trying to figure out the rationale of an irrational person.

"Kaggo, you okay?" Kennedy said.

Bob turned. "Hey, Hampster. Yeah, I'm fine. Tired of watching little Miss Righteousness like a hawk to make sure she doesn't accidentally synthesize a dose of arsenic to put us out for good."

"She was putting the moves on you pretty slick there," Kennedy said.

Bob felt his ears burning. "What moves?"

Kennedy grinned. "You don't know much about women, do you?"

I know a whale of a lot more than I'm going to tell you. Bob cleared his throat. "What are you trying to tell me?"

"Just thinking that you could catch more flies with honey than vinegar."

"I'm not interested in catching flies."

Kennedy raised an eyebrow. "And she just happens to have birth-control pills packed away in her personal kit. Now why do you suppose that is?"

"I don't know and I don't care," Bob said. "But I'm still trying to figure out why you'd vote for her. You don't trust me, do you?"

Kennedy shrugged. "I trust you a lot more than I trust her. But I trust me more. Sorry, nothing personal, but you *were* the guy who set off the bomb."

"It was an accident!" Bob said.

"And Valkerie was nowhere near it."

"Somebody put it there. Bombs don't just appear by chance."

Kennedy gave him a devilish smile.

"So you really think I put the bomb there?"

"I have no idea who made that bomb. But *you* set it off, Kaggo, and you did it after we told you not to touch those wires. Valkerie saved Lex and patched the ship. Can you honestly expect me to vote for you after that? I'd have to be crazy."

"So you're telling me we have a stalemate?" Bob said. "Because there's no way I'm going to vote for Valkerie. Ever."

"Maybe you could persuade her to vote for me," Kennedy said. "She seems to trust you."

For whatever reason, she doesn't trust you. Bob studied Kennedy. "I don't think she'll listen to me."

"So we'll deadlock," Kennedy said.

"Which means Nate has the tie breaker."

"Nate's not going to vote for you," Kennedy said. "You know that, right? He can't. For the same reason I can't. You set off the bomb."

Does everybody have to keep reminding me? Bob swallowed. "Okay, fine. Nate's not going to vote for me. So what's your point?"

"My point is that Nate has two real choices—me or Valkerie. Josh is going to have a voice in the decision too. And I get the impression he favors her."

"Did you see how he signed his notes to her?" Bob said. " 'Love, Josh.' Can you believe that?"

"On the other hand, Josh is a rational guy. He knows I'm the best pilot in the known universe—except for him, of course. I'm the best person to do the docking with the ERV. That means I should be the one who stays awake."

"I think I need to talk to him. He might be interested in hearing about an old college buddy of Valkerie's," Bob said. "Is he on Capcom shift right now?"

"He's around, even if he's not on shift," Kennedy said. "The guy's been a maniac down there. He already came up with the lifeboat idea. If there's any way to save our cookies, Josh'll find it." He pushed off from the wall and headed for the bathroom. "Gotta take a pit stop."

Bob grabbed the mike and keyed it. "Houston, this is Ares 10, Bob speaking, with a personal message for Josh Bennett. Over."

Minutes ticked by. The delay was getting on Bob's nerves. *We're lost in space.*

"Ares 10, this is Josh. Man, what a coincidence! I was just coming online to give you some news. Let me go first with the news, and then I'll wait for you. Nate wanted me to give this to you right away. The mystery man on Lex's e-mail is a guy named Ronald J. Anderson, a U.S. Air Force officer." Josh went on for about two minutes, giving details about Anderson.

Bob didn't really see the significance. Okay, fine, so Lex had a boyfriend. She could have one in every hamlet in the country, for all Bob cared. The only mystery was why she was keeping him a mystery.

When Josh finished, Bob took the mike. "Thanks for that info, Josh." *I don't see the point, but thanks.* He hesitated a minute. He had to phrase this in such a way that it didn't look like he was trying to influence Josh. "The reason I called was to ask your advice on something. You know we're going to be voting soon on who should stay awake while we're in a coma. For a lot of reasons, I'm not going to win that vote. No problem with that—I'd hate to be alone for that long anyway. Now my question is this. Can you get me the scores on docking maneuvers for both Valkerie and Kennedy? The reason I ask is because whoever stays awake is going to have to dock with that ERV, and I kind of want us to be in good hands, you know what I mean? Anyway, if you can get me that info, I'd be much obliged. Also, I have a request of a more personal nature. Strictly between you and me, okay? Valkerie mentioned dating a guy from Yale. Sidney Nichols. Could you do a little research on him? I need to know right away. It's important. Over."

Bob set the mike aside, feeling like an idiot, the way he usually did when he talked to an answering machine. He usually just blabbed and blabbed until he ran out of steam. It was kind of like praying. Except that, with prayer, God never answered His voice mail.

"Hello, Bob, funny you should ask about docking scores. I just checked over those this morning," Josh said. "Kennedy and Lex both have ratings of one hundred on docking maneuvers. Valkerie is at ninety-eight. And you are . . . pretty low. Seventy-one, I think. But don't worry about those scores. Frankly, the computer's going to do the docking just fine ninety-nine times out of a hundred anyway. There's not a dime's worth of difference between Kennedy and Valkerie on that. You should be making your decision based on other criteria. You need to evaluate their mental states. That's probably the most important thing. Who's least likely to crack up if they're alone for five or six weeks? As for the other question, I'll get on it right away. I knew you two were going to hit it off. Any other questions? Over."

Bob closed his eyes. He'd missed with the first pitch. The second had better be a strike. He keyed the mike. "Houston, this is Ares 10. Thanks for that input. Let me know on the second question as soon as you can. That's a big help in making my decision. Over and out."

Kennedy was nowhere in sight, but the *In Use* indicator was still showing on the handle of the bathroom door. Bob pushed off and floated down the stairwell and into the lab.

Valkerie was strapped onto the wall in her SRU. Bob floated over and studied her intently. Was she really asleep? Her chest rose and fell slowly. You could only just hear her breathing. A dull ache settled in Bob's gut. He wished Kennedy would quit the suggestive remarks about Valkerie. Sure, she was a nice-looking woman. But what was killing Bob was the way she seemed to read his heart, his thoughts, his past. *Like Sarah.* Valkerie could see through the tough shell he put up. And she didn't reject him. She even seemed to like him. Sort of.

If only . . .

Something hot welled up in Bob's eyes. He brushed at them madly. Never mind the what-ifs. The reality was that Valkerie might have put a bomb on this ship. *Probably* put it there. It was the only logical possibility.

And he couldn't afford to let her finish the job.

Bob checked Valkerie's eyes again, then gently pushed off toward the medical bay. He silently opened the drawer. *There.* He grabbed a syringe, eased it into one of the long pockets on his leg, and Velcroed it shut.

As he closed the drawer, he heard a noise in the stairwell.

"Misfire." Kennedy floated into the lab, looking irritated. "My guts are playing games with me again. Did you get hold of Josh?"

Bob nodded. "Yeah, he was in. I kind of felt him out on all that stuff we talked about."

"And?" Kennedy narrowed his eyes.

"Don't worry," Bob said. "It's taken care of."

CHAPTER 26

Monday, April 7, 2014, 11:00 P.M.
NATE

Nate hadn't been in his own office in days. Now he had a good reason to be there. He had to confront Josh Bennett about that stolen blueprint. And he needed privacy to do that. He drummed his fingers on his desk. Where was Josh?

"Nervous?" Perez said.

"I can't believe he'd do such a thing." Nate shook his head. "Josh's father was an engineer here during the Apollo years. Josh grew up eating, drinking, and breathing the space program. He loves NASA. He couldn't—"

A knock sounded at the door. It opened just as Nate got to it. "Hey, Josh, come on in." Nate thought his voice sounded ridiculously breezy.

Josh walked in, saw Perez, and took a second look at Nate's face. His eyes put up their phaser shields. "What's up, gentlemen?" He didn't sit down.

Nate pointed to a chair, then plopped into his own.

Josh sat down as if the chair were made of toothpicks.

Nate cleared his throat. *How was he going to say this?* "Josh, we've got a couple of questions about the Hab."

Josh licked his lips. "Um, sure, fine." He looked over at Perez, then back to Nate. "What kind of questions?"

Nate pulled a blueprint out of his drawer and spread it on the desk. "This blueprint found its way to a Japanese terrorist organization back in August of 2012. Remember that month? We had a lot of stuff going on then. Senator Axton was trimming our budget with a chainsaw. You had a little accident on your motorcycle." *And we axed you from Ares 10, remember?*

Josh managed a feeble grin. "Hey, some months you don't forget, right?" He wiped his palms on his filthy shirt.

"Okay, so I'll get to the point," Nate said. "This blueprint was sent electronically to Japan from here. We've traced it through an anonymous remailer in Finland."

"A... what?" Josh looked genuinely mystified.

"Anonymous remailer. It's some kind of an e-mail site where you can send messages, and it'll mail them on to any address you choose, wiping out all the information about who sent it."

"What's the point of that?"

Nate sighed. Josh was either a really good actor, or... what? "You can send things to someone through one of these remailers, and nobody will ever know who sent it. Including the recipients."

"And you say it came from inside NASA?" Josh said. "How do you know that if it's anonymous?"

"We had Interpol get a court order and open the records on the re-mailer in Finland," Nate said.

Perez just sat there, nodding. He wasn't going to help at all.

"Josh, the bottom line is this." Nate pulled out another document. "According to the records, that blueprint was mailed from your computer, using your e-mail address."

Josh's jaw sagged. "Mine? That's... crazy. I don't know anyone in Japan. Why would I want to send some terrorists a blueprint of the Hab?" He looked at Perez. "Dr. Perez, you don't believe I did that, do you?"

"We're just trying to get to the bottom of this, Josh," Perez said. "We thought we'd start by talking to you. Now if there's anything you'd like to tell us—"

"No kidding, there's something I want to tell you." Josh stood up. "I've been out there working my tail off on this project for something like eight years. I've done the roadwork, the classwork, the grunt work— and you guys canned me, and I'm still doing my job. And you know why? I'll tell you why. Because I... love... NASA."

"I've been dreaming all my life about putting a man on Mars. Or a woman, or whatever. Our men. Our women. United States of America. And if you think I'd do anything—*anything*—to hurt this project, you are brain-dead flipped-out crazy! I don't have to put up with this. I've got a crew that needs me." He turned for the door.

"Whoa, whoa, whoa!" Nate said. "Josh, we are not accusing you of anything. But the Fibbies have brought this to our attention and we need to resolve this question. And we wanted to be up front with you about it right from the start." He held the paper up in the air.

"Okay, fine. Be up front." Josh grabbed the FBI report and looked at it. "What's the date on this thing, anyway? Did you even think to check my schedule? I was out of town a lot that month, as I recall."

He scanned the paper. "Here it is. August 11, 2012, 7:00 P.M." He pulled out his PDA. "Look at this. I was in an airplane flying to Japan to visit the Japanese Space Agency. Sitting next to Dr. Perez and Dr. Abrams."

Nate felt a rush of relief. "Thank goodness! I'm glad to hear that, Josh."

Perez pulled out his own PDA and scanned it. "He's right, Nate. I remember now. On the way back, Roger and I dropped in on Valkerie in Alaska."

Josh plopped down in his chair, looking exhausted.

Perez put his PDA back in his pocket. "Josh, we didn't think it was you. We didn't see how it could possibly—"

"You know, we still have a problem," Josh said.

Nate stared at him for a second before it struck him. "Who broke into your machine and sent that e-mail?"

Josh put his head in his hands. "I hate to say it, but . . . it's most likely one of the crew. They were the ones with the easiest access to my machine."

"Not Valkerie Jansen, obviously," said Perez. "She was up in Alaska then, looking for bacteria."

"And I wish we'd left her there, instead of sending her up to die in space," Josh said.

Nate's heart lurched. *Josh wasn't giving up, was he?* "It seems likely that whoever sent this blueprint . . ."

" . . . was the same person who planted that bomb." Perez looked grim. "That's very likely, but not a certainty. However, it is an extra clue, and we'll take any we can get."

Nate pulled out a pad and began taking notes. "Okay, here's an action item for me. I'm going to check the schedules for Kennedy, Lex, and Bob to see which of them were in town on August 11, 2012. And Josh, an action item for you: Talk to the crew—individually—and try to pump each one of them for info on who might have known your password, or had the ability to get it."

Josh looked sober. "I hate doing this kind of thing."

"So do I," said Nate. "And . . . I'm sorry we had to bring you in to discuss this."

"I understand," Josh said. He gave a short laugh. "Better here than on the six-o'clock news, huh?"

"Speaking of which . . ." Perez said.

Nate looked up, startled. *Now what?*

Josh turned wary eyes on them both.

"Jane Seyler," Perez said, looking intently at Josh.

"Um, what about her?" Josh looked puzzled. "She's an anchor, isn't she, for one of the networks?"

"You haven't talked to Jane Seyler recently?" Perez asked. "In person?"

Josh's eyes narrowed. "If so, it had to be at one of our press conferences. But I don't recall seeing her here."

"No, she's a New York talking hairdo. We . . . had an interesting discussion with her recently," Nate said. "I did, anyway."

"Josh, have you ever talked to this woman in person?" Perez asked. "Ever called her?"

"Never called her, no," Josh said. "And she's never called me. Never met her in person that I can remember."

Nate didn't want to push this any further. "Okay, that's all we need to know. Go talk to the crew. Let's see if we can nail this blueprint thing down."

Josh got up and walked out.

Perez shut the door. "Do you believe him?"

Nate shrugged. *Of course not. Josh had to be lying through his teeth.* "Yes."

"Good." Perez picked up his briefcase and went to the door. "Because if you thought he broke that gag order, I'd throw him in jail faster than you can say 'Houdini.' "

Tuesday, April 8, 2014, 12:30 A.M.
VALKERIE

Valkerie plunged through dark corridors, tearing at the elastic pseu-dopods that held her down. Gravity. The tunnels were thick with it. She tried to push off a wall, but the pseudopods dragged her back down. *Beep-beep. Beep-beep . . .* She fought against the heavy tentacles. Kennedy was coming for her. She had to escape. *Beep-beep . . .* Something tickled at the back of her mind. The sound—it was an alarm. It meant something. Something important . . .

Decompression! Valkerie tore through the elastic bands that bound her. She sat up with a staticky rip. Where was she? She wiped her eyes and looked up. A room hung sideways above her head. She grabbed at the fabric that covered her legs and held on. Her stomach surged. The room spun around her like a surging sea.

Beep-beep . . . Valkerie squeezed her eyes shut—and listened. The sound was coming from the floor. She opened her eyes slowly and looked down at her watch. *Beep-beep . . .* She pressed down on the two left buttons and the alarm stopped.

"Oh no!" The time jumped off the watch face. She'd slept for over seven hours. Why didn't they wake her up? She needed to finish the synthesis.

Valkerie heard the faint murmur of voices coming from behind her—no, that should be overhead. Valkerie slipped out of the SRU and reoriented herself. She pushed off for the stairwell, listening intently. Bob and Kennedy were talking upstairs. Probably making plans. Some kind of alliance.

Valkerie pulled herself slowly up the stairwell. Kennedy was talking in a loud voice. She heard her name. She entered the upper deck and pulled herself to the left, keeping the stairwell between her and the voices.

"Copy that, Houston. I'd say she was very unstable. The tape we played you was her. She started screaming as soon as she fell asleep."

A long pause.

"Something about Kennedy." The voice was Bob's. "She's been show-ing signs of paranoia the whole trip. Especially where Kennedy is con-cerned. She doesn't seem to get along with him at all."

Valkerie stifled a gasp. They were talking to Josh. Trying to turn him against her. She moved silently along the circular corridor. If only she could hear what Josh was saying.

"Okay, I'll go get her." Kennedy's voice was startlingly close.

Valkerie froze. What would they do if they found her sneaking around? Things were already bad enough. She ducked into a cabin and pressed herself against the wall. Kennedy floated past in the corridor. Had he seen her?

Apparently not. Valkerie had dodged that bullet, but another one was coming. They were going to blow a fuse when they discovered she wasn't downstairs. What could she do? There was no way she could get downstairs ahead of Kennedy. He was already halfway down—

"Bob! You better get down here!" Kennedy's shout came rattling up the stairwell.

Valkerie heard a thump on the wall of the stairwell—Bob rushing downstairs with all the grace of a half-drunk bull.

Valkerie ran through her options. She could try to get off a message to Josh, but with the time delay, she'd probably get caught. Maybe she could . . . no. She pushed off down the hall toward the toilet. It was her only viable option—her bladder had decided for her.

Valkerie held herself down with the foot stirrups and readied the hose as fast as she could. They were probably searching the ship already.

She was just putting away her funnel tip when the toilet door exploded open. Her shriek wasn't an act. Neither was the bump in the head she got from jumping up in the five-foot-high compartment.

"What are you doing in here?" Kennedy yelled.

"What do you think I was doing?" Valkerie tried to sound defiant, but her voice came out squeaky.

Kennedy grabbed her roughly by the arm and dragged her from the bathroom compartment. "I've got her!" he shouted. "She was in the head."

Valkerie struggled to free herself, but Kennedy's grip dug in tighter.

"What were you sneaking around for? Didn't I tell you to stay in the bag?"

"My shift was supposed to end an hour ago. Why didn't you wake me up?" Valkerie kicked wildly with her feet, trying to find purchase on the wall behind her. Her right foot connected with Kennedy's leg.

"Oh no you don't." Kennedy grabbed Valkerie's other shoulder and lifted her with her feet held out away from him.

"Please, you're hurting me." Valkerie started to tremble. Kennedy's eyes were wide and unfocused—the eyes of a maniac.

"What were you doing?" Kennedy drew her toward his face. "Answer me now or—"

"Put—her—down!" Bob's voice boomed. Valkerie felt herself spinning forward in Kennedy's grip as he went sailing backward down the corridor.

She twisted free of his grasp and wriggled in the air, trying to make the world hold still. A strong arm circled around her waist and turned her back to upright.

"What did you think you were doing?" Bob's eyes flashed. Valkerie had never seen him so furious.

"I was just . . ." Valkerie swallowed hard. Bob was staring past her. Valkerie turned around. He had been talking to Kennedy.

"I found her hiding in the toilet compartment. I don't know what she was doing, but she was up to no good." Kennedy moved toward Valkerie menacingly.

Valkerie shrank back, clinging to Bob for protection. "I was just using the bathroom. You can check my funnel if you don't believe me."

Bob wrapped a protective arm around her. "And that's why you were shaking her?" he demanded.

Kennedy sneered. "Don't you see what she's doing? She's playing you. Look at her." He spat the words. "Suddenly soft and weak and clinging for protection. Where did that come from? All she wants is to turn you against me."

"No," Valkerie pleaded.

"Look at her! It's all an act. But her true self will come out when we're both asleep. You can be sure of that."

Valkerie looked up at Bob. His face mirrored the battle that raged inside. "Bob, please. You've got to believe me. I didn't do anything."

Bob took his arm back from around her waist and pushed her away. "I can't take this anymore. We have to make a decision. Right or wrong, we have to make it now."

"But I'm not done with the synthesis." Valkerie's heart sank. It was too early. She still had to talk to Josh. . . .

"I agree," Kennedy said. "Let's call Houston and tell them we're ready to decide. We can finish the synthesis later."

Valkerie looked up at Bob. If she refused, it would look as if she were afraid. Like she had something to hide. She nodded her acquiescence.

"Good." Bob sighed and moved down the corridor to the command center.

Valkerie followed and took her place at the conference table. The three of them hovered around the table for several minutes, staring at each other's faces. Trying to read each other's thoughts.

"Okay, how are we going to do this?" Bob finally broke the silence.

"Just like last time, but this time we write down the name of the person we want to stay awake." Kennedy got a sheet of paper from a stowage bin and tore it into three pieces.

"And Josh and Nate decide if it's a tie," Valkerie added.

"Nate decides alone." Kennedy handed out the strips of paper. "Josh took himself out of it. He called while you were asleep."

Valkerie went numb. Why was Josh distancing himself from the vote? Didn't he know how Nate felt about her? Surely he didn't believe Bob and Kennedy. He knew her—better than any of them.

Valkerie scrawled Bob's name in big letters and slid her strip of paper face up onto the table. She didn't care who saw it. Maybe Kennedy would get mad and vote for Bob just to spite her. Bob stared down at his blank slip of paper. His knuckles were white around his pen. What was he thinking?

Valkerie cleared her throat and caught his eye when he looked up. Bob stared back at her fiercely.

"Please," she mouthed the word. How could she make him understand? She was innocent.

Kennedy slid his strip of paper onto the table and held it face up so that the name was turned toward Bob. *Valkerie.* If Bob voted for Valkerie, then she'd be the one to stay awake. If he voted for Kennedy, then Nate Harrington would have to break the deadlock. But Valkerie already knew what Nate's decision would be.

Tuesday, April 8, 2014, 12:45 A.M.
BOB

Bob stared at his blank slip of paper. *Great, I get to decide. Kennedy or Valkerie.*

Until a few minutes ago, he'd been planning to vote for Kennedy. But the way Kennedy had been manhandling Valkerie . . . over nothing. That was scary. What if Kennedy went nonlinear while the rest of them were in comas?

Or more down-to-earth, what if one of them had a medical emergency? Valkerie was the one with the M.D. behind her name.

On the other hand, if she had a Kevorkian complex, the M.D. degree wouldn't be of much help to her victims.

Truth was, neither one of them was a good choice. *The best person to stay awake is me.* Valkerie saw that. But Kennedy didn't. Did that reflect on Kennedy's judgment? Or was Valkerie just afraid of Kennedy? Or . . .

Bob sighed heavily. This was not going anywhere. "Listen, guys, I know I was pushing to make a quick decision, but now I'm having a hard time." He wiped the sweat off his forehead. "Could I have just a few minutes alone with each of you? I need to talk."

Both Kennedy and Valkerie nodded. Not that they had much choice. They had to be agreeable here. Each of them needed his vote.

"Okay, Kennedy, I'll talk to you first. In my quarters. We'll leave the door open, so we can keep an eye on Valkerie."

Bob pushed off from the CommConsole and floated into his room. Kennedy followed.

"Why should I vote for you?" Bob asked in a low voice. "If I do, we deadlock and that means Nate gets to decide."

"And he'll decide on me," Kennedy said. "That's pretty clear. So I'll give it to you straight. First, look me in the eye."

Bob did. Kennedy's eyes looked bad—the left one bloodshot, the right one squinting, unfocused.

"I swear on a planetful of Bibles I'm not the bomber," Kennedy said. "You know that, don't you?"

Bob nodded. He was sure of it.

"Second, I don't care what Mission Control tells you, when we dock with the ERV, we need an experienced pilot to manage it. Most dockings go okay. But when one goes wrong, it goes *really* wrong. I've got six hundred hours in the docking sim, and Valkerie has maybe twenty. Clear?"

"Keep talking."

"Third, our problems started the day Valkerie arrived. She's got opportunity, motive. . . . It doesn't take an expert to see that she's paranoid. She took a dislike to me early on, and she's been challenging my authority ever since launch. The only reason I'm voting for her is to force a tie and give the tie breaker to Nate. Nate will vote for me—you know he will. I'd vote for you, but you breathe too much oxygen, big guy."

And you're paranoid too. So am I, probably. Lex isn't, but she's out for the count. The guy we need on board right now is Josh, and that just isn't possible.

"That's all I have to say." Kennedy pushed himself back through the door. "I know you'll make the right choice."

Right, but you don't trust me enough to vote for me, you gutless little Nazi.

"Okay, Valkerie, go on in there and make your points," Kennedy said. A minute later, Valkerie came floating in. She just looked helplessly at Bob.

"The clock's ticking," he said.

She looked up at Bob with big watery doe eyes.

For crying out loud, just what I need.

"I'm sorry," she said in a whisper. "I'm acting like an idiot. Bob, I'm afraid of Kennedy, and that's all there is to it. I don't believe he put that bomb out there. But I didn't do it either, and I know you didn't."

"So who did?" Bob asked. "It didn't just grow there by itself." He managed a laugh. "Maybe it evolved from a long succession of smaller bombs, each more complex than the last—"

"Bob, please. Could you just lay off?" She smeared her eyes with her sleeves. "This may all be an amusing little academic exercise to you, but I have to live with my faith . . . and my doubts . . . every day. Don't think I don't struggle with it. If you think I'm burying my head in the sand, you're dead wrong! I understand the way the world works. Only too well. You know what I'm worried about right now? I'm afraid that Kennedy is going to . . . I'm afraid that he might take advantage . . . Bob, he scares me to death."

"Look, Kennedy's not going to . . . you know. Do anything wrong."

Valkerie covered her face again. "Kennedy's got a bad streak, and I don't trust him. But I do trust you—enough to take the chance that you'll use up all the oxygen while we're asleep. Have you thought about what that means? It means I'd rather run the risk of dying than leave him loose around me."

So you'd die for your principles. You and Sidney Nichols both. Which is just what I've been saying. You've got the terrorist mentality.

Valkerie uncovered her face. She looked tired, defeated. "That's all I have to say. I don't . . . know anything else to tell you, but if you had half a heart, you'd pick me."

The problem is that I have a whole brain. Bob shook his head. "Just give me a few minutes to think about this." He felt strangely dizzy.

So. Valkerie was human after all. She had doubts. And fears.

And she trusted him. Which was bizarre, because he had treated her like dirt. Now he had to decide. His heart told him one thing, his head another. Valkerie *looked* so sweet and innocent on the surface. But she was the only one of the six who had a motive. The only plausible answer to this riddle was that she was a fanatic, someone who put her religion above her common sense.

So why was her religion failing her now? Valkerie wasn't acting like a single-minded killer. She was acting scared, lonely, confused.

Just like me.

So it came down to this choice. Play it safe with Kennedy, who was clearly halfway around the bend—or trust Valkerie, who was either perfectly trustworthy or all the way around the bend and banging on heaven's gate. Of course, voting for Kennedy would force a tie, and Nate might decide to . . . no, a vote for Kennedy was a vote for Kennedy—if Josh had finished his research assignment.

Kennedy pushed off from the CommConsole and floated toward the door. "Any more questions for me?"

Bob made his decision. "All right, all right, we're finished." He grabbed the doorframe and propelled himself to the conference table.

The other two followed him.

"Ready to vote?" Kennedy asked.

Bob grabbed his sheet of paper. He heard Valkerie suck in her breath and hold it.

Do it now. Bob picked up his pen and wrote down his vote in large block letters.

KENNEDY.

Because when all the money was on the table, it was always better to play it safe. Bob's heart had betrayed him before, but his head had never let him down.

NATE

Nate was dozing on his cot in the war room when the door burst open. It was Josh Bennett.

"They've voted," Josh said. "And they're deadlocked."

"Already?" Nate rubbed his eyes and fumbled for his watch. "I thought they still had another step in the synthesis."

"They decided to vote now. And they're stalemated but good. You have the tie breaker."

Nate swore. "How am I supposed to decide if they can't?"

"Well, don't look at me. I'm Capcom. I've got to be the advocate—for all of them."

"Just let me go through the options with you, okay?" Nate stood up and began pacing to get the blood moving. "First off, I think Bob's out because of his higher oxygen requirements. Better to be safe than sorry—know what I mean?"

"Good point," Josh said.

"Secondly, I'm concerned by the reports I'm getting on Valkerie's mental state."

"Those reports have to be taken with a grain of salt," Josh said. "Neither Kennedy nor Bob is an unbiased observer."

"Yes, but they *are* observers, and I'm not," Nate said. "And furthermore, they're in agreement. That tells me something. Third, there's the fact that Kennedy is the better pilot."

"Statistically irrelevant," Josh said. "That is the wrong criterion to be making a—"

The phone rang. Nate lifted the receiver and dropped it on the hook.

"Shouldn't you take that call?" Josh asked.

"If it's important, they can bother me some other time," Nate said. "I don't need the distraction."

"Do you think Valkerie put that bomb up there?" Josh asked.

Nate scratched his head. "Who's to say?" He kept pacing. "Do you?"

A brief pause. "No."

"Why not?"

The phone rang again. Josh shrugged helplessly and grabbed it. "Bennett." He listened, then nodded. "Yeah, I'm talking to him now."

Nate waved his hands and shook his head. "I'm not here."

Josh handed him the phone. "It's Agent Yamaguchi. They've traced that blueprint e-mail."

Nate's heart began pounding. He grabbed the phone. "Crystal? What's the word?"

"We've found the smoking gun," Crystal said. "Definite proof."

"It's Bob, right?"

"We did a trace of the exact time the e-mail was sent," Crystal said. "Then we tried to pinpoint the locations of the three suspects during that time."

"I don't care how you worked it all out," Nate said. "Just give me the answer. I've got a big decision to make. Is it Bob?"

"It's Kennedy Hampton," Crystal said. "Beyond all doubt."

Nate dropped the phone and sat down weakly on the cot. "Josh . . . the Hampster sent that e-mail."

"Kennedy?" Josh stepped closer to Nate. "You're telling me Kennedy broke into my machine and sent an e-mail in my name?"

Nate nodded. "Yamaguchi says they've got absolute proof."

Josh slammed his open palm on the table. "That filthy little Machiavelli! I can guess why he did it too."

"Josh—"

"He was trying to frame me, wasn't he?" Josh paced back and forth in the small room, his face red with fury. "And it worked! He found a way to bump me off so he could be commander!"

"Josh, there were a lot of other reasons—"

"Oh sure!" Josh turned and stabbed a finger at Nate. "Sure, there were other reasons. But if you poke around behind those so-called reasons, I bet you'll find that little weasel's paw prints."

"Josh, I'm sure you've got a point." Nate stood up and rubbed his bleary eyes. "But right now, we've got a crew to deal with. It's obvious we can't let Kennedy take care of the others. But here's my question. Do we tell Bob and Valkerie about this?"

"They have a right to know," Josh said. "There's a chance Kennedy could be dangerous, but if you want my opinion, he'd be twice as dangerous if he knew we've blown his cover."

"Right." Nate reached for the doorknob. "Okay, let's go. If Kennedy's not there, I'll tell Bob and Valkerie. Otherwise, I'll . . . try to act normal."

"Break a leg."

BOB

"Ares 10, this is Houston. Mission Director Nate Harrington speaking. Sound off, crew. I want to hear each of you speaking. Over."

"This is Kennedy Hampton, sir."

"Kaggo present and speaking."

Valkerie hesitated. "This is Valkerie. As for Lex, she's still unconscious, but she seems to be stable."

"Over," Bob said, because Valkerie had forgotten.

The minutes ticked by as they waited for the radio signal to travel to a pale blue dot millions of miles away.

"Ares 10, this is Nate. With me are Steven Perez and Josh Bennett. We have discussed the situation and we are in agreement. Let me emphasize this is a unanimous decision based on compelling reasons."

"That's correct, this is unanimous." The voice of Steven Perez crackled in the speaker.

"Ditto for me," said Josh. "We're a hundred percent in agreement."

"Get on with it," Kennedy muttered under his breath.

"Let me also emphasize that our decision is final," Nate said. "This is a direct order from your Mission Director."

Bob was dying inside. *You'd better say Kennedy, you crazy fools.*

"We direct that Valkerie Jansen shall remain conscious and care for you, Kennedy, and you, Bob, while you submit to a chemically induced coma until your rendezvous with the ERV. Please acknowledge. Over."

Bob's mouth dropped open. *No.* How could they foul up like this? Had Josh forgotten to research Sidney Nichols?

Kennedy scowled, hesitated. Then he said, "Houston, this is CDR Kennedy Hampton acknowledging that order. Valkerie Jansen to remain conscious."

"MS1 acknowledges," Valkerie said.

Kennedy pointed the mike at Bob.

"Um . . . Josh? Did you get a chance to run down that piece of information I asked for? Over." Bob looked at the table to avoid Kennedy's and Valkerie's questioning looks. Should he bring up Sidney Nichols now? Would they think it was a ploy? Four minutes passed.

"Affirmative, Bob." Josh's voice sounded enthusiastic. "I can say with 100 percent confidence that you have nothing to worry about from that quarter. I guarantee it. Over."

"Um . . . thanks, Josh," Bob mumbled into the microphone. "Over."

Except that it wasn't over. Bob folded his arms across his chest. An order was an order. You had to obey the order.

Unless it was a matter of life and death.

Well, fine. He would cooperate. He would help Valkerie administer the drug to Kennedy. And then . . .

Bob felt for the little bulge in his pocket. When Kennedy was out, he'd give Valkerie a little surprise. And why should that bother her? She had voted for him, hadn't she?

She was going to get her wish.

Tuesday, April 8, 2014, 11:00 A.M.
VALKERIE

"Thanks for trusting me, Kennedy. I won't let you down." Valkerie set the flow rate on the zero-gravity IV pump to deliver an initial bolus of 150 mg sodium pentothal per minute. "You saw how easy it was with Lex. Nothing to it."

Kennedy lay still inside his SRU. His left arm was strapped to the side of his bunk—rotated palm upward to expose the IV tube that fed into a taped, bulging vein. His brow was furrowed, and his eyes were almost hidden in the tight folds of a pain-filled grimace.

Valkerie didn't know what else to say. Her supply of civility was at an end. The drug would have to calm him down. He wouldn't believe anything she said anyway.

Valkerie injected the drug into the IV bag and shook the solution vigorously. The solution flowed slowly into her patient's vein. In less than a minute, the drug started to take effect, gradually soothing the worry lines from Kennedy's face. After ten minutes Valkerie set the pump for a delivery rate of 500 mg/hr. In two hours she could slow it down to 25 mg/hr and add the Raplon. She checked his vitals. Perfect. He looked better than she had seen him in weeks. At least time would pass quickly for him. She doubted the same would be true for her.

Valkerie readied a syringe for the next dose. If her calculations were right, she had just enough drug to last. She frowned and checked the vial of Raplon again. Hadn't they synthesized a lot more sodium pentothal than that? Apparently not. She and Bob had measured it three times and got the same result each time. Almost two cc's less than she had originally calculated. Well, that's what she got for working on too little sleep.

Valkerie marked the syringe carefully and put it in her kit. Spread out over several days, the dose of Raplon was fine, but taken all at once it could kill a man.

"Is he going to wake up from that?"

Valkerie turned to face Bob. He was floating nonchalantly in the doorway with his hand stabbed into one of his pockets.

"You're supposed to be getting ready. This is your last chance in a long time for a shower."

"That's okay. I just wanted to see how the Hampster was doing."

"Worried that I was going to plant a bomb in his IV? You can check it if you want. As you can see, he's perfectly content."

Bob moved toward the bunk. "I don't know if I'd say content, but he looks a lot better. After what we've been through, I don't know if five weeks of sleep is going to be enough."

Valkerie laughed but stopped abruptly when she caught the look in Bob's eye. He seemed nervous. Poor guy. He was probably terrified.

"It's okay. I'm going to take good care of you. I promise." Valkerie tried to think. What could she say that would make things easier for him?

"You know . . . when I was a little girl, I used to be afraid of the dark."

"So want me to stay awake instead?"

"Actually I was afraid of being home at night. I told my friends my house was haunted. I'd invite myself over to my best friend's house every chance I got and begged her mother to let me spend the night. Sometimes, I'd climb out the window before dark and sleep in the garage. One time I even snuck out with a sleeping bag and spent the night in the woods."

Valkerie looked up at Bob, expecting him to ask a question, but he didn't seem to be paying attention. Sweat beaded up on his forehead. He looked like he was in pain.

"You see, I wasn't really afraid of my house. That's just what I told everyone. I was afraid of my mother. My father traveled a lot for his business, and when he was gone my mom would start drinking. I didn't know it at the time, but she had been an alcoholic for years—ever since my brother died."

Bob's eyes searched the room restlessly. Was he bored or just too nervous to look her in the eye?

"Um . . . she never hurt me. She wasn't even particularly mean. But it was like she was another person. And that person scared me to death. I thought she hated me—that she blamed me for my brother's death. He died when he was four. I wasn't even born yet, but I still felt like it was somehow my fault. Like she would have been happier with him instead of me."

"Why are you telling me this?" Bob sounded miserable—almost angry.

"I don't know. I just thought you might like to know the real reason I've never drunk alcohol. It's because . . . I didn't want to be like *her*. I've never told anyone about her problem before—not really. I mean, people knew. My mother talked about it all the time after she started going to the new church. In fact that's one of the reasons I never wanted to go to church with her. It was too embarrassing. I could hardly stand to be around her. My father and I never talked about her drinking. It just seemed better to pretend that it never happened." Valkerie bit her lip and waited for Bob to respond. She was gabbling like an old hen.

"So how much, uh, what'd you call it, Raplon? How much Raplon did you give him?" Bob grabbed a ceiling strap and thrust his hand into his pocket. His veins stood out all over his arms. It would certainly be easy to get the IV needle in him.

"None so far. I'll inject two cc's in about two hours—right before I intubate." Valkerie tried to get back to her story. "You know my mother—"

"Two cc's. And for someone smaller, you'd have to adjust the dosage, right?"

Valkerie frowned. Why was he so eager to change the subject? What was he trying so hard to avoid? "Actually the dosage isn't that critical at the concentration it's delivered in."

"Good." Bob moved in closer. He looked as if he was mad at her.

Valkerie turned away. He was trying to change the subject, but this time she wouldn't let herself get sidetracked. She had a point to make. "You know, Bob. Sometimes what we think we're afraid of is very different from what we're actually afraid of."

Tuesday, April 8, 2014, 11:15 A.M.

NATE

Nate paced behind Josh. Right now, twenty-four million miles away, Valkerie was putting Kennedy down for a long winter's nap. Bob would be next. Nate clenched his fists. This had better be the right decision.

The phone at the Capcom station rang. Nate grabbed it. "Harrington."

"Nate, it's Crystal." Her voice sounded tight, controlled.

"You okay?" he said. "You sound a little upset."

"Who's going down first?" she asked. "Kennedy or Bob?"

"Kennedy volunteered. Bob and Valkerie are putting him out right now, and then Bob goes next. What's up?"

"You remember we did a thorough investigation of the crew's schedule during the month of August 2012?"

"Right." Nate swallowed. "So what's the problem?"

Crystal paused. "There was a break-in to a NASA computer back then that was never explained. An access from a university in Japan—a very quick in-and-outer."

"Keep talking." *Don't tell me this. I don't want to know.*

"We noticed a pattern and took a wild guess—and we got lucky. We've been able to show that Bob initiated that access through a cutout account. Furthermore, he had the combination to Josh Bennett's lab."

"I knew that."

"We believe he's engaged in a systematic pattern of violation of NASA rules."

"Me too—lately. Everything I've done since we launched has gone against NASA rules. So sue my socks off. What's the problem?"

"We believe Bob may consider himself outside the law."

Nate sighed. "He *is* a little beyond the reach of the county sheriff right now. What's your point?"

"The life-support team wanted to get the numbers exact on their little simulations, so they got some of the medical people to reanalyze all the oxygen-uptake requirements for the crew."

"Bully for them," Nate said. "Hold one second, will you?" He covered the phone. "Josh, any word from Ares 10?"

Josh shook his head. "Still hailing them."

"Okay, I'm back, Crystal. So what's the word?"

"The word is this. Bob's basal metabolic rate is a bit higher than one would expect for a person of his body weight. Your people ran the new

253

numbers on him, and he comes up way short."

"Short? Meaning what?"

"Meaning the crew wouldn't survive if he were the person remaining conscious."

"Yeah? No big deal, right? Valkerie's doing the honors. Bob's going to be in a coma."

"He is unless he decides to take the law into his own hands one more time," Crystal said. "You make sure you talk to him and let him know it would kill them all, okay, honey?"

"He's not gonna do that," Nate growled. *"Honey."*

"Just make sure, okay?"

"Right." Nate slapped the phone down.

"Ares 10, this is Houston, come in." Josh looked frustrated.

"Josh, when you get our boys and girls on the line, just pass one little extra fact along." Nate filled him in on the details.

"Don't worry," Josh said. "Bob's smarter than to try something like that." He keyed his mike again. "Ares 10, this is Houston, come in."

Tuesday, April 8, 2014, 11:30 A.M.
BOB

"Shouldn't we answer that?" Valkerie said. "They've been hailing us for the last twenty minutes." She gave one final look at Kennedy, then moved toward the door.

Bob blocked her. "They can wait. I want to talk to you first." Anything to stall for time.

"*You* want to talk?" She stared at him. "Okay, fine by me. Go ahead."

Now what? If only he weren't such a coward. He had had plenty of opportunities to give her the injection, but he couldn't seem to force himself to do it. He hesitated for a long moment, then blurted the first thing that came into his mind. "If you're the bomber, I may not have much time left. Maybe I want to . . ." *Good grief, this isn't making sense.*

"To what?" She studied him intently. "Do you need to clear your conscience, Bob? If so, we have plenty of time. Go ahead and talk."

Maybe it was just his imagination, but Valkerie seemed to have relaxed a little, now that Kennedy was out for the count. Bob tried to think, but his brain had gone into neutral. What was he going to say?

He didn't have anything on his conscience. He stared at her, feeling stupid.

"Bob, can I tell you something first?"

Bob nodded.

"I know I've offended you in a lot of ways, and I just wanted to say I'm sorry. I think it would have been better if I hadn't accepted this mission. I just came barging in, wrecking a great team, never quite fitting in. And the reason I did it was to gratify my own stupid ambition." She wiped at her eyes.

Ambition? Valkerie?

"I've never felt like I was good enough, ever since I was a little girl. I think I've been trying to prove myself to my daddy, and maybe Mom too, I don't know. But it's never enough. The M.D. wasn't enough. The Ph.D. wasn't enough. And then, when Dr. Perez came along and offered me Mars, I jumped right in without thinking about why I wanted to go." She wiped her nose on her sleeve. "Am I talking too much? Would you rather—"

"Go on." Bob felt a huge lump in his throat.

"I don't know what to say. I was out of control. It was all a big ugly ego trip. All I thought about was the headlines. Valkerie Jansen, first woman on Mars. Valkerie Jansen, first to discover evidence of life on Mars. I was so blind. I never even considered the alternative. Valkerie Jansen, first astronaut to die in interplanetary space. I just realized—"

She closed her eyes tight. Bob could see little tears forming at the corners.

"Ares 10, this is Houston, come in. We have an urgent message for you. Ares 10, come in."

Bob closed the door to shut out the distraction. "You just realized what?"

"That it's not worth it. My ambition is responsible for a lot of what's gone wrong here, do you realize that? Don't answer; I know you do. If I hadn't been here, you wouldn't have been so suspicious of me, and you could have spent more time dealing with the ship. And Kennedy too. So I'm sorry, Bob." She put a hand on his arm. "Can you forgive me?"

Bob sighed heavily. It was a nice little speech. Went right to his heart. He wanted to believe it. Wanted to forgive her. Wanted to trust her. Wanted to . . . what? What would she think of him if she knew what he'd been planning? He wanted to tell her everything. To come totally clean . . .

And yet, who else could have placed that bomb? Who else had the motive? Who else?

"Bob?" she asked in a small voice. "Can you forgive me?"

"Sure, um, Valkerie. I . . . forgive you."

Something hot broke inside Bob's gut. He gasped.

"Bob, are you okay?"

"I'm . . . fine," he mumbled. Which was a lie. Something had just cracked inside his soul.

Valkerie put her hand on his arm again. "It's okay," she said. "Let it out."

Like he had a choice.

He wiped his arm vainly against his eyes, trying to stop it. But there were some things you couldn't stop. And bawling your brains out was one of those things.

Valkerie didn't say anything for a long while. Bob kept his eyes shut and endured the shame of crying in front of a woman—this woman. What would she think of him?

He heard the sound of a tissue being yanked from a dispenser. She pressed it into his hand. He wiped his eyes and blew his nose and sighed heavily.

It was weird, but he felt different. Lighter. Cleaner . . .

"You're a really special person, Bob. I've always thought that."

"Thanks." His voice sounded horrible, almost a grunt.

She came closer and hugged him. "Now, what did you want to tell me?"

He shook his head fiercely. "Never mind. I'll tell you . . . later."

"Oooookay." She drew the word way out. "Ready to be put into your bunk?"

Absolutely not. Now is the time. Step up to the plate and hit a home run, Kaggo. This is your survival on the line. Grab her and administer that drug. Do it now!

Bob opened his eyes and realized he couldn't. Something had gone horribly wrong. He had forgiven her—had not just said the words, but really and truly forgiven her—and that meant . . . something. For starters, it meant he couldn't force her to do something she didn't want to do. He just couldn't. And if that meant he was going to die, well . . .

"Let's go." He swished the door open and pulled himself out and around the corner into his room. *You're a fool, Kaggo! You're letting her sweet-talk you.*

Bob floated into his SRU and Velcroed himself in.

Kaggo, you're a moron.

Valkerie floated into the room. "Okay, you saw the drill with Kennedy. I'm going to poke your arm with a little IV needle and then put the sodium pentothal in the bag."

Bob held out his arm and closed his eyes. He hated needles. Now he was going to be living out of one for the next five or six weeks. He felt the sting of the needle. Valkerie taped it in place. A dull throb settled into his arm. Even that would be gone in a few minutes.

Valkerie smiled encouragement. "Anything else before I put the drug in the IV bag? Did you want to say anything, or. . . ?"

Bob narrowed his eyes and studied her. The real question was, would she murder them all or not? He had no way to know. But there was one thing for sure. If he was about to go down for good, if this was the end, then he did have one thing left to do.

"Yeah, I want to say something." His throat felt cracked and dry.

"Yes?"

"There's a woman named Sarah," Bob said. "Sarah McLean. Tell her . . . I forgive her."

Valkerie's eyes widened. "Sure, Bob, I'll do that. Anything else?"

Bob shook his head and looked up at her.

She seemed disappointed. "Okay . . ." She pulled out a syringe with the drug and injected it into the IV bag. "Pleasant dreams . . . Kaggo."

Bob closed his eyes and felt his whole world shake. Never in all the world had he expected to forgive Sarah. Never. Now he had. And it was sweet. Soft. Gentle.

He heard Valkerie humming quietly to herself. It was a tune he hadn't heard in a long time, and he couldn't quite place it. His brain felt murky, sluggish. From very far away, he thought he could hear his mother's voice singing.

"Amazing Grace, how sweet the sound that saved a wretch like me. I once was lost, but now am found, was blind, but now I . . ."

CHAPTER 28

Tuesday, April 8, 2014, 12:30 P.M.
VALKERIE

Silence. Complete and absolute. Valkerie watched Bob's still form, searching for even the slightest indication of life. Nothing. She palpated his carotid to assure herself that he was still alive, that blood was still reaching his brain. Now check his respiration one more time . . . perfect.

"He's fine." Her whispered words broke the silence like a shout. "This is stupid. Everything is fine. There's nothing to worry about." Nothing to worry about but being alone. For thirty-eight days. Twenty or thirty million miles away from the closest conscious human being, hurtling through space in a tiny ship that was slowly running out of oxygen.

She took Bob's hand in hers. It was a strong hand. Warm, callused— a smidge of grease painted gray arcs across the tips of his nails.

"Ares 10, this is Houston, come in." Josh's voice broke in over comm.

Valkerie flung open the door and dove from the room. She grabbed the mike. "Josh, this is Valkerie. Come in." She held her breath and then let it out again. The time delay. She might as well report. "Josh, I've just put my last patient under. Repeat. Lex, Kennedy, and Bob are all sleeping soundly. All vitals look good."

"Ares 10, this is Houston, please come in. We have urgent information concerning Bob's metabolism."

Valkerie's heart sank. There was a problem with his metabolism? She knew she should have checked in with Houston first. "Josh, this is Valkerie. Please, what's your information? Should I continue administering the drug?" Valkerie waited, drumming her fingers on the console.

"Valkerie, that's great news! Glad to hear it. How are you holding up?"

Great news? How am I holding up? "Josh, what is your new information on Bob's metabolism? Repeat. What is your information? Is Bob in any danger?"

A long pause. "That's affirmative, Valkerie. Continue administering the drug. We have no relevant information. Over."

"Affirmative? Bob's in danger and you want me to do nothing?" Valkerie shouted into the microphone. "What do you mean you don't have any information? You just said you had important information concerning Bob's metabolism." Valkerie pounded on the console. What was going on down there? She waited impatiently.

"That's a negative, Valkerie. As far as we know Bob is not in any danger. Repeat. Bob is not in danger at this time."

"At this time? Will somebody just tell me what's going on? I'm not a baby. If something's wrong, I want to know it!" The minutes ticked by.

"Valkerie, this is Josh. Don't talk, just listen. Our communications have gotten out of sync. Remember that there's a two-minute delay each way between messages. Please wait four minutes for us to reply or you may confuse a response to an old transmission with a response to a later transmission. Understand? Please acknowledge with the phrase 'Roger, Houston. Acknowledge the transmission delays.' Over."

Valkerie blushed. "Roger, Houston. Acknowledge the transmission delays. Sorry, I remember the protocol—just got excited when I thought Bob was in danger. Standing by for a full update." *One, one thousand. Two, one thousand.* She counted down twice the time delay. Maybe the protocols weren't so stupid after all.

"Everything is fine, Valkerie. Bob's metabolism data indicated that he wouldn't have had enough oxygen if you decided to let him stay awake, but of course that data is irrelevant, since Bob is sleeping soundly. Repeat. There is no problem with Bob. The only thing you need to worry about is shutting down the last of the ship's remaining systems. We've figured out how to turn off ninety-five percent of the emergency lighting and are sending you an e-mail with instructions. It also has instructions for shutting down and powering up comm. You should power up the radios every forty-eight hours to check in with us." The message continued after a short pause. "I guess that's it. Good luck, Valkerie. I—we're all—praying for you. Please end transmission with a confirmation. Over."

Valkerie took a deep breath. This was it. "Okay, Houston. Bob wouldn't have had enough oxygen if he had stayed awake. You've e-mailed instructions for taking down comm and turning off most of the emergency lights. And I'll check in with you every forty-eight hours for updates. Thank you—for everything. Don't forget about us up here. Over..." Valkerie wracked her brain for something else to say, but nothing came. "... and out."

Valkerie pulled off the headphones and moved to her computer. So much for her last conversation. Cold, impersonal computer-speak. *Don't forget about us?* What kind of a good-bye was that?

She clicked on the e-mail message and started to read it. The first instruction was to print out the full message and power down the computer. Only the systems controller would continue to run. Great. She wouldn't even have access to a computer. All those electronic books, all those DVD II's—for nothing. She'd have no books, no movies, no experiments, no conversation, nothing to do but lie on her bunk and try not to breathe.

Valkerie printed out the instructions and powered down the computer. Next came the communication systems—her last link with Earth. She tried to think of an excuse to contact Houston. Anything. She couldn't let it end on a cold, impersonal report. If she just had one more message ...

Valkerie grabbed the mike again. "Houston, this is Valkerie. I'm just about to switch off the communications system, but I promised Bob I'd send back a message. He asked me to tell a woman named Sarah Mc-Lean that he forgives her. It was his last request as he was going under. Please try to locate her. I promised him you would. And please could you send one last message to my father? Please tell him that I love him—and I'm sorry. He'll know what I mean. And—well, I guess that's all. I love you all. Thanks for your prayers. Over." Valkerie counted down the long transmission delay. Surely they were still listening. They had to be.

"Valkerie, this is Houston." Jake Hunter's voice broke through the static. "We'll make sure Sarah McLean and your father get the messages—and um, we love you too. Over and out."

Valkerie wiped her eyes with the back of her sleeve. Well, that was that. She flipped off the communication power switches and moved to the bus that controlled the emergency lights.

"One off, two off, three off, four off..." She went down the row of tiny microswitches on the circuit board and held her breath. She flipped the eighth switch, and the ship plunged into darkness.

Easter Sunday, April 20, 2014, 6:00 A.M.
VALKERIE

Valkerie lay on her back, searching the darkness for a trace of sunlight. The slow "barbecue roll" that maintained the even heating of the surface of the ship had swept the sun across the porthole twenty-nine times since she'd woken up. One more dawn and she'd allow herself to check her watch.

A faint glow lit the corner of her doorway. Close enough. She lit her watch. 6:02. She groaned out loud. She still had twenty-eight hours before her next check-in.

"I can't do this!" Her shout echoed through the empty ship. "Do you hear me? I can't take it!" Her voice seemed dead, muted. Swallowed up by the emptiness of space.

Valkerie yanked herself back down on her bunk and cinched the draw straps of her SRU tight around her. It seemed like she had been in the dark forever. If there really was a God, if He really was the God of love, why was He letting this happen to her? Why the explosion? Why wasn't Lex wearing her pressure suit? The whole universe seemed so cruel and heartless. Pain, death, destruction. This was supposed to be the fingerprint of a kind, loving God?

It was easy to believe that it was all an accident. A tiny blip in a vast fabric of chaos. Maybe she was just a fleeting intermediate in an eternal series of chemical reactions. No reason, no design, no purpose. Complete and absolute futility. What did it matter that she was hurtling through space, alone in a leaky tin can? Who cared? Certainly not the physico-chemical universe. Did God care? If He did, then why was He leaving her rescue up to the laws of the universe? If they did manage to dock with the ERV, would it be fair for God to get the credit even though the laws of physics did all the work?

And that was another thing. Physics and chemistry, they were at least predictable. Even biology was predictable—on a good day. If God was such a constant, why couldn't you rely on Him to come through? Honestly, did she even know of a single time in her life where He had come through? Would a God who wanted people to know about Him really work so hard to cover His tracks with coincidence? Coincidence—another name for blind, random chance.

But where did art and beauty fit in? Was it just a by-product of survival—organisms moving toward positive stimuli and away from the negative? What about love? Hormones to precipitate mating? Good and evil? Instincts evolved to increase the survival of the species? God, was it all just an illusion? Was it all wishful thinking? A fantasy we made up because we couldn't deal with the futility of reality?

"Okay, God, if you're ever going to say something, now would be a really good time." Valkerie flung out the words. "You're the one who's supposed to want the relationship. If it was worth a son, why isn't it worth a few stinking words?"

She pressed the heels of her hands into her eyes. "I'm sorry," she whispered. "Please forgive me. I'm so sorry."

"Arggh!" Valkerie balled her hands into fists. It didn't make any sense. She had no rational reason to believe in God, but the irrational part wouldn't let go. She took so much pride in being a rational, intelligent scientist, but she couldn't shake the most irrational part of her life. Was it a psychosis? Her upbringing? It shouldn't be. She hadn't grown up Christian. Not really. The religion thing hadn't kicked in until her mom started going to the other church. But Mom *had* stopped drinking. . . .

"God, I'm sorry. I just want to understand. How can I convince Bob if I don't understand it myself? I'm not even sure I believe it. God, convince me. Help me to understand. Help me to—"

A dull thud echoed through the ship. Valkerie tore off her Velcro restraints and hurtled for the door. "Bob? Lex? Is that you?"

She spun around the doorway and glided into Lex's room. Lex hadn't stirred. Valkerie started to check her vitals but was interrupted by another thud.

"Bob? Kennedy?" She moved cautiously toward the door. "Bob?" She reached for the light switch, but of course it was dead. The corridor was lit by a few low-wattage LEDs. Barely enough light to find the doorways. Valkerie paused at Bob's door and searched the gloom within. A shadow lay stretched out on the bunk—like a cadaver. "Bob?" Her voice was a hoarse whisper. "Dear God, please help me." Bob wasn't moving.

Valkerie turned back to her room and grabbed her flashlight. It was supposed to be for emergencies, but this would have to do. She shined the light up and down the circular corridor and pushed toward Kennedy's room. Pausing at the door, she searched the entire room with the light. Kennedy was still there.

"Kennedy?" She gripped the flashlight like a club and steadied herself in the doorway. No movement. She crept toward him, holding her flashlight out in front of her like a talisman. Still no movement. She reached out a cautious hand and checked his pulse. Nothing. She tried the carotid. It was faint but steady.

Valkerie took a deep breath. Must have been thermal expansion—or something. Whatever it was, it certainly got her worked up. She played the light across the IV bag and checked the battery-driven pump and tube connections. While she was checking the needle, she noticed some red blotches on the fingers of Kennedy's left hand. "That's odd. Why didn't I notice that before?" His index and middle fingers seemed to be broken out in some kind of a rash.

An image leapt to her mind. Kennedy reaching his finger into the small micrometeorite crater in the foam hull of the ship. Ridiculous. He was wearing gloves. Decontamination was just a precaution. Nothing could survive the cold vacuum of space. It was a rash, that's all. She'd keep an eye on it and report it at her next check-in.

Valkerie checked her watch eagerly. 6:10. Only twenty-seven hours and fifty minutes to go.

CHAPTER 29

"Okay, Bob, let's say you're right. Say love *is* irrational. Does that mean you could love somebody you hate? Could you love somebody you were trying to hurt? If that's true, what does love really mean? Is it a hormonal addiction brought on by familiarity? What about love at first sight?" Valkerie sat in the dark, squeezing Bob's hand to her cheek.

"Okay, maybe that's hormones. But what about the love you feel for a stranger? Somebody of the same sex? Has that ever happened to you? Have you ever met somebody and known right off that you were going to be friends?" An ache stabbed through Valkerie's heart. Gina-Marie Davis. She had only known her for two months, but that was more than enough time to cement a friendship that would last a lifetime. What was Gina-Marie doing right now? Worrying? What had NASA told the newspapers? Did the people know that the Ares 10 astronauts were going to die?

"God, why couldn't I have had a sister? Even a brother, God? Why did he have to die?" Danny Jansen. He was only four years old when he died. Four years old and cute as a kitten.

"No offense, God, but your universe really stinks!" Valkerie blurted out the words and felt immediately uneasy. What if Houston were listening in? What if they had active microphones on board to monitor her condition?

"Hear that, Harrington?" Valkerie shouted at the ceiling. "I'm cracking up. If you're wasting our power listening to this, the least you could do is let me receive messages as well. Gina-Marie Davis. She's a postdoc at MIT. Couldn't I talk to her? What about my father? Just ten minutes. Is that too much to ask?"

Valkerie released Bob's hand and pushed off for the command station. She had a transmitter. What was Harrington going to do, fire her? She felt for the transmitter switches. This was an emergency, wasn't it? If she couldn't talk to anyone, she was going to pound a hole in the hull with her forehead. That definitely qualified as an emergency.

Valkerie fingered the switches nervously. What if there wasn't enough power? What if they ran out of oxygen before the ERV could dock? *Sorry about that, Bob. You'll just have to hold your breath. I blew all our power on a long-distance call.*

Valkerie pushed away from the switches and headed for the dining area. She wasn't hungry, but maybe a snack would help anyway. She grabbed her flashlight and dug through the packets in the food bin, ignoring the names on the labels. Here it was. Blueberries and cream. Ohta 4–17. Lex wouldn't mind. She had already missed that meal anyway.

Valkerie carried the packet to the hydration station and stabbed through the valve with the needle. Two and a half ounces of water—a half ounce less than called for. She shook the packet impatiently and retrieved her plastic spoon.

Good enough. She peeled back the foil top and took a bite.

"Gross!" Valkerie spat the food into her hand. It tasted like rotten mushrooms. She pulled out her light and checked her spoon. She had been a little lax about washing lately, but it looked fine. Maybe it was a bad packet.

Valkerie dug through the bin and found Kennedy's packet of blueberries and cream. She added water and tasted it, not waiting for the blueberries to hydrate. Rotten mushrooms again—if anything, the taste was even more intense.

"Don't tell me the food is going bad." Or even worse... She dispensed some water into a clear plastic bag and shined her light on it. It was definitely cloudy. She dipped a finger in and tasted it. Rotten mushrooms.

"No..." Valkerie plunged down the stairwell and pushed her way to the lab. The bioreactor filled the corner of the room. A huge incubator filled with layer upon layer of filters and bacterial cultures. She turned on her microscope and dotted a slide with a sample from the effluent. Sure enough. The sample was crawling with bacteria. She flipped to a higher magnification.

"Huh?" The bacteria were too small. Too conical. She'd never seen anything like them. Valkerie flipped to an even higher power. They certainly weren't from the bioreactor ecosystem. Where had they come from?

A scraping noise made her jump. It seemed to come from the next bay. Valkerie sucked in her breath. Nothing to worry about. It was just the ship. Uneven expansion of the floor or a wall panel. She aimed her flashlight at the door and waited for the sound to repeat itself. Of course it wouldn't. She was being ridiculous.

Valkerie crept toward the door and beamed her light through the corridor. Nothing. The sound had come from the right, but she took the left loop. Might as well rule the other rooms out first. She moved slowly around the circular corridor, checking each room with her light. Nothing.

By the time she arrived at the decontamination room, Valkerie was feeling better. She played the light about the room. Nothing but the lockers and decontamination equipment. There was nothing to worry about. It was a ping—uneven expansion.

Valkerie inspected the blowers and then each locker in turn. When she came to Kennedy's locker, she hesitated. She opened up the top compartment and poked her flashlight at his gloves. They tumbled in the air, revealing a slight discoloration on the fingertips—the fingertips of the left glove.

They'd never decontaminated the gloves. They'd been too busy with the explosion. There hadn't been time.

"Impossible!" Valkerie scolded herself. The micrometeorite didn't even penetrate. It couldn't have been bigger than a couple of grains of sand. And what about the vacuum? The radiation?

Valkerie pushed the gloves back into the locker with her flashlight, careful not to touch them with her hands. Not that they could really be contaminated. That was absurd. But hadn't somebody found a Bacillus bacterium inside a salt crystal two thousand feet underground? The spores had remained viable after 250 million years.

Kennedy's rash. His erratic behavior. The water. Valkerie slammed the locker shut. Her light was beginning to fade. She pushed off for the door and started up the stairwell. No. The microscope. She had forgotten to turn it off. Reluctantly, she turned herself around and pulled herself back down the stairs. Her flashlight was a dull orange spark. She switched it off and pushed her way into the lab, guided by the light of the microscope.

"Please, God. Please be with me." Valkerie switched off the microscope, and the room went black. "Help me not to be afraid."

A faint groan sounded right behind her. She fumbled for her flashlight and turned it on, but the orange spark faded immediately to black.

Thursday, May 1, 2014, 7:00 P.M.

NATE

Nate's phone rang just as he was about to leave for the day. Carol was already gone. Nate grabbed the phone. "Harrington."

"Mr. Nate Harrington? The Mars Mission Director?"

"Yes, this is Nate Harrington. What can I do for you?"

"Um, I'm sorry . . . you don't know me, but . . . I mean, I saw you on the news last night and I've been trying to work up my nerve all day to call you."

Nate drummed his fingers on the desk.

"Anyway, my name is Sarah McLean, and . . . well, you were asking for me to call you."

Nate sat up straight, his mind instantly racing. "Yes, thank you for calling, Miss McLean."

"Actually, I'm a Mrs."

"Beg pardon, Mrs. McLean."

"It's Mrs. Laval now."

Nate blinked. "I'm afraid I don't understand."

"My maiden name was Sarah McLean. You were asking on TV for anyone by that name who knows Bobby to call you."

"And I take it you know him."

"I guess you could say that."

"You guess?" Nate leaned back in his chair. This had the feel of a crackpot call, but he might as well play it out. In three weeks of digging, nobody in NASA had been able to figure out anything about the mysterious Sarah McLean. "Mrs. . . . . Laval, may I ask how well you know Dr. Kaganovski?"

"We were engaged to be married."

Nate's brain started buzzing. *Kaggo? Engaged? Why didn't he ever say anything about that?* "Oh."

"So, um . . . why did you want me to call?"

Nate gave a short laugh. "Well, actually, I'm hoping you can help me figure that out. As you know, Bob Kaganovski is on his way to Mars—"

"Mr. Harrington, is he going to make it?" Sarah's voice quivered with fear.

"We think so," Nate said. "It's going to be very tight, but as long as nothing goes wrong, our lifeboat plan has a good chance."

"Oh, I'll be praying that nothing will go wrong. God loves Bobby. He'll take care of him; you'll see."

Nate was beginning to see some other things. "Sarah, I have a sort of private message from Bobby to you. He asked specifically that we should tell you this."

"Yes?" Sarah sounded breathless.

Hold on a minute, Harrington. How do we know this isn't the National Enquirer *calling?*

"Um, Mrs. Laval, I hope you won't mind, but I kind of need to make sure you are who you say you are."

"But . . . who else would I be?"

"Well, that's just the point. You could be anybody, and . . . this is a very personal message from Bob. Is there any way we can verify your identity?"

"He's still mad at me, isn't he?"

"What?" Nate studied the slip of paper. *Tell Sarah that I forgive her.*

Silence. Then the sound of quiet crying.

"Mrs. Laval?"

"I'll call you back." The woman hung up.

Nate stared at the phone in his hand. *I didn't get her number. Her hometown. Nothing. What a hash I've made of this.*

Friday, May 2, 2014, 10:00 A.M.

VALKERIE

Valkerie dumped an armload of food packets into the supply bin in Bob's room and unhooked the oxyacetylene torch from her belt, transferring it to her left hand. With her right hand she adjusted the three flashlights at her belt. No way was she going to be caught in the dark again—especially not downstairs. That noise had scared her to death.

Thermal ping or not, her head was still ringing from her collision with the corner of the stairwell hatch.

Valkerie tied a cargo net across Bob's open door and tested it to make sure nothing bigger than a kitten could get through. Not that she was worried, but why deny herself a little peace of mind? There was precious little peace of mind to go around these days. Besides, there was always the possibility that Kennedy's IV would come loose while she slept. In her state of mind, if she woke up to an unexpected encounter with him, she'd light him up like a torch.

"Okay, Bob. I'm going to get a little snack. Mind if I eat your apple pie?" Valkerie rummaged through the packets, searching for a package that was prehydrated. She hefted a small packet. It felt like apple pie—or was it a little heavier? It was so hard to tell without gravity. She opened the packet and the smell of cold beef stew filled the room. Great. Not exactly what she wanted, but she'd have to eat it anyway. Most of the packets were dehydrated, and she needed the water bad.

"You're lucky you get an IV," Valkerie said around a bite of stew. "Wanna trade?"

Bob didn't say a word. He was quite the gentleman now that he was unconscious.

"I know, but to be honest I wouldn't mind a little sodium pentothal right now."

Bob ignored her.

"Selfish toad!" Valkerie forced down the last bite of stew and tossed the empty container into the corner. She was so thirsty she could spit. Of course she was too thirsty to spit, but that wouldn't stop her from trying. She had to go downstairs soon. There was a radiation sterilizer in the lab. It would only sterilize a few ounces at a time, but it would be enough to get by on. Why was she putting it off? There was nothing down there. That was a fact. She was going to have to go sooner or later. Might as well make it sooner, while she was still capable of semi-rational thought.

"Okay, Bob. Hold down the fort. I'm going downstairs to borrow a cup of water from our ghost." Valkerie untied the cargo net and moved down the corridor with an unlit flashlight in one hand and the welding torch in the other.

The stairwell was lit by a dim emergency light—not enough light to read by, but almost blinding to Valkerie's sensitive eyes. She waited at the lower hatch for her eyes to adjust again to the darkness. There was an emergency light downstairs too, but it was on the side opposite the hatch.

Valkerie listened carefully before kicking off for the lab. So far so good. She flashed her light inside the small room. Everything seemed to be okay. A flashlight hung in the air by the bioreactor—her dead flashlight from her last visit to the lab.

"Okay, here goes." Valkerie took a plastic sample tube from a bin near the door and moved toward the bioreactor. She dispensed some water into the vial and held it to her nose. Still rotten mushrooms. She searched the lab with her flashlight. Surely she wasn't imagining . . . no, there it was. The sterilizer was mounted in a rack of instruments that lined the far wall.

Valkerie turned on the power and inserted the sample tube. Ten seconds should be more than enough. She started the sterilizer and counted down the seconds on her watch. Time!

Valkerie waited a couple of minutes before removing the vial. That should do it. She cracked the vial and sniffed. Rotten mushrooms.

Of course, it was still going to smell bad. Killing the bacteria wouldn't kill the smell. She waited a few minutes and added a drop of hydrogen peroxide to the vial, holding it up to the light. Impossible. The sample bubbled away.

Valkerie dispensed a new sample and put it in the sterilizer for a full five minutes—enough to carbonize a steak. She took the sample out and tested it again. So much for NASA's twenty-year warranty. The bacteria were still alive.

Valkerie felt sick to her stomach. What if the sterilizer wasn't broken? What if? She took another water sample, but this time from one of the bacteria rings in the bioreactor. She checked the sample under the microscope. Good healthy bacteria—the kind that were supposed to be there. She popped the sample into the sterilizer. Ten seconds for the first test, then she'd ramp it to sixty. She took out the sample and added a drop of peroxide. No bubbles. The bacteria were dead.

Valkerie examined the sample under the microscope. Yes, dead. She couldn't believe it. If the sterilizer worked, then that meant . . . radiation-resistant bacteria? How? Why? Could they have survived a trip through space? It was too incredible.

Valkerie turned off the microscope and headed for the upper deck in a daze. Life on other planets? The implications were staggering. She thought she had been prepared for this. Wasn't this what Mars exploration was all about? She had reviewed the evidence, had thought it possible, had even hoped, but now that it was staring her in the face . . . why was she so disturbed by it? The Bible said nothing about life outside planet Earth. But . . .

"God, why? Why would you create life on other planets?" Valkerie entered Bob's room and tied the cargo net across the door. "What's this going to do to the church—to creationism?" She felt for Bob's hand in the dark and squeezed it tight. "I know. I know. Genesis is full of figurative language—it doesn't rule out an evolutionary process. But life on other planets? They've been preaching creationism for a hundred years. What's it going to do to people's faith? What's it going to do to my faith? Aren't you going to leave me with any reasons to believe?"

Valkerie squeezed Bob's hand tighter. She felt sick—like she was going to throw up. Was it her nerves or—

"Oh no!" Valkerie slung Bob's hand away from her. The rash on Kennedy's hand. What if he'd been infected? Could that explain his erratic behavior?

Valkerie jumped up and fumbled with the cargo net. A knot slipped and she squirmed out through the upper corner of the doorway. She was at Kennedy's side in an instant. Good, he still had a pulse. She checked his fingers. The rash was gone, but that didn't mean anything. She rushed back to get her medical kit and started an examination.

"Why didn't I do this before?" She took a throat and nose culture and examined his ears. So far so good. At least nothing was visible.

Valkerie spread open Kennedy's eyelids and peered into his left eye with the scope. An awful lot of floaties, but otherwise normal. She looked into the right eye and almost dropped the scope. The inside of his eye was laced with a ghostly pattern. The retina was detached and fully degenerated. Kennedy was almost certainly blind—at least in that eye.

Valkerie took a deep breath. Was it the bacteria? Why would it stop at one eye? Was the other eye next?

She hurried to the medical station and searched for the Ceftriaxone. If the bacterium was extraterrestrial in origin, then there was no reason on earth why it would be resistant. Of course, there was no earthly reason why it should respond to Ceftriaxone either. What if its membranes were completely different? She grabbed up two more antibiotics and started searching the bin for a 10-cc syringe. Where were they? She only needed one. . . . A vague fear dropped into her belly like a lead weight.

The blueberries. She'd ingested a ton of the bacteria. What if she—

A bright red flare streaked across her eyes. What was that? Was it coming from inside or out? She closed her eyes and waited. Another flash. She wasn't imagining it. This time it tracked with her right eye.

"Dear God, please help me!" She grabbed four syringes from the bin. At this point the size didn't matter. Both of her eyes were sparkling like the night sky on the Fourth of July.

CHAPTER 30

"Ares 10, this is Houston, come in," Josh said. A sweaty sheen covered his forehead.

Nate felt a lump of lead in his gut. "Keep trying," he said. *Come on, Valkerie—answer!* Maybe she was asleep. It wasn't the normal hailing time. They were supposed to talk every forty-eight hours, and she wasn't due to check in for another twenty-three and a half.

But this was an emergency. A solar flare had blown off from the surface of the sun a few hours ago. They'd detected it right away, when the gamma radiation from the sun shot way up. That wouldn't be a problem for the astronauts—the dose was too low. The problem would come in a few minutes, when a hailstorm of protons moving at a few percent of light-speed hit the ship. The prompt radiation dose from that could give the crew a serious case of radiation sickness in hours if they didn't take shelter. Why wasn't Valkerie responding?

"Ares 10, this is Houston, come in."

Nate began pacing. "Is it possible she turned off the receiver on the emergency channel?"

Josh shook his head. "Valkerie's too smart for that. Ares 10, this is Houston, come in."

Nothing.

Josh's phone rang. The flight director picked it up, then handed it to Nate. "For you."

"Mr. Harrington," Carol said, "I have a caller, a Sarah McLean Laval who wants to talk to you. She won't leave a message on your voice mail, and she won't leave a number."

"I'll take it." Nate hauled the phone as far away from everyone else as he could. "And Carol, in the future, I want you to transfer her to me, right away, no questions asked, is that understood?"

"Right, Mr. Harrington. Sorry, she's not on your list." The line beeped.

"Hello, Mrs. Laval?" Nate sat on the floor, leaned his back against the flight surgeon's desk, and turned to the right to face the wall.

A slight pause. "Um, hello? Mr. Harrington?"

"Yes, this is he. You can call me Nate. That's what . . . Bobby calls me."

A long pause followed. "Sarah? Are you there?"

"Yes, I'm here. I heard some noise. Are you alone?"

"Sort of." *Two dozen engineers don't count, do they?*

"Did you get the e-mail I sent you last night?"

"Yes, I did, and thanks for that, Sarah. I checked with the registrar at Berkeley, and she confirmed that information you gave me. I'm satisfied that you are Bobby's Sarah McLean. I'm sure you understand why I needed to be cautious."

"What was the message Bobby had for me?"

Nate lowered his voice. " 'Tell Sarah that I forgive her.' "

"Oh my!"

Nate wondered if she was going to start bawling again. That was all he needed.

"Thank you, Mr. Harrington. That's such a precious gift."

"I, um, understand." Nate didn't have a clue what she was talking about.

"I always loved Bobby, you know. In a way, I still do."

"He's a great guy," Nate said. "Everybody here thinks the world of him."

"Is he going to be okay?"

"We're hoping so." *Oh yeah, she had sounded pretty religious last time.* "He's in our prayers, Mrs. Laval."

"Mine too," she said. "I haven't stopped praying for Bobby and his friends since I heard that horrible news."

Nate wondered if he should ask for more information. On the one hand, his curiosity was killing him. On the other hand, did he have a need to know? This was something private, wasn't it?

"Do you think . . ." Sarah's voice broke. "Mr. Harrington, do you think he's really forgiven me? What I did was so awful, I just . . ."

I'm not a psychiatrist. What do I say? There followed the sound of quiet weeping. Nate just listened. What else was he going to do? He couldn't exactly order her to get control of herself. Even the Mars Mission Director had some limits to his power.

Sarah sniffled loudly. "I'm sorry, you must think I'm a silly fool."

Well, yes. Nate cleared his throat. "No, not at all. I understand."

"Could you give Bobby a message for me?"

"Not right away," Nate admitted. "Bob's in a drug-induced coma right now to conserve oxygen. But we'll be bringing him out in a couple weeks, and I'll be happy to give him your message in person if you want. Whatever you say. If you'd like, we could even patch you through on a private line."

"Oh no, I don't think I could face talking to him in person," Sarah said. "But you just tell him this, will you?"

Nate pulled his PDA close and pressed the Record button. "I'm ready."

"Tell him I'm so, so sorry. And that I love him, and I've been praying for him."

Nate waited till he was sure she had finished, then clicked off the recording. "I'll pass that along to him."

Another long pause.

"Mr. Harrington? There's something else you need to know."

Nate waited. "Yes?"

"I think I need to send you another e-mail."

"That's fine. You've got my address."

"I'll send it right away." Sarah hung up.

Nate stood slowly. His back was in a knot after sitting twisted on the floor like that. He put the phone back on the Capcom desk. "Any luck, Josh?"

Josh shook his head, then spoke into the mike. "Ares 10, this is Houston, come in."

"Can I borrow your computer?" Nate pointed at Josh's machine. "I need to check my e-mail."

Josh nodded and stood up. "Ares 10, this is Houston, come in."

Nate pulled up Josh's e-mail app and sourced it to his own account. He had twenty messages unread. A new one appeared when he clicked on the Refresh icon.

From sarahlaval@spidernet.com. The subject line said, *My Picture.* Nate turned to Josh. "E-mail from Sarah McLean Laval. Want to look?"

Josh nodded.

Nate double-clicked on the message.

A window popped up with a JPEG image of a woman with frizzy blond hair.

Josh emitted a low whistle. "Amazing!"

Nate stared. Sarah McLean looked an awful lot like Valkerie. Not quite twins, but they could have been sisters.

"Ares 10, this is Houston. Come in."

Friday, May 2, 2014, 10:45 A.M.

VALKERIE

Red lights exploded inside Valkerie's head. She stabbed the syringe into her thigh and pumped her leg full of a cocktail of every antibiotic they had.

"God, please help me. Please . . ." She scrambled for Bob's room and fought with the net across the door. It was flimsy, but without anything to push against, she couldn't tear it down.

"Bob!" Valkerie pulled herself up the net and squirmed through the gap in the corner. "Okay, buddy. Maybe you're not infected, but I'm taking no chances." She flipped on all three of her flashlights and left them hovering in the air above her patient.

That's funny. She didn't notice the flashes as much in the light. Maybe they were going away. Valkerie turned off the lights and the flashes returned. That was strange. If the source was physical, why didn't she notice it in the light?

"Calm down, Valkerie. Think," she panted. "Something's wrong here—you don't want to misdiagnose!" Valkerie fumbled for a flashlight and turned it on. It was radiation. Solar flares. It had to be. All that training and she had missed it. They had to get to the stairwell. The double walls that surrounded the stairwell were filled with water—a shelter against solar storms.

Valkerie tore at Bob's tie-downs, but her fingers were too shaky. She swung the light desperately around the room and her eyes settled on the torch. She dove for it and turned it on. No time for niceties. She burned through the cords that attached Bob's SRU to the cot, and the smell of burnt plastic filled the air.

"Come on, Bob. Let's go!" Valkerie burned through the net at the door and dragged Bob into the corridor. The IV bag and pump trailed behind him like a knotted kite string.

Valkerie rounded the corridor and shoved Bob down the hatch into the stairwell. "Stay there! I've got to get the others." Seconds later, she reached Lex's room with the torch and cut Lex from her cot. Lex was in no condition to be moved, but she couldn't be left out in the storm. If the flashes in Valkerie's eyes were any indication, they'd absorb a fatal prompt dose in a few hours. How much time had she already wasted?

Valkerie maneuvered Lex through the corridor and pushed her into the stairwell. She pushed off from the wall and rebounded down the circular corridor. A kick and a thrust brought her to Kennedy's bed. The straps parted at the heat of the flame. A cloud of smoke cloaked the sides of the bag. Smoke didn't rise in zero-g. She started to fan it with her free hand, but the bag burst into yellow flame. "Kennedy!" She beat at the flame with her hands, but it wasn't helping.

Valkerie threw herself on the fire, smothering it with her outstretched body. Her stomach burned, but she pressed her body even closer, until she was sure the fire was out. What had she been thinking? A flame used up oxygen at an incredible rate.

Valkerie dragged Kennedy into the stairwell and shut the hatch behind her. Bob and Lex floated in the tube like zombies. Arms extended out at the shoulder. Mouths gaping open. She switched off her light and shut her eyes. There were still a few red streaks, but definitely not as many.

Valkerie let herself drift to the lower level of the stairwell and pulled the hatch shut. A rectangular hole was cut into the metal door, but it probably didn't matter. Valkerie moved the others into the upper section of the stairwell and looped her arm around one of the folded-up stairs. Radiation from the flares might take a couple years off their lives, but if the stuffiness of the air was any indication, none of them would live long enough to notice any difference.

CHAPTER 31

Friday, May 2, 2014, 4:30 P.M.
VALKERIE

Valkerie lay still, floating in a glimmering sea of foil packets and shadow. Her breath came in gasps. *Come on, Valkerie. You've got to think. Think! What else can you do? What?* Valkerie drifted into a wall and tensed.

Okay, calm down. Breathe slowly. In . . . out . . . in . . . out . . . She was missing something. What? The solar storm was over, but without NASA to warn them of new flares, they were safer where they were. Besides, there was a light in the stairwell, and she had already brought in enough hydrated food to last her through docking. If only they could live that long.

Okay, I've given them their antibiotics. Their checkups, their IVs, the pumps, the flashlight batteries . . . Valkerie raced through her checklists. What else? There had to be something. Did she need more water? She checked the stoppered flask that floated by her side. It had taken forever, but she had managed to run three liters of the contaminated water through a tiny one-micron Millipore filter. She was fine for now.

"Okay, now what? There has to be something." Valkerie shut her eyes, trying to concentrate through the storm of thoughts that swirled in her head. Nothing. Just the gentle rustle of floating food packets. And the staccato beat of her own pounding heart.

Relax. Come on relax. Calm, soothing thoughts. Come on, concentrate! Her heartbeat refused to cooperate. *Traitor!* It was out of control, and she couldn't do a thing about it.

"What more can I do?"

Silence.

Well, if she had done all she could do, wasn't the rest up to God? Valkerie started to relax, but then jerked to alertness. She was falling helplessly though space. What if God didn't catch her? What if they couldn't dock with the ERV?

Then they would die. There was nothing she could do. She had to trust in God.

Just like that? Was that what faith was all about? Grasping at hope after all other options were used up? That wasn't faith. That was willful self-delusion. Ignorance.

"God, it doesn't make sense. Give me one good reason why I should believe in you. I can't think of one good reason!" Valkerie shouted her frustration at the circular walls.

She bit her lip and listened. What was she doing? Waiting for an answer? She was so brainwashed it was pathetic. Nothing but a sniveling coward, too scared to face the truth. There was no God. She was just too self-important to live in a universe with no purpose. Too needy to live life cut off and all alone.

"God, I can't do it anymore. My whole life is a lie. I can't believe without a reason. Sorry, but I just can't." Valkerie shut her eyes and went limp. The swirling packets made a gentle rustling noise, like the sound of leaves on a late summer afternoon. She could remember her mother, laughing and trying to cover her with leaves. She could remember winning her first robot competition. Her father had swooped her up on his shoulders and carried her all the way back to the pit area.

"God." Valkerie swallowed back a lump in her throat. "It doesn't matter, does it? I'm going to believe whether I want to or not. No matter how illogical it might feel." Valkerie chewed on the thought. Wasn't that proof enough? She never worried about proofs that her mother had existed. Maybe it was just that simple. Somehow, she had met God, and that meeting had changed her. How could she argue with that? The knowledge was deep down in her spirit—too deep to be argued away. It was a part of her. She didn't have a choice.

Or did she? Couldn't she choose not to follow? Hadn't she been doing that ever since her mom died? How long had it been since God was a real part of her life? She felt suddenly uncomfortable.

"But why didn't you tell me? Why didn't you make me follow? If you had just said something, I would have listened. You spoke to a fig tree and a storm, why don't you speak to me?"

The answer came like a kick to the head. The storm had obeyed. The fig tree had withered. God spoke and the universe sprang into being. They had no choice. God's word was reality.

Valkerie felt dizzy. Overwhelmed. She lay back and watched the shimmering packets, trying to take it all in. Maybe it didn't all have to make sense. Their oxygen was running out. They'd been exposed to radiation from a solar flare. They'd been infected with an alien bacterium from God only knew where. She was forty million miles away from the nearest conscious human being. There was nothing that she could do about any of it, but somehow she was at peace. Happy even. Did that make sense?

Valkerie smiled and swatted playfully at a packet of food, sending it glittering through the dim light. She actually felt happy. Let Bob explain that.

She drifted into the edge of Kennedy's dangling SRU and was surrounded by the smell of burnt plastic. It had been her fault, but somehow she was beyond self-reproach.

Why hadn't they warned her about using the torch? They'd put everything else on the list, why not the torch?

Because it wasn't on the official manifest. It was part of Bob's personal weight allotment.

Valkerie spun around, and scrambled up the stairs, stopping suddenly to keep from getting tangled in Bob's IV tube. "You're a genius!" She planted a kiss on Bob's cheek. They hadn't considered the torch because it was part of Bob's personal luggage. And it had a canister of compressed oxygen. It wasn't much, but it would help. It had to.

Valkerie opened the hatch and pushed out into the upper deck. The torch was still in Kennedy's room where she'd left it. She hefted the oxygen canister. No it wasn't much at all, but it would do. Maybe. And if it didn't ... well, she was okay with that too. She was forty million miles away from Earth, but she was not alone.

Saturday, May 3, 2014, 1:00 P.M.
NATE

Nate sat sweating at the table while Perez finished making his statement to the press. If this wasn't the loneliest seat in America.

" . . . no real news to report," Perez said. "Our last contact with Dr.

Jansen indicates that she's doing as well as can be expected and that the crew is alive and healthy. At this time, we'll entertain questions from the floor."

A dozen reporters were on their feet, bleating for recognition. Perez pointed to the science reporter from New York.

"Hank Russell, *New York Times*." Russell waited for the TV camera to swing around and focus on him. "Mr. Perez, what does that mean—'as well as can be expected'? Under the circumstances, I'd expect that ship to be a little house of horrors. Would you honestly describe Dr. Jansen as 'doing well'?"

Nate leaned forward toward his mike. Perez nodded to him. "It means," Nate said, "that Dr. Jansen is doing a lot better than you or I would under similar circumstances. She and the other crew members were specially chosen to be stable in a harsh environment. She's been trained to be tough—both mentally and physically. She is doing *very* well and has adapted to what we're now calling a 'routine crisis.' "

Nate pushed the mike back and radiated confidence at the reporter. Everything he'd said was true—and a lie. Valkerie had been alone now for over three weeks, and cracks were starting to appear. But only the Capcoms knew about that, and they weren't going to say anything. Because if they did, all four of them would be out of a job just as quick as Nate could plant a twenty-pound boot in their fat little behinds.

All around the room, Nate saw reporters feverishly jotting notes, as if he'd just told them the crew was solving the Unified Field Theory in their spare time. *Routine crisis.* You could see it in their eyes that they liked that one. If you wanted to fool the press, feed them an oxymoron and act like it made sense, and they'd treat it like the gospel straight from Buddha.

A week or so later, the press had moved on from "routine crisis." Tonight, it was an hour-long documentary on Valkerie Jansen's life. They'd dug up every teacher back to kindergarten.

Yes, I remember Valkerie. I always knew she'd go far.

Valkerie Jansen—best student I ever had.

She was strong—a real competitor, and never gave up.

Nate shook his head and turned off the tube. Today, she was getting the hero treatment. Tomorrow, if she messed up the mission, they'd haul out those same teachers to remember what a know-it-all little piece of plastic Miss Jansen had been.

————

Eventually the reporters got to Bob—the least interesting of the crew. Somehow a news jerk had dug up the story of Sarah McLean. Before you could say "Kaganovski," the *Enquirer* was running one of those stupid "Separated At Birth?" stories, with side-by-side pictures of Valkerie and Sarah. Nate wanted to puke.

Monday, May 12, 2014, 1:00 P.M.

NATE

"Mr. Harrington, we got that Sabatier scrubber working."

Nate looked up from his desk on the floor of Mission Control. It was one of the hotshot engineers, a kid named Howard something-or-other. The kid was grinning as if he'd just won the Nobel prize. Nate tried not to scowl, but he was exhausted. "What are you talking about?"

Howard motioned to the door, and three engineers wheeled in the most lame-brained Rube Goldberg contraption Nate had ever seen. "What is that thing?"

"Sir, when you launched Operation Lifeboat, you tasked us to put together a Sabatier-process carbon-dioxide scrubber using only materials on the Hab. We did some research and found that the metal they use for speakers in laptops makes a very efficient catalyst. We've put together a procedure that Dr. Kaganovski can use to build a scrubber. The process is exothermic, and it costs practically no energy—as long as they have some excess hydrogen. And they do, in the fuel cells." Howard grinned at Nate. "Pretty cool, huh?"

Nate had been taking heat for weeks, and all of a sudden he felt it busting loose in his gut. "Cool? Yes!" he bellowed. "Useful? No! Have you kids been asleep for the last few weeks, or what? Our crew is going to dock with that ERV in three days, and they'll have all the energy they need. We do not need this . . . contraption." Nate stood and jabbed a finger at the scrubber.

Howard looked stung. "Um, sir, what do you want us to do with it?"

"Junk it!" Nate roared. "And get working on something useful!"

The kids wheeled the monstrosity out of the room. Nate collapsed back in his chair. Why didn't they teach the young engineers to *think* about what they were doing?

Wednesday, May 14, 2014, 4:00 P.M.
NATE

"Nate, we've found the smoking gun."

Nate looked up from his desk. Crystal Yamaguchi stood beside Josh Bennett. Behind them were a couple of Fibbies, each holding a plastic crate full of papers. "What smoking gun?" Nate asked.

The Fibbies dumped the crates on Nate's desk. "We got a court order to search Kennedy Hampton's apartment," Josh said. "He seems to have an unusual interest in psychology."

"That's not a crime." Nate picked up one of the photocopies. An article by Roger Abrams on crew psychoses in restricted environments.

"These are all papers by our shrinks," Josh said. "Abrams. Hartmann. Avery. All about teamwork indices and how they're computed. Psychometric analyses. Crisis-adaptability predictors."

Nate shook his head. "Josh, it's not against the law for astronauts to study psychology papers. And you can't tell me this had anything to do with the Kaganovski interview."

"Yeah?" Josh plopped a thick sheaf on Nate's desk.

Nate looked at it suspiciously. "What's this?"

"That," said Josh, "is what led to the Kaganovski interview in the first place."

Nate picked it up as if it were on fire. "Interview with Kennedy Hampton, August 8, 2012."

"Read it and roar," Josh said. "The little weasel knew exactly what buttons to push. Exactly."

Thursday, May 15, 2014, 1:00 P.M.
NATE

"Hank Russell, *New York Times*." Russell pointed his perfectly coiffed mug toward the cameras. "Mr. Harrington, when the crew comes out of their comas tomorrow, what sort of physical condition will they be in?"

I have no idea. Nate cleared his throat. "We've given that a lot of study, Mr. Russell. As you know, a microgravity environment causes loss of muscle tone and bone density. In typical missions, crews are able to recover much of that within a few weeks."

"Yes, but this crew is entirely different. They'll be coming out of complete inactivity into a microgravity environment."

"So we expect the transition to be somewhat smoother," Nate said. "We'll still have forty-eight days left for the crew to get buffed into condition for Mars gravity, which is only a third of earth gravity. We've got a volunteer on the International Space Station who just spent the last month recovering from a weeklong total inactivity regime. Based on his experiences and a supercomputer physiological model, we've put together a rehabilitation program that we project will bring the crew back to ninety percent of baseline by the time of Mars orbit insertion."

All of which was probably bogus, but it was the best NASA had been able to come up with. Nate didn't expect anyone to challenge him. He'd said the magic word—supercomputer. That automatically put the imprimatur on any kind of scientific work, no matter how half-baked.

Russell nodded sagely and sat down. Next week—count on it—he'd be running an article quacking about how great supercomputers were, featuring interviews with all the big names in computational physiology.

In the meantime, God help our boys and girls, because they're going to need more than some stupid supercomputer model to put life back into their poor little spaghetti muscles.

Friday, May 16, 2014, 3:00 A.M.
VALKERIE

Valkerie pushed Kennedy through the lower hatch and Velcroed his SRU to the wall of the lab. The effort left her panting—as if she had just finished a 440-yard sprint.

"Kennedy... if you can... hear me." Valkerie forced out the words between breaths. "I'm sorry I... didn't trust you. Forgive me for the fire. I did... my best." Valkerie pulled herself slowly to the stairwell. The oxygen level was getting lower. They wouldn't last much longer. Spreading the crew throughout the ship would buy them a little more time, but only a little. She had to call Houston now. If they couldn't dock in the next twenty-four hours, they weren't going to make it.

Valkerie powered up the radios and plugged her headset into the transmitter. "Houston . . . this is Valkerie. How close is the ERV?" She took a few shallow breaths. "O_2 levels are getting low. We aren't going to make it much longer."

Valkerie caught her breath and braced herself for the nine-minute wait, but a reply came almost immediately. "Ares 10, this is Houston, come in. We have the ERV at nine hours fifty-five minutes to docking."

"Houston, how . . ." Valkerie swallowed. There was no way her signal could have reached Earth that fast.

"Ares 10, this is Houston, come in. We have the ERV at nine hours fifty-four minutes to docking."

Valkerie waited impatiently as the Capcom's voice ticked down the minutes. Ten hours was cutting it close, but it was doable. They hadn't even tapped into the oxygen supply in the EVA suits.

"Good to hear from you, Valkerie!" Josh's voice replaced the drone of the other Capcom. "The ERV is on target and speeding to your position. We're uploading docking instructions now. You should begin preparation for docking."

Valkerie's heart sank. They were expecting her to pilot the docking. She should have realized that before. Of course, Kennedy couldn't pilot the docking. He was blind in one eye, if not both—even if he could recover from the coma in time.

"Copy that, Houston." Valkerie fought down her panic. *God, help me. I don't want to do this alone.* "Um, Houston? I'd like to request permission to wake up Bob for the docking. I could bleed the oxygen from Lex's EVA suit to sustain us for a few more hours. Over."

Valkerie drummed her fingers on the console. *Please, God, I have to be able to talk to Bob before docking. There's so much I have to say to him. If something were to happen . . .* Valkerie bit her lip. She shouldn't have requested permission. She should have insisted. She—

"Copy that, Valkerie. Commence bleeding oxygen from Lex's EVA suit and bring Bob out of his catnap. He's been sleeping on the job long enough. It's about time he started earning his paycheck. Your next check-in will be in three hours at 6:00 A.M. Please confirm. Over."

Valkerie responded with a thankful confirmation and shut down communications. "Yes!" She dove down the stairwell and pulled Lex's unused EVA suit from the locker. A minute later, the Hab's thinning atmosphere was being replenished with a high-pitched hiss.

Valkerie hurried up to the command center. Bob lay sleeping serenely on the wall. He was a lot thinner and a little scruffy, but he looked pretty good with a beard. The zero-g-induced edema of his face and neck had gone down, and his now prominent cheekbones gave him an angular, rugged appearance. He actually looked better than he did on Earth. Zero-g seemed to agree with him.

Valkerie switched off the IV pump and carefully removed the needle from Bob's arm. His forearm was bruised and swollen. He had been on an IV for an awfully long time.

"It's okay. It's all over now," she crooned as she rubbed life back into his arms and legs. "Don't worry, I'm right here." Carefully she extracted the tube she'd inserted to protect Bob's airways from excess stomach acid. Just because he was in a coma didn't mean that his stomach stopped producing acid. She wiped his mouth with a towel and brushed his hair back from his forehead. Considering what he had been through, he was in amazingly good shape. She brought a hand to her face. She knew that she didn't look nearly as good. She hadn't seen a mirror in weeks. Much less a hairbrush.

"I'll be right back." Valkerie pushed off for her cabin and rummaged through her clothes. Where was it—the shirt she was saving for the post-landing press conference? Bob would be asleep for hours. She'd have plenty of time for a shower.

CHAPTER 32

Friday, May 16, 2014, 3:30 A.M.
BOB

Bob floated in a vast and peaceful sea, barely aware. Warmth bathed him, soothing his heart, caressing his face. Waves of . . . something lapped at his mind, forming a lazy puddle of good feeling. Bob let himself drift in it.

Time passed. Slowly, awareness built into a conscious thought.

I am loved.

He drowsed in it, unable to move.

Who am I? Where am I? Why am I here? Each question formed slowly, nibbled at his consciousness, and then dispersed like fog in the warmth of the sun.

The sun warmed him. Love. Peace. Contentment.

All the world was fuzzy, the past an indistinct blob, the future a shadow, the present an endless sea of peace.

He heard a voice. Until now, he hadn't remembered that there was anything in this universe besides himself. The voice was soft and clear and quiet.

"And, God, please show Bob how much you love him. Please just . . . let him know you're there."

The feeling of warmth intensified. Something in Bob reached out to it. *More of that peace.*

Two human arms wrapped around Bob and hugged him tightly.

Sarah? The name sprang to Bob's mind from some nameless void. He could not remember having learned the name, and yet he knew it.

Warmth flooded through him. He wanted it to last forever.

"Okay, Bob, I need to go take care of the others. I'll be back in a little bit." Something soft brushed his cheek.

The warmth left him. He would have shivered, but his body could not. He lay there, desolate, alone, dying. Alone for a vast age, while the universe spun. Somewhere, far away, tiny indistinct voices crackled and popped. Bob strained to understand them. Frustrated, he gave up.

Where am I? Why am I here? Is this purgatory?

He heard motion near him again. "It's okay. It's all over now." Sarah's voice. No, not Sarah. Valkerie. Now he remembered.

Warm, strong hands began rubbing his arms, his legs. Sweet Valkerie. He'd treated her so badly, so . . .

"Don't worry, I'm right here." Her voice made him feel . . . warm inside. So comfortable. So good. Then her hands lifted.

"I'll be right back," she said.

Bob wanted to open his eyes, to call after her to come back, but his eyes were frozen shut, his lips still locked. The chemical. Valkerie had made it—had saved his life, saved all of their lives. And he had treated her like a criminal.

And yet . . . she had forgiven him. He knew it. Could feel it. He was alive, awake from the dead. And with that knowledge came joy, bubbling up inside his guts, filling his whole heart, warming the cold places in his soul.

Had God answered their prayers? Bob knew he couldn't prove it, like a theorem. And yet he felt it. God, the great God of the universe, Maker of heaven and earth, the one who didn't answer His e-mail—that God had come through for them.

Thank you . . . God.

"I'm back."

Bob's eyelids flickered open—just a hair—enough to see the shadowy outline of a face hovering above his. With all his concentration, he strained to open his eyes further. Slowly, a millimeter at a time, they came open. Valkerie was studying him.

"I'm back," she said again. "Are you. . . ?" She suddenly looked embarrassed, then pulled away from him. "I'm sorry, Bob. I didn't realize you'd be coming out so soon. I didn't mean to scare you."

I'm not scared. He tried to say the words, but his mouth wouldn't work. *Valkerie, I'm not afraid of you anymore.*

"Can you talk?" Concern etched her eyes. "I guess you can't yet. Blink your eyes if you're awake."

He blinked—sort of. It took forever, but he blinked.

"Okay, good, the drug's wearing off." She sounded businesslike now, not warm and kind like she had a little earlier. But she looked . . . good. Fresh. Clean. Like she'd just stepped out of an April shower and was ready to break out into May flowers. Or something.

"Just rest a little." Valkerie patted his forehead. "You've been out of it for a long time. We're going to dock with the ERV real soon now, and I need you to help me with it. Lex is never going to pilot again, and Kennedy . . . well, he's got a big problem in one of his eyes. It looks like it's blind. So I need you, okay?"

Bob felt panic surging through his chest. *Me, dock the ship? I'm about as strong as a jellyfish.*

"I'll fill you in on the news while you wake up all the way," Valkerie said. "It's been a bit over five weeks since I put you and Kennedy out. NASA's doing everything they can for us, but they're a long way off. We went through a solar flare storm, and I didn't get the warning in time, but I started seeing these little flashes in my eyes like they told us in training—so I brought you guys into the storm shelter. We all got some prompt radiation, but only a few rems. Like living in Denver for a few years, I guess.

"Anyway, Nate found your friend Sarah McLean, and she has a message for you when you're feeling a little stronger. Am I talking too much? Sorry, but I got used to just jabbering on while you guys were out. It gets kind of lonely when the nearest person awake is fifty million miles away."

Bob yawned. It surprised him that he could.

"Oh, I'm sorry, was I boring you?" She smiled.

"No," Bob whispered. He wanted to say that he'd never be bored listening to her again. Wanted to tell her . . . a lot of things. But not right now, when a single word was a struggle.

"Okay, I'm going to need your help in docking," Valkerie said. She grabbed one of his hands and started massaging it. Bob didn't protest. He knew the massage wasn't going to do any good. He could no more fly this ship than a rabbit could hop the English Channel.

But let her work on him if she wanted to.

It was . . . nice.

Friday, May 16, 2014, 12:45 P.M.
VALKERIE

"Houston, this is Valkerie. The radar is on, and we are pinging and watching for the ERV. Over." Valkerie switched off the microphone and sat panting for several minutes in the command chair. She reached out to take Bob's hand. She had floated his cot up beside the command station. He knew the ship better than anyone. Even if he couldn't move, he could still answer her questions—and without a nine-minute time delay.

"Okay, try squeezing again," she said.

Bob applied a gentle pressure, but it quickly faded to nothing. The effort left him gulping for air. Their oxygen was running out fast. She wondered if she had done the right thing to wake him.

"That's a lot... better." She smiled reassuringly and squeezed his hand back.

"Okay, Ares 10, this is Josh. By the time you hear this, the ERV will be about ninety kilometers out. We have been applying a series of burns to slow it down, relative to you. By now, it should be coming in easy at about 200 meters per second. Transferring control to you. Let the computer bring it in. Be aware that the ERV is very low on fuel, so you may need to do a small burn with the Hab to match velocities. Your computer knows how to do that, so just sit back and enjoy the ride. You should be docking in about fifteen minutes."

"Roger that, Josh." Valkerie studied the display. The interface was identical to the one she'd practiced with on the simulator. "Computed range is eighty kilometers—still no sign of the ERV on radar." She turned to Bob. "When do you think we'll pick it up?"

"I'm not sure," Bob said. "Ideally, the range of that radar is tens of kilometers. Assuming it's properly boresighted, the ERV should be coming into our radar cone in a couple—" His mouth fell open. "Whoa!"

Valkerie spun to look at the display. A blip appeared on the screen—way closer than she'd expected. The range estimate on the display suddenly switched from seventy kilometers to twenty. "What's going on?"

"It's coming in too fast!" Bob hissed. "Switch the ERV to manual and give it a good burn."

Valkerie's hands flew over the controls. The ERV didn't respond.

"It's out of fuel!" Bob said. "They shaved the rendezvous too close."

"I'll try to slow it down some with its RCS jets and make up the difference with our engines." Valkerie fired up the Hab's engines. "Hang on, Bob."

A crash against the far wall told her Bob hadn't found a handhold.

"Keep going, Valkerie. Don't worry about me."

"It's going too fast!" She fired the Hab thrusters again—a long, steady burn.

"Watch your fuel!" Bob shouted from the wall.

"I think I see it on camera. It's coming this way fast!"

"Okay, match its velocity, but don't let the fuel level go below the red line on the display. Understand?"

Valkerie fired the main thrusters. She could hear Bob rolling across the wall, but she didn't take her eyes off the white blip on the screen. It was still too fast!

"Valkerie! Understand? Don't go below the red line!"

She checked the fuel indicator. *God have mercy!* "Bob! The fuel's already below the red line, what do I do?"

"Stop!" Bob's shout came from the back wall. "That's our reserve for orbital capture at Mars."

Valkerie released the thrusters. "But if we don't rendezvous, we're going to run out of oxygen. We have to try."

"No!" Bob shouted. "Don't burn another ounce."

"Ares 10. This is Houston! The ERV is out of fuel. Repeat, the ERV is out of fuel. If you can see the ERV on your radar, you'll have to try to match velocities manually, but watch your fuel. You must not go below the red line."

Valkerie sat frozen, watching as the blip on the radar screen passed by, only twenty meters away, but going far too fast. The range numbers kept changing on the display. One kilometer away. Two. Three.

She had burned too much fuel. And the ERV was gone.

CHAPTER 33

Friday, May 16, 2014, 1:00 P.M.

NATE

Nate stared at the radar display on the giant TV screen, mesmerized. So close. Around him, reporters were going nuts.

"Mr. Harrington, Mr. Harrington!"

A huge hole seemed to have opened in Nate's gut. Dully, he turned to face the wolves.

"Mr. Harrington, what does it mean?" shouted a reporter.

Nate pulled the mike in close. "It means . . ." He stopped and choked, unable to get the words out. *Control yourself.*

"It means . . . they're going to die." He shrugged helplessly. "I'm sorry. There's nothing more we can do. We cut it too close and ran out of fuel on the ERV. We missed the rendezvous. There's no partial credit."

He turned and walked quickly off stage, wiping at his eyes, just in case there might be a tear or some other sign that he was still a human being.

There was none.

Friday, May 16, 2014, 1:00 P.M.

BOB

Bob simply couldn't believe it. So close. So far. You couldn't just jam the two ships together at a relative velocity of 100 meters per second. It had to be inches per second.

"I'm sorry, Bob." Valkerie's voice betrayed her agony. "I did my best." A high-pitched whistle sounded close to Bob's head. The last of the oxygen from Lex's EVA suit.

"It wasn't your fault," Bob said. "The ERV ran out of fuel. We couldn't spare any more of ours. As it is, I don't see how we'll be able to circularize our orbit when we capture into Mars. The Hab is a lot bigger than that itty-bitty capsule we'd use for Earth—"

"The Earth-landing capsule on the ERV!" A stunned look flashed across Valkerie's face. "It has an engine, doesn't it?"

Bob saw it right away. "Yes! You have control of the ERV. Release that capsule and bring it back to us." He pushed himself off from the wall and floated back to the console.

"Found it!" Valkerie said. "It's deploying . . . now."

"Bring it in slow," Bob said. "That thing doesn't have much fuel."

"It's time we don't have," she said. Her eyes seemed to bore holes in the monitor. "Come on—hurry!"

"Hey, Valkerie?" Bob paused to catch his breath. "Relax, okay? You're going to do fine."

Valkerie nodded tightly. Sweat stood out on her forehead. Suddenly, she twisted her head to look at him. "How many weeks of life support are on that thing?"

"About seventy-two hours."

She looked deflated. "That's not nearly enough. What's the point?"

"It has a methane/LOX engine." Bob squeezed his eyes shut. He was starting to get dizzy. "Hundreds of pounds of liquid oxygen. We can cannibalize it if you don't burn it all up now."

"But how do we get it?"

"You'll do a spacewalk—and cut out the tank."

Valkerie shook her head. "That's crazy! It can't work."

"It has to." Bob gulped at the thin air. His chest was on fire. "If it doesn't . . . we die."

Friday, May 16, 2014, 1:30 P.M.
VALKERIE

Valkerie twisted her glove onto the sleeve of her EVA suit until it locked. She had to pause to catch her breath. The oxygen level was too low. Bob wasn't going to make it if she didn't hurry. "Are you sure we can do this?"

Bob floated next to her like a ghost. He nodded grimly. He was so weak he could hardly move, and she was leaving him in control of the ship?

"If you need more oxygen, just bleed it from Kennedy's EVA suit, okay, Bob?"

"I can't. We bled both his and mine down to an hour of oxygen. That bought us all the time we can spare. Get moving."

Valkerie set the bubble helmet over her head and clamped it in place.

Bob adjusted the oxygen-flow control on her chest panel and donned a headset. "Don't worry. I'll be here—every step of the way."

Valkerie took a few deep gulps of pure oxygen. It felt so good to breathe. She felt almost guilty.

"Got your instructions?" The sound of Bob's shallow breathing filled Valkerie's helmet.

Valkerie checked to make sure she could read the instructions through the clear plastic sheath on her sleeve. "Check."

"Flashlights, torch, cutter, and crowbar."

"Check, check, check, check."

"Okay, good luck. I'll be . . . praying for you."

Valkerie swung around to search Bob's expression. Was he making fun of her?

Bob shrugged noncommittally and nodded in the direction of the airlock.

Valkerie clambered into the chamber and sealed the hatch. She hit the evacuation control and readied her tether line while she waited for the chamber to evacuate. What was taking so long? Was the pump working? It was taking forever.

The needle gauge settled to zero. Valkerie spun open the external hatch. Space opened up all around her. Black as midnight. Bright and startlingly clear. She fell forward, teetering on the brink of a vast bottomless pit. Valkerie grabbed at the hatch and clung to the locking wheel, while fiery points of light spun around her. Slowly her head began to clear.

"I'm a little agoraphobic, but I'm out. Didn't realize how much living in our little closet would affect me."

"Do you see it?"

Valkerie clamped her tether to a trail bar and pulled herself hand over hand along the exterior of the ship.

"I see it! Halfway around the ship from the hatch." Valkerie shielded her eyes against the glare of the sun. The back of the tiny Apollo-style capsule blazed like a torch, while the front was lost in shadow. "Are you sure it's only five meters? It seems a lot farther."

"I've got it on the CamBot. Looks like five meters to me."

Valkerie attached a second tether to the rail. "It's too far away. I'll never make it."

"Want me to bring it in closer?"

Valkerie hesitated. If turbulence from the RCS jets damaged their solar panel . . . "No. That's okay. I'm fine."

Valkerie gathered her feet under her and pushed off. Her heart leaped out of her chest and hung for a sickening moment in the inky black void. Then she hit the side of the capsule with a dull thud.

Valkerie clawed at the capsule's smooth surface. There was nothing to hold on to. She was drifting away, propelled backward by the force of her collision. "Bob!" She unclamped a flashlight from her belt and flung it behind her to propel herself forward. She hung in space, reaching for the capsule. The handle of the hatch rotated slowly into view, if only . . . She stretched out her hand for the handle. Closer. Closer. There!

Her hand closed around the handle, and she held on tight. With her other hand she pulled the secondary tether from her belt and clamped it onto the handle. "I did it! The capsule is tethered!" Valkerie moved along the capsule, careful not to push herself away. "Bob?"

"That's great . . . Valkerie." Bob sounded out of breath. "Now cut . . . your way . . . to that oxygen tank."

Valkerie studied the diagram on her sleeve and located the indicated spot on the capsule. If she was off by four inches in any direction, she could puncture the LOX tank's vacuum jacket. "Okay, Bob. Here goes." She unhooked the crowbar from her Display and Control Module and jabbed it into the hull of the capsule. So far, so good. She took the oversized metal shears in both hands and cut a large circle into the thin metal skin. A spherical tank lay just below the surface. The LOX tank! Just where they said it would be.

Valkerie quickly located the valve on the feeder line and cut through the pipe that connected the valve to the engine. No LOX. The valve was holding. "Almost!" She quickly cut through the mountings that held the tank in place.

She tugged at the tank, and it drifted free. "I've got it, Bob! Hold on!" Valkerie pulled out the tank and reached for the tether line that connected the capsule to the Hab. Gripping the oxygen tank between her knees, she loosed the clamp from the capsule hatch and pulled herself back to the ship.

"Hold on, Bob! I'm at the hatch!" Valkerie climbed in through the hatch, pushing the oxygen tank ahead of her. "Bob? Answer me!" She closed the hatch and swatted at the repressurization controls. *God, please let me be in time. Please . . .* The pressure gauge moved slowly to cabin pressure, and she pushed herself into the Hab.

"Bob?" Valkerie braced the tank against the floor and opened the valve with her wrench. A stream of sputtering liquid oxygen spewed from the tank and filled the chamber with a white cloud. That was probably enough, but she didn't want to take any chances. They needed it to diffuse through the ship as fast as possible. She clamped back down on the valve and launched herself for the stairwell. In a leap and a bounce, she was upstairs at the command center, tugging the oxygen tank behind her.

Bob lay motionless, floating above the console. Kennedy's PLSS floated next to him, but the bleed valve still seemed to be closed. Valkerie released another blast of life-giving oxygen from her LOX tank, then removed her helmet and flung away her gloves. "Bob?"

He didn't move.

Tears clouded Valkerie's eyes. Bob had Kennedy's tank right there. Why didn't he use it? Why didn't he bleed off just a little more oxygen? She reached a trembling hand to Bob's neck and felt for his pulse. His pulse was shallow and weak. He was alive.

PART IV

Independence Day

"Furthermore, no matter how many backup plans and abort options the mission design includes, we must understand that in sending a crew to Mars, we are, one way or another, sending a group of humans into harm's way."

ROBERT ZUBRIN

"... an entry vehicle must walk a tightrope between being squashed and skipping out, between fire and ice, and between hitting and missing the target."

CONDON, TIGGES, AND CRUZ

"Greater love hath no man than this, that a man lay down his life for his friends."

JOHN 15:13

CHAPTER 34

OXYGEN

Friday, May 16, 2014, 4:00 P.M.
BOB

A soft touch tingled across Bob's face and stroked back his hair.

"Bob, wake up. Please. Don't do this to me." Valkerie's voice. She sounded like she was in trouble.

"W-what?" Bob opened his eyes. "Valkerie, are you . . . okay?"

"Bob, I was so worried. I thought you were going to . . ." Valkerie looked down into his face, tears glistening in her eyes. "Why didn't you bleed more oxygen from Kennedy's tank?"

"I didn't want to take the chance. His tank is down to fifty-eight minutes. We'll need every second when we land."

"When we land? We don't even know we'll make it that far! You could have been killed."

Bob shook his head. "Valkerie, please. We'll be fine, but we've got to hurry. We don't have much time."

"Why? What's wrong?"

"Did you get the LOX?"

Valkerie took a deep breath and nodded. "I don't know if it will be enough, but it seems like there's lots of mass left."

"Inspect the tank carefully. If the vacuum jacket is damaged, the tank could lose insulation and blow a burst disk."

Valkerie disappeared from view. When she came back her eyes were dry and full of determination. "The jacket looks fine. The valve looks good too. What else do we need to do?"

"Now we need to build a Sabatier scrubber."

"A what?"

"It's a low-power method of cleaning carbon dioxide out of the air. Nate sent instructions while you were in the airlock."

"I don't understand. Aren't we going to wake Lex and Kennedy?"

"Not till we're done. This is time-critical. Our current scrubber is costing us a kilowatt, and we won't have that for much longer."

"Okay, how do we get started?"

Bob checked the printout. "First, go get all the laptops in the ship."

Friday, May 16, 2014, 6:00 P.M.

VALKERIE

Valkerie attached a copper tube to the catalyst bed and soldered it in place. She looked expectantly toward the hatch, wondering if Bob needed help with the bathroom door. He'd been gone a long time.

"Valkerie! I just got a message from Nate." Bob drifted into the lab. "He's worried that Kennedy might be the bomber."

"Kennedy?"

"Apparently, Kennedy e-mailed schematics of the Hab to a student group in Japan—using Josh's computer."

"Josh's computer? I don't get it."

Bob shrugged. "Kennedy's apartment was full of psych articles by Abrams. They think Kennedy jiggered the psych interviews to get Josh kicked off the mission. If he was capable of that, he could be capable of anything."

"That may be true, except for one thing. Kennedy didn't plant that bomb out there."

"How do you know?"

"I just . . . know. I know Kennedy. No, I don't trust him—at least not in personal matters. But he's not the type to sabotage his own mission."

"If it's not him, then who?"

"I don't know, Bob, but I'm dead sure that nobody on board this ship set that bomb. There are ways of knowing that have nothing to do with facts. I don't expect you to understand that, but—"

"I do."

"What?" She turned to gape at him.

Bob's face reddened. "Valkerie, I've been doing a lot of . . . thinking. You have a real intuition for people and . . . a lot of other things. I've always respected that in you."

"You haven't always acted like you—"

"Please. Let me finish." Bob closed his eyes and held silent for a long minute. "While I was coming out of the coma, I could feel your presence when you were near me."

Valkerie checked the catalyst matrix to see if the glue had set yet.

"And when you weren't there, I could feel another presence," Bob said. "It was weird. It was love and acceptance and . . . just a lot of things. I couldn't get away from it."

"And?"

"And what if it was God?"

She gave him a tentative grin. "Did He leave you an e-mail?"

Bob shook his head and smiled. "If you mean, did He give me some cold, hard fact that I could grab on to, no. But I experienced something warm and close and intimate. I . . . almost feel like I was born . . . um . . ."

" . . . again?" Valkerie's heart hammered in her chest.

His face hardened. "I have a knee-jerk reaction to that phrase, you know."

"Sorry."

"When someone tells me they're 'born-again,' what it means to me is they've got this blind faith, they've made up their mind, and don't confuse them with the facts. And I've always hated that kind of thinking— that kind of nonthinking. But you know what I realized?"

Valkerie slid the catalyst matrix into the flow chamber, afraid to say a word.

"I realized that cold logic isn't much better than blind faith. Because the problem with logic is that one fact can change everything. Kind of like, back in the 1920s, one simple experiment showed that electrons can interfere with each other just like they were waves, and all of a sudden, quantum mechanics was born and changed the way we look at the whole world."

"I've never understood all that quantum stuff," Valkerie said.

"Neither do I," Bob said. A goofy grin slid across his face. "Nobody does. You know why? Because you *can't* understand it. You can *accept* it, but it flies in the face of logic. No, not logic. I'm sure it's all logical to God, but it flies in the face of our intuition, our experience of everyday life. Electrons are particles, and yet they can be in two places at once. That's impossible, right? Well, unfortunately, that's just the way the universe is."

Valkerie soldered the endcap onto the flow chamber.

"Anyway," Bob said, "I finally realized that somewhere between blind faith and cold logic—that's where God is. And . . ." He didn't say anything for a long moment. "And I just wanted to say that I'm sorry about a lot of the things I've said to you. You were right after all."

Valkerie tightened down the nuts, locking the tubes into the endcap. "Not as right as you imagine. I think I've been running away from both faith and logic. While you were asleep, I asked a lot of questions that I didn't have any answers to. Finally I just gave up and tried to stop believing."

"I'm sorry. I didn't mean to—"

"It's okay," Valkerie said. "I tried not to believe, and I found that I couldn't do it. I guess it was going against my intuition. My experience of everyday life. Even so, I still have my doubts. I can't seem to escape them."

"You can't have faith without doubts," Bob said. "And you can't have doubts without faith. That's just the way the universe is."

"Well, it's not a very comfortable universe."

"The truth usually isn't comfortable. If you go looking for the truth only where things are comfortable . . . well, maybe it's like looking for a bomber on the Ares 10." Bob closed his eyes. "I don't know about you, but I'm exhausted." His eyes blinked several times and then finally closed.

Valkerie floated him to the wall and strapped him into an SRU.

"Pleasant dreams . . . Kaggo."

A serene smile slid across Bob's face.

Sunday, May 18, 2014, 6:00 P.M.
BOB

Bob floated in midair, doing isometric exercises with his arms. If he was ever going to get his strength back, he'd have to work out like a madman for the next several weeks. He'd been out of the coma for two days now, but he still felt almost helpless.

Kennedy and Lex were in even worse shape. Valkerie had brought them to consciousness this morning, after working thirty-six hours straight on that Sabatier scrubber. And now she had three invalids to care for. Kennedy seemed to need more attention than a newborn babe.

It was disgusting. And Lex. She was conscious now, but she still couldn't move, couldn't even talk. About all she could do was blink her eyes and sleep. And take up Valkerie's time.

Bob looked at his watch. Time for their meeting. It would be their first since waking up, and like it or not, he was in command. He pushed across to the command center. Kennedy floated motionless near the NavConsole, his face haggard—furrowed with exhaustion. Valkerie sat at the meeting table, working on an adapter that would allow them to transfer oxygen from the LOX tank to the emergency breathers. Lex floated next to her, clinging to a foam exercise ball.

"Okay, team, let's get started. The good news is we're going to make Mars," Bob said. "Thanks to Valkerie, we've survived this far, and hopefully we'll have enough oxygen. And if we start running low, one of us could volunteer to go back to sleep for a while longer."

Valkerie shook her head. "I'm afraid not. We don't have enough drugs. I used everything we had to keep Lex and Kennedy asleep that extra day, and we're completely out of raw materials. We can't synthesize more."

"Well, we'll just have to make do with what we have. We've turned off the oxygen generators. We also turned off the four-bed molecular CO_2 scrubbers, because they were burning a kilowatt we couldn't spare. Howard Spears at JSC came up with a procedure to build a Sabatier scrubber, and that's costing us only about twenty watts."

"I nominate Howard for a Silver Snoopy," Valkerie said.

"Give him two," said Kennedy.

Lex blinked twice.

"I'll tell Josh on the next comm link," Bob said. "The bad news is, we spent all of our fuel margin and more trying to dock with the ERV."

"I'm really, really sorry," Valkerie said. "I shouldn't have tried to—"

Bob held up his hand. "You saved our lives, and that's more than we had a right to ask. But we've got to change plans. We had intended to aerocapture into an elliptical orbit on July third, then do a couple of burns to circularize the orbit at a 500-kilometer radius and deorbit into Mars on July fourth. We don't have the fuel to do that. We'll have to execute an aeroentry from Earth-Mars transit directly into our base camp on the surface."

Kennedy looked skeptical. "That's going to be tough. The timing needs to be perfect."

"It will be," Bob said. "Cathe Willison came up with a series of very small corridor alignment burns that we've already programmed in and will be executing over the next few weeks. They amount to just a few dozen meters per second total, which is all we have left. It's not much, but we've got seven weeks for it to add up. We know the time we'll get there, to the second, and we know the insertion angle to within a few dozen millidegrees. The rest is up to you and the flight software, Hampster."

"No sweat. This thing flies like a brick, but it flies."

"We've got all the oxygen we need waiting for us on Mars," Bob said. "But you'll need to land as close to base camp as possible. Two of us will do an EVA to get the rover, then bring it back for the other two."

"I can land this baby on a dime if I have to," Kennedy said.

"We're going to kick up a lot of debris when we do our descent," Bob said. "If we land closer than two hundred meters, we're going to damage the base camp."

"And that means we've got to get you guys built up," Valkerie said. "Coming out of microgravity is pretty debilitating. On Earth, twenty-four hours bed rest is the norm. Mars gravity is only one third of Earth's, so that'll help, but we'll have to immediately do some hard work. It's going to take at least two of us to go get the rover. So whoever's in the best shape gets to go. Kennedy, how are you feeling?"

"Like road kill." His voice was a dry rasp.

She narrowed her eyes. "How's your eyesight?"

"As good as before."

Bob's ears perked up. *What was this all about?*

"Um, Commander, I did a physical exam on each of you while you were in a coma. You, sir, have a detached retina in your right eye and you can't see a thing."

Kennedy didn't blink. "I know."

"And you're saying it's as good as before?" Valkerie looked annoyed. "Listen, I'm your doctor. Don't hide things from me. We've got some kind of a bacterial contamination on board here, and I think it infected your eye and—"

"No." Kennedy wheezed as he spoke. "My eye ... something happened to it when we launched. I think it was all that vibration."

"When we launched?" Valkerie's eyes went wide. "You mean you've been suffering with a detached retina for *three and a half months*? Why didn't you tell me? I could have done something. We could have—"

"No!" Kennedy coughed. "If I'd told you, you'd have insisted that I get it treated."

Valkerie nodded. "Well, of course."

"You can't do that kind of surgery here on board."

She shook her head. "No. We'd have had to return to Earth."

Kennedy closed his eyes. "We'd have scrubbed the mission. I couldn't do that."

"So you . . . sacrificed your eye for this mission?" Valkerie stared at him.

Bob was beginning to understand a lot of things.

"It was worth it," Kennedy said. "I wasn't going to make us lose Mars."

The crew was silent for a long moment. Then Bob cleared his throat. "Um, guys, I have something to say." He felt his face getting hot. The others looked at him. "I . . . kind of said a lot of things about Valkerie after the explosion. Really stupid things. Blaming her."

Bob wiped at his eyes. *Keep going. Say it all.* "And Valkerie just took all that and turned the other cheek. Then when we were all in a coma, she took care of me, and all of us, and . . . well, I just want to say that I trust her now, and I respect her very highly. I don't know what the rest of you think, but I say she ought to be the first man on Mars. She's earned it. We'd be dead without her. Dead three times over. She's saved this mission. What do you all think?"

Valkerie blushed. "Bob, you don't have to—"

Kennedy nodded. "You're right, Kaggo. Lex, what do you say? Blink your eyes if you agree."

Lex blinked rapidly, five or six times.

Valkerie was stammering now. "G-g-guys, let's not even think about this—"

"You're overruled, Valkerie," Bob said. "You deserve it. Take it—please. We . . . love you, and we haven't got anything else we can give you." *Shut up, Kaggo, you're embarrassing yourself.*

Valkerie covered her face with her hands. "I don't know what to say."

"Just say, 'Thank you.' "

She was crying now. "Okay." Sniffles. She wiped her nose on her sleeve. "Thanks, guys. Thanks, Lex. And Kennedy? I know I said some angry things to you, and I complained about you to Houston. I thought you were paranoid, and I was so scared and . . . I'm sorry. You must have been feeling horrible with your eye like that."

"Forget it," Kennedy said, his voice gruff. "But let's backtrack. You were talking about a bacterial infection."

"I thought that's what attacked your eye."

He shook his head. "The eye was gone when we left Earth orbit."

Bob leaned forward. "Valkerie . . . are you telling me we've got another problem?"

Her face went pale. "I'd forgotten about it, what with all the panic about getting the new scrubber online. But yes. We've got a bacterium infesting our bioreactor—the whole ship, in fact. I've never seen anything like it. It's heat-resistant, radiation-resistant, and . . ."

Bob raised his eyebrows. "And?"

Valkerie bit her lip. "And it may be an extraterrestrial form of life."

Monday, May 19, 2014, 11:00 A.M.

NATE

Nate clenched his fists and tried to smile for the cameras. Was his life going to be one endless press conference?

"Hank Russell, *New York Times*." Russell wore a look of appropriately deep concern. *Filthy hypocrite.* "Mr. Harrington, are we, or are we not, out of the woods yet?"

Nate cleared his throat. "We've dodged one bullet, but there may be more. Thanks to quick thinking by Dr. Jansen and Dr. Kaganovski, we were able to salvage LOX from the earth-landing capsule engine. They've completed work on a low-energy Sabatier scrubber to remove carbon dioxide from the Hab. We believe that may be enough to bring the crew very close to Mars."

"Close?" Russell looked as if he was going to start salivating all over the microphone. "How close is close?"

Nate wanted to strangle him. *Just kill me and hang me out to rot, why don't you?* "We don't know. Listen, people, Scout's honor, swearing on a stack of Bibles, I am giving you every scrap of information I have. The crew is in bad shape. That artificial coma kept them alive, but Commander Hampton and Dr. Kaganovski are in very weak physical condition. Dr. Ohta remains in serious condition, but she is now conscious. So let me lay it all out for you. A lot of things are going to have to go right in order for the crew to land safely on Mars."

Nate held up his first finger. "For starters, that cannibalized LOX is going to have to last till they get there. We don't know how much they have, but we do know it's tight."

He held up a second finger. "Then, Commander Kennedy needs to land that ship direct from Mars transit—there won't be time to do a parking orbit. I don't need to tell you it's going to be a delicate operation."

Another finger. "Third, the ship needs to have no further mechanical problems. Dr. Kaganovski just simply cannot do repairs right now. He can barely move."

The pinkie. "Fourth, the crew will need to get into far better physical condition. Once they land, they'll have only a few hours of oxygen left— at least, we hope they'll have that much—and two of them will need to walk to the base station to get the rover so they can rescue the other two."

Nate raised his thumb. "Fifth . . ." He looked down at his notes. *What was fifth? Oh yeah, the bacterial invasion.* That was the scariest of them all. Valkerie had no idea what that was all about. But if her hypothesis was correct . . . the press would go nuts with it.

Nate folded down his thumb and gave a sorry-I-goofed shrug. "Oops, I miscounted. There's only four."

I hope. Because if Valkerie's right . . . our boys and girls won't be coming back—ever.

Monday, May 19, 2014, 1:00 P.M.

VALKERIE

Valkerie broke off a tiny piece of dehydrated ice-cream sandwich and placed it in Lex's mouth. Lex managed a weak smile and blinked twice with her eyes. Valkerie grinned back. She felt closer to Lex now than she ever had when Lex could talk and move. She wondered if God had felt the same way when she was floating alone and still in the dark stairwell.

"Okay, those are just the repairs we know about," Bob said. "There may be more. Ever since the explosion, the computer sensor diagnostics have been a little squirrelly." He caught Valkerie's eye. "I'm going to have to rely on Valkerie to do most of the repair work until I'm up on my feet again. She's going to have a lot on her plate. Repairing the ship. Filtering drinking water. Taking care of an invalid crew. Making sure Kennedy does his exercises . . ."

"I was moving around faster than you," Kennedy growled.

"And don't forget characterizing the bacteria that's infecting the ship. I really need to work on that. It's important," Valkerie added.

"What about recharging her EVA suit?" Kennedy asked. "She may need to do another spacewalk. Did Houston say anything about that?"

"Houston's looking into it, but they aren't making any promises. We may not have the energy and LOX for it. All the more reason for us to get back in shape as fast as possible. My suit and Kennedy's are the only ones with enough oxygen to get us to the base camp and back—assuming we can land close enough."

"But I thought we agreed that Valkerie would be first."

"As I said, Houston's looking into it," Bob said. "Right now we have more important things to worry about. We all agree that we can trust each other, right?"

"Definitely." Valkerie looked around the cabin. Kennedy nodded and Lex blinked her eyes three times.

"Are you sure?" Kennedy looked at Valkerie pointedly.

She nodded. "Positive. I just wish you had told us about your eye earlier. I was interpreting your pain as some kind of psychosis, but now that I understand—"

"Okay, we all agree that we can trust each other," Bob cut in. "That means that someone or some group of people on the ground planted that bomb."

"Well, I think we can rule out Josh," Valkerie said. "Nobody's fought for us harder than Josh. The whole ERV rendezvous was his idea."

"Absolutely. I think we can rule out Nate too. Besides the obvious lack of motive, he's been every bit as supportive as Josh." Bob looked hard at Valkerie.

"But he's the one who said it had to be one of six people. He's the only one left on the list."

"Well, he's obviously wrong. Whoever planted the bomb was very good. He was also an insider. He could have gotten around the security cameras just like he covered his tracks after stealing the explosives. I'm one hundred percent convinced that the explosives were stolen from JSC, and whoever did it covered his tracks brilliantly."

"Which brings us to another point." Kennedy turned toward Bob. "You never did tell us how you knew about that."

Bob's ears turned hot. "I did a little human engineering on Nate and got him to tell me there'd been a break-in at Energy Systems. Then . . . I hacked into the ESTL database and checked inventories." Bob looked down at the floor. "I guess I was a bit of a geek when I was in high school. Back when hacking was considered cool."

A broad smile spread across Kennedy's face. "I suppose that makes two of us. Think we could do a little snooping on our asynchronous ground connection? It's tied into the JSC network."

Bob shook his head. "Too slow and way too dangerous."

"Too dangerous? Why?" Valkerie wasn't following. What was so dangerous about doing a computer search?

"We know one thing for certain. Whoever planted that bomb wasn't waiting around for me to set it off with a multimeter. That was a total fluke, and it probably saved our lives. If it had gone off any other time, we wouldn't have been able to get into our EVA suits fast enough. Lex is proof of that." Bob looked around at each of them. "So the bomb was either wired into the ship to go off when a certain system got activated, or it was wired to go off at a command sequence sent from earth."

"So you're saying there may be another bomb?" Valkerie was incredulous.

Bob shook his head. "I'm saying that there's a good chance that the saboteur can transmit command sequences to this ship. If he thinks we're on to him, he may be able to figure out a way to get to us from the ground. Up until now, we've been as good as dead, so there wasn't any reason for him to take the risk. But now that we're out of danger— well, let's just say that we may be in more danger than ever."

CHAPTER 35

Wednesday, June 4, 2014, 10:00 A.M.
BOB

Bob had been on the treadmill only ten minutes, but he felt as if he'd just finished the Pike's Peak Marathon.

"You're slowing down," Valkerie said. "You can do better than that, Kaggo."

She called me Kaggo. Bob picked up the pace a little. It was nice having your own personal trainer. The bad part was knowing you had a deadline to meet. Four weeks from tomorrow, he and Valkerie would have to go traipsing across Mars to get the rover. Two hundred meters, if they landed perfectly. Four hundred if Kennedy hiccupped on entry. And if it was more than that . . . you could kiss this mission good-bye.

Valkerie floated over to inspect Kennedy, who was doing isometrics upside down. "Come on, Hampster—I want fifty reps of those! Did you do fifty?"

"Give me a break," Kennedy groaned. "I need a recovery day. You're working me to death."

"We need you in shape for that landing," she said. "You're doing great—just keep it up, okay? You'll have to fly us in, and you won't get to stop for a breather halfway through the aeroentry."

Bob felt himself slowing again. *God, help me. I'm not going to make it at this rate.*

Valkerie moved on to Lex. "How you doing with that squeeze-ball? Make a fist for me, okay?"

Sweat stood out on Lex's forehead as she squeezed.

Bob felt sorry for her. She'd been in a coma longer than any of them, and on top of that, she'd been down to almost full vacuum. Lex was lucky to be alive. They all were. He grabbed his sports drink and took another pull. This treadmill was torture, but it was going to save his life.

Hopefully. Valkerie had hacked up exercise charts for all of them, and had made them promise to hold to the schedule. Bob was keeping his promise—barely.

Valkerie floated back to him. "How you doing, big guy? Keeping the pace up?"

Bob nodded, panting. "How much . . . longer?"

She checked her watch. "Another five minutes should wrap you up for this session. That way you'll be fresh for your strength workout tonight."

Bob groaned. He didn't want a strength workout. Didn't want aerobics. *Just kill me now—it'll be an improvement.*

Which was a lie, of course. He wanted to live. Wanted Lex and Kennedy to live. And Valkerie.

Especially Valkerie. If only he could find a way to tell her . . . if only he knew what to say. So far, everything he'd ever said to a woman had ended up backfiring. Ever since Sarah . . .

Don't think about Sarah.

"Keep that pace, Kaggo!" Valkerie said. "And, Kennedy, was that fifty reps? I want fifty! Lex, don't give up yet. Try the other hand if that one's exhausted. Come on, guys. Please. Our lives depend on it."

Finally, the torture was over. The treadmill was in the unpowered coast mode, so Bob didn't have to turn it off—he just staggered to a stop. He fumbled with the bungee cords, searching for the release. Half undone, they tangled. He swore, then felt his face flushing. "Oops. Sorry, Valkerie. Bad habit."

She floated over, braced herself on the treadmill, and helped him untangle the mess.

"You worked hard," she said, feeling his sweaty shirt. "Good job, Bob."

"I'm exhausted." He floated up out of the harness. "I have got to take a little nap."

"You need to get cleaned up first."

He groaned. "You're killing me."

"Come on, you need to wash up. You'll feel better."

"I didn't wash when I was unconscious."

"You didn't smell like this, either." Valkerie wrinkled her nose. "Good grief, do I need to drag you again?"

Bob shook his head. "I'm a big boy. I know how to take a shower. I'm just . . . can't I do it later?"

"No way. Come on." Valkerie grabbed his wrist and pulled.

Bob let her herd him off to the bathroom. As he passed Kennedy, he thought he saw a trace of a smile on the Hampster's face.

"Work those quads!" Valkerie barked. "You haven't got gravity to fight against, so go for speed. I want you working against your own inertia. Do it! Fifty reps! Lex—you're looking good. Keep it up."

———

Twenty minutes later, Bob was clean and dressed in fresh clothes. "You were right, Valkerie," he said. "I do feel better."

"Next time, you can put your shirt on by yourself," she said. "I've got two other babies to take care of too."

Bob suppressed his urge to smile. *Nobody's stopping you.*

Kennedy was on the treadmill now, dogging along, looking like one of those Bataan death-march survivors.

"Come on, Hampster, give me some leg speed!" Valkerie said. "Lex, how are you doing?"

Lex was asleep, upside down, having drifted against the wall and up into a corner. She was sleeping about twenty hours a day—which was good for her.

"How much longer?" Kennedy asked.

Valkerie floated over to the treadmill and looked at the indicator. "Good, half a mile. That's your record. Take a break."

Kennedy cut the treadmill and collapsed under the force of the bungee cords, groaning.

"You need a shower too, Hampster." Valkerie turned back to Bob. "Bob, I still need you to help me figure out how to fill those breather bottles from the LOX tank."

"Hey, Valkerie, give me a hand on these bungees?" Kennedy asked.

She floated back to him, hit the release, and hauled him out. "Now go take a shower!" She gave him a shove, and he went spinning toward the bathroom.

"But, Mommy, you carried Bobby. Why can't you carry me?"

Valkerie shook her head. "Cut the baby talk, okay, sweetie?" She turned back to Bob. "Ready to work, champ?"

He looked at his watch. "We're due for a comm link in six minutes."

"I'll get the radio switched on and boot the computer." Valkerie floated toward the CommConsole. "Can you check on Lex?"

Bob pushed off toward Lex. She was breathing slowly, evenly. Bob gently pulled her down and floated her over to her SRU. He Velcroed her inside and patted her gently on the head. "Sweet dreams, kiddo."

When he reached the CommConsole, Valkerie had a little smile on her face. "You've changed, haven't you?"

"Ummm," he mumbled, flushing.

"Ares 10, this is Houston, and top of the morning to you all! Come in, Ares 10!"

Grateful, Bob reached for the mike. "Houston, this is Ares 10. Nice to hear we still have a few fans down there. This is Bob, and Valkerie's right here. Kennedy's taking a shower after a tough workout from Taskmaster Jansen, and Lex is asleep." He held the mike to Valkerie.

"Morning, Josh!" she said. "Great to hear from you again. My boys are working hard, and they might even be able to beat me at armwrestling in a few more weeks." She grabbed Bob's biceps and squeezed. "Then again, maybe not. What's on the agenda today? Over."

They waited for the return message. After a couple of minutes, Valkerie suddenly let go of Bob's arm. "Sorry," she said.

Bob felt his ears starting to glow again. "Um . . . no problem."

The seconds ticked slowly by. Nine minutes. Ten. Eleven. "Okay, Ares 10, how did the breather-refilling project go yesterday?" Josh's voice sounded a little strained.

Bob wiped his forehead with his arm. "Negative, Houston. We had our hands full with the IMU. It glitched on us again and we had to resync a couple of times."

Valkerie leaned in close. Bob could feel her body heat. "Also, Lex had some problems with her breathing. I had to give her some epinephrine. Things got a little tense for a while. We're hoping to get to the breathers today. Over."

Another eleven minutes of silence. "Okay, keep us posted on that, then. Bob, I've got some baseball scores for you." Josh rattled off scores for a couple of minutes. It was a little fiction Houston maintained that Bob cared about sports scores. A touch of normalcy in a battle zone.

"Cubs win again! Roger on that," Bob said. "Anything else we need to know? Nate hasn't gone off and retired on us, has he? Tell the old coot he needs to finish out this mission. And say hi to Dr. Perez, okay?"

They sat close together, hunched over the mike, waiting out the comm delay. Finally Nate's voice came rasping over the speaker. "Hey, Kaggo, this old coot heard that. I'm not gonna retire till you lazy bums either finish blowing yourself up or get your tails back here so I'll have someone to cry at my retirement party. Hang on, here's Perez."

Bob heard the sound of a mike changing hands. "Hey, team," said Steven Perez. "Great to hear from you all. Just want you to know that we're all praying for you down here. Valkerie, I have big news! Trident erupted Monday night. Roger talked to Dr. Wiseman and made me promise to tell you that your old cabin is now sitting under six feet of fresh lava. And Kaggo, guess what? When you get back, the Cubs manager has invited you to throw out the first ball. So you just get that arm into shape, okay? We can't have you embarrassing NASA. And I had a call from the pope yesterday. He's going to lead a special prayer service for you guys on Pentecost Sunday. Anyway, I know you have lots to do, so I won't hold you long. I don't want you to waste any more of your juice running the radio. Here's Josh again."

"Be well, guys," Josh said. "We're gunning for you down here. Over and out."

"We love you too," Bob said.

Valkerie had a big smile on her face. "Talk to you tomorrow. Over and out." She turned off the radio and shut down the computer. "Let's get to those breathers." She pushed off and floated toward the stairwell.

Bob followed her, wondering what in the world she was smiling about.

Thursday, June 19, 2014, 10:00 A.M.

NATE

Nate studied the laptop carefully. "You're sure about this, Cathe?"

Cathe Willison nodded. "The telemetry data is super slow and flaky, but it's consistently flaky. The primary aerobrake-deployment system is showing a busted hydraulic line."

Nate stared at the big wall calendar. *Two weeks till landing, and now this.* "Does the crew know?"

"They haven't had time to run diagnostics in weeks. Bob's a week behind in his exercise regime, Kennedy's about ten days behind, Lex is still totally out of it, and Valkerie is mothering them all, like, twenty hours a day."

"Okay, Josh, what's the crew's mental state?" Nate said. "What do we tell them and when?"

Josh studied his hands. "It's a question of whether they need to know," he said slowly. "If the backup system is good, then we tell them to go with the backup and explain why."

"What's the scoop on the backup?"

Cathe shrugged her shoulders eloquently. "No way to know. The diagnostics on it are powered down."

"Which means . . ."

"Not much. Everything on that ship is powered down." Cathe shook her head. "It's anybody's guess if that backup is functional."

"I don't want guesses. I need an answer!" Nate stood up and began pacing. "If they can't deploy an aerobrake, then they're dead. If so, we'll have to let Perez know about it."

"But not the press," Josh said.

"That's his call," Nate said. "He's the one always going on about free and full flow of information."

"If the press knows, the crew's going to find out," Cathe said. "They get e-mail."

"They'll find out eventually, when they try to land and go splat," Nate said. "The question is, do we tell them?"

"Can they fix it?" Cathe asked.

"They'd have to do a spacewalk," Josh said. "And normally, that's a two-man job. Lex can't go. And Bob and Kennedy aren't up to snuff yet."

"How long would it take Valkerie?" Cathe said.

"At least six hours of EVA, but her suit's way short on oxygen. She already did two EVAs." Nate blew his nose. "The system's almost inaccessible—that's why we have a backup. The point is, we need to find out if that backup is working. If so, then it's all a mute point."

"Moot point," said Cathe.

"Whatever." Nate pointed to Josh. "On the next comm link, get them to power up diagnostics on that backup. But don't alarm the crew. This is important. We don't want them to panic."

"So you're just going to leave them in the dark?" Cathe said. "Let them think they can land it, even if you know they can't?"

"We'll cross that bridge when we fall off of it. When's the next comm link, Josh?"

"A couple of hours."

"You should tell them," Cathe said. "Tell them everything."

"Duly noted, Miss Willison." Nate waved Josh toward the door. "Okay, Capcom, go find out whether we have a problem. And this time—bring me some good news."

Thursday, June 19, 2014, 11:00 A.M.

VALKERIE

Valkerie clipped the panel back in place and checked the Sabatier scrubber fixes off her to-do list. She wiped her forehead with her sleeve and let herself relax into a zombie position. Someone was definitely trying to kill them, but it wasn't some faceless saboteur. It was Josh and Nate and a team of five thousand engineers. She had seven more tasks on her list before check-in—and check-in was in less than five minutes. Valkerie shook her head and grabbed Bob's tool bag. A visual check of the bioreactor was a small job. Maybe if she hurried, she could squeeze it in before her report.

"Valkerie!" Bob's voice echoed down through the stairwell.

Great. So much for the bioreactor. She hurried upstairs and found Bob struggling with his penguin suit. He didn't seem to be struggling very hard. "Finished your run already?" she asked.

"One point four miles." Bob grinned triumphantly. "Can you give me a hand with this suit?"

"That's great!" Valkerie helped him pull his arms out of the bungee-corded sleeve of his exercise suit. "I've got to run. I want to look at the bioreactor before check-in."

"Uh, Valkerie?"

Valkerie swiveled to face him. "What's wrong? Are you okay?" Bob's face and neck were flushed. His eyes locked with hers.

"Thank you."

Valkerie searched Bob's face, losing herself in the mystery of his expression. Bob caught his breath and stared steadfastly back.

"I, um . . . you're welcome." Valkerie turned slowly away. She had work to do. Had to fix the . . . what was it she had to fix? Whatever it was, it would have to wait. Nature called.

Valkerie pulled her way around the stairwell. Yuck! The boys had been awake only four weeks and the place was a wreck. She picked a jumpsuit, some sweats, and a pair of damp socks out of the air and opened the door to Bob's cabin. If he thought she was going to repair the ship and provide maid service too . . . Her hand closed around a pencil-shaped object in the jumpsuit. Engineers. She opened the pocket and pulled out . . . a syringe.

Valkerie gasped. It looked like . . . sodium pentothal. Why. . . ? Valkerie felt suddenly queasy. No wonder he had been acting so weird. He hadn't been afraid of being put in a coma. He had been planning—to put her in a coma instead? Valkerie stared at the syringe, letting the revelation sink in. He really had believed that she was the saboteur. That she would kill him in his sleep. What had happened? Why didn't he follow through with it?

Something creaked behind her. She threw the dirty clothes in Bob's cabin and hid the syringe in her pocket. Pushing through the corridor, she drifted over to the CommConsole. Bob sat at the conference table, watching her with haunted eyes.

All those questions. He had learned every detail of how the drugs were administered. He could have easily overpowered her—but he didn't. In his mind he was risking death rather than force his will on her. Valkerie shook her head. It was unbelievable. It was . . . She checked her watch. Check-in time. They were two minutes early, but there was no point wasting time. She switched on the transmitters.

"Houston, this is Valkerie reporting in. We have successfully repaired the Sabatier scrubber and verified the StarTracker. Um . . . we have deferred checkups on the coolant loops, Nav software, and all avionics diagnostics. I'm sorry, but I just don't have time to do everything on your lists. Over."

Bob floated up alongside her and braced himself against the console. Valkerie turned away from him. They waited in awkward silence.

"Ares 10, this is Houston. Copy on that progress report. We're updating your task list. Things are going smoothly down here. Real smoothly. How are you guys doing with the exercise?"

"Hi, Josh. This is Bob. We're doing great. Kennedy is up to a mile per session, and I'm almost up to a mile and a half. Valkerie is a drill sergeant, but we're hanging in there."

"Don't listen to him, Josh," Valkerie said. "I only had Bob scheduled for a mile run. I'm so easy on them that they're doing extra just to keep from being bored."

"Sir, yes sir. Whatever you say, sir!"

Valkerie smiled awkwardly and scooted farther away from Bob.

"Speaking of drill sergeants, what else do you have for us to do? We've still got a ton left on the list, but I don't suppose that's going to stop you from giving us more. Hugs to all you guys. Over." Valkerie looked up at Bob.

Bob studied her with a puzzled look and brushed his fingers through his hair. "You really like him, don't you?"

"Who? Josh?" Valkerie bit her lip. What could she say? A few months ago she wouldn't have hesitated, but now . . . now she wasn't so sure. "Of course I like him. He's a great friend."

"A friend?" Bob raised an eyebrow.

"Of course. Don't tell me you don't trust him anymore." Valkerie looked down at the console. What was she supposed to say? Bob was getting so . . . personal.

"I . . . well, I trust the people on this ship a whole lot more than any-body down there."

Valkerie didn't reply. If he was going to get paranoid again, she didn't want to encourage that kind of thinking. The minutes ticked by in si-lence.

"Ares 10, sounds like you're having a great time. Wish I was there. We're e-mailing you a new schedule that should take some of the load off you. These are some routine system checks we want to make re-motely. No big deal. Just routine. We need you to power up some of the diagnostic systems just before the next check-in, and we'll scan them by telemetry. That should save you guys a big block of time and get you ready for Mars entry. Next check-in time is in three hours at fourteen hundred hours. Have everything ready and we'll get these routine checks done and then you can power them off again. Please confirm."

Bob reached for the mike. A frown creased his face. "Josh, what's going on?" His expression changed. "Um . . . going on down there? You didn't give us any baseball scores. Anyway, we're confirming check-in at fourteen hundred hours. Out." He powered down.

"What's wrong?" Valkerie asked.

"Didn't you hear him? Something's wrong. He used the word 'rou-tine' at least twice. Maybe three times. Bring up that e-mail."

Valkerie brought up the message and scrolled down to the end.

"Wow, look at all the stuff on this list. Can we afford to power all those up?"

Bob scanned the list. "Most of these are just small sensors—a few watts apiece. Coolant loop sensors. Heat-exchanger diagnostics. The bioreactor time-history data analyzer. We can afford to bring them up for a few minutes."

Bob froze. "Wait a second . . . this one doesn't fit the pattern."

"What pattern?"

"Most of these things are diagnostic only. *All* of them are, except one." He pointed at the middle of the list. "They want us to power up the backup aerobrake-deployment system."

"The aerobrake has a backup? I must have missed that one somewhere along the way."

"Not the aerobrake—just the deployment system. There's a hydraulic line that moves the whole aerobrake system out of the solar panel bay on a mechanical arm and prepares the inflatable shell for deploy—" Bob's face froze in an expression of horror. "Oh no!"

"What?"

"If someone were to deploy the aerobrake system right now, it would knock out what remains of our solar panel."

"But they can't do that. There's got to be some kind of a fail-safe, right?"

"The fail-safe for the backup system was damaged during launch. I mentioned that to Houston before we left Earth orbit, but it's not mission critical, so nobody worried about it."

"Could somebody on the ground initiate the backup aerobrake-deployment system right now?"

"No, we have it powered down."

"But now Josh wants us to power it up."

"*Somebody* wants us to power it up," Bob said. "We don't know who put it on that list."

"What are we going to do?"

Bob scratched his chin. "We'll give them what they want, with a little surprise. We'll power up the system but pull the controller board. Then we'll see what they do. We can watch their commands in real-time on the monitor."

Bob pushed off and floated over to a wall panel. He unlatched it and reached far inside. "Okay . . . got it. I've pulled the board." He held it up for Valkerie to see. "Now we'll see what our little saboteur does, whoever he is."

CHAPTER 36

OXYGEN

Bob lunged toward Kennedy at top speed. Kennedy threw up both arms. Bob piled into him, spun his legs up and around, kicked off the wall, and flung his missile—right through Kennedy's arms and into the makeshift goal.

"Score!" Bob shouted. "Fifty-four to fifty-two! Woo, woo, woo!"

They were playing space hockey in the stairwell, a game Valkerie had invented to take some of the tedium out of getting back in shape. They liked it so much, she usually had to force them to quit.

Kennedy picked up the "puck"—a large round mesh bag stuffed with sweaty clothes. Bob retreated to cover his own goal. Kennedy eyed him for a moment, feinted left, right, left again. Then he launched himself.

Bob didn't move. Kennedy had accidentally given himself a bit of cartwheel. *Sorry, you lose, Hampster.*

Halfway across, Kennedy's foot lashed out, caught the side wall, and spun him back toward the center—feet first into Bob. Bob grabbed his feet, but that gave Kennedy leverage to swing around him and dunk the puck into the net as softly as a butterfly kiss.

"Score!" Kennedy shouted. "Watch out, Kaggo, I'm on your tail."

"Boys!" The door swung open and Valkerie floated in. "Time to quit for the day. Houston's going to call in half an hour, and we need to get all those sensors powered up."

"Who's on Capcom shift right now?" Bob floated up the stairwell and past Valkerie into the common area. Kennedy followed, dribbling the puck ahead of him.

"Still Josh." Valkerie floated in and took up a station at the CommConsole. "It's only been three hours since we talked to them last."

"Okay, let's all keep our story straight," Bob said. "We'll tell them that the backup aerobrake-deployment system is down and we're working on it, but we don't think it'll be up in time."

"Here's the list," Valkerie said. "Get busy powering these sensors up."

They each worked rapidly for the next twenty-five minutes.

"Ares 10, this is Houston, come in."

All three of them turned to stare at the radio. Nate's voice! Why was he coming on the air? He wasn't a Capcom.

Bob keyed on the mike. "Nate, this is Bob, how are you today? Where's Josh? Hope he's not sick." He turned off the mike and looked at the others.

"Must have a pretty big announcement," Kennedy said.

"He sounded kind of uptight." Valkerie's eyebrows knotted.

"He's always uptight." Bob switched on the computer so Houston could do their data uplink. "That's his job, to be—"

"In case you guys are wondering, Josh is fine and he's here with me now. Say hello, Josh."

"Hey, guys, who's ahead in the space hockey wars?" Josh asked.

"Okay, crew, listen up," Nate said. "You'll be landing in a little under two weeks, and we just need to go over procedures." He cleared his throat. "Protocol, and all that. Kennedy, you may not remember this, but there's still the question of who's going to be first on Mars. I'll need your decision in the next few days, or those reporters are going to eat me for lunch."

Bob relaxed a little. Okay, that was typical of Nate, to be sweating over the TV jerks. Let him sweat.

"Second, we'll be wanting to do a show with you as soon as possible after landing. The president will want to give you her congratulations, and if you can possibly get us a video feed, it would ... make my job easier. I'd kind of like to get the ratings high enough so we can afford to bring you back." He gave a brittle laugh. "Just kidding."

Sure you are. Bob kept his eyes on the computer console. He had set things up to intercept and display the commands in real time as they came across the monitor. *Query power level. Query CO_2 level.*

"Well, that's enough about protocol, kids," Nate said. "I'm proud of what you've done so far. Bob, could you go get Lex? I'd like her to hear this next announcement. I'll give you about three minutes. Meantime,

Josh has a message to Valkerie from her father."

Bob didn't move. Lex had gone to sleep less than an hour ago, and he didn't want to wake her up. And besides, he wanted to watch the command stream.

"Hey, Valkerie," Josh said. "Your dad says you don't have to name any more bugs after him. I guess the *National Enquirer* found out about that bacteria you found in Alaska, and they ran a big story on your dad. Quoted him out of context, ran a bad photo, the works. Over."

"Daddy thinks all his pictures are bad. Send him my love. Okay, here's the report . . ." Valkerie began giving a rundown of what she'd done for the last three hours.

Bob squinted at the monitor. What was that command? *Activate backup aerobrake hydraulic arm.* He stared at the screen for several seconds, unable to believe it was really happening. Someone was trying to destroy their ship. He'd been afraid of it, had suspected it, but he hadn't quite believed it. Until now. *Kissinger was right. Even paranoids have enemies.*

Bob reached forward and cut the data link.

Valkerie kept talking for a few seconds, but then her voice trailed off and she stopped speaking in midsentence and turned to stare at Bob.

He flicked off the mike and pointed to the monitor. "Somebody tried to sneak in a command sequence to activate the hydraulic arm on our backup aerobrake-deployment system."

"I can't believe it—right when Nate decided to play Capcom." Sweat stood out on Kennedy's forehead. "Bob, I think you're right. Somebody's messing with us big time."

"Um, what do we do about the comm session?" Valkerie said. "They're going to be wondering why I quit talking."

"What I want to know is, who's behind this?" Bob said. "Do Nate and Josh know somebody's monkeying with us?"

"Of course they don't know. I can't believe it. Any of it." Valkerie looked stunned.

"Just wait." Bob held up his hand. "Let's see whose side Nate's on."

"He's on our side," Valkerie said.

"That remains to be seen," Kennedy said. "Let's see what he says next."

There followed a long silence while they waited for Houston to respond.

"Ares 10, this is Houston, come in!" Nate said. "Crew, we are getting no vox. Do you read me? We are not getting vox. Please respond if you copy. Over."

"No vox," Bob said. "You notice he doesn't say anything about the data link? I shut that down first, but he's only talking about the vox. He's not being honest here."

"Ares 10, this is Houston, come in. Valkerie, do you read me? We also need to begin a checkout of those sensors we mentioned this morning. Those are mission-critical systems, and we still need to begin looking at those. Ares 10, come in."

"Begin?" Valkerie looked at Bob. "Am I hearing right? Did he say they need to begin looking at those?"

"He's lying through his pointy little fangs." Kennedy put his hand on the radio power switch. "I say we cut off this conversation right now. Any objections?"

"Do it. We need to conserve power," Bob said.

Valkerie nodded. Her face had gone pale.

Kennedy flicked the switch off.

"Nate's in on it," Bob said.

"That's . . . crazy," Valkerie said. She didn't sound convinced.

Kennedy smacked his hand on the console. "There's no other interpretation. Nate lied to us, pure and simple."

"And if Nate's in on it, Josh has to be too," Bob said. "They were working out of the same playbook there."

Valkerie covered her face with her hands. "This is so . . . unbelievable."

"From now on, no more data links *and* no more vox," Kennedy said. "We won't even listen for their transmissions. We turn the radio off completely and we save our juice for reentry."

"From now on . . . we're on our own," Bob said. *And may God help us all.*

Thursday, June 19, 2014, 2:30 P.M.
VALKERIE

Valkerie stumbled to her room, pushing through the haze that shrouded her vision. It was true. Someone really was trying to kill them. And Josh was in on it. Nate too. They all were.

Valkerie swung herself through her door and slammed it shut behind her. She hung in the darkness, convulsing with the force of her sobs. Her body tingled with the pricks of a million needles, but she was too numb to care. It didn't matter. Nothing mattered anymore. They all were as good as dead.

A knock sounded at her door.

"Go away!"

"Valkerie, it's me. Bob."

"Leave me alone." She flung back the words, not caring what Bob thought. It didn't matter anymore. She just wanted to be left alone.

"Valkerie, please. It's okay. Everything's going to be okay. You have to keep believing that."

Valkerie didn't say anything.

The door slid open. "May I come in?"

Valkerie wiped her face and nodded. Turning to her mirror, she raked back her hair with her fingertips.

"Valkerie, I know what you're going through. Believe me, I know how it feels." Bob's voice was soft. Tender. Valkerie glanced back at his face. He looked miserable.

Valkerie turned back to the reflection in her mirror. "How?"

"How?"

"How do I feel?"

"Betrayed." Bob pulled himself to the corner of the cabin and turned to face her. "You feel like you gave your heart away, and he threw it back in your face—trampled and broken and crushed and torn. . . . You gave him your trust, and he twisted it to use against you. You . . ." Bob's voice quivered. "You hurt more than you ever thought possible."

Valkerie searched Bob's face with wondering eyes. "Is that what you've been feeling?" Valkerie reached out and took his hand. "Bob, what happened? Can't you please tell me? Can't you let me help?"

Bob looked at the floor and took a deep breath. "Her name was Sarah."

"Sarah McLean?"

Bob nodded silently. "It was my second year at Berkeley. She was . . . outgoing, sociable, attractive . . . everything I'm not. But she liked me anyway—with all my flaws."

Valkerie squeezed Bob's hand and nodded for him to continue.

"Valkerie, I loved her so much it made me sick. I couldn't sleep. I couldn't think. I lost weight. . . . When I asked her to marry me, and she said yes, I . . . I couldn't believe it. She was so beautiful. So perfect." He sniffled softly.

"But then I had to go to Boston for an APS conference. That was in June, and we were going to get married in August. I was only gone about a week. And when I got back, she'd . . ."

"She'd met someone else?" Valkerie enfolded Bob's hand in her own and hugged it to her chest. "Bob, I'm so sorry. I can't imagine . . ."

Bob shook his head and looked back down at the floor. "One of her friends took her to a meeting at a church over on Dana Street. When I got back, all she could talk about was how she'd met Jesus and gotten saved. You know . . . born again."

Valkerie nodded. The puzzle pieces were beginning to fall together now. Everything was beginning to make sense.

"She had some friends over at her new church," Bob said. "And they kept working on her about how she couldn't be unequally yoked. If you don't know what that means—"

"I know."

Bob breathed in deeply. "We had some terrible fights about it, and then . . . two days before the wedding . . . she broke it off. I'd paid for the tuxes, the church, the plane tickets to Cancun. . . ."

Valkerie leaned forward. "Bob, I'm so sorry."

"It's okay. I'm . . . over her now."

Valkerie looked deep into Bob's eyes. "Are you sure?"

"I'm sure." Bob nodded solemnly. "I met someone else." A fragile smile spread itself over his features, then darkened suddenly and faded to a frown.

"Bob, what's wrong?"

Bob took a deep breath. "I know that the evidence looks bad, but maybe Josh isn't in on it. I can't believe he would ever hurt you. You've got to keep believing. He's not like Sarah."

Valkerie stared at him. "What kind of a relationship do you think we have? I told you we're just friends."

"Just friends?"

Valkerie's heart pounded at the expression of wonder that filled Bob's eyes. She turned to look away, but it was too late. She could tell by his face that Bob had already seen her smile.

Thursday, June 19, 2014, 2:30 P.M.
NATE

"You're sure it's broken?" Nate asked.

Cathe Willison pointed to her laptop. "Here's the return message. We sent a command to activate the aerobrake hydraulic system. All we wanted to do was to interrogate it electronically. It's got a full range of diagnostics."

"And?"

"And it's busted." She snapped shut the laptop. "They don't have a backup. And they don't have a primary."

Nate buried his head in his hands. "So I'll ask you guys again, do we or don't we tell the crew they're dead?"

"We don't have a choice," Josh said. "They aren't responding on vox. I have a Capcom out there hailing them continuously, and they are not responding."

"Bad antenna?" Nate asked.

"I doubt it." Josh tapped his pencil on the table. "It was working fine when we talked to them. Then, boom! Off it went. I think they may have gotten suspicious of us."

"You should have told them up front what your concerns were," Cathe said.

Nate spun around on her. "Miss Willison, we do not need—"

"She's right, Nate," Josh said. "We fouled up—tried to do an end around and got nailed. Astronauts are smart. I betcha Bob caught on to us."

Nate sighed heavily. "Guys, it doesn't matter who caught on. It doesn't matter who messed up. The only thing that matters right now is we got four boys and girls heading toward a brick wall without any brakes. And they don't even know it. We have to get hold of them before July third. We *have* to."

"The problem isn't on our end," Josh said. "We can talk all we want. If they don't want to listen . . . there's nothing we can do."

Valkerie floated in the semidarkness of the musty stairwell, staring up at the failing emergency light that painted the three faces around her with streaks of orange and dull red. They had been floating in the stairwell for days, conserving energy. Buying time. The oxygen from the earth-landing capsule was running out quicker than expected. Probably a result of all their exercise and repair work.

Valkerie looked up at Bob. He nodded back and returned her smile.

A hand slipped into Valkerie's and squeezed. Valkerie pulled Lex closer and draped an arm around her shoulders. Lex looked up at her with a grateful smile. "Thank you again." The words were barely audible, but they thrilled through Valkerie with the force of a scream. Tears formed in Valkerie's eyes, warping the faces around her into shimmering blurs. A strong arm wrapped around Valkerie's shoulders. Another reached out and took her by the hand.

Valkerie shut her eyes and floated in the warmth of the embrace. How different from her ordeal while the others were unconscious. How totally different, and yet somehow, now that she looked back, it felt exactly the same. *Thank you, God. Thank you.* She repeated the words over and over, trying to hold on to the feelings that welled up inside. She was free. She was totally dependent, but somehow, deep down inside, that knowledge made her free. She tried to understand, to wrap her mind around the feelings and trap them in a cage of reason, but they slowly faded, slipping away between the insubstantial bars.

"It's okay, Valkerie. Don't worry. We're going to make it. I know we are." Bob pulled her in closer under his arm. His voice dropped to a whisper. "God's taken care of us so far. I can't imagine Him stopping now."

Valkerie swiped her arm across her eyes and looked up at Bob. He looked down at her with a goofy grin. Valkerie smiled. That grin used to irritate her to death. "I'm not worried." She looked around at the faces of her crewmates. "I'm just happy to be with you guys. I love you. A lot. All of you."

"We love you too, Valkerie," Kennedy reached across the circle and clasped her arm. "Oh man, I've been in this tin can too long. I'm starting to sound like the Tin Woodsman."

Bob laughed. "So what do we do now, Dorothy? Lex brought some ruby slippers in her personal gear. Maybe if you put them on and tapped the heels together three times—"

"I am not the wicked witch!" Lex exclaimed in a hoarse whisper. "You better watch it, you toad, or I'll turn you into a charming prince."

Valkerie laughed until she couldn't breathe. They had been frantic for so long. She had almost forgotten what it felt like not to have the threat of death hovering over her head.

"Okay, y'all. We've got to be serious." Kennedy's voice dampened the mood like a storm cloud rolling across the sun. "We've got to work out our strategy for landing. If Bob's calculations are right, we'll make our landing with less than two hours of energy left for the fuel cells. We're not going to have much to breathe. It's going to be very tight."

Everybody went silent. Valkerie wanted to kick Kennedy. Why couldn't he have let them enjoy themselves for just a few more minutes? What would it have hurt?

"I think we should talk to Houston." Lex broke the silence after a long pause. "We don't have to do a data link, but we could at least ask their advice."

"Every minute of transmission time is fifteen seconds less that we can power the ship," Bob interjected. "It costs too much energy. We can't do it."

"Please, just one quick transmission." Lex sounded desperate.

"Lex. Given what you already know about our situation"—Kennedy let the words hang—"would you trust the advice Houston sent back?"

Lex stared off into space. Valkerie watched her in alarm. Was she in pain? She seemed so distant—so sad.

Valkerie pulled her close, but Lex dropped her gaze. Valkerie could feel her slender frame shaking.

"I guess not." Lex's whisper trembled on the thin air.

Valkerie held her tighter. Something was terribly wrong. If only she would . . . *Oh no* . . . She remembered back to the first time she had met Lex. It seemed like so long ago, but Lex had been with Josh! Could Lex be in love with him? That would explain everything. Valkerie felt sick to her stomach. No wonder Lex had been so distant. If only she had said something. If only . . .

Kennedy cleared his throat. "It's going to take two people to travel on foot to the base camp and get the rover. After five months of weightlessness, it's going to be a very demanding expedition, even if we manage to land close to the base. Valkerie is the doctor. I say we let her decide whether it's going to be Bob or me that goes with her."

Valkerie shook her head to clear her mind. "But my EVA suit is completely out of oxygen."

"I'm almost done modifying the hose," Bob said. "We should be able to transfer oxygen from one of our suits to yours. The question is which one."

"But the fitting isn't perfect. Aren't we going to lose oxygen in the transfer?"

Bob nodded. "A little, but I'll tape up the hose good and tight. It should be able to withstand the pressure."

"But what if it doesn't? What if we lose too much oxygen? We only have fifty-eight minutes."

"That's not going to happen," Bob said emphatically. "But if it did, we'd still have it to breathe in the Hab."

"But we'd be left with only one charged EVA suit. One person can't go out alone."

"That's not going to happen," Bob declared. "We're not going to lose nearly that much."

"Okay . . ." Valkerie looked each of her crewmates in the eye. "And you all agree to abide by my decision?"

Lex and Kennedy nodded their heads.

"Of course we do, Valkerie," Bob said. "You're the only reason we're still alive. We trust you with our lives."

Valkerie took a deep breath. *So much for fame and fortune. . . .* "Okay, I've decided. Bob and Kennedy will do the EVA. They've worked—"

"But you're supposed to be first," Bob broke in.

"I'm deciding, Bob," Valkerie said firmly. "You and Kennedy have worked very hard since you woke up. You both are at about ninety percent, so strength isn't really an issue. The important consideration is the oxygen transfer between suits. If we lose too much oxygen during the transfer, we're dead. This way we don't have to worry about that. Bob will be able to stop kludging a transfer hose and start working on getting us down in one piece."

Valkerie looked up at Bob, defying him to argue. He gazed down into her eyes. At length he smiled and nodded his head slowly.

She looked at Kennedy and received his nod before turning to Lex. Lex was still looking down. Both of her eyes glistened with unshed tears.

CHAPTER 37

Thursday, July 3, 2014, 10:00 A.M.
BOB

Bob looked at his watch through the faceplate of his breather mask. Less than two hours till they entered the Martian atmosphere. And they had about two hours—maybe a little more—of oxygen left in their breather canisters. If he was going to get the ship up and operating, he had to start now. He pressed the power switch to boot the computers.

These breathers were a pain in the neck, but there was no choice. They had run out of the LOX Valkerie had rescued. Now all they had left was the emergency bottled oxygen and whatever remained in the EVA suits. *Dear God, let it be enough.*

Bob cracked his knuckles and looked over at Kennedy. Both of them were wearing their MAG diapers and Liquid-Cooled Garments. Once they landed, they'd have to jump into their EVA suits and *sprint* to the base camp. If Kennedy landed them within two hundred meters, it was doable.

Okay, good, the computer was coming online. He could hear the soft murmur of voices back in the stairwell. Lex and Valkerie were talking.

He wished he could have a few minutes to talk to Valkerie. Alone. In a couple of hours, they were going to land on Mars. Dead or alive, they would reach the Red Planet. And he desperately wanted to tell Valkerie—

A warning message flicked on the screen. The IMU was fritzing again. There wasn't time for this kind of nonsense. He'd have to resync it with the backup. This was going to waste energy. And time. He didn't have much of either to spare.

He synced up the IMU. The computer made final calculations and recommended a couple of burns. The first would increase speed right now by a few inches per second. Bob keyed in the commands to fire the RCS vernier jets. He hung his PDA in the air. The burn was so tiny, he wouldn't be able to feel it. But he'd know it when the PDA started moving. Inches per second, but measurable.

The last few days had been priceless. They'd huddled together in the stairwell, talking little, but saying much. Valkerie had talked about her alcoholic mother and cried. Lex told them about finding a picture of the father she'd never known—and burning it. Kennedy had talked about growing up in the South in a family that still thought the wrong side won the War Between the States. And Bob had told them all about Sarah McLean.

The talking had brought them all closer together. Slowly, slowly. Imperceptibly.

Bob's PDA started drifting toward the wall. That told him the burn had worked. He grabbed the PDA and stuffed it in his pocket.

There was one more thing Bob wanted to talk about. With Valkerie. Just her.

But there hadn't been a convenient time, and now it was too late. He'd waited too long. If they burned up on entry, if the parachutes failed, if Kennedy hovered too long and they ran out of bipropellant before touching down, if the fuel cells ran out, if any of a thousand failure modes went poof, then Bob would never be able to tell her.

He punched the buttons to begin bringing in the solar panel. From now on, they'd be living on whatever power they'd managed to save up in the fuel cells—maybe a couple hours' worth.

Something blurred Bob's vision. He brushed at his eyes madly. He had a job to do. Kaggo the Robot had to perform. There wasn't time to be human.

Thursday, July 3, 2014, 10:30 a.m.
VALKERIE

Valkerie carefully checked the patches on the shrapnel punctures in Bob's EVA suit. This was the fourth time she had checked it today. She hoped they held. Maybe she should reconsider and do the EVA herself. If one of the patches failed . . . no, it was too late now. There wasn't enough time to modify the oxygen-transfer hose. Besides, NASA had put a lot of work into the patch kits. Bob would be fine. He was strong, and he knew the workings of the rover better than anyone.

"Is that the last one?" Valkerie could barely hear Lex's whisper through her breather.

"I sure hope so. Here, see if you can find any more of those little stainless-steel splinters." Valkerie pushed Bob's suit across the stairwell. Lex took it with a melancholy nod and bent over it with a magnifying glass.

"Lex, did you know that Bob almost died while I was bringing in the capsule's LOX tank? He refused to breathe from Kennedy's suit, because he was afraid fifty-eight minutes wasn't going to be enough. He was willing to sacrifice himself to give us a better chance."

"Bob is a . . . special guy," Lex whispered back. "I'm not surprised."

"The guys want us to take some of the oxygen from their EVA suits for our breathers—so we'll all have equal amounts." Valkerie paused. *Did she dare go on?* "But . . . I've been thinking. What if they don't have enough? Bob and Kennedy are going to be weak and dizzy once they hit Mars gravity. I don't think they have any idea how hard it's going to be. What if they run out of oxygen? Then we'll *all* be dead. For sure."

Lex nodded slowly. "We have to . . . give them our share." Her whisper was barely audible.

Valkerie moved across the stairwell and put her arm around Lex. "Don't worry. It'll be all right. I've—"

Lex pulled away from Valkerie. "Is that what you think? That I'm afraid? Don't you think I considered the odds when I signed onto this mission? I'm not afraid to die. I just wish . . ." Lex buried her face in her hands. Her shoulders shook.

Valkerie reached a hand out to Lex's shoulder but drew it back again. She felt so helpless. What could she do? She was the last person that Lex would want to comfort her.

"I just wish we could send a message home. Just one message . . ."

Valkerie nodded and took a deep breath, steeling herself to ask the question that she had been putting off for so long. "You want to send a message to Josh, don't you?"

Lex looked up. "What?"

"You're in love with Josh, aren't you? I'm so sorry. I should have known. I don't know how I could have been so stupid. I never would have—"

"What are you talking about?"

"Lex, you have to believe me. If I had known you were interested in Josh, I never would have gone out with him. I'm really sorry."

"Josh and I are just friends. I'm certainly not in love with him."

"Well, then who . . . I mean, why do you want to send back a message?"

Lex lowered her head. She was silent for several minutes. Valkerie bit her lip, watching the struggle that played across Lex's dimly lit features.

"My . . . husband," she said at last.

"Your husband!" Valkerie gasped. "I didn't know you were married."

"Nobody does," Lex admitted to the floor. "We kept it a secret. They wouldn't take married people in the Ares program. I didn't want to lose Mars, but it wasn't just me. I did it for his career too. . . . He was moving up in rank so fast, and he needed to be able to go wherever they sent him."

"The officer at the last visitation," Valkerie said. "I was wondering why he left without talking to anybody."

Lex nodded. Her brow was creased with pain. "We had a fight. It was my fault. I insisted that we give each other freedom. But when he finally . . . when he . . . took me up on it, I . . ." Lex buried her face in her hands and sobbed.

Valkerie pulled Lex close and held her gently as she cried. *God, please let this be okay. I know we're running out of time.*

After a time, Lex grew quiet and finally pulled away.

"Lex, I can check the suits. Go write a letter. I'll convince Bob to let us send it."

Lex sniffled. "Thank you, but I'm okay. I've already written a long one—just in case." Lex retrieved Bob's EVA suit and fell to examining it with the magnifying glass.

"Lex, maybe this is none of my business, but when we searched your cabin, I noticed . . ."

Lex looked up at Valkerie.

"I'm sorry. It's really none of my business."

"No, it's okay. What's your question?"

"Well, Flight Med put me on birth-control pills, but I . . ."

Lex pushed Bob's suit away. "I was such a fool. I wanted so bad to make something of myself. As soon as I got out of college . . . the first thing I did was have an operation."

"And now?"

"And now . . . I think you and I both know what's really important.

And it's not something we're likely to find on Mars."

Valkerie nodded slowly and turned to leave.

"What about you? Are you in love with Josh?" Lex whispered.

Valkerie turned around at the hatch and considered Lex's question. "No . . . I mean, I like him, and maybe at one time I thought something might develop, but now . . ." She shrugged. "Now I'm definitely not in love . . . with him."

"Good," Lex said with relief.

"What do you mean, good? What's wrong with me liking Josh?"

"Well, for one, he's dating Karla Faust."

"*The* Karla Faust—the one at Stanford?"

Lex nodded. "I guess you *would* know her work."

"Well, of course. Bob told me once that Josh had a girlfriend in Antarctica, but he didn't tell me it was *her*. And I thought Bob was just . . . making it all up. Anyway, Josh told me he broke up with her a long time ago."

"Well, he never told me. Not that I'm questioning him. Karla wasn't his type at all. I always assumed he was stringing her along because he needed help with his research."

"Research?"

"Yeah. She brought him back all kinds of specimens to practice on."

"Specimens? From Antarctica?"

"Yeah. Bacteria and stuff. They were supposed to be drought-resistant. Didn't he ever show you any of his work?"

Valkerie could see Josh's lab in her mind's eye. A PCR thermal cycler. Dozens of parafilmed Petri dishes. A stainless-steel canister. *Stainless steel?* Valkerie grabbed Lex's arm, her brain suddenly in high gear.

"Valkerie? What's wrong?"

Valkerie kicked off the wall and dove through the hatch. "Bob!"

Thursday, July 3, 2014, 11:15 A.M.

BOB

Bob ticked off the last item on his checklist and looked at the time. Thirty minutes to spare. "Okay, Hampster. She's good to fly. Your move, buddy."

Kennedy gave him a thumbs-up. "I've got Lex's seat set up downstairs, and the others are locked down over in the command center. Better get the girls and help them strap in. Lex is going to need a lot of help."

"Roger on that." Bob started toward the stairwell. Lex would ride on the lower deck so they wouldn't have to carry her down the stairs after the landing. It was going to be tough getting used to gravity. Bob wondered if maybe they shouldn't have tried to set up all the seats on the lower deck. Oh, well . . . maybe after they finished getting Lex situated, he would get a chance to talk to Valkerie alone in the stairwell. Maybe.

Before he reached the hatch, it flew open. Valkerie sailed out, her face flushed.

"Bob, listen, I've got something to tell you."

"I've got something to tell you too. I—"

"Bob, I know who the saboteur was."

"You . . . what?" Bob stared at her.

Lex drifted out of the stairwell, pushing feebly off the walls. "Valkerie, are you sure about this?"

"Yes, I'm sure." Valkerie's face shone. "We don't have much time, so just listen, everyone. After the explosion, we detected stainless-steel chips embedded in Bob's suit, right? And nobody knew where they came from, because there isn't any stainless steel out there on the hull. It's all composites. You with me so far?"

"Keep going," Bob said.

"And Josh has a girlfriend in Antarctica. Lex was just telling me about her—"

"Karla Faust. I told you about her a long time ago," Bob said. "You wouldn't believe me."

"We don't have time!" Valkerie said. "Just listen. I saw a stainless-steel cylinder in Josh's lab once. A small one, but large enough to hold a few hundred cc's of biosample."

"We've got to get Lex strapped in. We're running out of time." Kennedy took hold of Lex and started to move her toward the stairwell.

Bob helped Kennedy maneuver Lex through the hatch. "Keep talking, we're listening."

Valkerie followed Bob and Kennedy downstairs and helped them guide Lex to her seat. "Okay, it's simple, really. Josh once asked me what I thought of life on Mars—whether we'd find it. I said I doubted it, but I didn't know. I remember now how urgent he seemed to think it was. Said if we didn't find life, the Ares program would crash and burn, and NASA wouldn't survive."

"That's ... nuts," Lex whispered. "Valkerie, are you going to send my message?"

"I'm getting to that." Valkerie pulled a strap over Lex's head and cinched it down tight. "But listen. Josh's girlfriend is a microbial ecologist, a real heavy hitter. She specializes in hardy life forms in Antarctica. They're drought-resistant. Ergo, radiation-resistant."

"How does that follow?" Bob handed Valkerie a side strap.

"It's the same thing, really," Valkerie said. "Desiccation damages DNA in much the same way that radiation does. The same systems that repair DNA after freeze-drying can repair DNA after exposure to radiation. See? Josh told me once that if we didn't find life on Mars, the mission was dead. Now here's where the guesswork starts, and I admit it's a guess, but it's plausible. Suppose he decided to bring along some insurance, just to make sure he found what he needed. What NASA needed."

"That's crazy," Bob said. "Somebody would figure it out eventually."

"Maybe not," Valkerie said. "People would probably argue for an Earth-to-Mars transfer via meteorite blast—you know, the reverse of the process that sometimes brings Mars rocks to Earth. Anyway, it would buy him some time—years, maybe. In the meantime, maybe somebody would find the real McCoy. I'm just guessing here, but my gut tells me it's right. Josh loves NASA. He'd do anything to save it."

"He'd kill us to save NASA?" Bob shook his head. "Josh is a zealot—sure. But he's not a maniac. Not a murderer."

"No, you dummy! Of course not! He never intended that thing to go off in space. That had to be an accident. I wouldn't be surprised if it was built to arm itself after the solar panels got reeled in. He never expected us to do a test deployment in low-Earth orbit, then bring them back in, then redeploy. Anyway, just supposing I'm right, there are only two bays where he could have hidden his goodies."

"The solar-panel deployment bays," Bob said.

"Right. Everything deploys out of those two bays. The solar panels. The parachutes. The inflatable aerobrakes. Everything. I'm betting he stuffed in that little stainless-steel cylinder with some pyros set to go off just before landing. He wanted to seed the area with life. And then we'd find it. He wasn't counting on us blowing it up out in deep space. And now the whole ship is infected with this weird bacteria. Radiation-resistant bacteria. You guys still following me?"

"So ... there was no saboteur," Bob said.

"Right. It was an accident. Nobody on Earth ever tried to kill us. Now do you get it?"

Bob nodded. "Yeah, I guess so."

Valkerie pushed off toward the lower deck's CommConsole. "Can I turn the transmitter on from here?"

"Why would you want to do that?" Bob said. "We can't spare the power."

"Twenty seconds," Valkerie said. "Tell me we haven't got twenty seconds to send a message. If we don't survive the landing, there are people on earth who deserve to hear our final words."

Bob flicked the switches to power up the radio. "Okay. Maybe we can spare a minute."

Valkerie grabbed the microphone.

"Houston, this is Ares 10," Valkerie said. "We are twenty minutes from entering the Mars atmosphere. We are alive and well and transmitting final words before landing." She handed the mike to Kennedy.

"This is Kennedy Hampton, CDR of Ares 10. We have very little oxygen but hope to transfer to base camp immediately upon landing. The operation has a roughly fifty-fifty chance for success. For the record, the crew has been exceptional—every one of them."

Valkerie handed the mike to Bob. He took it and stammered. "Um ... well, this is Bob Kaganovski. Um ... live long and prosper." *What a stupid thing to say.*

Valkerie took the mike. "Valkerie Jansen here. We love you all, and we're sorry we've been on radio silence for the last two weeks. We kind of freaked out when we saw you trying to query the backup aerobrake-deployment system. Don't worry, guys, it was fine, but it doesn't matter because we'll be using the primary. Anyway, we now know that we have nothing to fear from any of you. Hugs to you, Josh Bennett. We know how desperately you wanted this mission to succeed, and the extraordinary steps you took to make it so. Please don't blame yourself if ... something happens to us. We know you did everything you could, and we love you. Alexis Ohta has something very special for someone." She held the mike down to Lex's lips.

Lex swallowed hard. "To my husband, Ronald J. Anderson, United States Air Force ... I love you. I love you. I love you." Her eyes fell shut. Kennedy and Bob gasped.

Valkerie took the mike and floated back toward the CommConsole.

"We're about to land. We'll catch you on the flip side in about an hour." She shut the radio off.

"Okay, kiddies." Kennedy pushed off for the stairwell. "Fifteen minutes till the ride begins."

Thursday, July 3, 2014, 11:45 A.M.
NATE

Nate's biggest fear yesterday was that he'd break down in front of the cameras. He knew now that he had nothing to fear on that score. The hot TV lights did nothing to warm the freezing cold in his gut. *We lost 'em.*

It was July third, one day short of the day he'd been dreaming about for the last eight years. Now the starlight had faded to ashes.

Thanks to Newton's equations, Nate knew exactly where his crew was—just entering the Martian atmosphere. But they were going to burn up when they reached it. Why, oh why, had they broken contact two weeks ago? Radio malfunction? Paranoia? Or was it Kennedy?

Steven Perez stepped to the podium. Nate knew what the press could only suspect. Perez was going to resign over this. Nate would too, of course, but he'd been planning on taking early retirement when the mission ended anyway, so it was no skin off his nose. But Perez was still young. This would destroy his career. And worse, it would keep them both awake every night for the rest of their lives.

"Fellow Americans," Perez began. His eyes glistened with real tears. *Perez is still a person, the lucky slob.* "Ares 10 is just now passing the point beyond which we can no longer talk to her. We know that neither aerobrake-deployment system on the ship is functional. Two weeks ago, we lost radio contact with the ship, for reasons unknown. It may be an equipment malfunction. It may be simple paranoia. Or it may be that they chose to end it all. What seems certain is that, at this moment, the ship is reaching Mars and will burn up in the thin atmosphere of an alien planet. Please join with me in four minutes of silence in honor of Kennedy Hampton, Alexis Ohta, Robert Kaganovski, and Valkerie Jansen—two men and two women who have shared their lives with us throughout their remarkable journey. Right now, their only hope of survival is a miracle."

Perez bowed his head. Nate could see his lips moving. Praying for that miracle?

Nate tipped his head down, but kept his eyes open. The only miracles he believed in were the kind his engineers pulled out of their hats. Movement caught his eye. He looked up. Josh Bennett was waving excitedly from backstage. Nate stood up and tiptoed out as quietly as he could.

Josh looked stricken. "We did the best we could, but they won't get it in time."

Nate stared at him. "Get what in time? Who won't?"

"The crew," Josh said. "We just heard from the Ares 10." He pulled out a PDA.

Nate listened to the recorded message. By the time it finished, Josh was crying like a baby. "I'm . . . sorry, you guys. You'll never know how sorry I am."

Nate stared at the PDA. "Their backup aerobrake was functional! Did you tell them the primary is out of commission? They're dead meat unless they switch to their backup. And they have to know that in advance. They won't have time to deploy with the primary, detect a failure, clear the bay, and deploy with the backup. The whole aeroentry is timed down to the second."

"I tried," Josh said. "I sent them a message right away. Here's the log."

Nate stared at the time on the log. 11:37 CST. "And what time were they going to enter the Martian atmosphere?"

"Eleven forty-five," Josh whispered. "Maybe five minutes ago." Tears streamed down his face. "I'm sorry, Nate. The one-way radio delay is eight minutes, twenty-five seconds. Even if they left their radio on to listen, the message couldn't have got there before they entered the atmosphere. By then—"

"Twenty-five seconds," Nate whispered. "We missed 'em by twenty-five seconds."

CHAPTER 38

Thursday, July 3, 2014, 11:38 A.M.
VALKERIE

Valkerie looked around the cabin. Kennedy was on her left, at the Flight Console. Bob was strapped in on her right, typing feverishly at the NavConsole. And Lex . . . Lex was all alone downstairs. When they left, she had been drifting in her seat like a fragile ghost. Her eyes were closed, but she was smiling. Probably remembering something precious. Something Valkerie had never experienced.

A pang of regret shot through Valkerie. She'd worked hard all her life and had so little to show for it. No husband. No family. No friends. If she died, who but her father would truly mourn her? Even Gina-Marie barely knew her. They had just gotten to be friends before Gina's work took her back to MIT. Besides her father, the only people Valkerie felt really close to, the only people who really appreciated her, would die with her—without ever knowing how much she really cared. She had to make sure that two of them would survive.

"Bob?" Her breather pressed her microphones tight against her lips.

Bob didn't respond. He didn't give any indication that he even heard.

"Okay, y'allf. Seffen minuff till enffry. Frrrff in tight. Frrf gonna be a bumphy riffe." Kennedy's voice vibrated through Valkerie's headset. The comm links sounded terrible. The microphones weren't designed to be worn inside breathers.

Bob leaned over and shouted to Valkerie, "Can you hear anything? I'm getting nothing but static."

Valkerie lifted off her breather. "Kennedy said seven minutes till entry. Are you getting anything at all in your headset?"

340

Bob shook his head and switched off his mike. "Must be busted. I'm taking it off. I can't hear a thing with it on." He lifted his breather and pulled off his Snoopy cap.

"Bob, I just want you . . . to know that I . . . I really . . ." Valkerie felt light-headed. Out of breath. "Bob, I . . ."

"T-minuh siff minirrr," Kennedy's voice blared in her headset. "Frrrrr fffrrr ffrr see ffrr monitors. Ffrr ffrr ffrrrr spectacular."

Valkerie pulled her mask back on and took a few panting breaths. Her heart pounded in her chest. *Dear God, please help me. I don't know if I can go through with it.*

Valkerie turned back to Bob. His eyebrows were creased in a pensive frown.

"What's wrong?" she shouted through her mask.

"I've been thinking," he said slowly. "If nobody's trying to kill us, what was all that hocus-pocus with the backup aerobrake-deployment system?"

"Maybe they were just curious. Maybe they didn't think it was important enough to mention it."

"Ffrrr-frrrrf! Ffrrr-frrrrf!" Lex's voice buzzed in Valkerie's ears.

"Lex, are you okay? I can't hear you. What's wrong?" Valkerie tore at the buckle of her harness.

"John Glenn." Lex's whisper was faint but clear.

"What? Keep whispering." Valkerie lifted her mask so Bob could hear. "What about John Glenn?" she shouted into her mikes.

"He was . . . my hero," Lex's voice buzzed through the static. "His first . . . mission. 1962. They thought his heat shield was broken. So they asked him in . . . a roundabout way . . . to check on it."

"Lex? Are you—oh no!" Valkerie threw off her flight harness. "That explains everything!" She pushed out of her seat. "Bob, switch to the backup system. The backup aerobrake-deployment system. Do it now!"

Bob froze, his fingers hovered rigid over the keyboard. "I can't. It's offline. Besides, the primary system is fine. The diagnostics—"

"The diagnostics are wrong. The primary has to be broken. Why else would Houston have been asking about the backup?"

"But—"

Kennedy twisted in his seat, pulled off his breather, and turned off his mikes. "Get back in your seat. It's too late. The solar panel is almost all the way back into the bay. We've got four minutes to entry!"

"Bob, please, do you trust me?" Valkerie asked.

Bob swallowed hard and nodded.

"Why else would they be so sneaky? They realized the primary system was out but didn't want to alarm us until they knew for sure that we had backup. Now help me get the backup system online!"

Bob's eyes lit with sudden realization. "You're right!" He unbuckled his harness and leaped toward the instrument wall on the far right side of the command center.

Valkerie was at his side in an instant, prying at the access panel.

Bob pulled a circuit board. "Now reach back there in the back and override that interrupt we put in."

"Three minutes!" Kennedy cried out. "The solar panels are all the way in. I've got to deploy the aerobrake now!"

"Just a few more seconds!" Valkerie reached into the cramped space. Why had they put the switch so far back? "Bob, I can't reach it."

"It must be snagged." Bob reached in and pulled a bundle of cables to the side. "Now try!"

"Two minutes, thirty seconds! I've got to deploy using the primary." Kennedy's voice hammered into Valkerie's brain.

"Don't you dare!" Valkerie dug though the cables. The switch had gotten tangled in the middle. She could already feel the ship starting to quiver.

"Valkerie!"

Valkerie's hand closed around the switch. "Got it!"

Valkerie felt herself pulled back out of the access panel. Bob handed her the board and she slammed it into place. "It's in. Ready to deploy!"

"Get to your seats!" Kennedy shouted. "Powering up the backup now. We're already hitting upper atmosphere."

Bob grabbed the access panel and aligned it. Valkerie locked it in place, then turned and pushed off for her seat. Missed! Instead of a straight line, she curved toward the floor. "We're decelerating! I can't get to my seat!" She smacked into the far wall and slowly drifted to the floor, flailing her arms.

"The aerobrake arm is fully extended. Firing the pyros!" A ping sounded through the ship. "Inflating, inflating!" Kennedy shouted. "Fully deployed!"

"Valkerie, stay still!" Bob shouted.

She turned and saw Bob push off toward her. He flipped and hit the wall feet first beside her, bending his knees on impact. He gathered her in his arms and lunged back toward her seat. Valkerie clutched her seat and scrambled in. The deceleration was getting stronger by the second. The sound of wind began to build up outside the ship.

Bob yanked her harness in place and cinched it home.

He lifted his breather away from his face and leaned in close. "I love you, Valkerie." His words mingled with the rising wind outside. Warm lips brushed across her cheek. She shut her eyes, letting the rush of warmth fill her. Caress her. She felt her body pressed against her harness.

"I . . . love you too." Valkerie breathed out the words. She opened her eyes, but Bob was gone. She looked frantically to her right. Bob lay twisted in his seat, clinging desperately to the armrest with one hand while the other hand tugged his harness into place. Had it locked? The rushing wind outside became a gale.

"I love you!" Valkerie's shout was washed away by the high-pitched roar. Bob didn't answer.

Thursday, July 3, 2014, 11:45 A.M.

BOB

Bob's right arm was trapped beneath him. He lay twisted in the seat with three and a half gees of inertial forces pushing his body into the seat. He had only managed to get part of his harness buckled before the ship's deceleration took over, rendering his hands and arms useless.

The roar was terrific. The ship bucked and pitched around him like one of those hideous mechanical bulls in a Houston bar. Bob could hear nothing, see nothing. Had they peaked on the deceleration curve yet? *Oh, God, help!* His heart was going to explode under the pressure, and he was going to die without knowing. He had said the words. He had kissed her on the cheek. What did she think? Was it too soon? Had he finally driven her away? Did it even matter?

The force began decreasing, and the shaking gradually faded. The roar of the wind died with it. From very far away, Bob thought he heard Kennedy yelling—something about a parachute.

Slam! Then silence.

"Bingo, guys!" Kennedy sang out through his breather. "The chutes are open and they are beautiful. Everybody okay?"

Bob groaned. "Just . . . get us on solid ground." They were now in Martian gravity, just over a third of a gee, and floating downward through the thin atmosphere toward the Red Planet.

"Releasing chutes and aerobrakes and . . . activating landing engine . . . now!" Kennedy said. A low roar throbbed below them, and the gravitational force seemed to increase a notch.

"Okay, we are hovering," Kennedy called out. "Distance to base camp is . . . uh-oh!"

"What's wrong?" Valkerie said.

"We're . . . off target a couple of klicks." Kennedy's voice sounded tight. "I'm on it, don't worry."

Bob opened his eyes and tried to raise his head. *This gravity thing was gonna be a bear!* He felt as if an elephant had quietly decided to invade his body. His head had to weigh fifty pounds, and his arms were lead.

"Um . . . guys, we're getting closer," Kennedy said. "We're about thirty meters above a rocky plain. I have the base camp on visual. It's about . . . fifteen hundred meters. We're down to . . . one hundred twenty seconds of bipropellant. I'm gonna bring us in as close as possible and lay us down like a baby."

Bob lay back and closed his eyes. Fifteen hundred meters was too far. He couldn't walk a mile in this gravity wearing an EVA suit. Not in half an hour. He just couldn't.

"Sixty seconds, and we are one thousand meters from base camp. Eat your heart out, Neil Armstrong. I'm gonna make you look like an amateur—with one eye tied behind my back."

The Hampster probably even believed it. All pilots thought they had the rightest stuff in the known universe. Which meant that all but one of them was wrong.

"Thirty seconds, and seven hundred meters to go. Yes . . . baby! We're at ten meters altitude, guys, so keep cool. If the engine conks out, we don't have far to fall."

Valkerie was praying audibly now. Bob would have joined her, but he couldn't speak.

"Slowing down lateral motion. Ten seconds of fuel left and we are skimming the tops of those rocks. Six hundred meters to base camp. Prepare for landing."

Bob's heart pounded in his ears. His breath was coming in great gulping pants. His breather . . . He was running out of oxygen.

"Five seconds of fuel, and we are at four meters altitude. Three meters. Two. One. Fifty centimeters. Ten."

There was a gentle thump on the floor.

"Zero seconds of fuel left, zero centimeters of altitude, five hundred and forty meters to base camp. Ladies and gentlemen, say hello to Mars."

Bob ripped the breather off his face and gulped at the thin air in the Hab. It wasn't enough. Not nearly enough. He had gotten so close, but he wasn't going to make it.

Thursday, July 3, 2014, 11:55 A.M.

VALKERIE

"Is everybody okay?" Valkerie fumbled at her flight harness with leaden fingers. "Nice landing, Hampster! Bob? How much time—" Valkerie froze. Bob lay in his seat, panting like a fish out of water. His breather was gone.

"Bob!" Valkerie flung off her harness and leaped to her feet. Too fast. The world spun around, filling her ears with a high-pitched ring. She collapsed to the deck floor, then pushed herself to her knees through the tingling haze that fogged her senses. Ripping the breather from her face, she reached up and pressed it to Bob's face. "Bob, it's okay. Calm down. Just breathe. Breathe into the mask."

A crash sounded behind her. Swearing.

"Kennedy, get over here! Bob needs help!"

Bob's breathing started to slow. Valkerie relaxed. "Okay, Bob, can you hear me?"

Bob nodded at her through the mask.

"I'm going to take the mask for just a few breaths, then I'll give it back. Understand?"

Bob nodded, lifted the breather from his face, and held it out to Valkerie. Their eyes met. For a moment Valkerie forgot all about the breather. He'd said he loved her.

"Bob, I don't know . . ."

Footsteps sounded behind her. "We're running out of time, people." Kennedy put his own breather on Bob's face. "Let's go get our suits on!" He hoisted Bob to his feet and put a shoulder under Bob's arm. "Just stand still a minute, buddy, and let your blood pressure stabilize."

Valkerie slipped the breather over her face and stood up slowly.

Kennedy was already walking Bob to the stairwell. She hurried to catch up but stumbled and fell.

"Valkerie!" Bob broke free from Kennedy, turned, and lifted her to her feet. "Are you okay?"

Valkerie nodded. The cabin started to spin. "I'm fine. I just stood up too fast. Go with Kennedy. Get into your suit."

"You don't look fine. Let me help you." Bob put his arm around her and started leading her into the hatch.

"Go with Kennedy. Please! You've got his breather."

"But . . ."

"Go! I'll be down in a second." Valkerie pulled away from Bob and pushed him toward the stairwell.

Bob rejoined Kennedy. Together, they stumbled through the hatch, sharing a breather. Bob looked back once, and then they disappeared down the stairs.

Valkerie dropped to her knees and lowered her head, waiting until the dizziness stopped. After a few minutes she rose slowly to her feet and clomped to the hatch. The dizziness was almost gone. She descended the stairs one painful step at a time. Maybe she only weighed forty pounds on Mars, but it felt like four hundred. How was Bob going to make it five hundred meters in a suit that added half again to his weight?

Valkerie was panting and out of breath by the time she reached the decontamination room. Kennedy was just helping Bob into the upper half of his EVA suit.

"Valkerie, are you okay? I was just about to go up looking for you." Bob started toward her, then jerked back. His pack was still mounted on a stabilizer rack.

"Valkerie, can you give me a hand?" Kennedy lay on the floor struggling to work his feet into his boots.

Valkerie looked up at Bob. She hadn't gotten a chance to talk to him. She wanted to let him know, to tell him how she felt.

Bob looked into her eyes and gave a slight nod.

She gave him an apologetic smile and turned to help Kennedy hold up the lower half of his suit while he burrowed up into the top half.

Valkerie glanced back at Bob. He nodded and pulled on his gloves. Before she could even think of what to say, he placed his helmet over his head and snapped it in place.

"Gloves!" Kennedy's shout broke Valkerie out of her daze.

Valkerie helped Kennedy with his gloves, but all she could think about was Bob. She didn't know if it was true, but she wanted to tell him she loved him. That she was *in love* with him. Could it really be true? It must be. Why would she want to tell him if it weren't true?

Kennedy handed Valkerie his breather and reached for his helmet. "You'll have to refill it. I think it's about out." He pulled the helmet over his head and snapped it in place.

Valkerie turned. Bob was right beside her, holding out a transfer hose—the hose they had rigged to refill their breathers from the EVA packs. Bob motioned to the back of his pack and turned to join Kennedy, who already stood facing the airlock. Valkerie stared at the hose, then at the backs of the two men. No more indecision. No more doubts. She knew what she had to do.

Valkerie stepped back and peered through the doorway, holding the transfer hose up where Lex could see it. Lex looked down for a few seconds. Her shoulders rose and fell in a deep sigh. When she looked up, her eyes blazed with determination. She nodded her head. *Yes.*

Valkerie turned and fumbled with the back of Bob's and Kennedy's backpacks, going through the motions of filling her breather. She moved between them and gave them the okay sign. Kennedy and Bob rocked back and forth in a nod and stepped toward the airlock. Kennedy walked through the hatch. Bob started to follow, but he turned back for a last look at Valkerie as if he wanted to tell Valkerie something but couldn't say it.

Valkerie stripped off her mask and tiptoed to plant a kiss on his visor. Then, before he could waste any more time, she pushed him though the doorway and began securing the hatch. As she locked it down, the emergency lights went black. The fuel cells had run out.

Valkerie wondered at her equanimity as she felt her way through the tomblike chamber back to Lex. The two women huddled quietly in the darkness. Clasping each other's hands. Whispering words of comfort and love.

Valkerie wasn't afraid anymore. She hadn't gotten a chance to tell Bob how much she loved him, but she had been able to demonstrate that love in a way that words could never equal. She didn't have proof that a loving God existed, but she knew it in her heart in a deeper way than she could ever understand.

Thursday, July 3, 2014, Noon
BOB

Bob leaned against the wall of the airlock. She had kissed him. He still couldn't believe it. He had told her he loved her, and she had given him a kiss. His pulse pounded in his ears. Adrenaline rushed through his veins. He had to hurry. Valkerie was depending on him. Valkerie and Lex. He couldn't let them down.

Bob checked his watch to baseline his time. They only had twenty-nine minutes of oxygen, and they had already wasted two. What was taking the airlock so long?

He turned to Kennedy. "Hey, Ken—" He froze. His comm link was busted. He had meant to trade Snoopy caps with Valkerie, but in all the excitement he had forgotten. He shoved Kennedy's shoulder. Kennedy was staring back through the glass plate of the hatch. The other side was completely dark.

Kennedy turned and pointed to the airlock light and slashed his pointer finger across his neck. Bob nodded. The fuel cells were dead. The airlock pumps were dead. The ship was completely without power. Bob released the lock. The pressure differential popped the hatch open like a New Year's Eve cork, yanking Bob out with it. He staggered forward, tripped, and landed hard. A cloud of ultrafine regolith flew up around him.

Dizzy and bruised, he pushed himself up onto his hands and knees. Even the weak Martian gravity was exhausting after five months in zero-g. Gloved hands grabbed him by the shoulders and hoisted him to his feet. Bob gave Kennedy the thumbs-up sign and they took off toward the base camp as fast as they could lumber. *Six hundred yards to life.*

Step, step. Rest. Step, step. Rest.

They staggered across the tan-colored plain, lurching over bowling-ball-sized rocks, kicking up spurts of dust. The sun looked small and anemic in a washed-out peach sky. The horizon seemed absurdly close. Bob felt disoriented, dizzy. All the proportions were wrong. He veered to the right when he meant to go straight. He ran into Kennedy when he thought he was standing still.

Bob looked at his watch. They had covered a couple of hundred yards in . . . ten minutes. Not fast enough! He motioned to Kennedy to walk faster. Kennedy nodded.

Step, step, step. Rest. Step, step, step. Rest.

Kennedy began lagging behind. Bob looked at his watch again.

Twenty-two minutes gone. They'd never make it. A bolt of panic knifed through his body. *Valkerie!* He couldn't wait for Kennedy.

Bob picked up the pace to a slow walk. Then to a shuffling jog. His breath rasped in his ears, echoing through his helmet in a ragged scream of unorchestrated agony.

At last, base camp. The rover was parked just outside, a six-ton behemoth with eight wheels and plenty of room for four people. It had been waiting here for two years, and it was long since fully loaded up with methane and LOX. Bob yanked open the doors to the airlock, reached up, grabbed the handle, and pulled.

He raised his body a few inches, then fell back. Exhaustion shivered through his body. He didn't have the strength to pull himself up. Where was the Hampster?

Bob looked back. Kennedy was shuffling along in slow motion, ten yards behind. *Hurry!* Bob risked a glance at his watch.

No! Thirty-nine minutes had elapsed. His air should have run out ten minutes ago. How. . . ?

Kennedy reached him and pressed his helmet against Bob's. "We're too late!"

"I know!" Bob said. "They must have given us a little extra air. In the rover, quick, before we run out!"

He grabbed the handle and pulled. Kennedy got underneath him and pushed upward. Slowly, Bob clawed his way into the airlock. He turned and grabbed Kennedy's right hand. Thank God, Kennedy was lighter. They pulled together. Up, up, up . . .

Kennedy lost his grip on the handle and fell backward. Bob hung on to his other hand. *Hurry!*

Kennedy grabbed the handle again. Bob anchored his feet. Pull! The Hampster slowly battled up into the airlock. Bob pulled him in all the way and yanked the hatch shut.

Bob jabbed the pressurization controls. The gauge quickly rose to 950 millibars. He checked the temperature. Fourteen degrees Celsius and climbing.

Bob popped open the inner door and stepped forward into the rover, unlocking his helmet and unsnapping his gloves. He stumbled forward blindly to the driver's seat and checked his watch. They'd been gone forty-five minutes, and their tanks still weren't empty. The realization hit him like a charging linebacker. Valkerie hadn't done the transfer. She hadn't taken any of their oxygen.

"Come on, come on, Hampster!" Bob punched the starter button and the engine roared to life. Kennedy staggered forward and fell into a seat. "We're too late. Bob, I'm sorry, I should have landed closer to—"

"No!" Bob jammed the gearshift into drive and punched the accelerator. The rover's tires spun madly in the dust, then took hold. The rover jerked forward.

"Get out of your suit!" Bob shouted to Kennedy. "We'll need to bring the girls in as soon as we get there, and you need to be mobile!"

Bob pounded on the steering wheel. The rover had maxed out at its top speed, fifteen kilometers per hour. The beast lumbered and creaked over the rocky plain. At this rate, it would take only two or three minutes to reach the women. Which was as good as forever.

Kennedy detached his suit at the beltline. "They gave us all their air." He leaned far forward and let gravity pull the upper half of his EVA suit off, then yanked off the pants.

Bob felt numbness creeping over his body and into his mind. His hands were blocks of wood, his heart a cold mass of dry ice. Kennedy was right. They'd been gone almost fifty minutes, and the girls had only the dregs from their oxygen bottles to breathe. If they lay really still . . . No, that wouldn't work. The only hope was that he had miscalculated. Maybe they had more air than he thought.

His body was running on autopilot now. *God, you can't let them die now, not when you've brought us so far.*

But God hadn't *let* them die. They had *chosen* to sacrifice themselves. Just as Bob himself would have chosen. Had already chosen.

Dear God, forgive me. I should have let Valkerie go. I should have insisted. I should have been the one to die. Not her. God, please, don't let her die. I couldn't bear it.

They were almost on top of the Hab. Bob angled in close, then skidded to a stop just outside the airlock. He set the brake and punched the button to deploy the rover-to-Hab connector. Thank God NASA had made this thing dockable. Kennedy stood waiting by the airlock doors with a flashlight, drumming his fingers on the door. "Hurry, hurry!" he shouted at the gauge.

The needle swung slowly up to full pressure. Bob yanked open the airlock door.

Kennedy raced ahead, now wearing nothing but his Liquid-Cooled Garment. Bob lumbered after him in his EVA suit, pawing frantically at the tears that would not stop gushing from his eyes.

The air in the Hab was close and stale, heavy with the smell of . . . death. An irrational dread surged through him. A cold sweat prickled down his arms and back. He felt nauseous. "Valkerie? Lex?"

He pushed forward into the gloom, running blindly after Kennedy's wavering light. "Valkerie?" He turned a corner and stopped. Valkerie and Lex lay huddled together on Lex's seat. Neither one was wearing a breather.

Kennedy fell on his knees next to Lex and started tearing at the flight harness that bound her to the seat.

"No!" Bob rushed forward and scooped Valkerie's limp form into his arms. "No. God, please no!" He carried her back to the rover, collapsing onto his knees to place her in the rear bay on the floor. He grabbed an oxygen mask and pressed it to her face, then felt her wrist for a pulse.

Nothing.

Kennedy raced in a moment later with Lex and gently lowered her to the floor near Valkerie. "I'll close the airlock."

Bob nodded and released Valkerie's wrist. Her skin was still warm. Soft. She had to be alive. He bent down over her, pressing his lips to hers, pinching her nose shut with his fingers. He blew into her lungs, watching her chest rise and fall with each breath.

He felt for her xiphoid and placed the heels of his hands on her sternum. Push, push, push . . . *God, please. I believe. I do believe.* Push, push, breathe, breathe. The world dissolved around him. He was alone in a blurry haze, pushing to the rhythm of his own pounding heart. Breathing into lips that stole all warmth from his own.

God, if you do work miracles, if you do interact with this world, please, I'm praying for a miracle. I'd give my life for hers, any day. Please!

Bob worked steadily, ignoring the chill numbness that seeped into his bones. At last, he stopped. A life had already been given. No other would be required.

A hand rested on Bob's shoulder. Bob turned, wiping his eyes on a bulky synthetic sleeve. Kennedy's eyes glistened, red, swollen. Tears streamed down his cheeks. He shook his head slowly and swallowed. "It's too late, Bob. We did our best."

Bob sighed deeply and admitted the truth he'd been fighting to change. "You're . . . right."

Kennedy took his hand and pulled him up. "Let's get back to base camp. And we have to call Houston. We have to tell the world"—his voice choked off with a sob—"about the sacrifice they made."

CHAPTER 39

Thursday, July 3, 2014, 11:50 A.M.
NATE

"Okay, Josh, get back to your post and see what else you can find out," Nate said. "NBC is milking this one for the bucks. They've got a show lined up on our brave boys and girls. Should take about an hour and a half. Then Perez and I are going to take the fall." Nate shook Josh's hand. "Take care of yourself." He turned and headed back on-stage. Perez was now speaking.

Nate figured there couldn't be a dry eye in the whole place. He dabbed at his own with a Kleenex. Well, okay, there were two. What kind of an emotionless Vulcan was he? His eyes were arid, his heart cold.

A giant screen behind Perez showed exactly what the rest of the world was seeing on TV—a picture of the Ares 10 team. Smiling and in their flight suits, coming out of the Astrovan back in January, on their way to the launch.

Perez sat down and the show began. Nate looked at his watch. Almost noon. *In an hour and a half, I'll be free of this job forever. But I'll never be free of my conscience, will I? If I'd just told them the truth. . . .*

The screen switched to a video that some TV whiz kids had done, showing the history of the Ares 10 mission. The early Ares program. Selection of ASCANs. Training. A tour of JSC. The Hab, the ERV, and all that. The base camp on Mars, with that juiced-up SUV rover. Then the Ares 10 crew, the launch, and repeated close-ups of the stabilizer fin nicking the tower. An interview with Nate, in which he gabbled something about "justifiable risk" and "calculated gamble." *Did I really believe that? What a moron.*

Finally, the segment wound down. Nate checked the time again—1:30 P.M., right on the button. TV people were good at that. And now, show-time . . .

The screen switched back to live TV, broadcast from right here in the Teague Auditorium. Steven Perez stepped to the podium.

"This is a sad day in the history of NASA. Four brave astronauts lost their lives, only miles short of their goal. When they entered the Martian atmosphere, we know that they had no functioning aerobrake-deployment system. We believe their deaths would have been very rapid."

That was a lie—but a kindhearted one—strictly for the families' sake. In reality, it would have taken several tens of seconds for the crew to die, while the Hab boiled hotter and hotter as it blazed down through the thin atmosphere.

Perez swallowed hard and wiped his eyes. "As Director of the Johnson Space Center, the deaths of these four men and women are my responsibility, and mine alone. We tried for too much with too few resources. I believe it was my own pride that was responsible, and . . . I beg forgiveness of both my nation and the families of the astronauts. Effective tomorrow at noon, I am resigning as—"

"Nooooooo!" Josh Bennett came flying down the left aisle of Teague Auditorium, holding something in his hand and screaming like a scalded cat. He leaped to the podium and whispered something to Perez. Perez stepped back. Josh held a small PDA to the microphone. He pressed a button and hissing static filled the room.

And then . . .

"Houston, this is Commander Kennedy Hampton, calling from the rover on the surface of Mars. Do you copy?"

There was a moment of stunned silence.

Then the room exploded. Screaming. Dancing. Papers thrown in the air. Hooting. Shrieking. Cathe Willison jumped up on stage, threw her arms around Nate, and kissed him. The *Times* science reporter, Hank Russell, was right behind her, shoving a microphone in Nate's face, sweating and bellowing something. Cameras flashed like solar flares. The whole place had gone nuts, just nuts.

The celebration went on for several minutes, then slowly began wearing down. Somebody began tapping hard on the microphone. Josh Bennett still stood at the podium, holding the PDA aloft, tears glistening on his cheeks.

Icy fingers closed around Nate's gut. He could see by the look on Josh's face that those were not tears of joy.

Thursday, July 3, 2014, 1:10 P.M.

BOB

Bob cradled Valkerie's head in his lap as the rover jolted and lurched over the rocky terrain. Kennedy had told Houston. It was final. Valkerie was dead. Gone forever. There was no going back. He stroked the hair back from her face and felt for her pulse one more time. Nothing. A huge lump formed in his throat. Tears streamed down his cheeks, splashing onto Valkerie's upturned face.

It was all so pointless. So unfair. NASA had traded two human lives for a dry, barren planet. Space exploration. What did it matter? There was more to Valkerie than a whole universe of planets. More to explore. More to appreciate. More to learn. He would have gladly dedicated his life to her exploration. He would have given all he owned. All he was. All he ever hoped to be.

Oh, God. Why didn't I see it before? He had squandered two years. His self-doubt, his pride, his fears. What were they compared to the opportunity he had wasted?

The rover rattled to a stop. Kennedy's voice sounded from the front of the rover. Another transmission to Houston. How could he do it? How could he endure talking to . . . *them*? Kennedy positioned the airlock for docking with the base module. The docking port locked in place. The hatch popped open with a swish.

Bob didn't move. All he could look at was Valkerie's face, peaceful now in death.

He felt Kennedy's hand on his shoulder. "She loved you, you know."

"She loved all of us." Bob looked up.

Pain creased Kennedy's face in deep lines that seemed to touch his very soul. "We need to go in now," he said in a soft voice. "This is our home for the next year and a half. We have a lot of work to do to get this place rigged for full life support, and not a lot of time to do it."

Bob sighed and a strange calm stole over him. He would be alone with Kennedy for two years. Another human being. A friend who needed his help. This time he would use those two years well.

Thursday, July 3, 2014, 1:40 P.M.

NATE

"Please sit down!" Josh shouted. "Friends, people, please sit down."

Teague Auditorium slowly quieted. The look on Josh's face made it clear that something was very wrong.

"Please . . ." Josh's voice cracked. "When we first heard from Ares 10, we responded right away. Seventeen minutes later, they sent back this reply."

A funereal hush settled over the auditorium. Nate sat down. He had known it was too good to be true.

Josh clicked the button on his PDA. "Houston, it is my sad duty to inform you that two of our crew, Dr. Alexis Ohta and Dr. Valkerie Jansen, gave their lives to save their fellow crew members, Bob Kaganovski and myself. Unknown to us, the women took no oxygen for themselves when . . ." Kennedy's voice broke completely. His sobs filled the auditorium. ". . . when Bob and I went to get the rescue vehicle. They gave it all to us. Because of the courageous sacrifice by Lex and Valkerie, Bob and I are still alive. We are returning to base camp with their bodies now. Over."

————

The amazing thing was how fast NBC reacted to it. Within thirty seconds, they were running a video clip eulogizing the two dead astronauts. Nate felt sick to his marrow at their ghoulish efficiency. When had they put these together? Last week? Last month? Before the launch?

Lex got the electronic embalming treatment first. A photo of her playing volleyball in high school, spiking the ball. Incredible—she must have had a three-foot vertical leap. The caption said *Alexis Ohta, Ph.D. April 1, 1979–July 3, 2014.*

They showed a long interview with Lex's mother, a cute little Japanese woman who must be about fifty, but didn't look much older than Lex. There was the usual TV song-and-dance about what a brave single mom she had been, how she'd overcome all obstacles, blah, blah, blah. Conveniently overlooked was the fact that the missing father was some rich kid from back East who didn't want to take responsibility. Nate hated people like that.

Finally the segment moved on to Lex at the Air Force Academy. Lex in graduate school at Stanford. Lex passing up a chance for the Olympic

Volleyball Team in 2004 so she could finish her Ph.D. work. Lex in ASCAN training, breaking Scott Carpenter's forty-year-old record for some fitness test. Lex in the Ares program. Lex waving as she strode into the launch vehicle. The whole thing ended, again, with the still of Lex and her last words, broadcast just before aeroentry.

Who would have believed Lex was *married*? According to the rumor mill, she'd gone out with half the guys in her ASCAN class. The networks had somehow tracked down this guy Anderson and they were interviewing him *live* on TV. And the poor guy was red-eyed and blubbering and the networks just had no mercy at all, did they?

Nate clutched his Kleenex. The tiny receiver that NBC had given him crackled in his ear. It was one of the TV execs, some twenty-six-year-old whiz kid in a five-thousand-dollar suit. "Great show, Nate! This is fabulous! The ratings are even better than if they'd—"

Nate yanked the earpiece out. What a moronic, freeze-dried piece of beef jerky that kid was. As if this were a show where the actors got up at the end to do another one tomorrow.

Now Valkerie's deathwatch. A photo of her in surgical greens, taken while she was at Johns Hopkins. *Valkerie Jansen, M.D., Ph.D. October 15, 1981–July 3, 2014.*

Nate wiped at his eyes again. Still dry. *Finish this segment and then it'll be over.* All over but the crying. If there were any tears in his locked-up, dried-out little heart. What was wrong with him, anyway?

Valkerie was born in Grand Rapids. Nate hadn't known that. Went to school at Yale, biochem. Then Hopkins for med school. Quit to take care of daddy after her mother died. Nice kid. Then on to Florida for her Ph.D. Wisconsin for a postdoc. Then Ares 10. *We grabbed her, trained her, and shipped her off on a wing and a prayer.*

The segment ended with the picture and her final words. ". . . Hugs to you, Josh Bennett, we know how desperately you wanted this mission to succeed, and the extraordinary steps you took to make it so. Please don't blame yourself if . . . something happens to us. We know you did everything you could, and we love you. We're about to land. We'll catch you on the flip side in about an hour."

The TV screen switched back to Teague Auditorium, live. Perez stepped slowly up to the mike and set a black book on the podium. "I'd like to read something right now, said by the man I admire most." He flipped the pages, wiping at his eyes. "I'm reading from the Jerusalem Bible, John 15:13. 'A man can have no greater love than to lay down his life for his friends.' " Perez closed the Bible. "Valkerie Jansen and Alexis Ohta proved themselves today to be heroes of the highest caliber. Heroes who will never be forgotten. They will be remembered—not for their dedication, not for their bravery or intellect or strength or charisma—but for a quality that far transcends all other virtues. They will be remembered for their love. Valkerie and Lex, we will never forget you. Thank you for sharing your lives with us all. . . ."

The room suddenly went out of focus. It took Nate a second to realize why.

He was crying.

Friday, July 4, 2014, 1:00 a.m.
BOB

Bob sat up on his cot with his head in his hands, waiting for his dizziness to pass. A dull ache settled over his heart. He didn't want to remember. Didn't want to think. He prayed that it had all been a terrible dream. A lingering nightmare that would fade away in the morning sun.

Bob pushed himself to his feet and braced against the wall. He took a few tentative steps. It was going to take a while to get used to walking again. But that was okay. He had nothing better to do with his time.

Bob slid open his door and stepped out into the circular corridor. He could hear Kennedy's raspy breathing through the thin walls. Bob slid Kennedy's door open and peeked inside. Kennedy lay on his back, snoring away. Funny, Kennedy hadn't snored on the Hab. Must be a gravity thing. Bob started to close the door, but paused for one more look.

A thunk sounded somewhere behind him. Bob stared down at Kennedy. Kennedy hadn't moved a muscle. Bob stepped out into the corridor and froze. The sound wasn't repeated. It must have been a ping—something settling. He circled the central stairwell, and stared at the stairwell hatch, listening. Had he heard something else? He couldn't be sure.

Taking a deep breath, Bob walked down the stairs, leaning heavily against the rail. A quick search of the downstairs level revealed nothing. There was only the rover, connected to the Hab through the airlock. The women's bodies were in there. He and Kennedy didn't have the heart to carry them inside yesterday, and they had been too exhausted to give them a decent burial.

Bob pulled a flashlight from its charging station on the decontamination room wall and stepped carefully into the airlock. His heart pounded in his chest, and his stomach surged as he spun open the hatch. He paused to catch his breath. He didn't want to go in. Couldn't go in. She had been so beautiful. So full of life. He wanted to remember her that way. What if she . . . what if her body. . . ? He didn't even want to think about it.

Bob took a deep breath and held it. Valkerie was gone. The . . . shell in the rover wasn't her. No more than an empty beer can was a beer.

Bob pushed on the hatch, and it swung open with a metallic groan.

Something moved inside the rover.

"Bob, is that you?"

CHAPTER 40

Friday, July 4, 2014, 1:10 A.M.
VALKERIE

"Bob?" Valkerie searched the dark chamber with blurry eyes. A metallic thunk rang out behind her, and an unseen object clattered to the floor. She tried to sit up, but a sharp pain pierced her rib cage. "Lex, is that you?"

A low, keening moan filled the tiny room. Blinding light stabbed though the darkness and fixed on her. A dark specter approached, tottering back and forth behind an erratic beam of light.

"Bob?" Valkerie rolled onto her side, crying out at the pain.

"Valkerie?" a strangled cry erupted above her. "I thought . . ." Valkerie made out Bob's shadowy features a tottering instant before he collapsed onto his knees, covering her in a trembling embrace.

"Bob, stop, you're hurting me." His body shook with convulsive sobs. "Bob?" Valkerie tried to pull away, but he clung to her tighter.

"Bob? What's wrong?" She reached an arm around his neck and held him, ignoring the pain in her ribs. "Is it Lex? Is she . . . is she okay?" A feeling of impending doom settled over her like a damp fog. She swallowed hard and waited for Bob's tears to subside.

After several minutes Bob pulled slowly away. His face was creased in pain. Tears streamed down his cheeks as he caught at his breath, fighting against the sobs that still shook his broad shoulders.

"Bob, please. You're scaring me. What's wrong? Where's Lex and Kennedy?" Gritting her teeth against the pain, she reached out and touched the side of his face.

Bob caught up her hand in his own and stared at her through

haunted eyes. "We thought . . . we thought you . . . were dead." He forced the words out between heaving breaths.

"Dead? Didn't you check? Didn't you read the note?"

Bob took a deep breath and wiped at his face. "N-note?"

"I pinned it to Lex's chair—with the needle of the syringe."

"What syringe?" Bob leaned in close. Tears still flowed freely down his face.

"The one with the sodium pentothal and Raplon."

Bob frowned and shook his head. "I thought . . . it was all gone."

"Bob, I'm so sorry. I explained it all in the note. I found the syringe in the pocket of one of your jumpsuits." Valkerie tried to sit up, but her ribs screamed out in protest.

"Are you okay? What's wrong?"

"I don't know. My chest. It feels like my ribs are all fractured."

"Dear God, forgive me. I'm so sorry."

"What? What's wrong?"

"I thought you were dead. I . . . tried . . . CPR." Bob hung his head.

Valkerie couldn't help smiling. "If I'd been dead, I'm sure it would have worked. It feels like you used a sledgehammer."

He looked timidly up at her. A fresh trail of tears ran down both cheeks. "I'm really sorry. I . . . I just couldn't . . ."

"It's okay. Don't worry about it. I'm fine. How's Lex?"

Bob's mouth dropped open.

"Bob, where is she? Tell me she's okay."

Bob shot a look behind Valkerie. "We checked her pulse. . . ."

"It's very faint. You have to feel the carotid. Right here on the neck."

Bob crawled out of sight. A few seconds later she heard a gasp. "I think I feel a pulse! I think she's—"

Valkerie squirmed onto her side and arched her neck to see Bob crouching low over a dark bench. "Is she okay?"

"Her eyes just moved. I think she's . . ." His voice trailed off as he leaned closer over the dark shadow on the bench. "Lex, it's Bob. Are you . . . awake?"

Valkerie could just make out a muffled cry and then Lex's faint voice. "Who was first?"

"Nobody was first," Bob said. "There weren't any TV cameras. As far as the world knows, Kennedy and I never touched the ground. Valkerie is still going to be the first man on Mars."

Friday, July 4, 2014, 11:00 A.M.

BOB

Bob stepped into his quarters, shut the door, and flicked on the encrypted comm link. Josh had set up an appointment for Sarah McLean to talk with him—him alone—at 11:00 A.M. sharp. Said it was urgent. Bob waited out the seconds until the hour. What in the world could Sarah have to say to him? He hadn't talked to her in almost twelve years.

Right on schedule, Josh's voice came over his headset. "Bob, this is Josh." His nose sounded stuffy, like he had a cold or something. There was a seventeen-minute comm delay right now, so Bob didn't bother trying to respond. "Here's Sarah Laval. She's got an important message for you."

Sarah Laval? Good for her.

"Hello, Bobby. This is Sarah. I just wanted you to know that your message meant so, so much to me. It's such a precious gift. I'm so sorry for what I did to you, and I'm thankful you're alive. I've been praying for you." A long pause. "I guess that's all for now. Bye."

That was it? The important encrypted message?

"Um, hi, Sarah. Thank you for your prayers. I, uh, really appreciate it. Now more than—"

"Okay, buddy, this is Josh again. We've got to talk fast. Sarah just left the room." Josh sniffled loudly. "Sorry to use her that way, but I couldn't think of any other way to talk to you in private."

"Listen, Kaggo, I never in a million years . . ." Another loud sniff. "Bob, I never meant to hurt you, but I . . . Kaggo, the explosion . . . it was all my fault." Josh's voice wavered and dissolved into a torrent of sobs and sniffles. Bob waited in agony, letting Josh get it out of his system. Confession was good for the soul—even for a well-meaning soul.

"Kaggo, listen, I never intended it to go off in the bay." The sound of a nose blowing. "It wasn't a bomb . . . I swear. Just a device to . . . seed Mars with life. Bacteria. *Harmless* bacteria. It was gonna be, you know, our . . . insurance. But . . . when I got bumped . . ." A deep sigh. "Please don't hate me, Kaggo. And please don't tell Kennedy and Lex. I think Valkerie already knows."

Bob grabbed the mike. "Josh, listen up. First of all, we already know. All of us. Valkerie figured it out yesterday. And we still love you—even Kennedy. *Really.* As far as we're concerned, there's nothing to forgive.

All you meant to do was save NASA by seeding a barren planet with life."

Bob wiped his eyes. "But listen, Josh, sometimes things just . . . you know, work out different than you expect. You wound up seeding a barren heart, and that's . . . something I'll always be grateful for."

Someone pounded on Bob's door. "Showtime, Bob!" Kennedy shouted.

"Listen, I need to go get suited for the Mars walk, but we'll talk again, okay? Watch the telecast—I've got something special for you. Over and out." Bob switched off the comm link.

Another knock at the door. Bob opened it.

"Hurry!" Kennedy said. "You've got fifteen minutes to get your EVA suit on."

Friday, July 4, 2014, 11:20 A.M.
VALKERIE

Valkerie relaxed, letting the stability rack hold up most of the weight of her suit. What could be taking Bob so long? How could talking to Sarah McLean be important enough to delay the big broadcast? Something twisted in the pit of her stomach. What if he had written Sarah about his experience coming out of the coma? What if—

Bob hurried into the EVA locker room. His eyes looked red and puffy.

"Bob, are you all right? What happened?"

Kennedy stormed into the chamber. "Okay, Bob, Nate wants you ready by eleven-forty." He spent the next fifteen minutes stuffing Bob into his suit.

"Bob, are you okay?" Valkerie caught his eye and smiled.

"Fine." Bob shrugged and let Kennedy fasten his suit at the waist.

Nate's voice sounded in her Snoopy cap and started running through the flags-and-footprints routine while Bob went through prebreathing. Valkerie tried to catch Bob's eye. What was wrong with him? What had Sarah said? Surely he wasn't still in—

"All right, boys and girls," Nate's voice growled in her ear. "Go earn us some gigabucks."

"And y'all remember to stay where I can see you from the window." Kennedy stepped to his spot behind the camera. "Nate says if we don't keep the TV people happy, we don't get to go back home."

Bob hefted his shoulder-mounted minicam. "We'll be fine, Hampster."

Valkerie waved to Lex. "We'll bring back lots of rocks."

Lex smiled weakly and lay back on the couch.

Valkerie stood up, clutching at her ribs.

Bob stepped to her side. "Are you okay?"

She nodded. "But you'll need to hammer in the flag."

"Okay, we're ready to roll." Bob switched Valkerie's comm link to the broadcast channel, then toggled his own to the same. "Bob, comm check."

"Valkerie, comm check." They moved toward the airlock.

"Loud and clear on both of you. We're going live . . . now." Kennedy flipped a switch and adjusted his mike. "Okay, Houston, this is CDR Kennedy Hampton calling from Mars. MS1 Valkerie Jansen is stepping into the airlock followed by MS2 Bob Kaganovski. . . ."

Bob closed the airlock and Valkerie punched the button. The needle swung slowly down to eight millibars, the ambient pressure outside. Valkerie turned and waved to the camera on Bob's shoulder.

She twisted the handle, swung the door open, and . . . Mars! It hit her like a blast of cold water. Alien. Bizarre. Breathtakingly beautiful. A whole world for her to explore.

"Dr. Jansen is now preparing to exit the Habitation Module," Kennedy's voice sounded in her head. Valkerie turned to make sure Bob was still behind her. He aimed the camera at her face and gave her a thumbs-up.

Valkerie stepped slowly down the metal staircase to the bottom rung, mentally rehearsing the line NASA had sent her.

She took a deep breath and stepped down onto the tan-colored dust.

"That's . . . one small step for a woman—one giant leap for humankind." Valkerie walked forward and turned to look at Bob. He was zooming the camera in on her footprint.

Valkerie turned around in a small circle, scanning the boulder-strewn horizon. "This is . . . incredible!" The Martian sky glowed amber through the tinted glass of her visor, painting the landscape with vivid clarity. The scattered rocks, the jutting ridge, the dusty sky, they were all so close, so solid. *Real.*

Valkerie went through the flagpole ceremony in a daze. The telescoping flagpole, the stiff, horizontally supported flag, the disembodied blow-by-blow narration in her helmet—it was so artificial, so surreal against the stunning reality of the Martian surface.

Valkerie picked up a rock and hefted it, suddenly overwhelmed by the vast distance they had traveled. She felt a tap on her shoulder. Bob pointed away from the Hab and motioned for her to follow.

"Bob, what's up? Do you see something?"

Bob reached out and flipped a switch on her chest Display and Control Module. Comm suddenly went dead.

"What did you do that for?" She held up her wrist mirror to locate her VOX switch, but Bob held up his hand and switched off his own VOX. He motioned again for her to follow.

Valkerie's heart pounded in her throat. Was he out of his mind? Houston was going to have a fit. She followed him uneasily. It was his conversation with Sarah. It had to be. Sarah had said something on that private comm link—something that really upset him. Either that or—

No. Valkerie stopped in her tracks and watched Bob continue forward with slow, hopping steps. He had *told* her he loved her. They had spent so much time together. Talking. Sharing. He *couldn't* still be in love with Sarah. He hadn't seen her in at least ten years.

Bob stopped in the center of a circular formation of rocks and beckoned to her. Valkerie held her ground. After the comas, they had all been a little loose with the word *love*. She had even told Kennedy she loved him. . . . Had Bob meant it in the same way?

Bob lowered his videocam and began waving wildly at her. Swallowing back a huge lump in her throat, she walked slowly toward him. *This is crazy.* When she reached him, he leaned over and touched his helmet to hers.

"Bob, what in the world do you think you're doing?" she hissed. "Six billion people are watching us."

Friday, July 4, 2014, 12:30 P.M.

NATE

The instant vox went off, Mission Control fell silent. Nate stood up from his chair. *Of all the tomfool, crack-headed stunts . . .* What had gotten into Kaggo?

A network exec rushed forward. "What's going on?" he demanded. "Get the sound back on right away—"

"Quiet!" Josh pointed at the big screen.

Bob and Valkerie stood helmet to helmet in a ring of Martian stones. "They're talking," Josh exclaimed. "And if I know Kaggo . . ."

Nate stared up at the screen. *Kaggo, you wouldn't . . .*

Bob stepped back from Valkerie, took her hand in his, and knelt down on one knee.

From somewhere nearby, EECOM squealed.

AUTHORS' NOTE

Humans could walk on Mars within a dozen years if we chose to. Technology is not an issue. Most of what we need exists right now, and the rest is well within our grasp. Money is not an issue either. If twenty percent of NASA's current spartan budget were put into a Mars mission, we could go. We have based this novel mostly on the "Mars Semi-direct" mission architecture popularized by Robert Zubrin, with some ideas taken from NASA's Mars Reference Mission Document and the Caltech Mars Society proposed mission. We have left out all glitzy gizmos and futuristic technology and have focused instead on a program that America could begin right now.

Humans could walk on Mars within a dozen years. Will we? And might the "first man on Mars" be a woman?

Glossary of NASA Terms

ASCAN	Astronaut Candidate
AU	Astronomical Unit—the distance from the sun to earth
Capcom	Capsule Communicator—the one person in Mission Control (other than the Flight Surgeon) allowed to talk to the astronauts
CDR	Commander
Delta-V	Change in velocity created by firing the rocket engines
EECOM	Electrical and Environmental Command officer
ERV	Earth Return Vehicle—a ship that flies unmanned to Mars, waits four years, then returns with the crew to earth
ESL	Environment Simulation Lab
ESTL	Energy Systems Test Lab
EVA suit	Extra-Vehicular Activity suit—NASA's term for a space suit
FDO	Flight Dynamics Officer (pronounced "Fido")
GNC	Guidance, Navigation, and Control officer
Hab	Habitation Module
IMU	Inertial Measurement Unit—a critically important navigation device
ISS	International Space Station
JSC	Johnson Space Center
KC-135	The Vomit Comet
KSC	Kennedy Space Center
Ku-band	The high-frequency radio band normally used for high-speed data transmissions
LCG	Liquid-Cooled Garment
LC	Launch Center
LD	Launch Director
LOX	Liquid Oxygen
MAG	Maximum Absorbing Garment—a diaper for astronauts

Max Q	The time of maximum dynamic pressure during launch
MCC	Mission Control Center
MECO	Main Engine Cutoff
MMD	Mars Mission Director
MS	Mission Specialist
MSR	Mars Sample Return—a proposed unmanned mission for returning samples of Martian rock to earth
NASA	National Aeronautics and Space Administration
NSI	NASA Standard Initiator—a space-rated explosive
ORU	Orbital Replaceable Unit—stowage bins for living quarters in space
PDA	Personal Digital Assistant
PLSS	Primary Life Support System—the backpack on EVA suits containing water, oxygen, power, and everything else needed for life support
PLT	Pilot
PT	Physical Training
RCS	Reaction Control System—a system of small gas jets that allows space vehicles to rotate in space
SAS	Space Adaptation Sickness
S-band	The low-frequency radio band normally used for voice transmissions and low-speed data transmission
SES	Systems Engineering Simulator
SRU	Sleep Restraint Unit—a sleeping bag with straps to restrain the sleeper's head
STS	Shuttle Transportation System—official name of the Space Shuttle
T-38	Supersonic Trainer Airplane, commonly used by astronaut pilots for maintaining proficiency
TDRSS	Tracking and Data Relay Satellite System
TELMU	Telemetry, Electrical, EVA Mobility Unit officer
TMI	Trans Mars Injection—the rocket firing maneuver that will take a spaceship from an orbiting pattern around earth to a trajectory leading to Mars
VOX	Voice radio transmission